Synergy Publications Presents...

A Dollar Outta Fifteen Cent III:
Mo' Money...Mo' Problems

Another Exclusive Novel by Caroline McGill

Published By:
Synergy Publications
P.O. Box 210-987
Brooklyn, NY 11221

www.SynergyPublications.com

Library of Congress Control Number: 2008910884
ISBN: 978-0-9752980-4-6
Cover Design: Matt Pramschufer of E-Moxie Data Solutions
Written by: Caroline McGill for Synergy Publications
Edited by: Lana Mac for Synergy Publications

www.SynergyPublications.com
Printed in Canada

Dedicated to Change

Yes, we can.

ACKNOWLEDGEMENTS

First and foremost, giving honor to God. Next, I'd like to thank my readers. I'm flattered by your loyalty, and inspired by your interest in my work. I'm grateful for all your emails, letters, and calls, and I want all of you to know that I really appreciate your support. There's no me without ya'll. Thanks for riding with a chick. I wish peace and blessings unto each and every one of you. Hey Sister Pam, hey Wendy Williams, hey Cleo, hey Sam (my protégé), and hey everybody! I love you all!

I'd like to thank my mother, Carolyn, my father, Carnell, my sisters, brothers, nieces, nephews, cousins, friends, homies, homegirls, the bookstores, book vendors, book clubs, libraries, wholesalers, distributors, and last but not least, the brothers and sisters in the penitentiary.

Shout-outs to Casino, Bless Bigz, Connie, Carleata (Keya) and Ty, Keiecha and Chris, Fanerra, NaQuanda, Jemik, Jaylin, ShaMauri, Zapanga Milan, the whole McGill family, the McKoy family, the Norfort family, Kishah B and the crew, Kendell, CJ, Fee-fee, Sparkle, Mo, Tammy, Paulette, Tara, Ice, Maisha, Lisa, Nicole, Tasha, Makeeba, Kadeasha, Kiana, Tashonda, Boobie, Lisa, Sandra, Terry, Jerry, Mighty, Otis, Sherron, Zayquan, K-Lo, Quick, Dun, Caine, Twan, White Bread, Tough Luck, Jehova, Gotti, Man Hood Entertainment, Diamond from VA, Ty, and Micah.

Mega shout out to the crew up there at Green Haven with my beloved brother Casino; Boom, LG, Gotti, George, Yusef, Kool-Aid, Butter, Life, etc. Shout to my other lil' bro Bless Bigz, and the whole crew from Collins, and Wyoming. What up, fellas? Lincoln at Eastern Correctional, what's good?

A special, double shout-out to Lucky. Thanks for the ideas, and inspiration. Love you. Jamie, welcome home, boo. Special shout out to Anthony Whyte and Jason Claiborne from Augustus Publishing, and Street Literature Review magazine. Thanks for the hot feature. Hakim from Black and Noble in Philly, K'wan, and Erick Gray. The staff at PPH Taxes on New Lots. To the whole country, thanks for holding me down. Special shout-out to North Carolina. If I forgot your name, please don't trip. I love every single one of you. Everybody reading this right now matters to me. Thank you all, and God bless! Brooklyn, stand up! Special Shout out to Raheem "Bounty" Hoyte, author of "Black Familia", and CEO of Street Money Publishing, and his partner, Tara Pugh. Welcome to the game!

Let me take a minute to honor the memories of those gone, but not forgotten... Grandma and Granddaddy, (Rosa McKoy and Cary Lee McKoy), and Grandma and Granddaddy (Zante McGill and Bennett McGill). Uncle Dake, Uncle James, Uncle Fred, Lindsay McDowell, Blue, Lloyd Hart from The Black Library Booksellers, my nephew-in-law, Davell Francis, Michael Norfort (Unc), Rab, EP, Kendell Lewis, Jesse Thomas, Kimyatta Ellison.

To all my deceased loved ones, and to all the fallen soldiers, rest in peace eternally. God bless.

P.S- In 2008, we, the people of the United States, elected our first African American president. Remember, brothers and sisters, the sky is the limit! Dare to dream.

CHAPTER ONE

When Portia and Fatima stepped on the elevator, they could feel those thirsty ass detectives' eyes on their backs. Both of their hearts were racing. Portia fought the urge to look back at Jay one last time. She was afraid her eyes would give her away. And she knew that under those circumstances, there was nothing Jay could do.

She and Fatima were both overwhelmed by a sea of emotions. Both of them were in shock. They couldn't believe Wise was gone. That shit was fucked up. But they couldn't grieve at the time, so they kept cool. Unfortunately, they had bigger fish to fry. They had to get rid of those hot ass guns.

When the elevator doors closed, Fatima spoke very quietly. "P, them mo'fuckas gon' be waitin' for us downstairs." Their situation was serious, and there was no margin for error. She and Portia had kids to get home to.

Portia knew Fatima was right. They had to think fast. She was so scared her stomach was doing flip flops. She could imagine her poor baby inside her, turning over and over. She told Fatima, "Yo, we gotta go up to the sixth floor, where Laila is."

Fatima said, "That's just what I was thinking." She quickly pressed the six button, and prayed the elevator went up first. She was glad she and Portia were on the same page.

They got lucky. The elevator went up. Fatima had an idea. She opened up her purse, and searched for something to block the elevator door from closing all the way when they got off. She pulled out the biggest thing she had in there, which was a small umbrella.

When the door opened, she placed the umbrella so that it would interfere with the door closing. That way, they could take the same elevator downstairs. Luckily, Laila's room wasn't far down the corridor.

When they got off the elevator, Fatima headed over to the nurses' station to create a little distraction. Something to take their attention off Portia. She clutched her throat, and loudly complained about not being able to breathe. She acted like she needed some medical attention.

Fatima said, "Please, help me! I think I'm choking! There's something in my throat! Help!" She staggered back and forth, coughing, and clutching her throat.

Fatima was as phony as a three dollar bill, but she was obviously pretty convincing, because the two nurses at the station moved fast to assist her with her "medical emergency".

While her homegirl was making all that commotion, Portia quietly slipped inside Laila's room. When she saw Laila all bandaged up, with all those tubes in her, and shit, she almost broke down and cried.

Portia's emotions were running over, and they were battling. Fear and grief were at each other's throats, going toe to toe. There was just so much awful stuff going on at the same time. But she was too afraid to grieve. She couldn't break down. Not yet. She bent down and placed a kiss on Laila's bandaged forehead, and whispered another prayer for her.

Next, Portia took those guns out of her pocketbook, and hid them underneath her poor, unconscious girlfriend's bed. After she got those guns off her, she took a deep breath, and tried to relax. But it was no use. Her heart was still racing. She said another quick prayer, and then she whispered something to Laila. "God's got you, babygirl. You gon' be ayight. I'll be back, Lay. I promise. Love you."

After that, Portia crept out of the room. Her objective was to get away from those hot ass guns ASAP. She would figure out a way to get them out of there later, when the heat died down.

Fatima saw Portia heading for the elevator, so she buried her act. She told the nurses she felt okay now, and thanked them for assisting her. They looked surprised at her sudden recovery.

Fatima hurried to the elevator. Portia was holding the door for her. They just nodded at each other. It was time for them to go. Portia pressed the button for the lobby.

Before those elevator doors opened, Portia and Fatima each took a deep breath. God willing, their plan was to walk on out of there. They both prayed that nobody had noticed that little shake they had just done on the detectives, to stash the guns. Portia just wanted to put as much distance between them and those weapons as possible.

As soon as the doors opened, they were rushed by a crew of police, and surrounded. Reporters and news cameras were everywhere, and the scene was abuzz. There was so much excitement in that hospital lobby, it was like a damn circus.

Portia and Fatima were forcefully apprehended. There were so many police, they could barely see. The ladies knew to cooperate. There was nothing they could really do to resist anyway. They were totally outnumbered.

Portia began to fear for her unborn child. She had to inform them about her pregnancy. "Wait a minute! I'm pregnant! Ya'll don't have to be so rough! Wait! I'm pregnant! If somethin' happens to my baby, I'ma sue the hell outta ya'll!"

After hearing that, a nearby reporter told her cameraman to make sure he got that on video. Portia and Fatima were not read their rights. And ironically, the blue and whites violated just about every Miranda Right they had. Their purses were snatched away from them and thoroughly searched without their permission, they were frisked and patted all over their private parts, and some of the police were violently shoving them around.

The pigs kept shouting, "Where are those guns? Give us those guns!" Some even gave Portia and Fatima a couple of spiteful jabs and blows.

Portia just bended over a little to protect her belly, and didn't resist. Fatima, on the other hand, felt like she didn't have anything to lose. Unfortunately, one black male officer tried to overdo his job. The "brother" was manhandling Fatima unnecessarily so, so she got fed up and screamed on him.

She yelled, "Quit grabbing on me like that, you sell-out, Uncle Tom, son of a bitch!" Fatima shoved him in his chest. Bam!

That bastard's expression told her he felt that shit. There

were so many emotions bottled up inside of her, she must've had the strength of ten men.

He responded with, "Fuck you, bitch!" And then he had the nerve to slap Fatima. He hit her in her face so hard, she stumbled backwards.

Portia watched that punk ass mothafucka smack her homegirl in straight disbelief. When Fatima stumbled, she caught her, and helped her regain her balance. After that, they simultaneously jumped on that nigga's ass.

Portia kneed him in the nuts, and Fatima hit him in the face. But the officer didn't just stand there. He fought them back, and hit them hard, like they were men.

The girls held their own, responding with windmill punches and jabs. But that pig was a big, broad shouldered dude about 6'2", and he wouldn't go down easily. He was swinging them around left and right, but Portia and Fatima managed to get some real good licks in. They went upside that mothafucka's head numerous times.

These two tough, dyke looking female officers, one Puerto Rican, and one White, tried to step in and be heroines. But Portia and Fatima wouldn't allow themselves to be subdued easily. They went head up with those bitches, and they gave those pig hoes a good fight too.

Portia and Fatima both got theirs, but neither of them went unscathed in the battle. The other officers didn't just stand aside, and let them fight fair. Those cops fucked them up pretty bad. Portia had a big ass knot on her forehead, Fatima's nose was bleeding, and they both had busted lips.

All of a sudden, this hateful, white cop pulled out his pepper spray, and sprayed it in their faces. Portia and Fatima were instantly blinded, and both of them went into uncontrollable coughing fits. That stuff burned their eyes and throats something awful. Their eyes got all teary up, and their noses started running like crazy.

Portia just prayed her baby was okay. She had taken quite a beating. Under normal circumstances, she would've just chucked it up, and shook it off, but she had a life inside of her. That bastards better pray her baby was okay. That incident was just fucked up. The pigs had assaulted them first.

$$$$$

Jay and Cas were still being detained by those two detectives outside Wise' hospital room. The shorter pig radioed downstairs to find out if his officers had obtained the guns. As the detective listened to the other party, his smug, confident expression changed. At the end of his conversation, he looked really disappointed.

Jay and Cas heard the discussion on the two-way. They said they hadn't found the guns. They also said there was a big fight going on down in the lobby between some officers, and the women they'd suspected were carrying the weapons.

Jay and Cas were immediately alarmed. They knew Portia and Fatima didn't have any wins against all those cops. They could just imagine how outnumbered they were. And not only were they women, one was a grieving widow, and the other was pregnant.

Jay and Casino knew their rights. Those pigs couldn't hold them without any weapons. Lucky for them, the detectives were anxious to get downstairs and see what all the melee was about. They told Jay and Cas they were free to go, but assured them they hadn't seen the last of them.

The shorter one said, "You two are lucky today. But don't sleep, 'cause we're gonna be on the two of yous wise guys like the black on your asses. Now get lost. Go on, beat it."

Jay and Cas didn't have to be told twice. They headed for the elevator. They had to get down there and check on the girls. Portia was pregnant, and Fatima had just lost her husband. They were in no shape to be fighting. Jay and Cas didn't know the whole story, but they were positive the police had attacked them first. There was no way Portia and Tima had initiated a fight with the police. They weren't stupid.

Jay bit his lip in anger at the thought of some fucking pig manhandling his pregnant wife. That was characteristic of the police. A lot of those dickheads felt like their badge was a license to just roughhouse mothafuckas. But not his wife.

When Jay and Cas got off the elevator, they couldn't believe what they saw. Portia and Fatima were getting jumped by about fifteen cops. And they got down there just in time to witness this cracker pig open up his mace on them. He was a "blue and white", and you could tell by his stance that he was a cocky bastard. He sprayed that shit right in their faces, with no type of remorse.

Jay reacted in a flash. And he didn't have to say a word to Cas, because his right-hand man was right by his side. Before anyone knew it, Jay's fist connected with the asshole cop with the pepper spray's jaw. That mace flew out of his hand, and he spun around, dazed, and surprised. He reached for his gun.

Jay saw him reach for his hammer, so he yelled to a nearby reporter, "Look, I'm unarmed! Yo, get this on tape, and put it on the news. The police 'bout to kill another unarmed black man! Sean Bell! Sean Bell! Fifty shots, America! See it for yourself!"

The reporter and cameraman were eagerly anticipating the officer's next action, so he thought the better of popping Jay now. He'd been on the job for close to twenty years. He wasn't trying to lose his pension over that black nigger, so he was lucky that day. Now had they been in an alley, or something, he would've filled that fucking 'coon with lead.

Jay saw the pig hesitate. He didn't think he wanted that type of press. At the time, Jay was a little more emotional than usual. Wise had just died, and they had assaulted his fucking wife. He knew he was out of control, but he snuffed that mothafucka again, and told him, "That's for spraying that shit in my wife's face, you fuckin' cocksucka!"

The officer was a tough redneck. He ate that blow, and yelled, "You fucking street nigger!", and then he swung back. Jay ducked, and gave him two solid gut punches. The pig doubled over in pain. Those body shots really slowed him down.

Jay could've easily beaten that cracker fair hands, but he had a lot of backup. The rest of those pigs tackled him like they were in the NFL finals. One of the vile officers placed him in an illegal chokehold, but his partner nudged him, and reminded him about the news cameras present.

While Jay was throwing hands with that redneck cop, Cas

had took it back to his Golden Gloves days. He was snuffing pigs, and throwing them around like a bully on a playground. When he and Jay got off the elevator, those bastards were handling Portia and Fatima like they were men.

Cas hated pigs anyway. Plus, he was so fucking angry about Wise' death, he needed to pound on somebody. He got off quite a few good punches before he was tackled.

Both Jay and Cas knew what a chance they'd taken by fighting with the police. Especially at the rate they were dropping unarmed black men lately. If it weren't for those news cameras rolling, someone probably would've taken a shot at their melons.

More police showed up. These pigs had on riot gear, with helmets and shields. After they arrived, the pigs finally gained control of the situation. They placed them all under arrest. Jay, Casino, Portia, and Fatima.

They were all led away in handcuffs. And the media took the opportunity to question Cas and Jay about Wise' death. Microphone after microphone was shoved in their faces, and the hounds fired questions at them like, "Is it true that the rapper, Wise, is dead?", "Are you all suspects in these murders?", "Is it true that Street Life Entertainment has ties with organized crime?"

Jay and Cas just kept their mouths shut, and they knew Portia and Fatima would do the same. The arresting officers handled them with unnecessary roughness. Jay was shoved into a police cruiser by the officer who cuffed him. He banged his head against the doorframe, and laughed crudely. Jay glared at him, and glimpsed at his nametag. He noted that prick's name. Cabarino.

Jay shook the pain off, but he knew he was going to get a knot from that shit. That cocksucka better be glad he had those cuffs on. But fuck it, it would match the other knot he had. He got that from another one of those pig pricks, who hit him in the head with his club.

They were all thrown in separate cop cars, and rushed to the precinct. No guns were found, but they were all going through the system. They were going to be charged for assaulting police officers. It was going to be a long, uncomfortable process. You didn't fight the police back like that, and just get away with it.

The pigs were always in cahoots, and they could make shit real hard for you. When it came to shit like that, they all stuck together. From the cops on desk duty, to the captains, and shit. They were all haughty, and took it as personal disrespect when people stood up for themselves and "defied the law".

CHAPTER TWO

Jay and Cas knew they had to go through the system. But as long as the cops didn't find those murder weapons, they weren't going to sweat it. They had both known the consequences of fighting with those pigs. But under the circumstances, they believed their actions were justifiable. If they'd just stood aside, while Portia and Tima got pounded on, they would have been less than men.

Jay and Cas were in a holding cell, but they kept on their poker faces, and appeared oblivious to the dudes, derelicts, and dope fiends surrounding them. The strong smell of underarms in there had started to pay off, but there wasn't anything they could do about it. They were all just waiting to get out of there.

Sixty three hours later, Jay and Cas finally got to the court room, to see a judge, and get a bail. They'd spent two nights in the bookings, and they were both aggravated. Those dickheads pigs had been spiteful, and shuffled their paperwork around like cards in a poker game.

Jay was tight, but he was more concerned about Portia's well-being. Especially since she was pregnant. He hoped their baby was alright. He wondered if Portia had been allowed to see a doctor. And he was concerned about Fatima too. He really hoped she was holding up okay.

Just then, Jay saw Portia and Fatima being led through a side door by two court officers. They were in handcuffs, just like him and Cas. The pigs had obviously "misplaced" their paperwork too. The girls looked a little messy, and had a few scratches on their faces, but they looked okay.

Jay greeted them with a nod. As soon as he caught Portia's eye, things started looking up. He was glad she was okay. Having each other just made everything seem a little easier.

Portia and Fatima were tough cookies, but they had really

suffered while they were locked up in that bull pen. When they finally heard their names called for court, they were so relieved they wanted to shout for joy. They had wanted to get the hell out of there.

Portia prayed she hadn't caught tuberculosis, or some other airborne disease that could be harmful to her baby. She didn't even want to sit down in that horrible, disgusting place. Fatima didn't either. Especially since there was this dope-sick broad in the cell with them, who'd kept on vomiting, and shouting to the police about needing her meds, because she was HIV-positive.

And Fatima kept on breaking down, and crying over Wise. That was a heartbreaking experience for Portia. Fatima told her that Wise was the love of her life. She said now that her love light was gone, she was just lost.

Portia's heart went out to her. The poor thing was devastated. She was just no good. Portia had comforted her best friend, but she'd also had to appear tough, so the other women in the cell wouldn't think about trying them.

When they were allowed to make telephone calls, they had informed Fatima's mother about their incarceration, and Jay's mother as well. Both of them had promised to look out for their grandkids, and Laila's daughter too. So their children's wellbeing was one thing Portia and Fatima didn't have to worry about while they were in the can. But they were pretty sure the kids were worried about them.

Portia and Fatima hadn't been angels all their lives, but that was their first time actually getting locked up. Cas and Jay weren't strangers to jail, but it had been a long time since either of them had been in there. All four of them were unhappy with the bullshit "assaulting a police officer" charges they had pinned on them, but they were all relieved that they were being released. That meant the pigs hadn't found those hot guns.

Jay and Cas' attorney, Solly Steiner, was at court front and center for their arraignment. The judge gave each of them a twenty five thousand dollar bail. Solly posted everyone's bond immediately, and they all went home.

$$$$$

When Fatima finally got home, all she wanted to do was take a hot bath. She rolled herself a nice blunt, and turned on the tub. Minutes later, she soaked her weary bones in a bubble bath, and reflected on her unexpected loss. She finally had a chance to cry freely, and she let it out.

She missed Wise so much the pain was unbearable. She yearned to hold him, and tell him how sorry she was for not forgiving him sooner. If she had, they would've had more time together. It was unbelievable how quickly he had just slipped away from her.

Fatima had spoken to her mother-in-law, Rose, and she'd informed her that Wise' body had already been transported from the hospital, to the funeral home she chose. With Fatima incarcerated, his mother said she'd been forced to make the decision alone. Fatima didn't have any beef with that. She was his wife, but they were all family. Rose did what she was supposed to do.

Fatima was tired and weary. She soon fell asleep in the hot tub. About an hour later, the phone rang, and woke her. When she realized she'd dozed off, she decided to get out before she messed around and drowned herself. Her daughter had already lost one parent.

That was Portia on the phone, calling to make sure she was okay. Again, she suggested Fatima stay with her for a few days, so she wouldn't have to be alone. Fatima declined, and told her she needed to be alone for a little while. She told Portia to get some rest, so she could come with her to the funeral home the following morning, to see Wise, and take the suit he would be buried in. It was a brand new, tailor-made Armani he hadn't even worn yet.

Portia told her Jay and Cas would accompany them as well. They wanted to see him too. Because of that incident with the police, none of them got a chance to see Wise after he passed. They all needed some type of closure before the funeral. Everybody was torn up about Wise' death. They had all loved him in their own way.

Fatima was glad they were all going together. She didn't want to see him by herself. She didn't think she could handle it. She said another quick prayer to maintain her sanity. Fatima knew her fear of God was about the only thing that kept her from being suicidal. That, and her daughter, Falynn.

She and Portia agreed that after they all left the funeral home, they would go to the hospital to see Laila. They had called the hospital, and her condition hadn't improved yet. It was very sad.

Macy was holding up pretty well after hearing about Laila, but Portia and Fatima knew she had no idea how bad off her mother really was. Macy wanted to see her, so they promised to take her to the hospital the following day.

Portia and Fatima discussed the kids' reaction to Wise' death. They were all sad about it. But Falynn was only three, so she didn't really quite understand what they meant by "your daddy's gone" yet. Fatima was glad her mother had taken her home with her. When she looked at Falynn, all she saw was Wise. It hurt so bad, she just kept on crying. She didn't want to put her baby through that. She had to get herself together.

A few minutes later, the girlfriends agreed to talk in the morning. They said goodnight to one another, and hung up.

After Portia hung up, she was still worried about Fatima. She just felt so sorry for her. She rubbed her belly, and prayed silently. Life was so uncertain. She prayed her kids' father would be around to see them grow up. Poor Fatima hadn't been that fortunate.

Portia felt like everything was okay, but she knew she needed to go to the doctor to make sure her baby was okay. That would be the third task on her agenda the following day. She yawned and stretched. She'd already eaten and taken a long hot bath, so sleep was very welcome at that point. She could really use a good night's rest. But she was so uneasy with all that was going on, that would be easier said than done.

Portia briefly entertained the thought of rolling herself a blunt, but she dismissed it. She'd quit smoking weed when she found out she was pregnant. And any second thoughts she had, she dismissed because she didn't feel like arguing with Jay. He didn't want her smoking through her pregnancy, and she'd promised him she wouldn't.

Speaking of Jay, he was downstairs in the rec section with the kids. She needed to go check on them. Portia headed down to join them for a little while. She was overprotective of her babies. She didn't have the power to do anything else, but she would smother them with love. She knew they were all hurting. Jay was too. He'd lost a brother, and he was fucked up about it.

When Portia got downstairs, she hugged all the kids and told them she loved them. Jazz, Macy, and Jayquan. They all hugged her back tightly.

Afterwards, Portia hugged her man. He held her tight, like he really needed that. She needed him too. They were in it together, come rain or sunshine. Portia prayed it would just stop raining. She didn't know how, but they would all get through everything. She said it aloud to her family to reassure them, and herself as well.

"We gon' get through this, ya'll. Together." Portia looked around at everyone's faces, and they all looked relieved to hear that. Like they wanted to believe her.

Portia was especially concerned about Macy. She loved that little girl like she was her own. She considered Macy her real niece. Her mother was in a coma, and her father was busy getting high. Portia felt totally responsible for her. That poor baby.

Portia wouldn't hesitate to nurture her as if she was her own, but Laila had to get well. There was no other like a mother. God knows Portia had learned that lesson the hard way, when she lost Patty Cake. God rest her mother's soul.

The sadness in the house was unbearable. It loomed around heavy, like fog on a London night. Jay suggested they all go to bed and get some rest. The kids were exhausted too. The poor little things had been on pins and needles since they'd been locked up.

It was unspoken, but understood between Jay and Portia that the older children, Macy and Lil' Jay, needed one on one talks about the unfortunate events that had recently occurred. When

Portia and Jay first came through the door, they'd bombarded them with questions about them being in jail. They'd put off the kids' questions, and asked them to let them get cleaned up first. Now the time had come to talk turkey.

Jay walked Jayquan upstairs to his room for a "man to man". He knew his son wanted some answers. And he was upset about his Uncle Wise' passing, and Laila's accident as well. She was like an auntie to him.

Portia and Jazmin walked with Macy upstairs to the guest bedroom she had been staying in while they'd been under Jay's mother, Mama Mitchell's care. She put her right arm around her shoulder affectionately, and they all walked side by side. Macy had just settled into the new house with Laila a couple of months ago. Portia doubted the poor child had time to adjust, the way she'd been moved around lately.

They were barely in the bedroom before Macy said, "Let's cut the chase." She paused. "Is my mother dead?"

Portia looked in her eyes, and assured her, "No! No, baby. Laila's not dead! She's gonna be fine, and you have to believe that. Have faith, boo. Just pray, and believe."

Macy crossed her arms, and made a face. She looked like she was angry. "I've been praying. I keep praying. Look, I wanna go see my mother. When I asked Mama Mitchell, she said "no". How come I couldn't go see her? It must be worse than ya'll say it is." She looked at Portia like she was waiting for an answer.

Portia sighed. She had to tell her the truth. "Macy, Mama Mitchell wasn't being mean to you. I asked her to wait, and let me be the one to take you to the hospital. I just wanted to be there with you. And Fatima did too."

Macy rolled her eyes. "No disrespect, Auntie, but I know my mother wanna see me. Don't you think that was a little bit selfish of ya'll to make me wait 'til ya'll got outta jail? I know ya'll meant well, but dang. How do you think she feels about me not coming to the hospital to see her? I'm her daughter!"

Portia excused all the attitude Macy was giving her at the time, because she had a right to be upset. The child didn't know what was going on. Quite naturally, she didn't want to be in

the dark. It broke Portia's heart to have to say her next words.
She took a deep breath. "Baby, your mother's in a coma. I was
praying that she would wake up before I had to tell you this."

Macy just shook her head, and tears welled up in her eyes.
When she spoke, her voice was barely audible. "Oh my God!
What if she doesn't wake up? What if she sees my sister, and
decides to go toward the light somehow? What am I gon' do
then? Huh, Auntie P? I need my mother."

Macy almost broke Portia down with that one. She wiped
away the fresh set of tears forming in her eyes. She had to be
strong because she was the closest thing that poor child had to
a parent at that time.

Portia wrapped Macy in her arms and hugged her tight, and
then she tilted her chin up to her, and said, "Don't talk like that,
lil' mama. Your mother's gonna wake up, and she's coming
home. She loves you, and that will give her strength. That, and
our prayers."

Macy wasn't the type to bite her tongue. She said, "Well,
God keeps letting everybody else die. What makes you think
He's gon' let my mother live? He took my sister, He took your
mother, Humble, and now Uncle Wise. What makes my
mother so special?"

Macy stared at Portia and demanded an answer, but she was
dumbfounded. She didn't have an answer for that child. In
fact, she felt the same way deep down inside. She was just too
afraid to say it out loud.

Macy kept on. "Everybody always talkin' about how much
God loves us. He must not give a damn about me. My father
is on crack, my little sister was murdered, and now my mother
is in a coma. What kind of damn love is that? You tell me."

Portia was stuck on stupid. Macy was really going in. All
Portia could say was, "God does love you, baby. Just have faith.
The only thing that can save your mother is faith, and prayer.
God is a miracle worker. Trust and believe, babygirl."

Macy just sighed heavily. "I'm trying, Auntie. I'm trying.
There's nothin' else I can do."

Portia hugged her again, and kissed her on the forehead. She
loved that little girl like she was her own. Lord knows she did.

Portia sent a mental telegram to her girl Laila. "Come on, sis. You gotta get better. Please! This child needs you."

Jazmin tugged on Macy's shirt, and attempted to console her. She said, "Its okay. Don't worry. Here, give me a hug."

Portia's heart melted. That was her angel.

Macy's heart melted too. She broke out into a big grin, and picked Jazz up and hugged her, and gave her a kiss.

Jazz was glad she cheered Macy up. She smiled at her, and said, "That's a good girl. Show me that pretty smile." She pinched Macy on the cheek affectionately. She was too cute, with her little grown self.

On a lighter note now, Macy asked Portia, "So how come all of ya'll been in jail for two days? You adults are always preaching to us about behaving ourselves. So you mean to tell me, ya'll don't know how to practice what you preach?"

Portia grinned, and shook her head. She didn't even know what to say to that. That little girl was something else. There was no point in lying, so she briefly told Macy about the scuffle they had with the police. She downplayed the events somewhat, because she didn't want Macy to think it was cool to fight cops. She made sure she told her how much trouble a person could get in for that. She also told her that Jay and Cas had been arrested simply for defending her and Fatima.

Macy said, "Wow, isn't that sweet? Uncle Jay fought for you, like a real man should. That's what you call true love."

Portia laughed. "Now, what do you know about true love?" She tickled Macy before she could respond.

Macy giggled uncontrollably, and begged her to stop. Jazmin played along with them, and they all shared a good laugh.

A few minutes later, Portia sat on the foot of Macy's bed, and told her she loved her. Macy said, "I love you too, Auntie P. Please pray for my mommy."

Portia promised her she would. She smiled at Macy for a second. She was so mature.

Macy said, "My Nana gave me a phone number for my father the other day. You think I need to call him? I called Nana and told her that my mother had a car accident. She freaked out, and wanted to come get me. But my mother told me not to tell

Nana where we moved, so it wouldn't get back to Daddy. So I
told Nana I was staying with you, until my mother gets better.
She wanted to speak to you, but I told her you were asleep. I
didn't wanna tell her you were in the "big house". You know
what I mean?"

She laughed. "Nah, Auntie, I'm just kidding." Macy looked
serious again. "My mother put me on her Sprint plan, and got
me a cell phone, so I gave Nana my number. If my father
wanted to call me, he could've got my number from her.
Right?"

Portia shrugged. "I guess."

Macy asked her, "You think I should call him? Or should I
wait for him to call me?"

Portia said, "Call him." Khalil was an asshole, but he was still
her father.

She made a face. "He's the adult! He should call to see about
me. Forget that." She yawned. "Boy, I'm absolutely beat. I'm
about to say my prayers, and then I'ma take it on down. Goodnight, Auntie Porsh. Night night, Jazz."

Portia and Jazmin said goodnight, and left Macy alone to
rest. They went down the hall to Jazmin's bedroom. It was
way pass her bedtime. Portia told Jazmin it was time to go
nighty night. Jazz said she wanted her daddy to tuck her in, so
Portia yelled downstairs for Jay.

Jay had just finished up his man to man with Jayquan. They
both came upstairs, and Jayquan went to his bedroom. When
Jay came in Jazmin's room, Portia reminded him to let Jazz say
her prayers, and she kissed her daughter goodnight.

She walked down the hall to say goodnight to Lil' Jay. She
saw him coming out of Macy's room. Portia smiled. He
must've gone to tell her goodnight. She loved how close the
two of them were.

She followed Jayquan in his bedroom, and asked him if he
was okay. He told her he was good, now that they were out of
jail. Portia laughed along with him. She was glad the kids had
senses of humor. Laughter was the best medicine. She hugged
her stepson, and told him she was glad to be back. She thought
about staying in there to talk, while he got changed, but she re-

membered Jayquan was growing up. She didn't want to embarrass him, so she gave him a kiss on the cheek, and left him to get ready for bed. He needed to get some rest.

When they were done with the kids, Portia went downstairs and relaxed in the living room. She was so happy to be out of that nasty ass jail cell, she just wanted to enjoy her home for a little while. She flicked on the television, and let up the recliner on the end of the sofa and put her feet up.

A few minutes later, Jay came downstairs to see what she was up to. He had just got out of the shower, and he was wearing blue pajama bottoms and a blue wifebeater. He sat down beside Portia on the sofa. She snuggled up under him, and he placed his arm around her.

Portia sighed, and inhaled his masculinity. It felt good being up under her husband. He always made her feel safe. She shifted positions and placed her legs across Jay's lap. He started massaging her calves and feet. She leaned back and relaxed. Her baby was so thoughtful. Portia loved that about him.

That foot rub felt so good, she wanted to repay him. A few minutes later, she proceeded to comfort Jay in exchange. She knew what he found most soothing, and it wasn't a foot rub. Portia got up, and started rubbing on something else.

Rocky sprang to attention. Portia gave Jay a little sly smile. The past couple of days had been rough for him. She kneeled in front of him, and freed Rocky from his boxers, and she gave him some TLC right on their three thousand dollar sofa. Jay handed her a pillow from the sofa, to place underneath her knees, so she wouldn't get carpet burn from the rug. He was always thoughtful.

Portia got comfortable on the pillow, because she didn't plan to get up until he was satisfied. She hand stroked Rocky a few times, and gave Jay the sexy eyes, and then she took him in her mouth. She knew just how he liked it.

Jay moaned, and took the scrunchie off her ponytail and ran his fingers through her hair. She looked sexy with her hair wild. Portia deep throated him, and squeezed on his tip. That head job was right on time. He was beat, but he was also tense. Portia knew him. She knew he needed to be put to sleep.

Fifteen minutes into a blowjob that would've probably put
Superhead to shame, Jay's toes were curled, and his volcano
about to erupt. There was no question, he was about to blow.
He knew how Portia felt about the whole "cum in her mouth"
thing, so he warned her. "Aahh. Ma, I'm 'bout to cum!"

To Jay's surprise, she kept on going, and going. Was she
about to swallow? If she did, that would be the first time ever,
since they'd been together. The thought of that made his ejac-
ulation more intense. He groaned, and pulled her hair.

When Jay was cumming, he pulled her hair, and let out this
animalistic sort of growl. Portia hung in there as long as she
could, but when she felt the first spurt of his man milk in her
mouth, she pulled back, and caressed him with her hand.

She held in her laugh. She would tease him about that weird
sound he'd made later. She was just glad he was satisfied. She
hoped he was feeling a little better now.

Portia loved her husband to death. She would do anything
for Jay. Well, except for one thing. She just couldn't bring herself to swallow that stuff. But he knew how she felt, and he
never seemed to have a problem with that.

She traced Jay's navel lightly with her fingernail, and asked
him if he was okay. He shivered from her touch, and nodded,
apparently too drained to speak at the moment. Portia felt
good inside. She did every time she knew her man was pleased.
She got up, and went to the downstairs bathroom, to pee, and
get some baby wipes to clean up the sticky situation she had
created.

When Portia returned, she laughed. Jay had dozed off, and
he was sitting there with his dick still out. Rocky was limp, and
lying lazily on the side of his leg. What if one of the kids had
seen him like that? He didn't usually slip like that. He was obviously really tired.

Portia leaned down and cleaned him up. Jay woke up while
she was putting Rocky away, and he gave her a lazy grin. She
smiled back at him, and told him to come and go to bed. Portia
turned off the television, and took his hand, and escorted him
up to the bedroom.

That blowjob was like a lullaby for Jay, and for her too. Por-

tia was tired as hell. None of them had slept well while they
were locked up, so it was time to catch up on their rest.

CHAPTER THREE

The following morning, Casino got up real early. He just couldn't sleep. He brushed his teeth, and took a shower in his futuristic bathroom with its automatic shower, sink, and toilets. When he was done, Cas chilled out in his boxers for a while before he got dressed. He stared out his glass terrace doors, over the pool, and tennis court out back. It was early November, so the leaves on the trees were starting to change colors.

Before Cas had moved out of the house with Kira, his mother, a seasoned real estate broker, had found him that huge penthouse. It was nice, and had a wonderful view, but to Cas, it was merely a shelter. Not taking anything from it, because it was modern architecture at its finest. It just didn't feel like home. He looked around the spacious, overpriced, avant-garde condominium, and just felt sad for some reason.

He had purchased that joint without even looking at it first. The day he left Kira, he had moved right in. Cas knew the real reason he had left was because he'd felt guilty about the fact that he was so smitten with Laila. He knew he had purchased their house, but continuing to stay there would have given Kira the impression that he wanted to work things out.

It was a lot easier to just go. He and Kira were over. Cas didn't want to work anything out with her. But he wanted them to be on good terms so they could raise their son together. He didn't want any bullshit.

Cas had bought a new house for Laila as well, but he had decided not to move in with her until they both got out of their current marital situations. That had been the original plan, but now Laila was in the hospital clinging to her life. Cas said another silent prayer for her. That was really wearing on him something terrible.

And not to mention Wise' death. That had almost destroyed him. He was devastated, and hated to even think about it.

Cas had a lot of built up tension. He kept on replaying that hospital parking lot shootout they had in his head. He kept on seeing Wise get hit. He wished he'd have done things differently. Cas was mad tight. He really needed to let off some steam.

And honestly, he needed some pussy too. But he wasn't in the mood to bother trying to score. It wasn't that he couldn't. There were a thousand bitches just a phone call away. He didn't live that type of lifestyle anymore, but it was nothing to get it popping.

Cas didn't feel like being bothered with any broads. Instead, he opted for a quick weight lifting session, and two hundred pushups.

As he bench pressed a few sets in his private gym, he thought about how much he was dreading attending Wise' funeral. Him not going wasn't an option, but he damn sure wasn't looking forward to it. After he busted out two hundred pushups, Cas still didn't feel quite at ease. He knew what it was. He needed to bust a nut. That was the only thing that would relax him.

Casino wasn't a sex-crazed dude, but it had been quite a few days since he'd relieved himself. He popped a porno DVD called "Big Phat Black Asses" in, and flicked on the flat screen on the living room wall. As the movie started up, Cas looked around at his crib. It didn't feel like home. He knew part of the reason was because he hadn't done any decorating yet, but he had the feeling he wouldn't be there long.

He focused back in on the porno. This was a new one he hadn't checked out yet. The girl in the first sex scene was kind of skinny, so he forwarded to the next. He didn't want to watch the whole movie. He just needed something to beat off to.

The next girl was a pretty, petite, dark skinned sister. She had a nice fatty on her, and sort of reminded him of Laila. Damn, he missed Laila. Cas sat back and watched the girl in action. She started out giving this dude some top. Her head game looked like it was lethal.

Casino pulled out his dick, and began stroking himself. Damn, homegirl was getting it in. The dude she was pleasuring leaned down and smacked her on the ass, and waves rippled over its abundance.

They switched up positions, and duke ate her pussy for a little while. After that, he flipped her over and hit it from behind. Her fat ass jiggled, just like Laila's did when he hit it doggy style. The girl threw it back on homie, and clawed the sheets. She moaned louder and louder, and Cas quickened the pace of his hand stroke. His breathing got heavier. Damn, he was about to bust. Casino imagined the palm of his fist to be Laila's tight, sweet box. The thought pushed him right off the cliff. When he came, he exclaimed, "Aaahhh! Oh shit!"

Cas cleaned up his mess with a hand towel he had nearby, and he sat there for a second and caught his breath. Now he felt relaxed. He wasn't all good, but he was definitely better.

It was almost ten A.M., and time to get the day started. He, Jay, Portia, and Fatima were all going to the funeral home to see about Wise, and then they were going to visit Laila. Cas called Fatima to see if she was ready, and told her he was on his way.

Less than thirty minutes later, he picked Fatima up, and they headed over to Jay and Portia's. When they got there, Jay was ready, but Portia was having a bout of morning sickness. Cas and Tima both asked her when she planned on going to the doctor to see about the baby. Portia insisted she was fine. She said she would go the following day. They had too much on their agenda that day. Cas reminded her that her baby was her number one priority, and told her they would take care of everything.

Jay told him he'd been telling Portia that all morning. He and Cas understood that she wanted to be there for Fatima, so they gave up. They just hoped she knew what she was doing.

They had gotten out of jail kind of late the day night before, so they didn't get a chance to retrieve those guns from under Laila's hospital bed yet. This influenced their decision to go visit Laila first. They really wanted to see how she was doing anyway. They would go to the funeral home afterwards.

Portia and Fatima agreed that they would go back to the hospital again later to take Macy to visit Laila. Portia threw up again. When she finally got her head out of the toilet, they all loaded up in Cas' Aston Martin and rolled out.

When they got to the hospital, everybody was quiet. There were so many bad memories there. Jay suggested Portia and Fatima go in Laila's room first, to check for the guns. He and Cas watched out for them in the hallway. They both wished they could've paid somebody to go in there and get the ratchets, but at the time there was no one they were willing to trust. The less people that knew about your dirt, the better off you were. That was one of the most important rules of life.

About two minutes later, Portia came back out the room looking confused. She shrugged, and mouthed the words "The guns are gone" to Jay and Cas.

They each gave her a questioning look. She shrugged again, and shook her head like she didn't have a clue. She motioned for them to follow her inside the room.

When they walked in, Jay and Cas both winced at the sight of Laila all bandaged up and full of tubes. It was heartbreaking. It really was. But they had to address those missing guns for a minute.

When he was positive no one else was in the room but them, Jay asked, "What you mean, "The guns are gone?" How, P?"

Portia sighed. "I don't know, baby. I put 'em right here under the bed, but they're gone now. All three of them. This shit is crazy."

Cas spoke quietly, but he was serious as cancer. "Whoever got those guns got the power to put us away for a long time, son. Real talk."

Cas glanced over at Laila. His heart went out to her. He was keeping hope alive, and praying that she would get well. He wanted her to come home, so he could take care of her. He couldn't do that if he was in prison. They had to find those guns.

Cas walked over and joined Fatima at Laila's bedside. He spoke as if she could hear him. "What up, Ma?" He traced the outline of her jaw, and leaned down and kissed her bandaged forehead.

The rest of them went outside to locate Laila's doctor, so he could update them on her condition. Their intentions were also to give Cas a moment alone with her.

When they found the doctor, Fatima called Cas out in the hall so he could hear about Laila's progress too.

The doctor told them that Laila had woke up, but she was so badly injured, they had placed her in a medically induced coma. He said her vital signs were strong, but his main concern was the damage that had been done to her spine. There was an eighty percent chance that she might not ever walk again. He said if she did, it definitely wouldn't happen overnight.

The doctor said he had one more concern, and asked which of the men was Laila's husband. Everybody just looked at Cas, so he automatically assumed it was him. To all of their amazement, the doctor informed Cas that his "wife" was two months pregnant. Everybody's jaw just dropped.

Cas just looked at the doctor for a second, like he expected him to say he was kidding or something. He couldn't believe what he just told him. Wow. Laila was pregnant with his baby. He was elated at first, but then he thought about the fact that she was in a coma, doped up with all that shit.

Cas didn't beat around the bush. He wanted to know the truth. He asked the doctor, "How much of a chance does the baby have, considering her condition?"

The doctor was honest with him. "The child would have a better chance if she were awake. For the baby to get the proper nutrition, she needs to maintain a healthy diet. There's no guarantee that the fetus will survive if its only being fed intravenously. But hopefully, we'll be able to bring her out sooner than later."

Cas thought positive after that. "So the baby does have a chance, right?"

The doctor saw how hopeful the young father-to-be looked. He smiled slightly, and nodded. But he was honest, and told Cas that Laila's spinal injuries would definitely complicate her pregnancy. He told him that, legally, he had to also let him know he had the option of aborting the child, because of the risks. He told Cas to think about it, but get back to him soon because she was almost eight weeks along.

Cas nodded, but he had pretty much made up his mind. It was a gamble, but he was a gambling man. He decided to roll the dice. He wasn't authorizing them to kill his seed. Hell no. There was no way. He addressed the doctor with a straight face, and said, "Thanks, doc. We'll take our chances."

The doctor nodded. He understood. That man was going to be a father, so he would do everything he could to make sure there were no mishaps. The doctor was a family man himself. He'd once had that same eager, proud look in his eyes.

Cas asked him, "How long before you can pull her outta that coma?"

"Six to eight weeks. By then, the sections of her spine and neck that the surgery was performed on will be reattached and mostly healed. Then we'll be able to remove the body cast."

"And she could walk again, right? It's possible. Right?"

The doctor said, "Anything is possible. But I must inform you, the chances aren't that great."

Cas nodded, and they all thanked the doctor. After he walked off, Casino was quiet for a minute. His exterior was cucumber cool, but his emotions were in a whirl. His heart swelled with pride at the thought of him being a father again. But he couldn't front, he was scared to death. He really needed to talk to someone, but he wasn't about to discuss it in front of the girls. He didn't want to show any weakness or doubt. He would holler at Jay about it later on. Cas looked at his Rolex, and asked everybody if they were ready to roll out.

Portia and Fatima glanced at one another. Neither of them could believe how Cas had just taken total control, and started making Laila's important life decisions. They were listed as her next of kin. They felt they should have had more of a say-so, but they both held their tongues for the time being.

Portia and Fatima were both torn anyway. They didn't even know what to say. The news of Laila's pregnancy was bittersweet. It was absolutely wonderful, but it would take a huge toll on her body. No disrespect to Casino, but he was a man. He had no idea what an extremely vulnerable state a woman's health was in during a pregnancy. And Laila had so many complications. Her body wasn't prepared to carry a baby at the time. The risks were frightening.

Portia and Fatima wondered if they should speak up. It was a real tough call. And how did they know that Laila would have wanted to have that child under those circumstances? They had both taken a back seat in the situation because Casino was the father. It was hard to believe Laila was pregnant. The ladies decided to keep their lips zipped for the time being.

One thing Portia, Fatima, Jay, and Cas had in common was the fact that they were all glad Laila's coma was medically induced. That meant she wasn't as bad off as they thought she was. They knew she had issues with her spine, but her vitals were okay. More than anything, they were just glad she was alive.

They all left the hospital and loaded up in the car again, and Cas took the George Washington Bridge from Jersey to Manhattan. They were headed to the mortuary Wise' mother had selected.

Nobody really said much on the way. It was truly a dreaded trip. Everybody in the car would've given anything to not have to go there to see Wise. It was still hard to believe that he was dead. None of them had a chance to view his body yet, because right after the doctor had pronounced him dead, they'd had that run-in with the law.

Nobody really wanted to go to the funeral home, but they had to make sure the mortician did him right. Wise' homegoing ceremony was going to be grand.

The drive wasn't long enough. Before they knew it, Cas was parking. When they got out of the car, all of their stomachs were doing flip flops. But nobody said anything.

Fatima placed the tailor-made Armani suit she wanted Wise to be laid to rest in across her arm. Portia grabbed her other hand and squeezed it. Fatima squeezed her friend's hand back to show she appreciated the support, and they all headed inside.

They had spoken to Wise' mother, Ms. Rose Page, along the way, and she told them she was already there. When they got inside, everyone hugged her and offered their condolences. Rose smiled feebly, and thanked them all.

Wise looked just like his mother. She was the female version of him, fit and good-looking. She had a bronzed caramel complexion, and wore her hair in a nice, short haircut. She looked real young for her age, but that day the poor woman looked like she hadn't slept in days. Her eyes were so puffy. You could tell she'd been crying a lot.

All of a sudden, Rose looked real serious. In a low voice, she told them she had to talk to them. She gathered everybody together in a huddle, and then she took a few seconds to say what was on her mind. From the look on her face, they could tell something was really wrong.

Rose took a deep breath, like it was hard for her to let out. She finally said, "I don't know how to say this. They say they had another man here by the same name as Wise, William Page, and one of the staff got them mixed up. So they told me they cremated Wise' body by mistake!"

Everyone's face looked like Jesus Christ just appeared in a thong. They said in unison, "What you mean, "they cremated him?!"

Rose nodded her head slowly, and spoke sadly. "Yes, I'm afraid so. I can't believe these people. His body was just here yesterday, and then when I get here today, they tell me this."

She pointed to a door on their far right, and said, "The owner's son is the director. He's back there in his office, and he keeps on saying they're gon' try to make it right. They're offering a settlement, so we don't go public."

Fatima just started crying. She couldn't believe what she was hearing. How the fuck could they have cremated Wise? She hadn't even got a chance to say goodbye to him yet. That shit seemed surreal. And why was his mother taking it so well?

Fatima wasn't taking it that lightly. She flipped. "Get the fuck outta here, I ain't try'na hear that shit! Hell no! Is these mothafuckas crazy?"

She marched straight over there to the director's office. Jay, Cas, and Portia were right on her heels. Rose ran behind them, trying to calm everyone down. Fatima swung open the door and screamed on the first person she saw. "What the hell happened to my husband's body?!"

That person just happened to be the funeral home director's assistant. The woman jumped up so fast, her glasses fell off. She quickly put her glasses back on, and cleared her throat, and told Fatima, "I'll get Mr. Hanson, ma'am." She just worked there, she didn't want any problems. She hurried in the back.

A few seconds later, a well dressed, light skinned gentleman came out and nervously introduced himself. He cleared his throat, and said, "Uh, hello, I'm Mr. Hanson."

Jay was the closest gentleman to him, so he extended his arm to him for a handshake. Jay looked at his hand like it was contaminated, and didn't shake it. He wasn't normally rude, but that nigga had some explaining to do.

Hanson looked at Rose like he was a little confused. He'd thought they had an understanding already, but he realized that he had to give the irate crew who had just stormed into his office some answers.

He clasped his hands in front of him, and pursed his lips in attempt at the sincerest expression of apology. "I'm very, very sorry, but there's been a terrible mix-up. We had another man here by the same name as Mr. Page, and due to a total error on our part, unfortunately, your loved one was mistakenly cremated yesterday. I can not express to you..."

Fatima cut him off right there. "Hold up. What the fuck do you mean, mistakenly cremated? Are you outta your fuckin' mind?"

She shook her head. "Nah, this must be some type of sick fuckin' joke. Am I being "Punk'd", or something?" Fatima looked around suspiciously for hidden cameras.

She didn't see any cameras, so she went berserk up in that bitch. She charged at Mr. Hanson like a raging bull. He ran around his desk to get away from her.

Cas grabbed Fatima, and stopped her from going to that man's ass. She screamed, "How the hell could ya'll make a mistake like that?! What type of sick organization is this? Oh my God! I'ma have this mothafucka shut down! Watch! You gon' regret this shit! You cremated my husband?! I didn't even get a chance to say goodbye to him! You selfish son of a bitch! Go to hell!"

Jay and Cas stood on either side of Fatima, and guarded her protectively. They let her vent, but they weren't with the talking stuff. They hadn't said anything yet, but both of their anger levels were simmering dangerously. It was hard to believe that so-called prestigious, bullshit ass funeral home had disrespected Wise' body like that.

Jay glanced over at Cas, who nodded at him. They were on the same page. That mortician mothafucka needed to be taught a lesson.

Casino politely pushed Fatima aside, and stormed over there and grabbed the director by his neck. He was so pissed off, he snarled, "That mistake gon' really cost you, man! Word. Possibly, with your life. How 'bout I fuckin' cremate you?" He twisted Hanson's arm behind his back, and threw him in a tight chokehold.

Jay reached under his shirt, and pulled out, and he shoved his hammer under Hanson's chin. When that mothafucka saw that gun, he looked like he shitted on himself. Jay narrowed his eyes, and said calmly, "Duke, that was my brother ya'll burned up. I should kill you." He hadn't raised his voice, but his demeanor told the man he was really contemplating doing it.

Portia could tell Jay was serious, and her heart was racing. She wanted to beg him to calm down and think about the consequences, but she knew it wasn't the time to get in his way. She knew better than to approach him in a situation like that. Those were some fucked up circumstances. Those mothafuckas had cremated Wise, so there was nothing she could say to him at that point. She just said a quick prayer that her husband wouldn't do anything crazy.

Rose saw how out of control things were getting, so she asked everyone to please calm down. She told Jay and Cas that there was a mistake was made, and them killing that man wouldn't undo that. She said it was an accident.

Mr. Hanson was clearly relieved to have an ally in the angry crowd. He nodded earnestly in agreement, and spoke as best he could with Cas cutting off his oxygen supply. "Yes, yes, it was a terrible mistake indeed. And I take full responsibility. But I assure you, we will make this right. You will be greatly compensated for your pain and troubles. I assure you." He nodded at them sincerely, with sweat rapidly forming on his brow.

Jay didn't want to hear that shit. It only made him angrier. "What?! There ain't enough money in the world to make up for no shit like this." He bit his lip, shook his head, and paused for a second.

"You better make that offer real sweet, duke. Or you'll be ya'll next client." The glare Jay gave him cemented his threat. He resentfully lowered his gun, and placed it back in his waist.

Casino reluctantly released the death grip he had on Hanson's neck. He felt like just snapping that shit. That chump was lucky. He'd almost been the nigga he took his frustrations out on. Cas was holding in a lot of shit too. And so was Jay, so Hanson was really lucky.

The funeral director was visibly shook, but he gathered his composure. He told them that he was the son of the owner, Mr. Robert Hanson Sr., and they would be in touch with an offer ASAP. He assured them it would be hefty.

Fatima just shook her head in disbelief. That man might as well have been talking Japanese. She couldn't stop crying. Rose and Portia comforted her, and led her outside. They both could only imagine her pain. She was a grieving widow.

Everybody was feeling it. They needed each other's strength. It was an extremely hard time for all of them.

Jay and Casino had no more words for Hanson. If he didn't do what he said, they would let their guns do the talking next round. Before they walked out behind the ladies, they gave him looks that told him they would leave him in an alley somewhere, with no remorse.

CHAPTER FOUR

The following morning around ten, Fatima was awakened by the telephone ringing. She rolled over to answer it, and a couple of the photos of Wise she had stayed up all night crying over fell to the floor. She reached down and picked them up, and said, "Hello?"

It was Rose, calling to tell her that the people at the funeral home had called. They said they would give them two million dollars, and plus carry out the memorial service of their choice for Wise at no charge.

Fatima was completely unimpressed. She sucked her teeth, and gave Rose her opinion. "You sound like you happy about that. That ain't shit."

Rose said, "Well, two million dollars ain't no chump change. And the funeral we planned would've probably cost over a hundred grand, with all the extras ya'll talkin' about having."

Fatima was getting tight. "Rose, please! I'm not happy with no doggone two million dollars! No! And you shouldn't be either. Hell, Wise left more money than that. I ain't pressed for no money. So I ain't gon' stop 'til them mothafuckas are penniless, and beggin' in the street. I wanna take everything from them. Look what they took away from me. No, I am not happy!"

Rose remained calm throughout Fatima's outburst. She just said, "Baby, that's still not gonna bring Wise back. Look, I just want him to rest in peace, Fatima. I want this thing to go away quietly, and not tarnish my son's memory. The media will make a circus out of something like this. That's the reason I don't wanna go public."

Rose paused for a few seconds to let what she was saying sink in, and then she continued. "When a black man dies, all the media does is bring up all the negative shit he ever did. Girl, have you seen the papers? They're already trying to crucify my baby's memory in the headlines. I'm so tired of these damn people in our family business. That's why I'm ready to just sign the release, and take the damn money."

Fatima shook her head in disbelief. "Wow, Rose. You are really something else. What about your granddaughter? Poor Falynn. Am I supposed to just tell her that her grandmother won't defend her daddy's honor? My God, Rose. Wise is your son! I do not stand with you on this. That's my final word. Now, no disrespect, but I gotta go. I'll talk to you later, Rose." After that, Fatima just hung up the phone.

She hadn't meant to be rude, but she was pissed off. That shit was like a nightmare. It was like Wise was just stolen away from her. Everything happened so fast. And now she'd never get the opportunity to tell him goodbye. She would never see him again. Their mistakenly cremating Wise was something that should only happen on television. It was unbelievable.

Fatima laid in bed, and thought about the day ahead. She was expecting Jay, Cas, and Portia a little later. Fatima remembered that they'd found out from Portia's doctor the evening before that her blood pressure was high.

Out of concern, Fatima called to check on her girlfriend. Portia was a trooper, and she was grateful for her, but homegirl had to take it easy.

When Portia picked up, she insisted that she was fine. She said she and Jay were about to get up now, and would be at her house around 'noon. She said Cas would probably show up around the same time.

Fatima told her they didn't have to come over so early. She knew they all needed some rest. She told Portia to lay down and chill out for a while. She reminded her about her too high blood pressure, and the fact that her ankles had swelled up the day before.

Portia agreed to rest a little longer. They agreed to see each other in a few hours, and hung up.

About an hour later, Kira called and told Fatima she was stopping by that afternoon to offer her condolences. Fatima appreciated the support. She knew everyone just wanted to make sure she was okay. It was really good to have friends.

Portia and Jay had insisted that she stay with them for a little while, so she wouldn't have to be alone. Fatima had refused, so Portia asked if she wanted her to come stay at her house with her. Fatima declined her offer because she needed to be alone to sort out some things in her head. She missed Wise, but she wasn't afraid to be in their home alone. If his spirit was in there, he would protect her, not frighten her.

Fatima thought about Laila, and the way her daughter, Macy, had reacted when she and Portia took her to the hospital. Macy was real mature for her age. She'd handled it a lot better than they had anticipated. Fatima would be glad when Laila got better. She needed to be there for her child.

Fatima thought about her little one, Falynn. She hadn't really spent any time with her since she'd been home. For a second, she felt a little guilty. What kind of mother was she? Her daughter had lost her father. Fatima was passing the buck of all of her maternal responsibilities on to her mother, and it wasn't fair. She reasoned that Falynn was so young she didn't understand what was going on. She probably just figured her daddy was out of town, or something.

Fatima hated to admit it, but the truth was that seeing her daughter made her really sad. Falynn reminded her of Wise too much. She looked just like him.

Wise' wake was scheduled for the following day. Time was moving by fast. But now that there was no longer a body for people to view, it would be more like a memorial service. And the day after that was the funeral. It would just be a closed casket ceremony, with a huge photo of Wise on display.

Fatima wanted to honor his memory, but she didn't want to face the fact that he was really gone forever. She reluctantly dragged herself out of bed. As much as she hated to, she knew she had to get on with her life.

$$\$\$\$\$\$$

Portia had dozed off for another hour after she spoke to Fatima. When she woke up, one of the first things she thought about was the fact that those guns were gone. She really couldn't believe it. Who the hell had taken them? She had absolutely no idea. Was it the police? Were they secretly lurking in the shadows with indictments, waiting to arrest them, or something?

Jay was already awake. He was laying there next to her watching the news. Portia rolled over, and snuggled up under him.

Jay leaned down and kissed her on her forehead. "Good morning, Kit Kat. How you feelin'?"

Portia nodded to let him know she felt okay. "How you feelin', baby?"

Jay didn't want to mess up Portia's mood, so he faked it. "I'm ayight, Ma", he lied. Truthfully, he was low because he'd been thinking about Wise all morning. He really missed that dude.

He rubbed Portia's belly, and they laid there together for a while. Jay silently prayed for the safety of his children. He really hoped he'd be around for them. His man Wise hadn't been so lucky.

"Look, Jay", Portia exclaimed, snapping him out of his thoughts. She pointed to the TV. "They're showing this shit again."

Together, Jay and Portia watched the news footage of Portia and Fatima fighting with the police for the umpteenth time. The media was wearing that story out. And they were definitely letting it be known that they were the wives of the famous, wealthy, deceased rapper, Wise, and wealthy record company executive, Jay Mitchell.

As usual, they found a way to blame it all on hip-hop. They tagged Street Life Entertainment to be the target of a heavy murder investigation. The press was having a field day with this shit. All the newspaper headlines read "FAMOUS RAPPER GUNNED DOWN IN DEADLY SHOOTOUT". The articles pointed fingers at Jay and Cas, and attributed Wise' demise to be a product of their company's name, Street Life Entertainment. They were saying Street Life's lifestyle had finally caught up to Wise.

Jay and Cas were so pissed at the articles, they had stopped reading the papers entirely. They kept telling themselves that it would blow over. And it would. They just hated the fact that the press was drawing so much heat to them. Heat they didn't need. Not that they were really doing anything illegal nowadays. It was their past activities they were more concerned about.

Jay and Cas were no idiots. They weren't sleeping on the law. Those crackers always let dudes blow up, and when they least expected it, they came trying to put them out of commission. Just like they had recently pressed, and tried to destroy Irv Gotti, from Murder Inc.

Jay remembered what the doctor said about Portia's blood pressure the day before. Thank God, she and the baby were okay. The doctor just said her blood pressure was a little high, and told her to take it easy. Jay was worried about her. Earlier that morning, he had got up and got the kids ready for school himself, so she could rest.

Jay had business to tend to at the office that day, but he'd delegated some of the tasks to his new assistant, Phil. Phil thought on his toes, and knew how to listen. Jay liked that about him, because he hated repeating himself. He wanted to stay at home more, and keep an eye on Portia and his kids.

They had been being constantly harassed by reporters trying to get their side of the story. And the paparazzi was violating them left and right. Jay had even found one of those bastards hiding in a tree the other day, trying to photograph him leaving his house. Those type of constant invasions of their privacy had influenced his decision to beef up security. Those mothafuckas had no respect. They crossed every line there was.

Jay shut the television off. That shit depressed him. He looked over at Portia, who looked deep in thought about something. He suggested they get up and take a shower together. They had to get a move on. The first thing on their agenda was to stop over at Fatima's to make sure she was okay, and then they would all go visit Laila again.

Jay thought about Cas. He decided to give him a quick call to make sure he was okay. He knew he had a lot on his mind, especially with him and Laila's new baby on the way.

Jay knew how complicated that situation was, but he was stay-ing out of it. Cas was married to his sister, but they were in the process of getting a divorce. Jay knew Kira would still be pissed when she found out about Cas' new baby.

$$$$$

A few hours later, Kira entered the gate and drove up the winding driveway to Wise and Fatima's estate. Along the way, her mind was flooded with reminders of Wise. She and him had always been cool. They had recorded their first hit record together, years ago when they first started out. Kira smiled at the memory. Damn, Wise was a good dude. She was really fond of him.

Kira thought about Cas. She was secretly hoping that he would be at Fatima's house as well. When she pulled up in the driveway, it looked like she had gotten her wish. His Aston Martin was parked right out front. She had seen him the day before when he came by to see about their son, but he and her had barely said three words to each other. Kira parked, and headed up to the door and rang the bell.

Jay opened the door, and he and Kira embraced. He hadn't seen her since before Wise had passed. His baby sister told him she was sorry for his loss. She knew how tight he and Wise were. Jay accepted her well-wishes, and walked her inside.

Kira said hello to everybody, and she hugged Fatima and told her how sorry she was. Next, Kira hugged Portia, and then she rubbed her belly and smiled. She was just starting to show.

Kira wanted to hug Cas next, but she was mad nervous. She didn't know why, because they were married. She just was. She finally got up the nerve and walked over to him. She wanted to be there for him. She knew he was hurting.

Kira took a chance, and she hugged Casino tight, and told him how sorry she was about Wise. But he only half-hugged her back. Kira realized that he didn't want her to be there for him. Not on the level she wanted to comfort him on. She was hurt, but she just played it off.

Everyone knew there was tension between Cas and Kira. In

effort to lighten up the mood, Fatima turned on the stereo and started bumping cuts from Wise' latest CD. It was still kind of early in the day, but she broke out a new bottle of Gran Patron Platinum and a fresh lime, and she offered tequila shots to everyone except Portia, because she was pregnant.

Within an hour's time, everyone was laughing and rejoicing about Wise. His death was untimely for sure, but they remembered the good times. They had really shared some great times. The world certainly lost a good dude.

Kira sat with them for a while reminiscing about Wise, but she was the first to break out. She had put up a good front, but even two tequila shots didn't take away the sting of Cas' rejection.

Fatima and Portia understood her plight. They both hugged her tight, and thanked her for coming by. So did Jay. Cas half-hugged her again, and told her he would see her the following day, when he came by to pick up his son.

Fatima locked the door after Kira, and remembered her conversation with Rose earlier that morning. She told Jay, Cas, and Portia about the offer the mortuary had made, and asked for their advice. She said she wanted to sue them for more, but she wanted to know what they thought she should do.

Jay and Cas told Fatima there would probably be a lot of interference from the media if they went public with it, but that was her prerogative. They said they would support her in whatever she wanted to do, but they reminded her that they were having a closed casket funeral, and going public with the lawsuit would let people know that the casket was really empty. And they told her to be prepared for a long, drawn-out battle. They said they would probably be in court for years.

Portia agreed with Jay and Cas. They weren't trying to dissuade Fatima. They were simply stating the facts of the matter. She had to know what they were up against before she made up her mind. Only then could she make an informed decision.

Fatima appreciated all of their advice. She decided to wait and see if the mortuary would sweeten the offer. Jay and Cas assured her that they would lean on them to make sure they did. Everybody agreed it would be best to wait a couple of days until after the funeral before they made a move. They all just wanted Wise to rest in peace. That was their main concern.

$$$$$

Wise' wake was the following day. The "prestigious" funeral home they had dealt with also had a Brooklyn location. The services were to be held there. Jay and Cas had hired security from The Nation of Islam, for the wake, and for the funeral the next day. They didn't want to take any chances, just in case things got a little rowdy.

They also had legal hammer-toting foot soldiers strategically placed throughout the joint. Not some trigger-happy, street corner knuckleheads. They were professional men with impressive résumés, and each played their positions well to earn the hefty paycheck they were receiving for the deed.

Mittens and Nifty, a well-known security team in the industry who worked exclusively for Beef & Broccoli, had offered to lend their services as well. Everyone knew Wise was good people, and no one wanted his memory to be disrespected.

Jay and Cas knew what a huge turnout they were expecting, so they weren't trying to have anyone's lives in jeopardy. They were realistic, so there was security all throughout the joint. Wise was killed in a gun battle, and he had taken the last of The Scumbag Brothas, bitch ass Mike Machete, with him. There was always the possibility of some street fame thirsty asshole with a death wish trying to get at them. Cas and Jay had agreed to never, ever sleep on anyone again. They refused to cut corners when it came to the security of their families.

It seemed like the whole Brooklyn came out that day and showed love. People lined up for blocks waiting to get inside and pay their respects. It was like a national holiday had been declared. Wise was an extremely well loved dude.

At Fatima's request, Wise' records played softly in the background during the viewing. It was hip-hop, but people were crying like it was sad, slow songs.

There were two designated bodyguards at the front by Wise' casket. The men were not to leave their post for any reason.

Their job was to keep an eye on the respect-payers, and make sure no one tried to steal anything. Everybody knew you couldn't take it with you, but it was traditional for dudes to pay their respects at a wake by dropping money or jewelry in the casket.

Wise' casket was closed, so dudes opted to place the valuables in a satin lined basket sitting on the side. That was their way of paying homage. Casino and Jay didn't mean to offend anyone, but unfortunately, there was usually at least one nigga scheming in the midst, so hence the bodyguards.

The wake lasted for five hours. With the strength of God, Wise' loved ones made it through day one of his services. That night they were all exhausted, so everybody went home at a decent time. The funeral was early the following afternoon.

CHAPTER FIVE

The church they held the funeral at was huge. It seated almost a thousand people, and it was packed to capacity. So many people came out that day to say goodbye to Wise, his funeral probably made black history.

The celebrity turnout alone was tremendous. Amongst the famous were Jay-Z, Allen Iverson, Kanye West, Jamie Foxx, Scarface, and Floyd Mayweather. Ludacris and T.I. were there, and Mariah Carey also came through. Jay and Cas knew Wise had secretly bedded her twice, but they never blew it up. Wise had bedded quite a few chicks in the industry.

Beef & Broccoli were also there. Broc had been up north with Wise. That was his man, even before all the rap fame and money. Everyone gave Jay and Cas pounds, and hugs, and expressed their deepest sympathies. Lots of folks had kind words for Fatima, and Rose also.

And Wise' fans came out in record numbers to see him off. There were so many women he had smashed there, it was incredible. Some of them were showing out too, competing for the spotlight. Some had chosen the occasion just to come out, and try to bag themselves another baller. And there were plenty money-getting dudes there for them to try to impress.

Fatima was oblivious to it all. She was preoccupied with her own grief. She spent the entire ceremony crying. She had been pretty strong considering the circumstances, but that day the levies broke. The tears just wouldn't stop coming.

Now, Fatima wasn't hollering and carrying on. She was entirely too weak. The fact that Wise was gone tormented her soul, and the pain was so overwhelming it silenced her. She sat on the pew next to Portia, Jay, Cas, her parents, and Wise' mother, Rose. Falynn sat on her granddaddy's lap. She cried a little, but mostly from seeing Fatima cry so much.

There were tons of flowers, and they were all beautiful. Amongst the lot was one that spelled out "WISE" in white roses. "STREET LIFE" was spelled out as well, but in red roses. Folks had sent some lovely plants as well, and someone got creative and had a big wreath custom-made of one hundred dollar bills. It had a sash across it that said "R.I.P. WI$E".

Jay, Cas, and Wise' former connect, Colombian Manuel had showed up with three non-English speaking bodyguards. After the service, he shook Jay and Cas' hands, and told them how sorry he was. He hugged Fatima and kissed her on the cheek, and wished her solace and peace. Afterwards, he handed her an envelope that Fatima would later discover was a gift in the form of a certified check for half a million dollars, to help ease her pain.

Amongst the funeral attendees were two dark shade wearing federal agents. They had played the background virtually unnoticed. When Manuel made an appearance, they believed they had something. They figured the pieces were starting to come together.

$$$$$

Later that evening, there was a big parade in Wise' honor. Jay and Cas had pulled a few strings, and personally reached out to the Brooklyn Borough president, Marty Markowitz. Markowitz got the okay from Mayor Bloomberg to shut down traffic in the whole 'hood for five hours. Streets were blocked off by police cars, and it was like one big block party in Bed-Stuy. Everybody in the neighborhood had on tee-shirts with Wise' picture on the front.

There was a candlelit vigil held at nine o'clock on the dot. The 'hood hadn't wept that much since Biggie got killed in '97. It was like the whole Brooklyn came out. Folks really represented, and proved BK to be the thorough borough for sure.

The memorial celebration lasted until twelve A.M. As soon as midnight struck, everybody put their lighters up and flicked them in Wise' memory. That was followed by another fireworks display, far grander than the first. After that, the festivities were over. Hopefully, Wise could rest in peace.

$$$$$

They had laid Wise to rest, but the days that followed were far from peaceful for his loved ones. Wise was a well loved family man, and a proud father. He was a good son that took his single mother out of poverty, he was a positive role model for young brothers in the 'hood, and a credit and hero to the community he grew up in.

But the media hounds only focused on the negative side of everything. They portrayed Wise as an unruly, troublemaking thug, and brought up every incident from his past they could to tarnish his good name. They dug up all of his priors from his younger days, and even that bogus rape charge that Melanie had later dropped.

The media insinuated that the record label, Street Life Entertainment, was just some type of front for violence and narcotics, and they portrayed its co-owners, Jay Mitchell and Caseem Brighton, to be former kingpins who had laundered dirty drug money to start up their company. It was all speculations and hearsay, but the family wished they would just let it be, and let Wise rest in peace.

$$$$$

That Thursday, Jay and Casino paid another visit to the funeral home, and they expressed their unhappiness with their first offer. The very next morning, the Hansons called Rose and Fatima, and doubled their settlement offer to four million dollars for their troubles.

This time Fatima agreed. She and Rose agreed to split the money evenly, two million apiece. Then Rose said she was giving half of her share to Falynn, who was her only grandchild. Her only request was that the money be put in a trust she couldn't touch until she was eighteen.

Fatima didn't have a problem with that. In fact, she believed that was a great idea. She decided to put her half of the money in an interest-bearing trust for Falynn as well. She appointed herself the guardian of the trust. She wouldn't steal from her own child. Wise had left Fatima set anyway, so she'd never have to touch a penny of her daughter's money.

Two days later, Fatima was given a big check, an urn full of Wise' ashes, and the Rolex he'd been wearing when he was gunned down. She kept her husband's ashes in a beautiful urn made of 24 karat solid gold, and trimmed with diamonds. She was unhappy with the way things had gone down, but at least that way she could keep him around forever.

CHAPTER SIX

Khalil often laid awake at night, tossing and turning, and struggling with the turn for the worse his life had taken. That night wasn't any different. He had gotten the news about Laila's car accident, and found out she was in a coma, and he felt horrible about it. And his daughter was staying with Portia and her husband, when she should've been with him. He was Macy's father. What kind of man was he? What had he become?

Khalil wondered what had happened. He was tempted to call Portia or Fatima to ask them a few questions, but he didn't even know how to face them. What could they possibly think of him at a time like that? Khalil wanted to get his shit together more than anything now. He needed to regain everyone's respect. It was crucial.

And he wanted to visit Laila in the hospital. He was torn up by the fact that she was in there. He mentally replayed the last conversation he'd had with her. He'd really been an asshole, on some real sour grapes shit. He knew he was wrong for telling her about that old ass incident with Portia. That was some foul shit.

Khalil got out of bed, and turned the light on. He looked over at the mirror on the back of his bedroom door, and didn't like the man he saw one bit. If a man was what you could call him. He was staying back at home with his mother now. She'd allowed him to move down in the basement. It seemed like everyone else had washed their hands with him, and she was only putting up with him because he was her son.

$$\$\$\$\$\$$

"Hold them legs open. Open them legs and gimme that pussy, girl! Don't run!"

Fatima held her legs open like Wise demanded. He was large, so all she felt was straight dick in that position. It was painful pleasure, and oh so good. She let him know how she felt. "You got the best dick in the world, daddy! Ooh yeah, baby. Give it to me. Fuck me, daddy. Just like that! Aahh! Oohh! Oh baby, I'm cummin'! Baby, I'm cummin'!"

Wise loved her facial expressions when she came, so he was looking right in her eyes. Her pussy muscles were twitching and contracting so much, now he was about to bust too. He leaned down and bit into her shoulder. "Aargghh! I'm cummin' too, Ma! Oh shit!" He humped a few more times, and slumped over her, breathing heavily.

Wise fell asleep right on top of Fatima, and she caressed his back and held him until she fell asleep too.

A few minutes later, Fatima opened her eyes, and sat up in bed. She was really groggy, and out of it, but one of the first things she saw was Wise' urn on her dresser. She remembered that he was dead, and grabbed her head. "Oh my God", she exclaimed. She could've sworn Wise had been in bed with her. They'd had sex, and a conversation, and everything. But how could that be?

Fatima drew the conclusion that Wise had come from the grave to pay her a visit. The thought startled her so much, she jumped out of bed and threw on a pair of sweat pants, and grabbed her purse. She ran downstairs and got her Bentley keys, and hurried to her car. Next thing she knew, she was driving down the winding driveway to Portia's house.

Fatima banged on the door, and rang the bell. Portia came and answered fast. She looked through the peephole and saw Fatima. She looked a mess. When she opened the door, she also saw that her friend looked like she was afraid. Tima looked like she had seen a ghost.

Portia's concern-o-meter skyrocketed. She said, "Fatima, what's wrong?"

She took a second to answer, and then she simply whispered, "He visited me from the grave."

Portia looked shocked. "What do you mean? Who, Wise?"

Fatima nodded, and said, "I made love to him, or I think I mean his spirit, last night."

Portia took her hand, and told her friend to come in and have a seat. Fatima followed behind her like she was in a daze. She sat down, and said, "Oh my God, Portia. It was so beautiful."

She placed her hand over her heart, and sighed. "Oh God, I miss him so much. I wanted to go with him, P, so we'd never have to be apart again."

Portia raised an eyebrow. That was when she started to worry. She had lost one dear friend, their girl Simone, to suicide, so she was being extra careful with her loved ones from now on. You had to really listen to what people said.

She spoke to Fatima in a soft tone for some reason, hoping she'd get through to her. "Tima, baby, it was just a dream. Wise is gone. That was God's will, but he wants you to be here, so you can take care of his daughter. Falynn needs you."

Fatima just started crying. Portia went over and hugged her. She felt so sorry for her. The poor child was cracking up.

Fatima must've read her mind. She said, "Portia, I'm telling you, I'm not crazy. Wise visited me from the grave. He was here! Word on everything I love. I'm not crazy. And he was inside of me! I felt him! I did! I did, P! I swear!"

Portia started crying too. Fatima was like her sister, and she was hurting. And she didn't know what to do for her. So she just sat there and cried with her. They sat for like thirty minutes without speaking. Fatima just kept on sobbing and shaking her head, like she was trying to convince herself that she wasn't insane.

After a while, she got it together. She got up and hugged Portia, and said, "Thanks, P. Don't tell nobody about this. I'm good." She picked up her Chanel clutch, and headed for the door.

Portia stopped her, and asked her if she was okay. Fatima gave her a weak smile, and nodded. She said, "I'll call you later, boo. Love you."

Portia said, "Love you too. Why don't you chill for a little while, Tima?"

Fatima refused, so Portia hugged her again real tight. She told her, "Be careful, sis. Take care."

Fatima nodded, and walked back out to her car. She ran out of the house afraid and confused earlier. She had to go back and confront her fears. Portia was right, that must've just been a vivid dream she had. Maybe Wise had visited her, but not physically.

Fatima headed back home. She couldn't run away from her house, and abandon everything she and Wise had worked so hard for. Her baby wouldn't have wanted it to go down like that. Not over a dream. But what a dream it was. She smiled to herself, and went on home.

When she got home, she decided to take a hot bath. She undressed, and looked at herself in the mirror. There was a mark on her shoulder she hadn't noticed the day before. She examined it closer, and to her surprise, it appeared to be a bite mark. She thought about the dream she had, and remembered Wise biting into her shoulder when he came. Fatima got a little spooked. She wondered if something like that was really possible.

She was kind of scared, but she'd enjoyed seeing Wise, and being with him again. That night, Fatima sprinkled some of his ashes between her sheets before she got in bed. Just a little bit. She would never tell anyone because she knew that was borderline crazy, but that was all she had left of him. And maybe she had a better chance of him visiting her again that way.

$$$$$

A few days later, Khalil decided to call Portia. His conscience was really eating at him. He wanted to go see Laila, but he didn't want to just pop up.

When Portia got the call from Khalil, she couldn't believe it. He had some nerve. She had wanted to tell him about his self anyway, so now she had the opportunity. It was all his fault that Laila was in her predicament, and now he was trying to act

like he was so fucking concerned. That phony ass mothafucka.
Portia stared at the phone with distaste. Khalil had the nerve
to ask her what happened to Laila. Her immediate response
was, "You almost made her get killed, that's what happened."
Khalil said, "What? How did I almost make her get killed?"
Portia told that nigga exactly what was on her mind. She did-
n't hold any punches. "Well if you must know, after you ran
ya' mouth and told her about that bullshit, she came over my
house all upset. She asked me if I'd been pregnant by you, and
of course I denied it. But I know she didn't believe me, 'cause
she ran off crying. She just jumped in her car, and sped off.
She didn't even give me a chance to talk to her. The next thing
I knew, the hospital called and said she was almost killed in an
explosive car accident. So I hope you feel real good about yourself."

Khalil was quiet for a minute. He knew he'd gone too far.
That was pretty dumb of him to tell Laila about that. But at
the time, he hadn't really been in his right mind. Damn, he felt
like shit. There was nothing he could say but, "Wow. I'm
sorry."

Portia just shook her head. "Yeah, Khalil. You really are",
she said quietly. After that, she just hung up on his ass. That
apology was too little, and too late.

When Portia hung up on him, Khalil just stared at the phone
for a second. He deserved that. Years ago, he and she had
agreed to never ever speak on that incident again. It wasn't fair
of him to blow shit up like that. Especially when he knew he
had forced himself on Portia that night. She'd been asleep in
her bed, and he had played himself.

Khalil felt low. He had violated Portia when he ran his
mouth too. And what about her and Laila's friendship? Those
girls had been friends long before he even got with Laila. That
was fucked up.

It seemed like everybody was disgusted with him, and had
reason to be so. He really had to earn his respect back. And he
would too, no matter what it took. Khalil knew he had to get
clean first. And he knew he had to go visit Laila too. He had
to go see her so he could apologize. He just had to.

$$$$$

After Khalil called Portia, she had trouble sleeping at night all week. She just couldn't rest thinking about all the things going on, that she wished she could change. Poor Laila's condition was in the top five. She was really mad at Khalil's stupid ass for running his mouth like that. After all that time. That was ridiculous. He did not have to go there.

The more Portia thought about it, she wanted some type of revenge. She had been blaming herself for Laila's ordeal since the accident, but it was Khalil's stupid ass fault that she was laying up in the hospital like that. At that point, Portia really couldn't stand that fucking dude. She was vexed, and she wanted that nigga to be taught a lesson.

Jay came in late that night, a little after one. He and Cas had gone out for a few drinks to take their minds off things. As he got ready for bed, he noticed that Portia seemed kind of uneasy. He asked her what was up.

Portia told Jay that she was still on edge, and worried about those hot guns resurfacing. She said she just wished she knew what had happened to them. She admitted to him that she kept imagining being handcuffed again, and carted off to jail while she was in her last days of pregnancy.

After that, Portia told Jay that Khalil had called and questioned her about Laila's wellbeing, and had fucked up her mood even worse. Then she explained to him that Laila had been in an argument with Khalil right before she crashed, so he was already on her shit list. She told him that she knew about the argument because Laila had called her and told her about the awful things he'd said.

Jay told Portia not to worry about it. He didn't say anything, but he had already decided to take care of it. He offered his wife a massage. He figured she could really use one. She was all worked up, and needed to relax. Portia had to be careful with that high blood pressure.

Portia accepted her husband's offer, and was dozing off in no time to the rhythm of Jay's strong hands kneading her tense back and shoulder muscles.

$$$$$

The following day, Jay told Cas about the argument Portia said Laila had with that nigga Khalil. Casino didn't really say much. All he said was, "Word?"

But Jay could tell from his homie's body language that he was uptight. He knew Cas. That was his man for over twenty years.

Jay knew Cas loved Laila, but he didn't know the depth. Unbeknownst to his right hand man, Casino was contemplating that mothafucka Khalil's murder for the news he just received. As bad as he needed somebody to blame for everything, he was looking forward to taking his aggravation out on that nigga. He would use his fucking face for target practice. That bitch ass nigga fucked with the wrong one. Laila meant a lot to him, and there was no doubt that chump was gonna pay.

Jay sensed that Cas was a little more uptight than he actually let on. He suggested they play a little chess that afternoon, to take his mind off shit. After all that had occurred, they were both somewhat stressed out. Especially Casino. As a way to escape for a minute, Jay challenged Cas to a lot of chess. Cas always stepped up to the challenge, so they both had a new hobby. They were both pretty good because they both enjoyed the game.

They'd also been playing a lot of golf lately. That gave them time to think too. The funny thing about it was they were both so on edge, they even strapped up and carried their guns on the golf course. They figured it was better to be safe than sorry. Past experiences had showed both Jay and Cas that death could be lurking around any corner. Their behavior could probably be described as a bit paranoid, but sleeping on dudes had caused them to lose Wise. They would never do that again.

$$$$$

A few weeks later, Jay accompanied Cas to the hospital to go see about Laila again. She was still in a medically induced coma, but the doctor told them they'd be bringing her out real soon. Both men were thrilled at the news. Cas' mood changed for the better. He just wanted Laila to wake up so she could nourish their baby. He thanked God to himself over and over.

Cas had visualized running into Khalil time and time again, and vividly imagined what he would do to that bastard. Lucky for him, that day he got his wish. When he and Jay were leaving the hospital, he spotted Khalil. That cocksucka was on his way to visit Laila! He was clean too. Cas was surprised to see him dressed up.

He began to wonder if the nigga had some kind of ulterior motives. Did he have some type of life insurance policy on Laila? Was he coming to try to finish her off, or something?

Casino felt particularly possessive of Laila, and protective of her too, because she was carrying his seed. He had never intervened in her "situation" before, but the way he saw it now, if Khalil had said something bad enough to make her crash, he didn't need to see her. Nah.

Cas started across the parking lot. He was gonna make that nigga stay the fuck away from Laila. Fuck that. He was about to shut that whole "visit" shit down. He stepped to that chump immediately.

Jay saw Khalil, and didn't ask Cas any questions. He followed him, because he had no choice. It was serious. He knew how Cas was, so it could get ugly.

Khalil saw Casino approaching him, and recognized him immediately. He recognized Jay too. That was Portia's husband. It was his familiarity with Cas that really stung, because their last encounter had ended with Khalil on his ass. He was ashamed to admit it, but that nigga had fucked him up. But in all fairness, he had been drunk and high when it happened.

Khalil had been clean for a few days. He was trying to get it together, so he knew he was a lot stronger now. And he had on a new outfit he had purchased solely for the occasion of going to visit Laila. Those two factors combined were a real self-esteem booster for him.

Khalil was feeling a whole lot more confident, so he told himself he was ready for round two with that nigga. And this time he would walk away the victor. Fuck that, he was no punk. And when he thought about the fact that Cas was smashing his wife, he felt particularly feisty.

Cas looked him dead in the eyes, and asked, "Yo, what's good?"

Khalil stuck out his chest and eyed Cas right back, displaying more confidence than he actually felt. "What's good? What up?" He glanced over at Jay, and nodded. They had met before.

Jay looked at him for a second. If duke was trying to line up an alliance, he had the wrong one. However, him being the laid back individual he was, he gave Khalil a little nod back. Cas was his main man, but that was Laila's husband. Jay was staying out of it. That was between those two men. He knew Cas could handle himself.

Cas commented on Khalil's surprisingly neat appearance. He told the nigga, "Yo, you clean up pretty nice. You even took a shower today."

Cas smiled at his own humor, and kept on. "Nah, you crispy, son. Nice crease, fresh pair of shoes on. Snakeskin, huh? Clean shave, and a haircut..." He nodded approvingly at Khalil's attire. He wasn't kidding. The last time he had seen duke, he looked a hot mess.

Khalil didn't find Cas' ball breaking comical, but he ate it. He knew he had looked dusty the last time he had seen him. But fuck that nigga.

Cas got to the point. "Yo, where you goin', man?"

Khalil made a face, like he was appalled that Cas had questioned him. "What?! I'm a grown ass man. But if you must know, I'm goin' up to see my wife."

Cas crossed his hands in front of him, and he kept calm. "That was the wrong answer. I don't think that's a good idea. Turn around, and go back to your car."

Khalil looked at him like he was crazy. "I ain't goin' nowhere. I said I'm goin' to see my wife."

Khalil had the mad screw face, but Casino was only amused by the expression wore. He'd never been into face fighting, and eye battling. Khalil's "tough guy" impersonation just made him laugh. But anyone who knew Cas knew that his laughter was a sign of danger.

When Cas laughed, Jay was a little alarmed. He knew he wasn't playing with a full deck when he got upset. He didn't want Cas to pop that nigga. Not over love. It wasn't that serious. Khalil wasn't even worth all that. And he was Macy's father, so Jay figured that was his E-Z Pass right there.

Casino didn't have all day to go back and forth with that lame. He was running out of patience. Seriously. He decided to give him one more chance. He addressed Khalil calmly again.

He said, "Turn around and leave, and don't come back here. This isn't a request. Stay away from Laila. You caused her enough trouble, and enough pain. She's better off without you, so just break out, man."

After that, Khalil got real tight. "So what the fuck you s'posed to be, Laila's keeper, or somethin'? Who the fuck is you?"

Cas clasped his hands in front of him. He was getting impatient. "I'm a very concerned person, who you should be very concerned about."

Khalil should've just taken that as his final warning, but his pride wouldn't allow him to. He screwed up his face even more, and told Cas, "Nigga, you better be concerned 'bout me!" He wasn't strapped, but he had faith in his knuckle game.

Casino was unthreatened by the four octaves Khalil's voice rose. That clown was just trying to come across as intimidating. Like he wasn't the same crackhead mothafucka he'd just knocked out a couple months ago.

Cas wasn't about to get into a verbal exchange. He didn't argue like no bitch. He didn't operate like that. He was short-tempered, and about ready to lay hands on that lame.

The more Cas thought about it, the angrier he got. He'd run out of patience. He was seething. He pressed Khalil aggressively, but he still didn't raise his voice. That wasn't his style. He said, "Nigga, stay the fuck away from Laila. You already upset her so bad, she crashed, and almost killed herself. You think I don't know about that shit? I should really fuckin' hurt you. Word."

Khalil didn't take Cas' words lightly. He knew how those niggas got down. He wondered exactly how much they knew. He prayed Jay didn't know the part about him getting Portia pregnant. He wasn't stupid enough to ask.

Khalil didn't have a death wish, and he didn't have any type of weapon on him at the time, but he wasn't about to punk out. He just shrugged, and told Cas, "Do what you gotta do. But I'm goin' up there to see my wife. And ain't nobody gon' stop me."

Cas was about to do something to that dude. Jay could see it. He already knew. He didn't have anything against that, but they weren't in the right place. He didn't want Cas to get locked up again, especially over no stupid shit. It was time to roll out. Jay through Cas a signal.

Cas knew they were in the wrong place. He reluctantly let it go, but he didn't take his eyes off Khalil. He smiled at him coldly, and said, "Ayight, man." Then he and Jay stepped off.

Khalil had portrayed himself to be hard, like he wasn't afraid. But there was something eerie about that nigga's grin. When they'd had that run-in before, he had smiled just like that. Now that evil grin made Khalil think twice.

But he stood there, and held his ground, until he saw them hop in this dark blue Aston Martin, and pull off. After they left, he headed on towards the hospital. Khalil assumed the beef would end there.

He stayed up there at Laila's bedside for about thirty minutes. It was really shocking to see how bad she looked. She was in a full body cast. He knew she couldn't hear him because she was in a coma, but he told her he was very sorry. He felt terrible. Damn. Laila was his heart. That woman was good to him. What had he done?

Khalil left the hospital feeling distraught. He got in his car, and just pulled off. He was extremely heavyhearted. He headed home with thoughts of his fucked up family situation floating through his mind. He knew he had thrown it all away, but he wanted his wife back. So he could take care of her. It wasn't a game.

Khalil was so deep in thought, he wasn't on point. He didn't notice the blue Aston Martin following him two cars behind. He didn't know Cas had decided to late-wait him, and follow him off the hospital property.

When Khalil got back to Brooklyn about forty minutes later, he parked at a nearby corner store in Bed-Stuy, and got out the car. He wanted to grab himself a beer.

On his way to the store, he looked up and saw Casino approaching him. Jay was right beside him. Oh shit, those niggas had followed him! Khalil's heart skipped a few beats. Were they try'na murk him, or somethin'? What the fuck was up?

Cas saw how nervous Khalil was, but had no pity on that fool. He smiled at him again. Casino was a man of few words, and reticent when he got upset. That infamous grin was an indication that his hands were going to do the talking. True to his reputation, Cas hooked off on that nigga.

That left hook connected with Khalil's jaw, and dazed him. Nonetheless, he put on a fighting stance and threw up his hands. That nigga sucker punched him, so he had no other choice but to thump with him now. He amped himself up, and boldly took a swing at Cas.

It was a fair fight, and Jay didn't intervene. He didn't feel the need to. He just wanted to make sure things didn't get too out of hand. He knew Cas was really mad, and he didn't want him to clap Khalil.

By now, there were a few bystanders watching. Casino was clearly the better, more skilled fighter. A blind man could see that. Khalil tried to front with a little fancy footwork, to impress the onlookers. That turned out to be a bad idea in the shoes he was wearing. He got off a few lucky shots and good hits, but Cas put him on his ass quick.

Khalil got back up fast, and looked determined to win. He was sliding around in those snakeskin hard bottoms like a dude in church shoes on ice. Nonetheless, he threw his hands back up. He swung first that time, but Cas blocked it, and countered with a powerful, blinding three piece. Bip, bam, bip!

Khalil backed up, and stumbled again. Cas was just too fast for him. It turned out to be another unsuccessful toe to toe round. He was completely embarrassed by his performance. He just had to admit it. His opponent was more powerful. Damn, that was the second time that nigga pounced him out. And this time Jay had witnessed his ass whipping too. Khalil's confidence level was at an all-time low.

Just then, Cas delivered the knockout punch. Khalil dropped, and he was out for a minute. Cas had energy enough to go some more. He was sort of disappointed that he dropped him so quick. He wanted to bust that nigga's ass again.

A bystander slapped Khalil awake. He looked up at all those people, and was ashamed. In effort to save face, and try to re-deem his "tough guy" image, he decided to bluff.

He got up off the ground, and brushed his shoulders off. He nodded at Cas, and said, "Ayight, son. You got that one. But yo', wait right here, nigga! I got somethin' for yo' ass! I'll be right back!" He clasped his hands and nodded again, and hurried to his car like he really meant it.

Casino didn't take kindly to threats. Now he was ready to lay that chump out for good. On impulse, he reached for his hammer.

When Jay heard Khalil's words, he knew what would come next. He knew Cas was strapped up just like he was. He looked at Cas, and just as he'd predicted, he saw him reaching. Jay stopped his man quick. It was broad daylight, and there were too many folks out.

Jay knew his bro was a lot like him, and would undoubtedly kill a dude for indicating that his life was in danger. In that case, you didn't give a person a chance to make good on their promise. The rule was not to let the opponent get to their gun. You had to take them out first. But Jay figured it was okay to let Khalil walk away. He was no real threat. That clown didn't really want it.

Khalil jumped in his car, and sped off. About eight blocks down, he made a right turn and pulled over. He sat there for a minute contemplating his next move. His pride was seriously hurt. The first thing he thought about was a quick fix to ease the pain. He needed a hit. The urge for the "medicine" over-whelmed him so much, he drove a few blocks over to Quincy and Nostrand. Them dudes had the best shit.

A few minutes later, Khalil copped, and went home and smoked himself into oblivion. While he got blasted, he mulled over the notion of killing that nigga Cas. It wasn't just about the fact that he'd gotten his ass beat for the second time. It was about the fact that that dude was standing between he and Laila's happiness. If he could just get him out of the picture, he felt like he would have another chance with Laila.

Khalil had never been a killer, but he was no sucker either. His pride was crushed. He couldn't believe that nigga had ordered him to stay away from his own wife. Now if that wasn't a reason to put some lead in a nigga, then what was? The more he thought about it, he knew that was what he had to do. He had to take that dude out. He didn't know how yet, or when, but that nigga Cas was gonna eventually be history. He just had to plan it the right way.

CHAPTER SEVEN

When Jay went home that night, he was in for a treat. While he sat on he and Portia's bed, describing the confrontation Cas had with Khalil to her, she started undressing him, and kissing all over his body. She was obviously very horny.

Jay hadn't been stressing Portia for sex that much lately, because he was concerned about her health. There was so much going on, and he'd listened to what the doctor said about her blood pressure. Jay imagined himself piping her, and causing her to be hospitalized for high blood pressure. He figured sex all the time was too stressful on her.

They still had sex, but they'd gone from three to five times a week, to about twice. But Portia was a good wife. She'd been giving him a lot of head lately. Jay loved it, but sometimes he told her to just relax. She was really starting to show, and he wanted her to take it easy.

But right about now, Jay was hard as hell. If she wanted some, he could definitely assist her with that. He knew from the few times they had done it lately, that thang was even sweeter while she was pregnant. Therefore, he had no objections.

Her belly was getting big, so they only had intercourse in positions he believed wouldn't hurt the baby. Portia loved when he came up behind her, and held her and caressed her. And he knew that, while she was pregnant, her favorite position was doggy style.

After she finished undressing him, Jay undressed her. When he was done, he admired Portia's naked body, and let out a whistle. She looked beautiful pregnant. He turned her around to get a good look.

Portia shook her ass for him, and he pulled her to him and squeezed it. She playfully slipped out of his arms, and ran to the doorway of their master bathroom, and stood there with her legs parted. She looked back at Jay, and theatrically removed the clip from her hair, and shook her hair and tossed it over her shoulder. Afterwards, she lifted her arms above her head, and seductively jiggled her ass. She gave him a little smile, and licked her lips at him.

Jay bit his lip. Damn, she looked good. She was so thick. He walked up behind all that juicy, chocolate Jello pudding ass, and rubbed his dick against it. He ran his hands along her belly, and gently nibbled on her ear and kissed her neck. He knew that was her weak spot.

He moved his hands up, and massaged her breasts. Not too hard, because he knew they were tender, but firm enough to please. He played with her nipples for a while, and had her creaming. Portia was breathing hard.

He wanted to taste her. Jay walked around in front of her, and kneeled down and spread her pussy lips apart. Portia smiled down at him. She loved getting her pussy eaten. He stuck his tongue in, and twirled it all around, and he ate her out until she grabbed the back of his head and cried out.

After that, he got up and leaned Portia against the wall. He ordered her to place her hands up on the wall like he was the police, and he bent down and licked the crack of her ass for a minute. She moaned, and squirmed with delight.

Jay got up, and he held her waist and slid Rocky in from behind. After a few strokes, she was literally purring. And her pussycat was dripping allover him.

Portia relaxed and enjoyed it. Jay was packing, but he was a gentle lover. He always loved her tender, and she loved him for that. He handled her with care, the way a man should. His lovemaking had her ready to climb the wall. She was in total bliss.

He bent her over just a little more, and stroked that thing from behind. He didn't go as deep as he normally would have, because of the baby. But Portia was on fire. She started throwing it back.

The intenseness of Jay's stroke combined with the crushing sensation of his balls slapping against her clit was enough to send Portia into convulsions. She ordered him to squeeze her nipples, and she started bucking and writhing, and moaning uncontrollably.

Jay squeezed her big, soft tities, and his eyes rolled back in his head. Portia was so hot and tight, he felt like he was melting in that pussy. Damn, that thing was right! It was simply overwhelming.

He couldn't hold it back anymore. He grabbed Portia's ass, and announced his "arrival". "Yo, P, I'm 'bout to cum! Aahh!"

She climaxed at the same exact time. That was what you called being in synch. When she came, she squeezed her vaginal muscles on Rocky, which caused Jay to lose his mind. He almost hit a soprano note.

Jay couldn't take it. Panting, he withdrew from inside of her. Afterwards, they both sat down for a minute to catch their breath.

After they were cleaned up, the couple got in bed. Portia snuggled up in the crook of Jay's arm, and he held her tenderly. He whispered a word of thanks in her ear, and nibbled gently on her lobe. They had each other. That was how they had gotten through all of the bad stuff that had happened. They gave one another strengths. Portia relaxed, and fell asleep in Jay's arms.

$$$$$

Christmas came, and went. And so did the New Year. Somehow, the gang managed to get through the holidays. They had tried to make the season joyous for their children, but the family's morale level was at an all-time low. It was mid-January of '08, and getting cold outdoors.

One morning, Fatima stood sideways in front of the huge wall mirror in her bathroom, staring at the spare tire gradually developing around her midsection. She frowned in disapproval, and squeezed the roll with her hands. She could pinch way more than an inch, and that was a damn shame. That was more than holiday weight. She was getting big as a house.

Fatima had been constantly overeating because she'd been

stressed out, and she gained more weight than Portia probably had during her pregnancy. Before she knew it, she was almost two hundred pounds. It was like she had put on forty pounds overnight. Enough was enough. Fatima knew she had to lose that weight.

She considered her options. She didn't want to go through surgery again. There was no way she was doing gastric bypass, and liposuction was painful. She had to lose the weight naturally, without going under the knife. Fatima was a smart girl. She knew what she had to do.

The very next morning, she went out and purchased a membership for a sports club. She took a change of clothes to the gym with her, and started working out the same day.

At the end of a thirty minute cardio aerobic workout she'd joined in on, she went to the locker room to freshen up, and she overheard some women talking about their weight loss secrets. The one Fatima found the most interesting belonged to this girl named Nadia. She had a real nice figure.

Nadia said her secret was, "I eat what I want, and then I just purge."

Fatima was curious, so she asked her, "What you mean, "purge"? Like drink some type of healthy detoxifying tea, or a laxative, or a colon cleanser, or something?"

Nadia laughed, and said, "No, girl. I mean purge." She motioned like she was going to stick her finger down her throat, and make herself vomit.

Fatima got what she was trying to say. That was some white girl shit. She disagreed, so she voiced her disapproval. "Girl, I don't think that's healthy."

Nadia placed her hand on her hip, and smiled. "Don't I look healthy? I'm a perfect size eight."

Fatima, nor any of the other women listening could dispute that. The girl did look good. Fatima didn't say another word.

She went home that evening with that quick weight loss formula in mind. She wasn't going to overdo it. She would only purge a few times, until she lost a little weight.

The following day, Fatima went to the gym again, and worked out. Later that evening, she rewarded herself with a greasy, fattening pizza from Papa John's, with extra cheese and ground beef. She ate like a wild hog.

A few minutes after she was done eating, she bent over the toilet and stuck her finger down her throat. The pizza, the orange juice and toasted bagel with jelly she had that morning, and everything else she ate that day came up immediately.

When Fatima was done barfing her guts out, she wiped the sweat from her brow with the back of her hand, and flushed the toilet. Then she got up and washed out her mouth. Now she was virtually guilt free about eating almost that whole large pizza. With her new purging method, she didn't have to starve herself. She could even overindulge every now and then.

Fatima thought about the addiction to food she had developed, and felt a little ashamed. It was ridiculous how she was trying to convince herself that her overeating was okay. She had been depressed, and moping around the house putting everything into her mouth. She was pitiful. She had to get out and start socializing more. It was time to break out of her shell.

Out of touch with the latest hot spots, she dug out her old phonebook and fished out the telephone numbers of some of her old party buddies. She had to find out what clubs were popping now. Fatima came across Charlene's number, and decided to call her first.

She and Charlene had worked together years ago at Black Reign Records, and Charlene had done her the favor of hiring Portia for a position in the fiscal department. That was before Fatima and Portia had abandoned ship to go onboard at Street Life Entertainment with Jay, Cas, and Wise, while the company was in its startup stage.

Fatima had attended a couple of "alternative" clubs with Charlene years ago. It was actually through her that Fatima had been exposed to her first lesbian experience. They had never done anything like that with each other, but they were cool. Charlene was a freaky bitch, but she damn sure knew how to party.

Luckily for Fatima, Charlene still had the same number. She answered her phone on the third ring. She was happy to hear from Fatima. She told her she was still single, with no children.

It was no secret that Charlene was a diehard lesbian, who didn't plan to have any. She acted like she was thrilled that Fatima wanted to hang out. They set a date for the following weekend.

Fatima hung up, and was so excited about the possibility of getting back into the swing of things, she headed upstairs to pick out a cute designer outfit. There was no point in going shopping, because she had a ton of things in her closet with the tags still on them. All the latest season too. She'd purchased them one day when Portia had attempted to lift her spirits, and dragged her out shopping on Fifth Avenue.

Fatima didn't want to buy a lot of stuff at the time because she had gained so much weight, but she had picked out some cute things. She had a nice set of hooters, and when she wore cleavage revealing blouses and showed off those bad boys, most men didn't seem to give a damn about her extra pounds.

Fatima smiled to herself. Saturday couldn't come fast enough. She was going to party hardy that night.

$$\$\$\$\$\$$$

Friday afternoon, Fatima stopped by Portia's house to have lunch with her. It was also an excuse to let Falynn play with Jazmin for a little while. They were both excited about the new dolls they got for Christmas.

Fatima's parents had brought her daughter home to her that morning, but she was taking Falynn to Rose's for the weekend. Rose had called the day before, and asked to keep her for a few days. She said she wanted to spend time with her granddaughter.

When Fatima had asked Portia what Jazz was doing home, she told her that she kept her home from school because she'd had a tummy ache that morning. Whatever bug she'd had obviously passed, because Jazz and Fay were running all over the place.

Fatima went to the bathroom, and Portia walked down the hall to check on the kids. When she walked pass the bathroom on her way back, she heard these sounds like Fatima was throwing up. "Poor Tima", she thought. She hadn't even looked like she was sick. Maybe it was something she had eaten.

Fatima was like her sister, so Portia didn't think twice about invading her privacy. She knocked once, and turned the doorknob and went inside to make sure she was okay. Girlfriend had her face stuck in the toilet, barfing her guts out. Portia gave her a second to finish, and recover.

When Fatima finally stopped heaving, Portia rubbed her back and smoothed back her hair. Full of concern, she asked her, "You ayight, ma-ma?"

After Fatima caught her breath, she wiped the sweat from her brow, and nodded her head. "Yeah. I'm alright, P. I made myself throw up." She gave Portia a little smile.

Portia was surprised, and the levels on her concern-o-meter rose, but she let her friend talk.

Fatima continued, "You saw how much food I ate, right? Girl, when I binge like that, I have to purge."

She'd seen the funny look on Portia's face, so Fatima regretted saying that. Sometimes her lips were too loose. She did not want to hear Portia's mouth.

Just as Fatima figured, Portia started going in. She said, "Bitch, are you crazy? You gon' fuck around and wind up with bulimia, or anorexia. That's some real "white girl" mess. Tima, how long you been doin' this stupid shit?"

Fatima rolled her eyes, like she wasn't in the mood. She said, "Not long. Okay, P? Don't start. Please."

Portia's pregnancy had her real moody lately. And on top of that, she was unable to puff trees. But she wasn't really that grouchy. She just lacked patience, especially for stupid shit. Short-tempered, she got right to the point.

She said, "Look, Fatima. Ain't no such thing as no "overnight weight loss method". Quit the dumb shit, bitch, before you wind up sick in the hospital, or something. You're the only living parent Falynn has now, so if for no other reason in this world, please think about her before you make stupid fuckin' choices. Are you trying to kill yourself? It ain't all about you no more, bitch. What the fuck is wrong with you?"

When Portia flipped on her, that tongue lashing was Fatima's cue to bounce. She hated when she tried to check her about her parenting skills, like she was Mary fucking Poppins. She took good care of her daughter. What did that have to do with anything? Portia really got on her nerves sometimes, with her sanctimonious bullshit. She wasn't perfect.

Fatima was glad she had kept her mouth shut, and hadn't told her about her weekend plans to hang out with Charlene. Portia would've turned into a real holy roller then, and probably started chastising her about the Bible, and what happened to the city of Sodom and Gomorrah all because of sin.

Fatima made a face, and sucked her teeth. She said, "Thank God, your baby will be born soon. Then you'll have somebody to fuss about and smother, Miss Mother. I am not your child, Portia."

Portia said, "No, you're not a child. So stop acting like one. "Purging" is something some dumb teenaged girl would do."

Fatima just rolled her eyes. After that remark, she kindly collected her little one, and told "Bootleg Oprah" she would talk to her later.

Portia didn't protest to Fatima bouncing. She kissed Falynn goodbye, and she told her silly mother, "Grow up. If I didn't love your crazy ass, I wouldn't say shit. Don't get mad because I fuckin' care about you."

Fatima just rolled her eyes again, and said, "Later, P." She kissed Jazz on the cheek, and burned it up. Falynn started crying because she wanted to stay and keep playing with Jazz, but Fatima pulled her along to the car.

Portia stared at her homegirl for a minute before she locked the door. She knew there weren't any hard feelings between them. Sometimes they just needed space. They knew when to back off each other. That was how they had remained friends for so long.

Portia and Fatima both knew they would be speaking again soon. They had no choice. The following Monday was the day Laila was scheduled to be brought out of her coma, and they both wanted to be there.

$$\$\$\$\$\$$$

When Kira first found out about Laila's accident, she couldn't help but hope she wouldn't recover. She didn't really want her to die, but she wouldn't mind her being crippled for the rest of her life. She didn't believe Cas would be interested in no cripple bitch. He would want to come back home to her.

Kira had found out from Jay that Laila was scheduled to be brought out of her coma that coming Monday. She had to admit she was disappointed at the news. She felt a little bit bad about that, but it was personal. Laila had stolen her husband. How could she possibly wish her well?

$$$$$

Earlier that morning, Jay and Cas had been informed by their attorney, Solly Steiner, that their record company could be the target of a huge criminal investigation in the future. He said it could be triggered partially by Wise' murder, and the fact that Colombian Manuel had showed up at his funeral.

Manuel was their former connect, but Solly didn't know the extent of their relationship. Jay and Cas weren't surprised at the news. They had seen two dark glasses wearing Federalis at Wise' burial. They knew those boys would probably be coming sooner or later. Every time a black man got up legitimately, along those bastards came.

On the low, Jay and Cas pulled Manuel's coat about the situation. He thanked them, and told them he had allies in high places just for stuff like that. The way Manuel figured, there wasn't a cop in the whole world he couldn't pay off. Manuel said that if one existed, then God help him, because he would sleep with the fishes before he'd let him take him down.

Solly warned Jay and Casino that the Feds could strike unexpectedly, and freeze all of their assets. So Jay and Cas were smart. They were two steps ahead of those sons of bitches. It was time to start moving money. They had recently discussed the possibilities of establishing some overseas accounts with their new business manager, a well respected, finance savvy dude named Tobias Rey.

Jay and Cas both agreed that it was time to make that move.

They had cleaned up their money pretty good through real estate investments when they first got in the game. They had been extra careful to avoid doing anything to incriminate themselves from the gate. They even had papers to prove that they'd sold legally "inherited" property to legitimately finance their record company start-up.

Being men of their stature, Jay and Cas had too many responsibilities to dwell on the possibility of a federal investigation. They just kept their noses clean, and continued living their lives, and handling their business. Their morals hadn't changed. "Take care of business first, but set aside time for family." Those were the words they lived by. The past year had taught them how easily a loved one could slip away. And both of them were also expectant fathers.

Speaking of babies, Cas was preoccupied with the excitement of knowing that Laila was scheduled to be brought out of her medically induced coma in two days. Needless to say, he was counting the hours. He just had to figure out the right way to inform her about the baby she was carrying.

CHAPTER EIGHT

Saturday finally came. It was Fatima's big day to step out. That evening, she took her time getting dressed. It had been a while since she'd been out. She knew what a party girl Charlene was, so for the trillionth time, she questioned her better judgment about hanging out with her. She hoped she'd made the right decision.

She knew Charlene was a lesbian, and they would undoubtedly wind up at some freak party, or something. That was evident when Charlene called and asked her if she had proof of being recently tested for HIV. Fatima would have never admitted it, but a small part of her reasoned that a one night stand with a woman was what she needed. Then she wouldn't be betraying Wise. She wanted to get her shit off but she didn't want to disrespect his memory by fucking some other dude. She didn't even want to have sex with another man anyway. She couldn't yet. But she was horny.

Knowing this influenced Fatima's decision to comb down her freshly straightened and wrapped hair, and step in her Louis Vuitton open toes. She grabbed her matching Louis clutch and her Bentley keys, and headed for the door. Fatima stopped short when she remembered that Charlene had mentioned that she should bring a copy of her latest AIDS test results. She hurried upstairs to retrieve the paperwork. She'd been tested two months ago during a routine physical, and she was proud to say that the results came back negative.

Fatima found the paper, and folded it up and stuck it in her clutch. She looked over at the mirror, and was pleased with what she saw. She still had a few pounds to shed, but like her girl Mary J. Blige said, "Work What You Got." Fatima was decked out in red, and that was the same color she planned to paint the town that night.

When Fatima arrived at Charlene's house in New York City, Charlene came out and informed her of their plans for the evening. She said a friend of hers had sent her an e-vite to a swing party. She was honest, and admitted that it was an "anything goes" type of party, and then she asked Fatima if she felt she was open-minded enough to attend.

Fatima thought about it for a second. If she went, it would be the first time she had ever done anything that crazy. She was already out of the house now, so she might as well roll. She was a grown woman. She didn't have to participate in anything if she didn't want to.

Charlene hopped in the Bentley with Fatima, and they headed to the Manhattan address she gave her. As Fatima headed for Chelsea on the Westside Highway, she actually got a little excited about the night to come. She was nervous, but she wanted to get her feet wet a little. She had been so stressed out lately. Maybe some unattached sex would do her body good.

An hour later, they were sitting in a dimly lit, modern, loft apartment that was located in a high-rise building, sipping on their second round of cocktails. Charlene had suggested that Fatima mingle a little bit, to see what type of flavor she savored. Fatima told her she would just chill out and observe for now. Charlene told her to do whatever she liked, and announced that she was going to do her.

Fatima finished her drink a few minutes after Charlene disappeared, and she decided to walk around and see what was popping. It was a split-level apartment they were in, and when she walked downstairs, she discovered there were freak shows going on everywhere. Including her and Charlene, there were about thirty people there, and most of them were openly engaged in fucking and sucking. And they acted like it was the most natural thing in the world. There were no holds barred at that party. Real talk.

The third room Fatima stepped in, she looked over in the corner and saw that Charlene was busy. She had her face buried between the thighs of some Spanish looking girl, who was holding the back of her head, and moaning in pleasure.

At first, Fatima was shocked by Charlene's boldness. Damn, homegirl hadn't wasted any time. But then she remembered that they were at a swing party. She was obviously the only person there with any sexual hang-ups.

She had to admit that seeing all that sex going on around her was beginning to make her horny too. Not horny enough to eat no coochie like Charlene, but she was tempted to let somebody do her. She left the room, and scanned the rest of the scene for a volunteer of her liking. Gender wasn't an issue, as long as the person had soft lips and knew what they were doing. Hell, she just wanted to get off.

All of a sudden, someone came up behind her and placed their hands over her eyes. The person was pretty tall. They leaned down and brushed her hair back, and breathed feather kisses along the nape of her neck. Their hands roamed south on her body, and stopped at her breasts. They fondled them gently, and firmly rolled her nipples with their thumbs and forefingers.

Fatima lifted her arms, and ran her hands along their shoulders. They were broad and muscular, so it had to be a man. Now she could feel his maleness growing hard on the back of her behind. He smelled good too. She knew that cologne. It was Gucci Pour Homme II. Wise used to wear that scent sometimes.

That stranger was seducing the hell out of Fatima. Her body temperature was rising. She moaned softly. She hadn't been wrapped in a man's arms since Wise had passed, and it felt good. Damn good. Fatima was so caught up in the moment she hardly noticed this young, slim, Asian girl approaching her.

The girl was high as hell on ecstasy or something, like most of the people there. She was drawn to Fatima, intrigued by the sight of her getting her big, beautiful breasts fondled. She wanted to assist that gentleman in pleasuring her, but she didn't say a single word. She just walked up, and ran her hands along Fatima's curves.

After a few seconds of caressing her sensually, she knelt down on one knee in front of Fatima, and lifted her skirt. The girl pulled her red thong to the side, and began kissing and licking her pussy. She went right in for the kill, sucking on her clit like it was a pacifier.

Fatima gasped, and parted her legs. She rolled her eyes in pleasure. She was losing control. The combination of the dude behind her playing with her nipples, and the girl eating her pussy was more than she could take. Her legs were getting weak. She leaned back on the gentleman for support, imagining him to look just like Denzell Washington. He held her tight, and nibbled on her earlobe. Fatima was dizzy with passion.

The girl spread Fatima's pussy lips apart with her thumbs, and continued pleasuring her. Homegirl was really going in. Her legs felt like they were about to buckle. She was going to cum. Fatima reached down and wrapped her fist in her hair, and held the back of her head. That shit felt so good, she didn't want her to stop. She was in ecstasy.

The girl didn't quit until Fatima's juices were running down her face. She licked up every drop hungrily, like she savored it.

The dude held Fatima, and caressed her breasts while home-girl's tongue sent her into convulsions. He knew she was cum-ming, and his dick was hard as a brick. After the girl gave her the appetizer, he was ready to give Fatima the main course. He led her to a nearby sofa, with his arm around her waist. The Asian girl followed them, and never took her eyes off of Fatima. She apparently liked the taste of her honey.

The guy pulled out a Magnum from his pocket. When he pulled out his dick, Fatima's eyes grew as big as fifty cent pieces. That thing was huge! It looked like a big fake, chocolate dick.

Homeboy proudly held it for a second while she admired it, like it was his most prized possession. After he rolled the con-dom on, he bent Fatima over and attempted to slide inside of her. She turned around to double-check the rubber, and ran her fingers along the latex approvingly. It was on right. Fuck it, she might as well go all out. Nobody there knew who she was. She looked at homeboy again. His face wasn't as attractive as Denzell's, but he had a nice body. She was about to fuck a total stranger. And he had a big ass dick.

Fatima bent over, but then she thought twice. Her better judgment kicked in. What the hell was she doing? That nigga could have herpes, or crabs, or anything. She stood up and moved, just in time enough to dodge that big black bullet. She turned around, and shook her head. She took a step back, and said, "I'm afraid I changed my mind. Sorry."

The guy was pretty cool about it. He was clearly disappointed, but he laughed it off. He had no choice but to respect her wishes. He zipped up his pants, and moved on to find someone willing to receive that big black pole he was working with. He was into guys sometimes too, so he didn't discriminate.

When he put that monster away, Fatima had to laugh. The term "well endowed" didn't do it for him. Homeboy was hung unnaturally, like a horse. That was beyond blessed. She was glad she had protested. That was too much dick. She didn't want to put that type of wear and tear on her pussy.

Fatima waved at him after he walked away. He winked at her, and kept it moving. She smiled. She couldn't front, the way he'd touched her had been amazing. It had been a long time since she'd been in the arms of a man, so she appreciated the comfort of their brief encounter. He had her creaming before that girl had even touched her.

Speaking of the girl, when Fatima turned around she was still standing there. She had taken her to ecstasy with her tongue, so she was alright with her. The girl must've wanted some more. She was bold, and said, "Why don't you lay down, beautiful, and let me taste you again? Your juices are really sweet."

Something about the way she asked encouraged Fatima to do it. Hell, everybody else was freaking. Oblivious to her surroundings, she sat down on a red chaise lounge to their right, and spread her legs. Fatima allowed the girl to feast on her essence. Homegirl placed her legs over her shoulders, and spread her pussy lips wide open. Fatima closed her eyes, and grooved to the beat of the techno music playing in the background while the girl expertly flicked her tongue over her clit, and tongue-fucked her into oblivion.

Fatima came again in less than three minutes. She couldn't take it anymore. She pushed the girl's head away and begged her to stop, but she refused. It was like she couldn't get enough.

She wrapped her arms tightly around Fatima's thighs, and sucked and licked her with fervor, from her clit to her asshole. She looked like she was really getting off, bucking and moaning like she was cumming too. And Fatima hadn't even touched her.

Fatima knew her shit was good, but damn. That chick really loved to eat pussy. Against her will, she pulled another orgasm out of her. One she didn't even think she had left. And it drained her too. Fatima was panting like she had just run a two-minute ten kilometer run. She came so hard tears came out of her eyes. All she could say was, "Damn! What's your name?"

The girl just smiled, and wiped her mouth. "I'm Cheyenne. I like you. We should keep in touch."

Although she probably should have protested, Fatima didn't. That Chinese chick could eat some pussy. They could exchange phone numbers. There was no harm in that.

Fatima had been so deeply engrossed in getting her pussy eaten, she hadn't noticed Charlene enter the room a minute ago. Charlene had just finished participating in a three-way "6-9" with these girls named Rosalind and Carmen. The latter of the two was the Spanish bombshell Fatima had seen her eating out earlier.

After Charlene had wrapped up her freak show, she went to look for Fatima, to make sure she was okay. Well, she could see that girlfriend was fine. And from the looks of things, she had really enjoyed herself.

Charlene had witnessed the last two minutes of Fatima getting pleasured, and she smiled on like a proud big sister. She was a diehard lesbian, and the thought of sex with men repulsed her. Charlene celebrated every new turnout that she witnessed. From the looks of things, that girl turned Fatima's ass inside out.

Charlene knew Fatima was no angel. She knew she'd had sex with a woman at least once, because it happened when they'd hung out at this gay club years ago, when they used to work together. But she also knew Fatima had gotten married. Girlfriend had taken the "straight" route. But now that her husband was gone, maybe Charlene could convince her to cross

over the "rainbow". In Charlene's book, there was nothing better than the vajayjay.

When Fatima looked up and saw Charlene staring at her,
she blushed. She quickly got up, and adjusted her clothing.
She didn't like the way Charlene was staring at her.

On the low, she took a business card from her purse and
handed it to the girl. Fatima didn't even remember her name.
She thanked her, and headed towards Charlene. For some reason, she felt a little ashamed. It was time for them to go.

Fatima informed Charlene that she was ready to break out.
That was enough excitement for her for one night. She had gotten out of the house, socialized a little bit, had a couple of
drinks, and got her shit off, all in one shot. Her mission was
accomplished.

$$\$\$\$\$\$$$

Monday morning, Jay, Cas, Fatima, and Portia all went to
the hospital together. They were sort of quiet during the ride,
each lost in their own thoughts. Ironically, all of them were
thinking the same thing. "What if something went wrong
while the doctors were bringing Laila out of her coma?" Nobody wanted to say it out loud, but they each sent up individual
prayers for Laila's recovery.

Inside the hospital, the doctor instructed them to wait in the
waiting room. He said he would be back soon to notify them
about Laila's progress. They all grabbed a seat. Everyone was
on edge. They all hoped everything turned out okay. More
than anything, they prayed Laila would walk again.

About forty minutes later, the doctor returned and told them
Laila was awake, and in recovery. He said they could see her in
a little while, but should be prepared for delayed responses
when they communicated with her. He explained that her
body had been shut down for months, and it would take a while
for her to regain all of her functional abilities. He said she
would have to learn to do some things all over again.

But on a brighter note, the sonogram he had just given Laila
showed that the baby was doing okay. He showed them the

pictures of the baby, and then handed them to Cas. The doctor said he hadn't informed Laila that she was pregnant yet. He was leaving that up to them, as they wished.

Casino stared at the pictures of his baby proudly. Technology was so amazing. He couldn't believe he was staring at photos his unborn child. The pictures and the news about the baby cheered everybody up. It gave them all hope.

It was sad to know that Laila would be unable to do certain things at first, but they all had faith in God that she would eventually be okay. They were all eager to do what they could to make sure.

About another thirty minutes later, a nurse came to the waiting room and summoned them to come with her. They all rose, and followed her. Each was nervous about seeing Laila awake for the first time in a while. Especially Portia, because she didn't know what Laila's first reaction to her would be. She wondered if Laila even remembered that bullshit Khalil had told her about him getting her pregnant.

Before they went inside, Portia told Jay and Cas she thought she and Fatima should go in first. She had her reasons for wanting to see Laila alone first, but she told them she just wanted to make sure she was decent. Fatima agreed, and they asked Cas and Jay if they minded. Neither of them did.

Cas felt like he needed another minute anyway. Laila didn't know about the baby she was carrying yet, but he knew he had to tell her. He couldn't front, he was a little nervous about the way she would react when she found out he was the one who'd made the decision for her to keep the baby. She might think he had crossed a line. That was her body. But that was his baby inside her too.

Portia and Fatima went inside the room, but they stood back for a minute. The last time they'd seen their girl, she was wearing a full body cast. At first sight this time, Laila looked like a shadow of her former self. She was thin, and she looked really weak. She appeared to be still in a trance. But thank God, she was awake. Her slanted eyes slowly opened, and she peered at them tiredly. She stared at them for a few seconds, and then they could tell she recognized them. She managed a weak smile.

Portia and Fatima hurried to her bedside. They kissed their best friend on the forehead and face, and stroked her hair. It was so good to see her with those bandages off. It had really been a long time.

They'd had to shave Laila's head on the side, to stitch up a huge gash she got in the accident. Her hair had grown back some, but you could tell that part was way shorter. Portia and Tima were already planning a salon visit for her, so she could get a chic hair cut.

Laila couldn't talk much, but she squeezed her best friends' hands to let them know she was okay. She was a fighter, and they knew that. Portia and Fatima smiled happily. They were grateful to God that their friend was okay. Laila was like their sister.

The first thing they told her was that they loved her and missed her, and were bringing Macy back to visit her in a little while. At the mention of her daughter's name, Laila smiled groggily.

Fatima told her that Casino and Jay were out in the hall, waiting to see her. At first, she looked a little hesitant. Then she let her guards down, and nodded a little, they guessed in approval. They hugged and kissed her again, and then told Laila they were sending in the men.

When Portia and Fatima came out and gave Jay and Cas the green light, they both went on inside. They smiled at Laila, happy to see her back in commission. Jay approached her bedside, and bent down and kissed her the cheek, and squeezed her hand. She smiled up at him.

Jay had mad love for Laila. The poor girl had been through a lot. They had really gotten to know one another when she and her children had come to stay with him and Portia, and he had learned that she was a real soldier. She'd managed to land on her feet every time she fell, and he prayed this time wouldn't be any different. Laila had a place in his heart, and there was nothing he wouldn't do for her.

Jay asked her if she was okay, and she nodded a little. He took that as a good sign. He looked back at Cas, and decided it was time for him to excuse himself. He squeezed Laila's hand again, and told her he'd be back. He wanted to give Cas some time alone with her.

After Jay left the hospital room, Casino stood back for a second. Every ounce of him wanted to rush over and take Laila in his arms, and hold her, but he hesitated for some reason. He just wanted to look at her. He felt so horrible about what had happened to her. He wished he could've turned back time. Then he would've protected her somehow, and prevented all that shit from happening.

Laila looked at Cas, and made eye contact for a second. She tried to be cool, but she knew her appearance was shot. She felt like she looked just awful. Her lips were peeling, and she knew her hair was tore up. That was probably the reason he was so hesitant to come to her.

Laila figured she had really turned Cas off. She unconsciously attempted to smooth down her hair. She didn't know exactly what she looked like, and she didn't even want to see any mirrors yet. That would probably make her feel worse.

Cas realized at that point that Laila was feeling self-conscious about her appearance. He walked over, and smiled at her assuredly. "Why you try'na fix your hair? That ain't necessary, Ma." He bent down and kissed her on the forehead.

"Welcome back", he said, and winked at her.

He got her to smile. Satisfied, Cas raised Laila's chin and forced her to look at him. "Hey, Laila. I missed you, girl. You look beautiful."

She looked away, seriously doubting what he said. Casino could tell, so he reassured her. "You heard what I said, baby girl."

Cas sounded so sincere, Laila's eyes watered up. She loved him. He was genuinely concerned, and that gave her hope. She was grateful to be alive. She had learned from her doctor a little while ago that she'd been out for about four months. It was hard to believe she had been stagnant for so long. She was sure glad to be back.

Laila couldn't remember many details about her accident, but she remembered that crash. She thought she was dead after that. But God was good. The only thing that worried her was the fact that she couldn't really move some of her body parts. The doctor told her it would take a minute for the medication to wear off. She couldn't wait. She hated that doped up feeling she was experiencing. She couldn't speak, and it was like she wasn't able to function.

Cas watched Laila closely, and he knew from her appearance that she wasn't ready for the news he had. Not yet. She was still pretty out of it. His eyes wandered down to her belly. He still couldn't believe his seed was in there. That was crazy.

Cas smiled at his baby mama. He was glad she was back. His heart went out to that girl. He would make it his business to not let anything else happen to her. That was word on their unborn child's life. He said a quick prayer that Laila would have a speedy recovery, so they could resume a normal life. She was the one for him. Deep in his heart, he felt it.

Two days later, Laila was doing a lot better. She was fully alert, and speaking coherently. The only sad part about her recovery was when she'd learned about Wise' passing. Her heart went out to Fatima. Laila wept openly, and even felt guilty because he was shot out in the parking lot of the hospital she was in. She felt that if she hadn't been in that accident, he might've still been alive.

Cas had barely left Laila's side the past two days. She was still bedridden, and the doctor was still unsure whether her paralysis was permanent. The tests they had run came back inconclusive, so there was still a fifty-fifty chance.

Cas sat by her bedside, and massaged her feet. He decided it was time to break the news to her about the baby she was carrying. He didn't see the point in waiting any longer. She really needed to know. He started out by asking her how she was feeling.

Laila looked at Cas, who had been by her side almost every hour since she woke up. She smiled at him, and nodded like she was okay. But honestly, there was little truth to her response. She was frightened beyond her imagination. She feared she would never walk again. But she was grateful that Cas was by her side, so she didn't want to scare him away with the truth.

Cas ran his hands along Laila's legs, and massaged her calves and ankles. He looked at her, and said, "Ma, I gotta tell you something."

Laila looked concerned. "What, boo? What's wrong?"

Cas looked away for a second. He had to get up the nerve. Damn, it was going to be a little harder than he'd guessed. "Fuck it", he thought. He looked at her sincerely, and came right out with it. "Laila, you're having a baby."

Laila looked surprised. She hadn't expected him to say that. Cas was mad upfront. They weren't ready for that yet, so she gave him a safe answer. "Yeah, maybe in due time, baby. But you know we have some issues we need to work out first. Like both of us getting a divorce, and me getting out of the hospital, and walking again."

Cas could see that she thought he was talking about in the future. He calmly explained to her that she was with child now. "Nah, Ma. I think you misunderstood. I meant you're having a baby right now. You're pregnant, Laila."

She looked at Cas like he was crazy. "What? Yeah, right."

Cas could see that she didn't believe him, so he said it more firmly. "Yo, I'm dead ass, Ma. You're pregnant. This is what the doctor said. You're about twenty weeks along."

Laila looked stunned. You could've knocked her over with a feather. Her mouth just hung open for a second. "But how?"

"How else? It had to happen before the accident", Cas said patiently.

Laila exclaimed, "Oh my God! Are you serious?"

"Yeah. We found out right after the wreck. They said you had "options", but I thought it would be a good idea for you to have it. I figured it was meant to be."

Casino paused for a second, and then he continued. "And obviously, it was." He looked at Laila earnestly, with love filled eyes. He was totally unprepared for what happened next.

Laila exploded. She hit the side of the bedrail angrily, and barked on him. "You thought it would be a good idea?! You can't be serious. Are you out of your fuckin' mind? Where the hell is my doctor? I gotta find out if it's too late to get rid of it. Oh my God! What the hell could I do with a baby right now?

Use your brain, Cas!" Laila couldn't believe she'd been so stupid. She really got pregnant at the wrong time.

Cas was a bit surprised. That was the first time Laila had ever spoken to him in that manner. He knew she was upset, so he let it ride. His response to her dilemma was, "You don't gotta do nothin'. Just have it, that's all. I'll take care of all the rest."

She flipped again, and spat, "Oh, it's that simple, huh? If you want a baby, mothafucka, you have one!"

Laila shook her head in disbelief. "Yo, I really, really hate you right now. As a matter of fact, could you please leave?"

Cas looked shocked. "What you mean, lea..."

Laila put up her hand, and stopped him. "Just get out! I need to be alone right now. Please, Cas."

Cas didn't like the way she cut him off when he was speaking, but he understood. He knew it must've been a real emotional time for Laila. But he wanted her to understand that he was there for her. Her pain was his. But he could tell by the way she was looking at him that right now wasn't the time to express this. He just got up, and left.

Laila watched Cas walk away, and as soon as he closed the door, her tears start to brim. Just when she thought her life couldn't get worse, it did. She was mad at Cas, and Portia and Fatima too, because they could've stood up for her and had the doctor perform an abortion. They knew that would have been in her best interest. Look at the circumstances. What the hell was wrong with those bitches? They had really sold her out.

When Laila spoke to her doctor later that day, he confirmed the fact that she was almost five months pregnant. She couldn't get an abortion that far gone. She spent the whole day and night crying about her situation. Portia, Jay, and Fatima came to see her before visiting hours were over, but she refused their visits. She told the nurses to tell them she didn't feel up to any company.

Laila continued this erratic behavior for the next four days. Cas, and the rest of the gang all came to visit her in the hospital, but their attempts were in vain. The only people Laila looked forward to seeing were the two physical therapists who came everyday and worked with her to learn how to get in and out of her wheelchair. They also assisted her with exercises to help strengthen her muscles, so she could walk again. She had been laid up for quite awhile. They designed a special routine for Laila, and they went at it everyday.

Other than that, Laila just wanted to shut the world out. Nobody understood what she was going through. They all acted like they were so concerned, but she didn't want to be around those phony mothafuckas. She just wanted to be alone, and wallow in self-pity. Laila felt like she was teeter-tottering dangerously on the brink of insanity. She'd been dealt a fucked up hand to play. How could she win? That pregnancy thing had her twisted.

Portia and Fatima wanted to know why Laila was bugging like that, refusing their visits and all. They called and spoke to Casino, and he told them what happened when he informed Laila about her pregnancy. He told them she flipped on him, and kicked him out. Him, or nobody else had seen her since.

On day ten of her retreat, Laila began to feel the effects of her loneliness. She realized how bad she wanted to get out of the hospital. Being confined in that room was driving her mad. And she hated all that damn medicine they kept shooting in her. She was a nurse, so she knew some of that stuff had side effects.

To Laila's delight, the doctor came in and told her he was releasing her soon. He said she could continue the therapy she'd been taking everyday at home. Laila was thrilled, but she knew she needed someone on the outside to make preparations for her to come home. She didn't have anybody but her friends, so she was forced to swallow her pride.

Laila's doctor called Portia, and told her Laila was being released in a couple of weeks. He asked her if Laila's residence would be wheelchair accessible. Portia told him it certainly would. As soon as she hung up, she went online and found a company that installed wheelchair ramps and handicap rails. After she set up an appointment for consultation the following day, she called Fatima.

Fatima was thrilled about the good news. Laila being released from the hospital was a blessing. God was so good.

They went back and forth over which of them she would stay with. Fatima gave in, and agreed to let Portia accommodate Laila temporarily. Her daughter, Macy, was staying with Portia already anyway.

Fatima didn't say anything, but Cheyenne, the Asian girl from the swing party she'd attended with Charlene, had been staying at her house a few nights. So she preferred that Laila stay with Portia, so she could still have her privacy. She didn't want her friends judging her.

Cheyenne had been eating Fatima out allover the house, and she'd started looking forward to it. Charlene had pulled her coat about Cheyenne. Her sources had revealed that she was a known for house hopping groupie in the industry. Fatima was all alone in that big ass house, so she didn't mind giving her a place to stay. Not as long as she could get off every single time she snapped her fingers. Cheyenne was her little "girl toy", there to service her whenever she wanted.

CHAPTER NINE

Biggie had said it well in that song, "You're nobody - 'til somebody - kills you." That sort of proved to be true. Wise was a popular dude when he was alive. His star had risen while he was there to witness it, but it shot through the roof after his demise. The weeks following his murder, his record sales had quadrupled.

Jay and Cas were proud of him. They really missed that dude. He'd worked hard on that album. It was sad that he couldn't be there to enjoy all the fruits of his labor. But his cut of the proceeds would go straight to his family.

Jay and Cas had scheduled a meeting with Fatima for the following afternoon. They wanted to discuss some financial matters with her. They had called Rose as well. They had to talk to her too. She told them they should go deal with Fatima first. Wise had left a will specifying who got what, and Rose said she was fine with what he'd left her.

Jay and Cas weren't shady businessmen like the average record company executives. They intended to pay Wise' family every penny that was due to them.

$$\$\$\$\$$$

The next day around noon, Fatima was in the house grooving. She had her stereo volume on ten, blasting one of the oldies CDs she'd been running lately. One of her favorite songs by The Supremes, "Someday We'll Be Together", was playing. Fatima did a little two-step, and sung along, careful not to spill the "Tima-tini" filled glass in her hand.

"Someday we'll be togeth-eh-eh-ther. Say it, say it, say it again. Someday we'll be togeth-eh-eh-ther. I know, I know, I know, I know. Someday, we'll be togeth-eh-eh-ther..."

She closed her eyes, and felt the music. Music was purging, and good for the soul. Before the song was over, Fatima had tears streaming down her face. She had been putting up a good front, but she was still fucked up over losing her husband. Lately she'd been partying, drinking, and smoking mad weed as a means of escape, but she missed Wise with all of her heart.

Just then, Fatima heard the doorbell. That had to be Cas and Jay. She was expecting them. She dried her eyes, and turned the music down a little, and she hurried to let them inside. Those two were Wise' truest friends. They had really been looking out for her. Fatima really loved those guys.

Jay and Cas were strong for her when she couldn't be. They were the core of her support system. Those dudes were like her big brothers.

Fatima opened the door and greeted Jay and Cas with big hugs, and then invited them inside. She blushed when they told her how good she looked with all the weight she had lost. After she took their jackets, she offered them a drink.

Cas looked at Fatima sternly, and said it was a little early to be drinking. He told her she was a bad influence, and then he laughed and told her to fix him a shot of Patron. Jay said he was good. He would be the designated driver.

He and Casino sat down and chilled for a while. They asked Fatima how she was doing, and asked where Falynn was. Fatima told them her daughter was staying with Wise's mother for a few days.

Before they addressed the business at hand, they all talked about Laila. She had just come home from the hospital a few days before. Laila had been staying at Portia and Jay's, but Fatima said she'd expressed wishes to go home to the new house that Cas had purchased for her. She said she wanted to go home, and be independent so she wouldn't be a burden on anyone. They all thought that was nonsense, but everybody understood her need to have her own space.

Cas hadn't seen Laila since she'd come home. It wasn't that he didn't want to, he was just unsure if she wanted to see him or not. He had gone to the hospital many times, only to have some nurse tell him Laila didn't feel well, and didn't want company. He was tired of her rejection, so he was just giving her space. He didn't want to upset her.

Cas had kept his distance for a few days, but he had made sure she had an accredited medical staff at her beck and call around the clock. He was glad to hear from Fatima that Laila wanted to go home to the house he'd bought her. He didn't say anything, but he'd already interviewed two live-in nurses he wanted to hire to look after her. That way she would never go unattended.

Fatima told Cas that she and Portia had taken Laila to the hair salon the day before, and she got a cute haircut. She hinted that he should go by and check it out. He told her he wanted to, but knew Laila was angry at him about the decision he had made about the baby. Fatima suggested he go over there, and make her talk to him. Cas thought about it, but he didn't respond.

Next, Cas and Jay talked to Fatima about the financial business they had come to discuss. Fatima appreciated them running everything down to her, and giving her the respect they did. They even asked her if she was familiar with Wise' accountant, or needed to be formerly introduced to him.

Jay and Cas didn't let on that they were concerned that she was drinking and partying so much lately. Instead, they casually suggested that it would be a good idea to keep a kind of low profile for a little while, for safety purposes. They told Fatima she was more of a target than she thought she was, and even wanted to hire a bodyguard for her.

Fatima thanked them, but she told them she didn't think that was necessary. She was okay. She didn't say anything, but she didn't want some big brute following her around and spying on her. He would just go back and report all of her business to Jay and Cas. The way she was living lately, that was a no-no.

While they were in the middle of their conversation, that silly bitch Cheyenne had the nerve to come downstairs wearing nothing but a baby doll tee-shirt and panties. At the worse time possible.

Fatima didn't know, but Cheyenne had looked out the upstairs window and seen a strange, expensive looking vehicle in the driveway. Cheyenne was a bi-sexual groupie, always aspiring to land a guy or girl even more prominent than the last. That was how she got by. Fatima was her current meal ticket, but she was always looking for a bigger payoff. That was the reason she came downstairs so scantily clad. She'd intentionally come down half-dressed, just to flirt.

Fatima hid her embarrassment well, but she wanted to kill that stupid ass girl. That bitch did not fucking listen. She had specifically told her to stay the fuck upstairs and out of the way, until her company left. How dare she come out and try to grandstand like that. She could've at least put on some damn clothes.

Fatima knew what that shit was about. She was throwing herself at Jay and Casino. Fatima doubted either of them wanted Cheyenne's drugged out, groupie ass. She wondered why she was even letting that bitch lay up on her. She knew she was using her.

Cheyenne was really wearing out her welcome. You could tell by her glassy eyes that she was coked up out of her mind. That's all the fuck that bitch wanted to do was snort coke. And smoke those stinking ass cigarettes. It was time for her to get the hell out.

Fatima was steaming, but she had to play it cool in front of Jay and Cas. She was sure they were both wondering what that was all about, so she had to say something. She turned around and addressed Cheyenne sternly, like she was her employer. "Did you clean the two bathrooms downstairs as well?"

Cheyenne pouted, and crossed her arms. She was no damn maid! But she saw the look on Fatima's face, and said, "Yes, I cleaned them. Master."

Fatima narrowed her eyes at her sarcasm, but she just said, "Thank you. Your pants should be dry by now. You should go put 'em back on."

Fatima dismissed that bitch with a wave of her hand. Cheyenne walked away, still pouting.

Jay and Cas played it cool, but they eyed each other. They were both thinking the same thing. "Who the hell was that half naked, Chinese looking broad?"

Fatima smiled at her company, and hoped the lie she was about to tell them sounded natural. "Ya'll, that's my house-keeper. She spilled something on her pants, and had to wash it out."

Fatima wasn't completely lying. She did make that bitch clean up the house sometimes. She just hoped she'd sounded convincing. It looked like they believed her. She made a mental note to slap that stupid slut for coming downstairs like that.

In attempt to continue where they left off, Fatima said, "So, as we were saying ..."

Laila must've been on Casino's mind heavy, because out of the blue, he announced that his next stop would be Jay's crib to see her. He said she was carrying his seed, so he didn't care if she was mad at him.

Jay busted Cas' balls, and asked him if that was that shot of Patron he drank doing all that bold talking. He and Fatima laughed. Cas had to laugh too.

Fatima said Laila still wasn't ecstatic about being pregnant, but she knew there was nothing she could do about it. She said Laila had barked on her, and Portia too. She had asked them how come they didn't intervene, and insist that the doctor give her an abortion.

They began to discuss the proceeds from Wise's career again. Fatima appreciated their honesty with her. She stuck to her guns about putting the bulk of the money in a trust for her daughter. She already had more money than she could spend, and more cars than she could drive. In fact, she had been think-ing about giving back lately.

Jay and Cas announced that they were leaving, so they hugged Fatima and told her they would be in touch. She got their jackets, and walked them to the front door.

As they drove away from Fatima's house, they were both thinking the same thing. But it was Cas who blew it up. He looked at Jay, and said, "Yo, son. You seen Fatima face when her little girlfriend came down? I thought she was gon' choke."

They both laughed. Fatima could front all she wanted, they knew what it was. But that was her business. And they figured that was better than her jumping into a relationship with some dude for comfort. Wise would've probably been glad she wasn't with another man.

$$$$$

Meanwhile, Laila was at Portia's house, and the two of them were privately discussing the alleged pregnancy Khalil had brought up before Laila's accident. Portia knew it was an issue that needed to be aired out before she and Laila could proceed with their friendship, but she was still nervous as hell when Laila bought it up.

It was the first time they had been completely alone together. Portia had pretty much been avoiding that. And Laila wasn't stupid. She knew. When they were finally alone, she told Portia she remembered what happened before her accident occurred. She said she'd waited until they were by themselves to talk about it, but she needed to know exactly what had gone down. She told Portia to look at her, and tell her the truth.

Portia felt horrible. At first, she couldn't even look at Laila. But she knew she owed her the truth. Especially after what she had been through behind it. Laila was her dear friend, and she didn't want anymore secrets between them. She just prayed she would find it in her heart to forgive her. Portia took a deep breath, and she sat down and confessed everything.

She told the entire story, starting with the way Khalil had shown up at the strip club she worked at, and requested a VIP. Portia told Laila that she didn't feel right about giving him a private dance, but he'd doubled the take, and she'd been money hungry, and agreed. She told her that afterwards, she had felt guilty, so she drank a bunch of Hennessy to try to relax and forget about everything.

Portia said she told herself it was just work, but she didn't dance anymore that night because she felt so low. She said a little later, the bartender called her a cab so she could go home, and she left the club drunk. She said when she went outside, Khalil appeared out of nowhere, and insisted on giving her a ride home. Portia told Laila he said he just wanted to make sure she got there safe, because she'd been drinking.

She said when they got to her building, Khalil walked her up-stairs, and acted like he was so concerned. She said that she was really fucked up, but when they got to her door, she thanked him and unlocked her apartment, and she ran to the bathroom because she had to throw up. She said Khalil told her good-night, so she was under the impression that he had left and gone home. Portia said after she threw up, she went in her bed-room and crashed. She said she swore on her mother's grave she didn't know he was still in her house, but then she awak-ened to find him inside of her.

Laila almost threw up. That story sounded too familiar. She didn't want to, but she believed Portia. She had been married to that bastard for almost fifteen years. She knew his sexual habits, likes, and dislikes. Entering her while she was asleep was something Khalil enjoyed. While they were together, Laila used to always go to bed smelling good, because it was common for her to be awakened by him penetrating her. And he also used to love to orally pleasure her while she was sleeping. She used to wake up smiling, with his face between her thighs all the time. It was a little game they played.

Laila's stomach turned at the idea of Khalil doing all that to Portia. The thought was nauseating, regardless of the fact that she didn't love him anymore. She felt like killing that fucking bastard. How could he? Despite her contempt for him, tears came to her eyes.

Laila just sat there quiet for a minute. As much as she wanted to hate Portia and blame her for everything, she knew it wasn't all her fault. Her no-good, trifling assed husband had played the biggest part in it. Laila remembered how quickly Portia had changed her lifestyle after that pregnancy. She had stopped dancing, and got a job and everything. Now Laila understood why. She had really felt bad about it.

Laila finally spoke. She said, "So he raped you. My husband. I can't believe this shit." Laila was unsure if she was crying be-cause she was more hurt, or more angry.

She couldn't look at Portia. A part of her hated her too, so not yet. She shouldn't have been such a fucking whore. Laila just asked her, "So why didn't you tell me?"

Portia sighed, and told her the God honest truth. "Because I kinda' felt like I deserved it. He had no business at my house in the first place. I should've never danced for him, and I never should've got drunk. I made some very bad decisions that I just decided to live with. That's why I got the hell out of that life, Laila. I felt so fuckin' low. I hated what I had become, and I believed it was my fault."

That's when Laila looked her in the eyes. Portia had tears streaming down her face, and she really looked sincere. That bitch got pregnant by her husband, but she was her friend. Damn, she couldn't hate her. Even after all that. They were best friends. And the thought of some asshole taking advantage of her made Laila very upset. Even if that asshole was her husband.

Laila would never forget about that incident, but she had to forgive her. They were like sisters. They had a long history together. And look what Portia had done for her. She had stood by her side when she was in that coma, and even took care of her child when she couldn't, and Macy's sorry assed daddy wouldn't. Portia was a real friend. Laila definitely had issues with what had gone down, but Portia was her homegirl. They'd been friends for the past twenty years. She was true blue. Regardless of what, she had already proved it. And those kind of friends didn't come a dime a dozen.

Laila was grateful to have Portia and Fatima. What would she do without her girls? She was pregnant, and half paralyzed. She needed them. She didn't have anyone else. She knew those two loved her. Throughout every storm in her life, those bitches had been right there.

Laila told Portia she forgave her, and said she wanted to put that in the past, and leave it there. Portia hugged her tight as hell, and neither of them could stop crying. The situation was just so emotional. And they were also both pregnant, and emotional themselves.

Portia was eight months now, and Laila was five. Portia was worried about Laila. She kept on saying she didn't want the baby. Portia tried to keep her spirits up, and kept assuring her that it was a blessing from God. It bothered her that Laila felt like she was doomed, just because she was having that baby.

Laila also kept saying she wanted to go home to her own house, because she felt like she was a huge burden. Portia told her over and over that was nonsense, but Laila kept insisting. Then she told Portia she felt horrible about the way she had treated Cas. She said deep down inside, she felt like he was going to leave her when he realized she would never walk again. She figured if she chased him away, she would have the satisfaction of knowing that he left on her terms.

Portia told Laila she understood how she felt, but she knew Cas loved her with all his heart. She reminded her that he was also risking a lot by making the decision he had about the baby. It couldn't have been easy for him. They were both still married, and all types of drama could unfold. She told Laila she really believed Cas' decision had come from the heart, and been based solely on love. Pure love for her, and their unborn child.

When Portia told her how Cas had sat by her bedside for hours, watching over her and praying for her recovery, Laila was touched. She told Portia she wanted to call him, and apologize, but she had to figure out what to say first.

Laila never got a chance to call Casino, because he came through about thirty minutes later. He said he'd come to check on her.

When Laila saw him, her heart soared. Good Lord, he was so fine. It felt so good when he hugged her, she almost melted. But she couldn't help but wonder why he was there. He could have any woman he wanted. What did he need with her crippled ass?

The first thing Cas told Laila was how much he loved her new haircut. After they talked, she realized that the love he had for her was just as strong as it was before the accident. She could see it in his eyes, so she was forced to let her guards down. She wasn't a naïve chick, but he made her believe his promise that he would take care of her. He told her that having that baby was the most precious gift she could ever give him.

After that, Cas assured Laila that she would be back in her house within a week. He said he was having some things done first, to make sure she would be comfortable. He didn't say anything yet, but he had even decided to stay there with her for a while. Just until he knew she was better. Amongst other things, he wanted to make sure she ate right. The baby's health was at stake.

Casino knelt down in front of Laila's wheelchair, and planted a kiss on her belly. He couldn't front, he really loved her. She was carrying his little blessing. Laila blushed, and traced the outline of Cas' ear. He stayed down on one knee, and just held her for a while. That was something they both needed.

CHAPTER TEN

A few weeks later, on one of those rare occasions Fatima had her daughter, she and Falynn sat in the den watching an episode of "Sponge Bob Square Pants" on Nickelodeon. She had gone and picked her baby up from her parent's house on Monday. She'd really missed her little one. She hadn't spent any time with her lately.

The last couple weeks, Fatima had hung out with her girls, Portia and Laila a lot. They must've been good influences on her, because being around them sort of made her want to be a better mom. Maybe it was because they were both good mothers. And both of them were expecting too. It was so cute. Laila wasn't thrilled about her package, but she would come around.

Fatima got fed up and told Cheyenne to get out weeks ago, because she was tired of having to talk to her like she was her child. That little incident she'd pulled, coming downstairs half-dressed when Jay and Cas were there visiting, got on her last nerve. That bitch got out of line.

Besides, Fatima felt like she had wasted too much time with her. It made her feel guilty about not spending enough time with her Falynn. Motherhood was a privilege, and she'd been handling it totally otherwise. Fatima had done some thinking, and she realized that she had been using Wise' death as a crutch. She was still grieving, but she was using it as an excuse for not being the mother she should be. Enough was enough.

During a commercial break from "Sponge Bob", Falynn said, "Mommy, guess what. I saw my daddy! He came to see me, Mommy. And Daddy said he loves me, and he will be back. And he gave me a biiig kiss. Like this!" She grinned, and hopped up and gave Fatima a big hug and kiss.

Fatima hugged her baby back tight. It broke her heart to have to tell her the truth, but she was forced to say, "Falynn,

Daddy's gone. But he does love you, baby. And don't you ever forget that." Fatima held her daughter, and fought the tears that were starting to well up in the corners of her eyes.

When Fatima let Falynn go, she started playing with one of her favorite dolls. When "Sponge Bob" came back on, she sat on her Dora the Explorer chair and looked at TV again. She held her doll in her lap like it was a real baby.

Fatima watched her little one with concern. That was the second time Falynn had said she'd seen her daddy. Fatima knew her daughter was smart, so she had to give what she said the benefit of a doubt. She was beginning to wonder if Wise had been visiting Falynn from the grave.

Fatima thought about that dream she'd had. It had seemed too real. Was there something supernatural going on? She was open-minded, and wasn't going to rule out the option. Wise' spirit could very well be walking amongst them. Sometimes children saw things adults couldn't. And Wise had loved his daughter so much, she wouldn't be surprised if he was checking up on her.

Fatima leaned back on the plush sofa and put her feet up, and she looked around the huge, extravagant house that was once their happy home. Wise's presence was surely missed. Emptiness loomed about the air now that he was gone. Fatima closed her eyes, and rested her head on the back of the chair for a minute. It had been months since he passed, but she couldn't seem to get over him. She doubted that she would ever find a man to replace him.

$$$$$

A few miles away at Laila's house, Casino sat massaging her legs and feet. He spent at least an hour doing this everyday. The doctor had told him that a massage was a good way to stimulate her nerves, and it could help bring back the feeling.

When Cas had first starting doing it a few weeks ago, their conversation would go the same every time he'd ask. He'd say, "Laila, do you feel anything?", and she'd answer, "No, Cas. I don't feel nothin' yet. I'm sorry." It crushed him to hear her keep apologizing, like it was her fault.

But God was good. The last few days, Laila had admitted to feeling little twitches and jumps in her legs. Cas took that as a good sign.

And just as sure as day, Laila's physical therapist had said that afternoon that she was doing a lot better. Cas smiled at her, and told her how proud he was of the progress she was making.

Laila didn't want to be negative, so she kept her thoughts to herself. If she had been honest, she would've told Cas to shut up and quit getting all happy about every little bullshit occurrence. To her, progress would be getting up out of that stupid fucking wheelchair and walking. She just wanted to walk. It was that fucking simple. And toting around that big ass belly didn't help any. Maybe if she wasn't so damn fat, she would've been able to move a little faster.

Laila tried really hard to keep the faith, but it was hard when God had put her in such a compromising position. Did He really love her? He had already taken her baby Pebbles away from her, and now she was paralyzed. It couldn't get any worse.

Laila smiled at Cas. He was a sweetheart. She was glad he was sticking by her, and she definitely didn't want to blow that by being a bitch all the time. She appreciated that man. She really did. She just wanted to hurry up and walk again, so she could be all the woman he needed. One of Laila's biggest fears was that Kira would win Cas back based on her inability to walk, and have sex with him.

That thought actually powered Laila's next move. She knew Cas was a man with needs, and she really wanted to please him. She was still cute, and Cas said she looked even better with her new haircut. The asymmetrical bob she was rocking now was something she probably would've never tried before, but once they'd whacked off the whole side of her hair to stitch her head up, she didn't have much of a choice.

Laila wasn't expecting Macy home for another hour. That gave her enough time to do what she had in mind to Cas. She looked over at him seductively, and stopped him from massaging her feet. "Boo, stand up for a minute."

Cas just looked at her for a second, like he was confused. He got up, and Laila took his hand and pulled him directly in front of her. He stood there sort of dumbfounded, while she lifted his shirt and traced along his waistline with her freshly French manicured fingernails.

Cas' dick was hard already. He wondered what she had in store for him. He didn't want to ruin it by running his mouth too much, so he just kept quiet, and savored the moment. It had been a while since he had any real action. He'd just been jerking off to new jack-off DVDs. He had accumulated an extensive porn collection.

Laila unfastened his belt, and then his jeans. She removed the lovely log from Cas' boxers, and massaged him gently. She leaned forward, and kissed the tip the way she knew he loved. She hadn't seen Cas' dick in so long, she was aroused as well. But Laila was unsure of how well she could perform sexually, so she focused her energy on pleasing him. Cas deserved some satisfaction, and she proceeded to give it to him.

She licked his shaft slowly, and then took the whole thing in her mouth. Or at least as much as she could. Damn, he had a big, long ass dick. Laila stared at it like it was a masterpiece. She had initially set out to please him, but she was enjoying herself as well. Pleasing Casino made her feel like a woman. She had her super powers back. Laila went in on that blowjob, and gave him the best head of the century.

Cas moaned, and ran his fingers through Laila's hair. Damn! Her throat was warm and soft, and her head game was on point. Babygirl was milking the shit out of his joint. Cas' heartbeat quickened. He felt his legs weakening, and couldn't hold it back a second longer. Damn, he was about to cum! He bit down hard on his back teeth. "Oh shit, Ma!"

Cas shot off a load. Laila pulled back just in time, but a few drops got on her face. She frowned at first, but then she smiled up at him, pleased that he was pleased. Cas laughed, and then joked that the vitamins in it were good for her skin. Laila shook her head, and just laughed at his nasty behind.

Just then, the phone rang. It was Macy, calling to ask if she could spend the night at her girlfriend, Briana's house. After Laila spoke to Briana's mother to make sure she didn't mind, she told Macy she could stay. It was Friday. Briana's mom said she would personally drive Macy home in the morning.

While Laila was on the phone, Cas went to the bathroom and got a clean, soapy washcloth for her to wipe her face. He smiled to himself, thinking what a nice surprise that had been. That blowjob was proper, but he wanted to sample that pussy. Cas knew the situation, so he didn't want to push it, but at the time there was nothing he would love more than getting up inside those sugar walls.

When he returned with the washcloth, he overheard Laila telling Macy she would see her the following morning. Cas was still thinking about that pussy. He walked over and handed Laila the washcloth to clean her face, and he knelt down and unbuttoned her shirt. He cupped her tities in his hands, and massaged them and squeezed her nipples.

That felt so good, Laila took off her bra to give him total access. His touch was remarkable. She wanted him. The oral she had given him had really turned her on.

After Laila removed her bra, Cas admired her topless for a second. Her tities were round and full. He leaned in and took the right one in his mouth, sucking the nipple hungrily. He was turned on again. Damn, he wanted to taste her. And he wanted to repay her for that banging ass blowjob. He picked Laila up from her wheelchair, and carried her up to the master bedroom.

Cas laid her across the bed, and took his time undressing her. Laila was nervous, but she was even hornier. She couldn't do any tricks or anything, but she was so turned on her pussy was soaked. Cas kissed her on her lips gently, and spread her legs apart. Seconds later, he kissed his way on downtown.

Cas licked and sucked her joy button skillfully, and Laila gasped in pleasure. Her pussy seemed to be working just fine, and that was for sure. She was aching for him. She needed him that second. Laila told him, "I want you inside of me, Cas. Put it in, baby."

Casino ignore her pleas, and kept his face between her legs until she shook uncontrollably. Afterwards, he came up and kissed her on the neck, and slowly lowered himself inside of her.

It had been a while, so she was real tight. The first few strokes felt like she had a suction cup on his joint. Real talk, Laila had some good ass pussy.

Laila laid underneath Casino, panting and moaning. She had forgotten how good that dick was. She didn't have any feeling in her legs, but the rest of her body was on fire. She clawed his back with her nails, and cried out, "Oh Cas! Baby! I'm about to cum! Ooohh!"

Laila was so fucking sexy. That shit pushed Casino over the top. He found her lips, and darted his tongue in and out her mouth. Laila sucked on his tongue like she had sucked on his penis. When he came, it felt like she drained everything out of him. Damn, she had a hot box on her.

After Cas ejaculated, he just laid there for a second. Not on no sucker shit, but he just felt real close to her that very moment. He was crazy about her. He really was. Laila was his heart, and she would walk again, even if he had to spend every penny he had.

$$$$$

Jay and Portia sat in their kitchen, eating lunch together, and discussing their son, Jayquan. Lil' Jay was thirteen now, and had obviously recently gone into puberty. He was getting more girl crazy by the day. That boy was about six feet tall now, standing almost as high as Jay, and his voice was getting deep too.

The kids were growing up too fast. It seemed like it happened overnight. Jazmin was in the first grade already, and Lil' Jay would be going to high school that fall.

And the baby on the way was growing fast too, according to the ultrasounds. Portia was nine months pregnant now, and she was big as a house. She was ready to drop that load. She was sick and tired of being knocked up. At the thought, Portia started humming a song she liked, "Knocked Up" by Lady Goines.

Portia remembered that she'd wanted to congratulate Jay about the company's recent earnings. They had done really well. On a positive note, she said, "Boo, I glimpsed over the books. This was a pretty profitable quarter, Daddy. Congratulations."

Portia threw her hands up in the air, and shook her hips from side to side. "Get money! Get money!"

Jay laughed at her bootleg Lil' Kim imitation. He shook his head, and said, "Yeah, but you know how it go. Mo' money, and mo' problems. It's real, P. This shit ain't no fairy tale."

Jay paused for a second. He looked real serious, like he was deep in thought. He had that cute little crease he got in the middle of his forehead when he was thinking.

He was sitting down, so Portia leaned over and kissed him right on that crease. And then she lovingly kissed the faint scars on either side of his face, which were a product of him getting shot the year before. Jay had grown out his beard to cover up the scars, so you could hardly tell. Portia found his imperfections sexy. Concerned about his mood change, she asked, "What's wrong, baby?"

Jay just shook his head, and said it was nothing. Just then, Portia's office phone rang. She had a separate business line, and luckily she had the cordless phone upstairs with her. She held her belly and waddled over to the coffee table where it was, and picked up the receiver. "Sinclair Lane Publishing. How may I help you?"

Strangely, it was a collect call from "Callie Benson". Portia recognized the name immediately. That was Simone's little sister, Callie! Portia hadn't seen her since she and her mother had that fight at Simone's funeral. Portia would never in her life forget that day. At the end of the fight, Callie had pushed her mother into Simone's grave.

Portia wondered why Callie was calling collect. And on her business line. She pressed 3, and accepted the call.

She and Callie greeted each other, and played catch-up for a minute. When Portia asked about her mother, she said they didn't keep in touch. It was good to hear from her but Portia wanted to know the real reason for her call, so she asked her what was wrong.

Callie told her she got her number from the back of her first novel, which she'd read and loved by the way. She said she saw that there was a contact number in the back of the book, so she called on a humble, and Portia just happened to answer the phone. She told her she was sorry for calling her collect, but she was in a fucked up situation at the moment. She said she didn't have a penny to her name.

Portia unknowingly took the bait, and asked her what happened. She wasn't just acting concerned. She really did care. That was Simone's little sister.

Callie went into a long story about how she was stranded in Miami with no money, and no place to go. She told Portia she was just getting out of an abusive relationship with a man she'd attempted to leave, but was badly beaten, and robbed of every dime she had in the process. She said she had moved down to Florida with her crazy boyfriend, but now she really wanted to come home. She told Portia she needed money to get back up top, and a place to stay for a little while, just until she got on her feet.

Portia felt funny about getting involved in someone else's drama. She hadn't seen Callie in years. But she couldn't turn her down. She was Simone's sister, so she was like family. Portia gave her the address, and told her she would wire her a thousand dollars through Western Union for airfare, food, and other travel expenses.

Portia hung up the phone believing every word Callie had said. She went and got her credit card, and called Western Union to send the money immediately. She felt so sorry for her. Portia started to call Laila and Tima, but she noticed her back was starting to ache pretty badly.

She told Jay her back was hurting, and he was ready to rush her to the hospital. Portia laughed, and told him it wasn't that serious. She said he was just thirsty for her to have the baby. Jay laughed, and shrugged his shoulders, knowing she was telling the truth. Portia reminded him that she had a doctor's appointment the following day. She was nine months, so they had her coming once a week now. She told Jay she would just lie down for a while. She decided to call Fatima and Laila to let them know about poor Callie later.

Unfortunately, most of what Callie told Portia was untrue.

Her intentions were to play on her kindness. She had located Portia through her first novel, but it was actually her no-good boyfriend that had supplied her with the information. Callie wasn't a reader. She had never even seen one of Portia's books before, until Smoke told her to check out her website. He told her to glimpse at the website, and read the synopsis so she would have some type of idea what the book was about.

Smoke, Callie's boyfriend, was in jail for a bullshit parole violation. He had been caught out pass his curfew several times, and his dickhead P.O. had it in for him. That cocksucka' violated him, so he had to lay up for about a year. He got a hold of Portia's first book, "It's Official", from a dude named Rell he was locked up with. Smoke read a lot of books to kill time, just like a lot of other dudes in the pen.

When he read the acknowledgements in the book, he noticed the author was from Bed-Stuy, and she gave a shout out, and said R.I.P. to a "Simone Benson". In fact, she had dedicated the entire book to her memory. Smoke knew Callie's last name was Benson, and he had heard her talk about her dead sister, Simone. He put two and two together, and came to the conclusion that there had to be an affiliation.

He called Callie, and asked her if she knew the author of the book, a chick named Portia Lane. Callie told him that was one of her sister's best friends, and she remembered her well. But she said she didn't know Portia was an author.

Always scheming, Smoke gave Callie the contact number listed in the back of the book, and told her to call and get reacquainted with Portia. He told her when she made the connection, and got a foot in the door, she should try to milk the situation as much as she could. He told her that if she played her cards right, she would have access to food, shelter, a vehicle, clothes, and money in no time. That would hold her down until he came home in a few months. Then she could stay out of the strip clubs and bars searching for vics. He told Callie that if she got in good, she should be on the lookout for anything she could take during her stay. Jewelry, cash, credit cards, and even I.D.

Smoke made it seem like his only concern was Callie's wellbeing. He didn't tell her about his ulterior motives. He could see from that bitch Portia's shout outs that she was also married to that dude, Jay, from that record company, Street Life Entertainment. That nigga Jay and them was getting it. He could see that him and Portia had a couple of kids too.

Smoke had heard through the streets that that nigga Jay, and his mans, Cas and Wise had been responsible for the work that killed these stickup niggas from Philly called The Scumbag Brothas. That nigga Wise was a big time rapper, and it was said that he died in that beef too. That shit was all over the news. Them dudes Jay and them had to have paper if they beat that shit. Them niggas must've had a dream team of lawyers, like O.J. Simpson did.

That made Smoke even tighter. Niggas was walking on bodies like it was nothing, and a dude like him had to lay up in the pen for some bullshit. Just because he had no bread stashed for legal fees. Smoke had that "jailhouse" mentality. He was a dude that would never learn, so he began to fantasize about robbing them niggas. If Callie could set that up, that would be the sweetest lick they ever made.

Smoke knew what Callie was, and wasn't built for. Especially after what had happened down in Miami. So he just told her to track Portia down, and get her to look out for her until he got out. He stressed the importance of her getting a ticket for the next thing smoking up out of there. She had almost gotten herself killed.

Smoke kept the rest of his plans to himself. First, he had to see if Callie was smart enough to pull the infiltration off. If she could just get in there, there would be no limit to the things he could manipulate her to do.

He had been controlling Callie for three years now, and the majority of the time he had been in the penitentiary. His game was so tight, he could get a female to do anything he wanted. And he had Callie do just about everything there was.

CHAPTER ELEVEN

The next morning, down in a small Florida town, on the out-skirts of Miami, Callie got up early, and picked up the money Portia had wired her through Western Union. She was already packed, so she went straight to the airport and booked a flight.

At a quarter past ten, Callie boarded a plane en route to Continental Airport in New Jersey. Her palms were sweaty, in anticipation of what was to come. She thanked her lucky stars for having Smoke again. He always took care of her. And when he wasn't around to do it, he pointed her in the right direction.

Back up north, Portia's water broke at around 10:30. She got up to go to the bathroom, and it just happened. But she didn't panic. She just yelled, "Jay! My water just broke! It's time, baby! "

Jay didn't respond. He must have not heard her, because he was still in the bed snoring. He'd been up late the night before, massaging her back. Portia had been having some really bad back pains the night before, and she'd mentioned to Jay that down there had also been aching for some reason. She realized now that she was in labor. She'd been having contractions! She wobbled back in the bedroom, and poked Jay in the ribs.

Jay popped up immediately, and Portia repeated herself. "Baby, it's time! My water just broke!"

Jay jumped up. Oh shit, Portia said it was time! She was about to have the baby! He was kind of scared for some reason, but he knew he had to keep a level head. He took a deep breath, and asked, "You ayight, Ma?"

Portia nodded, and told him she just wanted to take a quick shower. She wasn't about to go the hospital feeling unsure. Jay hurried to the phone, and called her doctor. Dr. Jacobs told him she would meet them at the hospital. She'd been Portia's gynecologist for years, and she wouldn't have anyone else deliver her baby.

Portia had packed a bag for the occasion weeks ago. Jay helped her to the bathroom, but she shooed him away and told him she was okay. He needed to get himself ready. It was time for them to go.

They both gargled with Listerine pre-brush mouthwash, and brushed their teeth side by side at their adjoining sinks. Afterwards, Jay jumped in one shower, and Portia got in the other. Portia had another contraction while she was washing, and she hollered out in pain. She would tell Jay later how funny it was when he jumped out of the shower naked, and ran over to see about her. He had suds all over him, and they were dripping off his dick. Portia wanted to laugh, but that contraction wouldn't allow her to.

After they showered, they got dressed quick, and headed to the hospital. Luckily, Jayquan and Jazmin were at Jay's sister, their Auntie Laurie's house for the weekend.

At the hospital, Portia's doctor confirmed that she had already dilated four centimeters. That explained why her coochie had been hurting so bad. She was having some serious contractions, but she told herself it was all worth it. God willing, she would soon cradle her precious newborn in her arms. She wondered if the baby would have her eyes, or Jay's.

Caught up in the miracle that was about to occur, she completely forgot about Callie coming in town. When Callie called Portia's cell phone to let her know she had arrived at the airport, Jay answered, and told her Portia was at the hospital having a baby. When Callie explained who she was, he gave her Fatima's number, and told her he was sorry but she should call her.

$$$$$

After Fatima got out of the shower that morning, she stood naked in front of her bathroom mirror. She ran her hands along her hips, satisfied with the twenty six pounds she had lost. And she did it in three months. She had just stepped off her digital scale. Only fourteen more pounds to lose before she reached her goal.

Her new weight loss regimen was working pretty well. Fatima was no longer purging, and vomiting every time she ate. She hadn't told anyone, but she'd been snorting a line of coke here and there.

She had discovered that cocaine took away her appetite. When she did it, she could go all day without eating. It was the complete opposite of weed, which gave her the munchies all the time. Fatima hated to admit it, but the first time she'd done it, she let Charlene convince her to try it. They hung out a few weeks ago, when Falynn had stayed the weekend with Rose.

While they were at the club, Fatima had complained that she didn't feel well. She drank too many margaritas, and the alcohol got to her. She told Charlene she was tired, and wanted to go home and lay down. Charlene had suggested that she just needed a little "wakeup", and pushed her a hundred dollar bill filled with snow. Fatima didn't know what had made her try snorting coke that night, but after she did it, she felt better. That shit was crazy.

Fatima was no dummy. She knew with friends like that, she didn't need enemies. She guessed Charlene was more of a "friend-nemy". But it wasn't like she had put a gun to her head. The telephone in Fatima's bedroom rang, snapping her out of her thoughts.

Still naked, Fatima hurried in the room to answer it before it woke up Falynn. It was Simone's sister, Callie. She said she was at the airport. Fatima wasn't expecting her, but it was nice to hear from her. Callie told her she was supposed to go to Portia's house, but she had just found out she went in labor.

Fatima gave Callie the address, and told her to get in a cab and come to her house. After she hung up, she wondered why Jay hadn't informed her about Portia having the baby. Just as she was about to dial his cell phone number, her phone rang again.

It was Jay, telling her that Portia was about to give birth any minute. Fatima was excited at the news. She asked Jay if he had told Laila and Cas yet. He said he had just got off the phone with them. Fatima told him she would be at the hospital soon, but to make sure he kept her posted. She told him she was expecting Callie. Jay said he knew, and understood. Fatima told him she was praying everything went okay, and they agreed to see each other soon.

About thirty minutes later, Fatima was dressed, and on the lookout for Callie. She had got Falynn up, bathed her, and got her dressed too. While she waited for Callie, she thought about Cheyenne for some reason. She had gotten tired of her, and told her to leave, but now she was feeling horny. She wished Cheyenne's face was nearby, so she could sit on it for a little while. That was all she was good for. Fatima unconsciously ran her hands along her breasts. She remembered her daughter was there, so she cancelled the thought of masturbating.

Fay was in the den watching T.V. Fatima went to check on her, and the phone rang again. That was Callie, letting her know that her taxi had just turned down this long, winding driveway. She said she wasn't sure if she was in the right neighborhood, and wanted to make sure she had copied the address down correctly. Fatima confirmed the address, and told her she was in the right place.

Callie sat in the back of her taxi, and looked around in disbelief. Fatima's house was located in a rich folk's neighborhood, and it was huge! She wondered if Portia's house was anything like that. If it was, there was one thing for sure. Those bitches were getting it. Callie was glad she had made contact with them. She could already tell this was going to be beneficial. She would make Smoke proud.

Fatima saw the taxi pull up outside. Callie was Simone's sister, so if she needed a place to stay because Portia was in the hospital, Fatima would ask no questions. She welcomed Callie with open arms. She had lots of space, so it would be her pleasure to accommodate her. Or so Fatima thought.

$$\$\$\$\$\$$$

When Jay called Cas and Laila, they were both happy about Portia having the baby. Well, at least Laila tried to be happy.

Portia and Jay were her friends, and she didn't want to rain on their parade. Laila felt bad, but Portia's giving birth just reminded her that she was next.

She'd been thinking about Pebbles a lot that morning, so her heart was heavy. It hurt to think about it, but she couldn't help it. That was something she would never forget. Her child had been raped, and murdered. To be honest, that was part of the reason she was unexcited about bringing another life into this cold ass world.

Laila wasn't in a great mood, but she faked it and pretended everything was everything. She did it more for Cas. He was right by her side, and trying so hard to make her happy. She didn't want him to feel like he'd failed.

She and Casino decided to go to the hospital a little later, after Portia actually gave birth. Laila had gone through it twice, so she knew firsthand that a woman could be in labor for hours. It was Saturday morning, and Macy would be home from her girlfriend's house soon. Then they could all go together. Laila knew Macy would want to see the baby. She loved kids. She was excited about the baby Laila was having too.

$$$$$

At the hospital a few hours later, Jay was in the delivery room watching Portia push out their new baby girl. Portia was irate because she was in a lot of pain, but Jay couldn't have been happier. In fact, he found all the hooting, hollering, and calling on the Lord that Portia was doing somewhat amusing.

He had made the mistake of smiling at her, and telling her everything was okay. Portia had cursed him out, and told him he didn't know shit. After that, Jay just held her hand, and pretty much kept his mouth shut.

It wasn't long before Portia had given birth to their 7 lb, 3 oz baby girl. She was a beauty, with a head full of curly black hair. She was perfect. Jay cut the umbilical cord himself. Portia was too exhausted to say anything, but she smiled weakly and watched the nurses clean the baby up, and hand her to Jay. He held his tiny little angel proudly, and showed her off to Portia.

After she pushed out that afterbirth, Portia was so exhausted she needed a nap. She dozed off listening to Jay telling her how happy he was.

When Portia woke up, everybody was there. Fatima, Laila, Cas, Jay's mother, and his sisters, Laurie and Kira. Portia knew Cas probably felt awkward around Kira and her family, especially since he was there with Laila.

But Cas was a man about it. He didn't flaunt it in their faces, but he wasn't trying to hide anything. Portia remembered that Cas and Kira's divorce was final, but she couldn't help but feel bad for all injured parties.

Portia was happy everyone had come out to witness the new addition to their family. She definitely felt the love they all showed. She especially appreciated Mama Mitchell's support, since her mother was gone and couldn't be there. Everybody said the baby looked like Jay, who grinned and ate it all up.

Laurie told Portia that she'd left the kids at home because of the hospital rules. They wouldn't have let Jazmin in because she was too young. Fatima said she had left Falynn at her house with Callie for the same reason. She said Callie said she loved kids, so she didn't mind.

$$\$\$\$\$\$$

Had Fatima used her better judgment, she wouldn't have left Callie unsupervised in her house. The only smart thing she did was lock her bedroom door. Just minutes after she pulled off, Callie had started rambling through her stuff. She gave Falynn some ice cream, and sat her in front of a "Backyardigans" DVD, so she would stay out of her way.

A former good girl, Callie always had an angle. She was grimy. Smoke had destroyed what was left of her innocence. He had changed her way of thinking, and made her believe it was them against the world. He had her so brainwashed that she handled everybody, good people and bad, as just potential victims to finance her and Smoke's lifestyle. Hooking up with that no-good ass nigga had made her rotten to the core.

Callie was looking through Fatima's photo albums when her

cell phone rang. She looked at the caller ID, and was glad it was the call she'd been eagerly anticipating all day. The number showed up as "Unavailable", so she knew it was her baby, Smoke. He was locked up on Riker's Island, so he was able to call her straight out, instead of collect.

The real reason Callie had been down in Florida was because she had gone on a run Smoke had directed from inside. In an unfortunate turn of events, the dude he had sent her after got hip to her intentions. Long story short, the nigga put a hit out on her. She had narrowly escaped an attempt on her life down in Miami, but she hadn't told Portia about that for obvious reasons.

Smoke was fucked up in jail, and unable to finance her getaway, but he had cleverly given her Portia's number, and told her to lay up on her for a while. At least that way she would be alright. Now she was excited to tell him that plan seemed like a good look.

Callie answered the phone all bubbly, "Hello?"

Smoke said, "What up, Ma? Tell me somethin' good."

Callie answered, "I'm in, daddy. And you ain't gon' believe this shit." She told Smoke about Portia going in labor, and her winding up at her sister's other friend, Fatima's crib. She told him she had been looking at old photos, and discovered that Fatima was married to Wise, that famous rapper who had just got killed a few months ago. She had seen their wedding photos. She said they had a little girl too, who was right in the other room watching a DVD.

Smoke already knew about Portia's affiliations with that dude Jay from Street Life, but the information she had just given him was even better. She was right up in there with that dead nigga Wise' widow. He knew that bitch had probably inherited an asshole full of money after that nigga died. He and Callie had really hit the jackpot this time. He just had to set shit up right so they could touch it.

Smoke told Callie that was good work, and instructed her to milk the situation for what it was worth. Callie told him not to worry, because she planned on milking her new cash cows dry. Smoke said he would be in touch, and they hung up.

Callie had a seat on the sofa, and put up her feet on the expensive marble coffee table. Everything around her looked like money. At one point in time, she would've thought twice about the plans she had for her deceased sister's best friends. But she was too far out there now.

Callie needed a big piece of change, so she could break out. She was leaning towards the west coast. L.A. seemed appealing, especially considering the recent east coast trouble she had acquired. She knew the danger she had encountered was based on karma. She knew she'd been living foul.

Callie took a second to reflect over her life. She had started out on the right track as a good kid. Determined not to wind up like her alcoholic mother, she had enlisted in the military. She served three years before she was dishonorably discharged for insubordination. She had busted her commanding officer in the head with an iron pipe. What was fucked up was, he had sexually assaulted her, so she was just defending herself.

Being unfairly kicked out of the army had landed her on the street, with no income, and lots of disdain for men. The only thing Callie got from the military was a bad habit. She was hooked on heroin. She was a snorter. She didn't shoot up, so she had maintained a scar-free body. And all the physical activity in the military had her in pretty good shape. That had helped her make a decent living as a stripper for a few years.

Then in a club, she met Smoke, the man who kissed her with death, and then saved her. He told Callie he saw something in her, and had used a strong-arm method to rid her of her heroin addiction. He had literally beaten her habit out of her. Smoke had lost it, and almost killed her on several occasions. The last time, he broke her jaw, and after that beating, she had never touched smack again. After that, Callie felt totally indebted to him.

So during the last few years, she had made a living by teaming up with him to set up dudes with big bread, and then rob them. Callie and Smoke played dirty. She would be sucking the shit out of some poor, unsuspecting schmuck's dick, and Smoke would step out of the shadows, and place his pistol on their temple. Then Callie would hold a switch blade to the dude's nuts, while Smoke robbed him. Afterwards, they would tie the vic up, and make sure they took his cell phone and I.D.

They had another con they played too. Callie would drop sleeping pills in dude's drinks. After they fell asleep, she robbed them of their cash, and credit cards. By the time the vic would wake up, she'd be long gone. Most of the time, the victim would be so ashamed, they'd just let it go.

But their last scheme had gone bad. Perhaps the dude was out of their league. Smoke had found out about this nigga named Pito, from this Florida cat he was locked up with, named Chuck. Pito was a well-known baller down in Miami, who was supposed to have all these millions in cash stashed in his house.

Smoke had expressed his interest to swindle the Miami dude, and promised Chuck a cut in exchange for the guy's information. The next day, he jumped on the phone and gave Callie an address, and a description of duke, and told her to get on down there and work her magic.

Smoke was in prison, and Callie was alone on the streets, so she had to fend for herself. But he figured he had taught her enough to work solo. Callie had eagerly jumped on the Miami mission. She flew down there, and she got hired at the strip club Smoke told her he frequented. Callie found Pito, and seduced him. She latched onto homeboy in no time. She had that effect on dudes. She could bag any man she set out to.

Pito really started digging her, and he trusted her a little too much. That was stemmed partially from his desire to impress her, because she was from New York. He took Callie to his house one night. It was just him, her, and a few big dudes he kept around for security. Pito cracked open a bottle of Cristal, and ordered her to dance for them.

Callie took the bottle from him, and she went to get three glasses from the bar in the corner. Earlier that day, she had crushed a whole bottle of powerful sleeping pills into fine powder. While she was over in the corner, she dumped the powder into the champagne and shook it up so it dissolved quickly.

She went back over, and filled champagne glasses for Pito and his "staff". Next, she proposed a toast to Pito. Callie laid it on real thick, stating how important, thorough, and handsome he was. Pito seemed to love every minute of it, but Callie was just stroking his ego. She thought of him as nothing but a big old country coon.

After her toast, everybody drank up their champagne quick. The fellows were in a rush to get right for the fun they thought was about to take place. Callie pretended to drink with them, but she wasn't really swallowing hers.

While they drank a few more rounds of champagne, Callie started dancing seductively. She held back her laugh as she watched the men struggling to keep their eyes open. It was funny, because their dicks were standing up, but their eyelids were going down.

Within minutes, all of them were knocked out. Pito, and his bodyguards. It was amazing. They were like menacing Rott-weilers when they were awake, but sleeping they were like harmless children.

Callie quickly searched the house for money and valuables. In a room upstairs, she opened a drawer and found four big stacks of hundred dollar bills, a Presidential Rolex, a huge diamond ring, and what looked like at least three kilos of cocaine. She grabbed a pillow from the bed, and stripped it of its case, and she dumped the stolen goods inside. She saw a safe in a walk-in closet, but she couldn't figure out the combination. If Pito had the type of cash and jewelry she had in her pillowcase just laying around, she could just imagine what was inside that safe.

Callie grabbed the pillowcase, and ran back down the stairs. Everyone was still out. She saw Pito's car keys on the coffee table, so she tiptoed over and quietly picked them up. Callie didn't know why she was being so careful not to make any noise. The dude she got those pills from told her they were the real deal. He had told her the truth, because those mothafuckas were knocked out.

The thought gave Callie a little assurance, so she went over and boldly but carefully removed the diamond flooded chain and Jesus medallion right from around Pito's neck. Afterwards, she grabbed the pillowcase, and she crept outside and hopped in homeboy's Benz, and drove off without looking back.

Callie wasn't stupid. She knew those sleeping pills would wear off sooner or later, and those niggas would wake up. She drove about thirty miles up the highway and tossed the auburn wig she was wearing. A few miles further, she ditched the car in a restaurant parking lot, and hailed a cab.

Callie headed for a nearby town, thinking she got away scot-free. She didn't know about the hidden cameras Pito had placed throughout his house. They had filmed her every move. But to her knowledge, everything had gone smooth when she robbed him.

Since Smoke and Callie had hooked up, they had screwed a lot of dudes. But they fucked the wrong one that time. After Pito saw the humiliating video footage of a stripper he'd welcomed into his home putting him and his crew to sleep, and robbing him, he was pretty slighted. There were definitely hard feelings on his part. Especially since Callie had stolen his chain right from around his neck, like he was some herb. She made him look like a real sucker, and then even stole his car.

In that bogus toast she'd proposed, right after she'd served them that spiked Cristal, Callie had mockingly said Pito was an important man. But she had clearly underestimated his caliber. She should've really asked somebody before she crossed him. Then she wouldn't have made the stupid mistake of sticking around after she robbed him.

Callie just wanted to get rid of the cocaine she had stolen, before she broke out. She couldn't take that much weight on an airplane. Not three kilos. She figured if she sold it dirt cheap, she could move it fast. She had hollered at some dudes who were interested.

Pito's money was long, and he had eyes everywhere. So he found out Callie's whereabouts with very little effort. She was staying in a five star hotel in the next town over. Pito even knew when she planned on leaving.

Callie had been in her hotel room in a deep sleep, when she woke up to find a pillow over her face. She tried to scream, but the pillow muffled her cries. She'd panicked, and put up a struggle in the darkness, but her assailant fired three shots through the pillow.

Callie didn't know if God was on her side, or what, but she shifted just in time. Two of the bullets completely missed her head, and the other one only grazed her ear. But she laid still and played dead, and prayed they would just take what they wanted, and leave.

As she laid there, she heard whoever it was ransacking the room. A minute later, she heard the room door close, and then it was quiet. They must've found what they were looking for. It couldn't have been hard. The money and coke was right in her suitcase.

Callie laid there frozen in fear for about ten minutes. She didn't hear anything else, so she slowly removed the pillow from her face. Her ear was bleeding, but she was okay. She was so afraid, she got dressed immediately, and grabbed her bags and got the hell out of dodge.

Whoever had invaded her hotel room, and tried to murder her had taken the money, jewelry, and the three kilos she had stolen. There was only so far she could get with the three twenties and eight singles she had in her change purse. Sixty-eight dollars. That was all she had in the world, but she was lucky to be alive.

Callie took that little bit of money, and took a cab to a cheap motel across town. Stranded out of town, with no money to get home, she awaited Smoke's call from jail. When he called, he was disappointed to learn that she had gotten the goods, and then lost them again, but he was glad she was okay. Smoke was always full of solutions. It was then that he gave her Portia's phone number, and told her to get at her. Callie was lucky Portia had answered the phone when she called. And girlfriend had even wired her a grand to get back up top.

Just then, Fatima's little girl ran in the room where she was, and snapped Callie out of her thoughts. She smiled, and listened to Falynn tell her what happened on the DVD she had just finished watching. Callie had to admit, she was a real cutie pie. She thanked her lucky stars once again that she had made it out of Florida alive, and she went to change the DVD for Falynn. She sat down and joined her, and they watched the next kid flick together.

Callie knew she could still be marked for death. Pito knew she was from New York, and could still possibly find her in New Jersey. She made up her mind to keep an extremely low profile. Pito was the wrong guy to sleep on. That dude was extremely thorough, and dangerous.

CHAPTER TWELVE

A few weeks later, Kira spent her Saturday evening sad, lonely, and depressed. She couldn't even concentrate enough to write any lyrics to the track she was working on. And she knew exactly what was bothering her. She was salty about seeing Cas with that bitch Laila at the hospital. Damn, their divorce was just finalized a couple of months ago. Was he living with that bitch already? Legally, Cas hadn't done anything wrong, but Kira felt like he really violated her. Both of those mothafuckas!

She couldn't believe Cas chose Laila's crippled ass over her. There was something really wrong with that picture. Kira couldn't front. Other than that, there was nothing bad she could say about Cas. He was a great father. He took up time with his son, and provided adequate financial support. In her divorce settlement, Kira got the house, and ten million dollars. And Cas still paid her fifteen thousand dollars a month for child support. Kira barely touched that money, so it was just piling up in a bank account.

The whole Cas and Laila thing didn't sit well with her. She was feeling real bitter. She felt like retaliating on those mothafuckas. She couldn't just let it go. She just couldn't. On impulse, Kira picked up the phone and called Cas to let him know what was on her mind.

Casino's cell phone rang three times before he answered it. He was driving along the Garden State Parkway at the time. He saw Kira's name on the caller ID, and hoped his little man was okay. He pressed a button, and spoke into his Bluetooth. "Hello?"

The first thing Kira said was, "Are you living with that bitch now?"

Cas started to say, "Don't call her that", but he just let it ride. That would've only made Kira get even more extra. He asked,

"Is my son okay?" That was the only reason she should've been calling him.

Kira said, "Yeah, he's fine. He's at my mother's house." She paused for a second, and then repeated her question a little more mildly this time. "So, are you living with Laila now, Cas?"

There was an awkward silence on both lines. Cas didn't have to answer to Kira. That was none of her business, but he just said, "Nah", and left it alone. That was somewhat true. He still had his condo, but he only stayed there when he had his son with him. He stayed with Laila most of the time, but Kira didn't need to know that.

Kira didn't respond, but she was glad he'd said no.

Cas sighed on the other end. "So, I'm driving right now. What up?"

Out of nowhere, Kira just blurted out, "I want us to try again. Let's make our family work, Cas. We ain't try as hard as we could have."

Wow. Cas didn't have an immediate response for that. She just didn't want to let it go. He felt sorry for Kira, but they were divorced, and he didn't love her that way anymore. To let her down easy, he said, "Who knows what the future holds. But for right now, we need time."

Kira listened to the mumbo-jumbo excuse Casino had just given her, and she regretted the fact that she'd even asked him. Fuck him! Kira flipped, and yelled, "Go to hell, nigga! I don't want yo' sorry ass no way!" She slammed the phone down, feeling like a woman scorned.

After she hung up, Cas just looked at the phone. He shook his head. That girl was seven-thirty. Kira obviously didn't know Laila was pregnant yet. If she knew, there was no way she wouldn't have brought it up. When he and Laila went to see Portia in the hospital a few weeks ago, Laila had been sitting down in her wheelchair, so it was hard to tell she was pregnant. She wasn't carrying that big. Cas was concerned about the baby's weight, but the doctor said everything looked okay.

Casino didn't want to deal with any more drama, so he wasn't about to tell Kira he had another kid on the way. She would find out eventually. The baby would be coming soon.

$$$$$

A few weeks later, Jay laid on his king-sized bed with one arm behind his head, and one hand resting lightly on his tiny newborn's back. He was just gazing at her, and watching her sleep. She was so beautiful. They had named her after Portia's mother, Patricia. Her name was Patrice Jayla Mitchell, and Portia had already given her a nickname. "Trixie" was sleeping peacefully on his chest, and Jay was awed by her preciousness. His heart swelled with pride.

His first princess, Jazmin, was laying right beside him on the bed. She loved her new little sister, and was trying hard to wake her up. Little Trixie must've been beat, because she wasn't trying to hear that. She woke up briefly, and stretched. She just opened her little eyes for a second and looked around, but she laid right back down on the pink receiving blanket spread out on her daddy's chest, and went back to sleep.

Jazmin laughed at the faces the baby made, and asked why she wouldn't wake up. Jay told her she was sleeping so much because she was growing. Jazmin made a serious face and nodded in agreement, like she understood. Jay told her that, in no time, Trixie would be running around behind her. Jazz found that quite amusing. She made a face at him, and laughed.

She was so cute. Jay leaned over, and kissed her on the forehead. He loved his kids more than anything in the world. As if on cue, his boy walked in the room. Jayquan was just waking up. He had slept late because his behind had been on MySpace chatting with girls all night. Jay knew what time it was. He grinned at his son affectionately, and greeted him. "What up, lil' man?"

"What up, Pop?" Jayquan came over, and sat on the bed next to his father and little sisters. Jazmin jumped on his back playfully. He tickled her, and gave her a kiss. Jay just laughed. Jazz liked to play rough. She could be a real tomboy when she wanted to.

Jayquan stood up, and lifted the baby from Jay's chest. He tried to wake her up too, with all these oochie cutchie coo sounds and baby talk, but babygirl was not ready to get up. She was only seven weeks old, but she was apparently big on beauty sleep, like her mama was. Lil' Jay smiled at her, and tickled her little thigh. Getting no response, he laid her back down on his father.

Jay asked him what was on the agenda for the day. Lil' Jay just shrugged. But when Jay announced that they'd be hanging out with him all day, he grinned. Jay told them to choose something fun to do.

He was keeping the kids that day, so Portia could get out of the house for a little while. She'd been a little down with post-partum blues, so he'd suggested she go out and go shopping, or something. Portia leapt at the opportunity. She told Jay she was going to visit her friends, Fatima and Laila, and then going shopping for the baby.

Portia wanted to check on Laila, because she was due to have her baby soon. She wanted to make sure her girl was okay. And Fatima had been on Portia's mind too, because she was going through some confused stage, and messing with girls. She had introduced Portia to her "friend" Cheyenne two weeks ago. Portia knew Fatima was grown, but sometimes she acted like a dumb ass teenager. Fatima told her she didn't want to be with another man since Wise had died, so she was trying something "different". Portia prayed it was just another phase.

Earlier, Portia had kissed her husband and babies, and told them she would see them later. Then she had pulled Jay's Phantom out of the garage, and drove to Fatima's crib to check on her crazy ass.

$$$$$

Fatima's girl toy was back, and she woke her up with a good twat tonguing early that afternoon. She licked her from clit to asshole over and over, until Fatima began to tremble. Cheyenne stuck her tongue inside her asshole, and sucked on the rim. Fatima humped her face, and spread her juices all over her.

Cheyenne zoomed back in on her clit, and sucked on it gently. Fatima caressed the back of her head, and stroked her hair

to her rhythm. She made her pussy feel wonderful. Fatima
could feel it building up. She was about to erupt. She grabbed
the back of Cheyenne's head, and fucked her face into oblivion.
Fatima cried out loudly when she came.

A few minutes later, Portia rang the bell. Fatima was just re-
covering from that powerful orgasm. She cleaned up fast, and
threw her robe on, and she headed downstairs to let her best
friend in. Fatima opened the door, and greeted Portia with a
sisterly kiss to the cheek. After that, she took a pack of cigarettes from her robe pocket. She lit up a Newport, and asked
how the kids were doing.

Portia told her they were fine, and she asked her about Falynn. Fatima told her Falynn was at her mother's house, but
she was okay. Portia didn't want to nitpick at her, but she had
to ask. "Since when do you smoke cigarettes, Tima?"

Fatima rolled her eyes impatiently. She took a long pull off
her cancer stick, and exhaled. She'd had a long night, and had
just got out the bed. She wasn't in the mood for Portia's nag-
ging, and shit.

Portia saw that Fatima wasn't going to answer her, so she left
it alone. They headed into the living room, and Fatima's little
Chinese freak, Cheyenne, appeared with a pink silk robe on.
Fatima could tell Cheyenne had an attitude, because she had
her arms crossed. She knew what that was all about. She didn't
like Portia.

Portia had met Fatima's lesbian lover one time, and she didn't
like her either. Not one bit. Portia could tell Cheyenne was
jealous of her and Fatima's friendship.

Fatima knew that too, and that really turned her off.
Cheyenne only hated Portia because she was her friend. Now
Fatima understood what dudes meant when they said broads
were "too emotional". But she didn't sweat it, because
Cheyenne knew to stay in her place. Since she'd allowed her to
come back, that girl had been tiptoeing around her.

On the other hand, Portia's main reason for disliking
Cheyenne was because she could see that her bad habits were
rubbing off on Fatima. That bitch even had her smoking cigarettes. Portia was annoyed by Cheyenne's presence, but she

tried to disregard that bitch. She looked right pass her, like she wasn't even there. Portia said, "Fatima, I gotta talk to you about something."

Cheyenne sat down on the couch across from them, and crossed her legs, and lit a cigarette. She did that like she was making some type of statement. Portia knew she was trying to be funny, so she addressed her directly. "Excuse me. I need to speak to my friend. In private, if you don't mind."

Cheyenne looked at Fatima to see where she stood on that. Fatima just nodded in agreement with Portia. She rolled her eyes, but she got her ass up and left.

Portia rolled her eyes at Cheyenne, and then she started fanning away smoke, like their cigarettes were really killing her. Fatima gave in to her dramatics. She knew her homegirl was a non-smoker. She didn't want to be selfish, so she smashed her Newport out in the ashtray. Afterwards, she smiled at Portia, and apologized.

Portia wanted to say more, but she kept her comments about the potential dangers of cigarette smoking to herself. She asked where Callie was, and Fatima said she was upstairs in her room, possibly still asleep.

Portia told Fatima the reason she had come over was that she wanted to discuss some new marketing strategies for their book publishing company. And Portia told Fatima she was ready to get started on her fourth book. She said she just needed an idea for the concept.

Fatima thought about all the action she'd been seeing at the swing parties she'd been attending lately, so she pitched the idea to Portia to write about something like that. They both knew that sex sold, and the raunchier and more exciting the material was, the better. Fatima told Portia she wouldn't believe some of the stuff that went on at those parties, and told her she had to go see for herself. She told her she was dragging her to the next one she planned to attend, which was a few weeks later. Fatima laughed, and said Portia had no idea what she was in for.

Portia agreed to go with her, for research's sake. Fatima told her she would need to have proof that she'd tested negative for

HIV/AIDS. Portia told her that wouldn't be a problem.
She'd just been tested right before she had the baby.

$$$$$

Every morning, Laila got up at seven to get Macy up for
school. She was proud of her daughter. Macy was going to the
tenth grade that fall. That girl was growing up too fast.

After Macy left for school, Laila usually spent the day with a
team of physical therapists. Cas stayed over most nights, but
he knew she liked to work with her therapy team alone. He
knew she preferred privacy with her therapists, so if he was
there, he stayed out of the way when they showed up.

Laila wasn't being mean. She just didn't want Cas monitor-
ing her progress. Especially when she felt like she wasn't making any. Casino was the one financing all the medical bills and
therapy her insurance didn't cover, but he was extremely understanding about her not wanting him there to watch. He realized that there were just some things he had to give Laila space
to work out on her own. And she handled him the same way.
She wasn't crowding or overbearing, and that was a plus.

Laila was trying hard to stay positive, because she really
wanted to walk before she had her baby. She didn't see how
she could pull off the "new mommy" thing again if she was confined to that wheelchair.

Now, Laila's chair was nice as hell. Cas had it custom-de-
signed, and had requested every type of special feature he could
think of. It did just about everything for Laila, except go to
the bathroom. That bad boy even had some nice ass rims on
it. Cas had purchased her the Rolls Royce of wheelchairs. But
it was still a damn wheelchair.

Laila was determined to walk, and already had her mind con-
ditioned to believe that anything short of that would be failing.
She was not prepared to accept the fact that she was paraplegic,
and truthfully, she wouldn't be happy until she was up and hopping around again.

Laila's life was good, considering. She had everything she
needed, and plenty of shit she didn't even really need. Her

house was absolutely fucking laced, and now Cas had it remodeled to fit her "temporarily" disabled lifestyle. Her kitchen cabinets were lower, all of the doorways in the house had been expanded so she could maneuver her chair in and out of every room without getting stuck, her master bathroom now had an electric lift in the tub and shower, and she even had an electric wheelchair lift that took her up and down the stairs easily.

Laila's plush, new living room furniture had remote controlled lifts in the sofa, loveseat and recliner. She could get out of her wheelchair, and relax with no problem. Her bed had been replaced with an adjustable one, making it easy for her to get up, or lay down.

Laila couldn't front, all those additions Cas had had done had helped her become independent enough to stay by herself. Being in the hospital under twenty-four hour care had taught Laila that "me time" was precious. That was the reason she told Cas she didn't need those fulltime nurses anymore. Now she just had part-time helpers. They assisted her with stuff like housecleaning, and laundry. And Laila preferred to cook for her daughter herself, but Cas had hired her an on-call cook to step in when she didn't feel like it.

Cas had hired two nurses, and a live-in assistant for her at first. He'd hired a whole staff of people, just in effort to make her life easier. But Laila told him it felt more like an invasion of her privacy. That was just too many mothafuckas in her house. Outside of her close friends, she was a very private person. She'd been raised to be furtive, and she didn't play that "strangers in her house" shit. And Laila didn't tell Cas, but she still liked to smoke a little weed every now and then, so she didn't want anybody all up in her business.

She just wanted to walk again. Cas had told her that if she wanted, he was willing to fly her overseas to have this world-renowned Swedish doctor perform a special operation on her spine. Laila had done some research before she answered him. There was a fifty-fifty chance that the surgery would work, and it would cost him about a million dollars.

Laila was flattered that Cas was willing to spare no expenses, but she had been in the hospital enough. She was afraid to go under the knife again, and she sure didn't want to fly all the way to Sweden to do it. And what if the operation didn't work? She just decided to keep the faith, and prayed that her therapy and hard work would finally pay off. There wasn't much time left until she had the baby. That was the reason she was doing her physical therapy sessions everyday. She was going hard.

Laila had just finished her Saturday session. After her team left, she had locked her doors, and gone upstairs to take a shower. She was home alone. Macy had spent the night over at her girlfriend's house again, and Cas had left a little earlier. He said he was spending the day with his son. Laila definitely didn't beef with that.

Right after Laila got out of the shower, she heard the doorbell ring. She was glad Cas had that new security system installed. There was an intercom, and a keypad she could punch a code in to unlock the front door, located in every room in her house. Being pregnant, and wheelchair bound, she was moving a lot slower, so that came in handy.

Laila pressed the intercom button, and asked who was at her front door. She was delighted to hear that it was Portia. She hadn't seen her in a couple weeks. She hoped she had the baby with her. Laila pushed in her four digit code, and unlocked the door, and she told Portia to come in and make herself at home. She told her she was upstairs in the bathroom, and would be down in a moment.

Laila got dressed as fast as she could, and went downstairs. She and Portia hugged, and asked where each other's kids were. After that, Portia filled Laila in on their crazy ass homegirl, Fatima, and the fact that she had a live-in lesbian lover.

Laila made a face, and couldn't believe it. Then she remembered Fatima had always been the one in the crew bold and crazy enough to try some different shit. Laila reminded Portia, and told her she shouldn't have been surprised.

Portia had to admit that was true. Fatima was the wild one. Portia used to be a stripper, and did some crazy things for money in her past, but Fatima had experimented with more freaky shit than she had.

Portia agreed with Laila that Tima was probably just going

through a phase, and then she asked how her divorce was coming along. Laila told her that bastard Khalil was still stunting,
and didn't want to sign the papers. She said she felt real bad
about this, especially since Cas had already divorced Kira. She
said she was thinking of a way to expedite the process.

Laila said he was still talking about "let's work it out", but
she told him she wanted to be alone right now, because she had
some work to do on herself. She told Portia she didn't imply
that it had anything to do with another man, but Khalil told
her he knew Cas was behind it. He was partially right. That
was one of the main reasons she wanted to end their marriage.
But Laila felt like it was unfair of him not to grant her a divorce
on those grounds. And it was him who had started it. He had
created a lot of bad blood between the two of them, especially
with the fucked up habit he had acquired. He had abandoned
her for crack! He wasn't willing to take any of the responsibility
for them breaking up, and that was the part she hated.

Jay had told Portia about the altercation Cas and Khalil had
when Laila was in the hospital, so she knew Khalil was aware
of Laila's new relationship. She agreed with her that he was
being really unfair. He had his chance, and he blew it. It was
that simple.

Laila said he wanted to meet with her in person to "talk, but
she was reluctant because he didn't know she was pregnant. She
said she just wished she could've planned that pregnancy, because she would've made sure it wouldn't have happened while
she was married to another man. Laila was old-fashioned, and
she thought that was really tacky. But what could she do? At
least Cas wanted it. He was standing by her, and that was a
blessing alone.

Portia told Laila she had come to scoop her up to go shopping with her, and she insisted. She would've suggested they
go to the hair salon as well, but Laila's do was tight as hell already. Every time she saw her it was. Portia was the one who
needed a wash and set.

She complimented her girl on her always perfect hair, and
Laila revealed her beauty secret. She told her Cas had hired her
hairstylist to make house calls now. Larissa came over twice a

week with all her supplies, and she kept Laila's wig piece look-ing good. And she also shaped her eyebrows once a week.

Portia grinned at her diva-licious homegirl. She really looked pretty. Laila was garbed in a desert colored pantsuit from Isaac Mizrahi's maternity collection. Her spirits seemed really high, and that heightened Portia's spirits. It was good to see Laila laughing again.

Laila agreed to roll out with Portia and go shopping, but she swore she wasn't buying any more clothes for herself until she dropped that load. She said she didn't want to ever see another maternity shirt again.

Portia said she still had fifteen pounds of post pregnancy weight to lose herself, so she wasn't buying any new clothes yet either. That being said, they agreed to go shopping for the kids.

CHAPTER THIRTEEN

"I don't know what they want from me. It's like the more money we come across, the more problems we see. Oh-oh-oh, what's goin' on? Somebody tell me-e-e..."

Right about then, it was like Biggie's hit song "Mo Money, Mo' Problems" was Jay's theme song. He turned the volume up, and crept along in his Rolls Road Phantom in late afternoon traffic. He wished he'd hired a helicopter to maneuver through the city that day. Hell, he needed to buy one. That damn traffic got on his nerves.

Jay had just left BET, where he had stood in for his deceased homie, Wise, and introduced his new video on "106th & Park". That was the last video he'd done before he passed away. Now he was running late for an on-air interview with the popular radio personality, Angie Martinez, down at Hot 97. He was tuned in, and heard Angie announce his expected arrival a few minutes before. When he got there, he also planned on mentioning the new clothing line they had in the works.

Jay thought about his main man, Cas. He was busy running around in the city too, going to have meetings with a couple of their associates. Cas was taking care of some inside stuff that needed to be done that day. Jay wondered if he would be where he was without him. He and Casino complemented each other businesswise. It was good to have a partner who thought on his toes. Cas was all business, all the time. That was the way he had always been. Ever since they were just young hustlers and crimies.

A little further uptown, Cas was driving along the FDR Drive, on his way to handle some company business. He was running a little late for a meeting, so he whipped his Maserati double the speed limit, with the precision of a professional driver. He had his radio tuned into Hot 97 as well, waiting to hear Jay talk to Angie Martinez.

The record that was playing, Biggie's "Mo' Money, Mo' Problems" had Cas thinking too. That shit was so true. Street Life was doing well. Especially at a time when CDs weren't really selling because musical downloads were so popular, and the economy was so shaky. He and Jay had their hands in a lot of stuff, so there was always a steady flow of dough rolling in. But it seemed like there was always one problem after another. Mo' money, mo' problems. Shit was crazy.

$$$$$

The time had come for Portia to go to that swing party with Fatima. Portia had asked herself over and over if she had the guts to go, but she wanted to do some research for her next novel. Being a new mom again had slowed her down a lot, but she had to get cracking. She needed to get started on that book.

Before Portia got ready for the evening, she fed Jazmin and the baby, and gave them both a bath. Macy was going to babysit for her for a while. She was staying over that night. Jayquan was supposed to be helping her do something to her MySpace page.

Macy was fifteen now, and she was a pretty mature young lady, so Portia left her in charge of the baby until Jay got there. Trixie had fallen asleep, so all Macy had to do was keep an eye on her. Jayquan felt like he was capable of taking care of the baby, but Portia felt better with Macy there also. She was a little older, and more responsible. And plus, Lil' Jay hadn't gotten pass his issues with changing diapers. He said he didn't even want to learn how. Macy, on the other hand, said she didn't mind changing "baby poop", so she won the babysitting position hands down.

Jay had called and said he would be there in about two hours, so the kids wouldn't be alone long. After Portia took a shower, she searched for an outfit for the evening.

Macy came in the room, and stretched out across the foot of Portia's bed, and she talked about the new baby her mother was expecting.

She said she couldn't wait until the baby came, but honestly, she was a little afraid of the way her father would react when he found out. She said she wished there was a way they could hide it from him forever, just to keep from hurting him with the news. She said she felt like she was stuck in the middle.

Portia told her not to mention it to Khalil. Macy told her Laila had already made that very clear, and said she wouldn't have anyhow. Portia told her not to worry about all that grown folk stuff, but Macy said that was easier said than done. She got up, and said she was going to the nursery to check on the baby. On her way out, she told Portia she should wear the green Vivienne Westwood dress she just took out.

Portia took Macy's advice, and decided to rock the Vivienne Westwood dress. It was sexy and fit her curves, but it wasn't too much. She didn't want to look like she was advertising her goods. They were going to a freak party, for goodness sake.

Portia walked back in her closet, and got her green Manolo Blahnik open-toes, and new green Balenciaga bag. Before she got dressed, she filled the bag with all her necessities, including her digital voice recorder. The weather was nice again, but it still got a little cool at night. She grabbed a cashmere Chanel shawl from her closet, to throw over her shoulders.

When Portia was done getting ready, she kissed the kids, and told them to lock the door. She reminded them to call her cell phone if anything happened.

Lil' Jay, Jazmin, and Macy all told her she looked nice. Portia blushed, and headed out the door to her Benz. She left a trail of Dolce and Gabbana's Light Blue perfume floating behind her.

When Portia got to Fatima's, she went inside for a cocktail. She needed to loosen up a little before they hit the party. It had been a while since she hung out, and she still couldn't believe she was going to a swing party.

Fatima looked real nice. She had on a short yellow Escada dress, yellow fishnets, and yellow Christian Louboutin pumps. The matching bag was sitting on the coffee table. She had a cherry "Tima-tini", and a freshly rolled blunt waiting for Portia, like she knew she needed to relax.

Cheyenne wasn't at Fatima's house, and Portia was glad. She did not feel like looking in that bitch's face. But it was nice to see Callie. She was downstairs chilling on the couch, watching Eddie Murphy's "Norbit". Portia hadn't seen her in a while. She asked Callie how she was doing, ands she said she was good. She told Portia she liked Jersey, and felt at peace. She said she was looking for a job, so she could find a place.

Portia wished her luck, and asked her if she wanted to hang out with them that night. Callie thanked her for the invitation, but said she didn't feel like partying. She said she was tired because she'd got up early that morning and gone job hunting, so she planned to turn in early. Portia remembered that Fatima did tell her she let Callie use one of her cars to go look for a job that morning.

Portia and Fatima had another round of drinks, and finished smoking the el. Afterwards, they were both feeling good. It was time to roll out. Fatima looked at Callie, and said, "Don't wait up, chick." She told her to lock the door behind them, and she and Portia said goodnight, and gleefully left the house.

$$$$$

Back at Portia's house, Macy and Jayquan were watching videos. Jazmin had fallen asleep already. When one of their favorites old videos, "Soulja Boy", came on, they got up and did the dance. Jayquan could do it even better than Soulja Boy himself.

Macy laughed at him, and thought about her younger sister. She said, "Jayquan, if Pebbles was here, she'd be killin' this shit. You know my sister could dance her ass off." She smiled affectionately at the memory.

Jayquan grinned, and nodded in agreement. "Word, Pebbles could dance." He thought about the time Pebbles had let him feel her tities. That was the last time he saw her alive. No disrespect to her memory, but he hadn't felt any that nice since. He had felt this white girl named Amy up at school, who was sweating him all the time. But she was skinny, with a flat chest, so that didn't really count. She didn't have anything, tities or booty.

Jayquan and Macy were as close as cousins because they'd
spent so much time together, and had been through so much
together. Jayquan felt like he could talk to Macy about pretty
much anything. He was getting older now, and he was having
these urges sometimes. He was curious about doing things
with girls. Sexual things. He and his friends had propositioned
a few girls at school to do nasty stuff to them, and some of them
loved it. Jayquan told Macy about the time Amy gave him, and
his homeboy Rashawn a blowjob under the bleachers in the
school gym.

Macy knew Amy was a white girl, so she acted like she was
disgusted with him. She told Jayquan, "Boy, yo' ass got "jungle
fever". You better keep yo' little thang outta them little nasty
behind girls' mouths. You gon' mess around and catch somethin' that your ass can't get rid of. Messin' with them old nasty
ass white girls."

Macy was concerned about Jayquan's health, but for some
reason, she was also a tiny bit jealous. She didn't appreciate
that news at all. To move away from the subject, she said, "Put
a movie in, dummy. Ooh, let's go watch "Dream Girls" again
on the theater screen."

Jayquan made a face. "Nobody wanna see that mess again.
Let's watch "Spiderman", or "Transformers.""

Macy agreed to watch "Spiderman". She followed Lil' Jay to
the theater on the other side of the rec section. She plopped
down in one of the reclining movie chairs, while he put the
movie on.

Lil' Jay made a discovery, and his eyes lit up. He looked back
at Macy with a mischievous grin. He had discovered a porno
DVD his father had obviously forgotten to put away. He didn't
tell Macy what he found. He just played that movie instead.

He had a seat beside her, and acted like nothing had changed.
The movie started, and it played for a minute before Macy realized what he had done.

She reached over and punched Jayquan in the shoulder.
Macy said, "You so nasty. What is wrong with you, boy? I'm
going to check on the babies." She got up, and walked away.

Jayquan just sat there watching the porno movie, and it got more interesting by the second. A few minutes later, Macy came back and sat down beside him. She didn't say a word, but she sat there and watched too.

Lil' Jay just smiled in the dark. He knew girls liked stuff like that too. He wondered why they were always fronting. He hoped that would change as he got older.

$$$$$

Fatima and Portia were barely gone five minutes before Callie ran upstairs and checked Fatima's bedroom door to see if it was locked. Her hopes soared when the knob turned with no problem. She had been checking that lock every single time Fatima left the house. She had considered just breaking it, but she knew Fatima would be able to tell.

Callie had lied about going job hunting that morning. She had used Fatima's car to go to Riker's Island in New York, and visit Smoke. Now she was anxious to accomplish something to impress him with. He was constantly on her, asking what type of progress she was making.

Callie went inside Fatima's room, and felt like a kid in a candy store. She ran over to Fatima's dresser, and opened the top drawer. Jackpot! It was filled with expensive jewelry. Callie sighed in awe at the sparkle from Fatima's gems. She wanted to just grab all those diamonds, and haul ass. But she had to play it smart. She couldn't do that. She had too much to lose. She really enjoyed living up in that house. She felt like she was royalty. She'd be a fool to run away from that. Plus, Smoke had told her to stay put until he got out, which would be in a few months.

Fatima had a good heart for letting her stay in her house. She had taken Callie shopping, and even let her drive one of her vehicles. She actually gave her the keys to her Mercedes. It was the least expensive vehicle Fatima owned, but she still had to trust her.

Callie couldn't resist the temptation. She decided to take just one thing. Something of worth, that she could pawn for the extra money she needed to do some shopping for Smoke, and put some money in his commissary. She carefully selected a chunky gold bracelet that was flooded with diamonds.

Greed wouldn't let Callie stop there. She noticed a pair of teardrop earrings. They were kind of small, so she figured Fatima wouldn't notice those missing. After that, she closed the drawer, and started searching for Fatima's important papers. Smoke told her that if she played her cards right, and got her social security number and credit profile, she would be able to become Fatima. Then she could buy them whatever she wanted.

$$\$\$\$\$\$$

Meanwhile, Portia and Fatima had arrived at the swing party. At the front door, they were asked to produce a photo I.D. and proof of a recent HIV/AIDS test. They waited patiently while their paperwork and I.D. were examined.

After they were approved, Portia and Fatima were given a green light, and then offered their pick from a box filled with colorful Mardi Gras type masquerade masks. There was a box right next to it that was filled with condoms, and little packets of Wet lubrication.

Fatima and Portia giggled, and picked out masks that matched their outfits. Portia didn't bother with the condoms because she wouldn't know how to explain them to Jay, but Fatima grabbed herself a handful. Portia just laughed at her crazy behind.

As soon as she put on her masquerade mask, she felt naughty. Portia could just imagine what went on behind those masks. The night had started out like some television shit already.

They walked through another door, and went inside the party. The whole place was lit with blue lights. Portia and Fatima ran right into Charlene, who was waiting for them at the front. Charlene was wearing a black and gold mask, and a black dress.

Charlene and Portia greeted with a friendly hug. Portia hadn't seen her since she left Black Reign, this record company she used to work for. Fatima used to work there too. In fact, she had helped Portia get the job.

It may have been Portia's imagination, but she could've sworn Charlene gave her this little knowing look. Maybe she was bugging, but it seemed like Charlene was thinking, "I knew you'd be getting down with us sooner or later." But Portia could have been just thinking about the time she'd hung out with her years ago. Some dude had slipped something in her drink that night, so Charlene had helped her out of the club, and drove her to her house to sleep it off. Portia had fallen asleep on her couch, and woke up to her feeling on her.

Portia felt like she needed another drink. She looked around, and checked out her surroundings. The further inside the party they walked, the more action she started seeing. It went from people just talking, to people just kissing, to topless people touching one another, to people engaged in oral, to people having actual intercourse.

Portia even saw a few dudes engaged in butt naked, sweaty, hot butt love. The "bottom", a dark haired dude, was bent over with his ass up in the air, moaning like a girl. The "top", a handsome blond dude who looked like he could be a model, was pounding that pink ass with force. To Portia, the live H.B.L. action was the most shocking sight so far. She really couldn't believe it. She used to be a stripper, and thought she had seen it all, but those mothafuckas up in there were on some real freak shit!

Fatima giggled at the way Portia was staring at the "fudge lovers", who knew they had an audience, and didn't care. Fatima told her girl to relax, and just have some fun. She told her not to be afraid to let her hair down that night. She promised Portia that whatever happened there, would stay there.

Portia looked at Fatima like she was crazy, and told her she didn't come there too "party". She said she was good, so she should go have herself some fun. Portia told her she was just going to walk around, and take some mental notes for her book.

Fatima just grinned, and told her she would see her later, and she and Charlene went off to the bathroom together. Portia saw Charlene sizing up this tall, slim chick walking in front of them. Portia shook her head, and headed in the other direction.

Portia walked upstairs to see what was going on up there. The lights up there were red. That probably indicated some real freaky stuff. She guessed that was where the "red light specials" were.

Instead of just open space like downstairs, the upstairs consisted of separate rooms. Up there, Portia saw all kinds of shit. In one room, there was a submissive girl begging this man to be her master. Portia watched as this male dominatrix began commanding her to do the unthinkable. The girl looked like she was enjoying it. She was really getting off on the dude, licking his boot toes, and doing everything else he said.

Portia chitchatted briefly with this decent looking guy, who seemed like he was just there to watch too. He wasn't even wearing a mask. They stood in the doorway of a room that had what looked like sadomasochism going on inside. In their conversation, she learned that there was a difference between bondage and discipline, and sadomasochism, respectively referred to as B&D and S&M.

Portia's conversation buddy told her that Bondage and Discipline consisted of acts that sometimes involved S&M, but Discipline could be just a level of suffering, without actual pain. Like a person being deprived of food or water, for instance.

The guy told Portia that the definition of Sadomasochism was "sexual gratification in the infliction of pain or suffering on or by another person". He said Sadists enjoy inflicting pain, and Masochists enjoy receiving pain, which didn't necessarily have to be sexual in nature. Then he said people who simply desire pain have a physical condition technically known as Algolagnia. According to him, Algolagnia caused a person to gain sexual pleasure by suffering pain, particularly to erogenous zones.

Portia appreciated the knowledge. She guessed that was what was up with the white dude to their left, who was presently getting thumb tacks and needles stuck in his scrotum, one by one. His poor nut sack had to be on fire, but homeboy looked like he was having the time of his life.

The dude who was schooling Portia kept a straight face the whole time. He was black, and she would've never guessed it from his appearance, but he had that shit down to a science. An articulate brother, who was obviously very into that type of thing, he had done his homework. Portia wondered what category he fit into. Regardless, she certainly found their conversation interesting. The knowledge made great research material for her new book. But some of that shit going on was a little scary.

The guy casually asked Portia if she was in the mood for a good spanking, or a choking, so she guessed he was a Sadist. She declined his offer, but was glad he had satisfied her curiosity, and let her know what his thing was.

She decided to walk back downstairs, to check out some more normal sex. Portia said goodbye to her freaky friend, and headed towards the stairs. Then she changed her mind. She hadn't just come to that party to witness the same old normal sex. She needed some more dirt. Portia turned around, and she saw some gay guys coming out of a big room on her left. She figured that had to be the gay section. There was sure to be some action over there.

Just as Portia thought, it was off the hook in that section. There were like three different orgies going on. Folks were carrying on like they had been in twenty-year marriages with each other. Portia didn't understand how anyone could be so comfortable with complete strangers.

Portia laughed to herself. She must've been getting old. Not long ago, she herself had made a living off discreet and anonymous sexual encounters with strangers sometimes. She had done it for money, but it was sort of like the same thing. Sex with a stranger was sex with a stranger. She hadn't gone all out with it like that, but she wasn't about to judge anyone. That would make her a hypocrite. To each his own.

Portia walked over to a mini-bar in the corner, and she ordered herself a stiff Cosmopolitan. The vodka in the drink was strong, so she held her breath, and swallowed that sucker quick. She hated the taste of alcohol, but she needed to loosen up.

This shapely girl about 5'7", with an Indian-like complexion, joined Portia at the bar. She introduced herself as Raquel, and she told Portia she found her very attractive. Portia blushed, and the girl apologized for being so bold. She told her she loved ample breasts, and would like very much to suck on hers.

She was so forward, Portia almost choked on her drink. She didn't know what to say to her after that. She just smiled politely, and said, "Sorry, but I'm not gay."

The girl laughed, and said, "Good, because I'm not either. I'm happily married. Going on six years now. I just have a breast fetish. Especially for beautiful, chocolate ones such as yours." She eyed Portia's breasts as she spoke.

Portia couldn't see her whole face, because she was wearing a mask too, but she seemed to be pretty. She was dressed nice, and didn't have any body odor she could smell. Portia wouldn't have admitted it to anyone, but a part of her actually wanted to say yes. She ordered another Cosmopolitan, and thought about it for a minute. Raquel insisted on paying for her drink for her, and promised her she would find the breast play pleasing.

Portia's curiosity got the best of her. She told Raquel she wouldn't mind, but only if they could go somewhere a little more secluded. Raquel smiled, and told her there were some more private rooms in the back. Portia took a deep breath, and followed her. She was careful to keep a few feet of distance between the two of them. For some reason, she felt like everyone was watching her, and knew what they were about to do.

Portia reminded herself that she was wearing a mask to protect her identity. And she was at a swing party. Everybody there was freaky, so nobody was thinking about her black ass. Who the hell cared if she got her tities sucked? That was light compared to some of the things she had witnessed.

Portia walked in the room behind Raquel. Inside, it was dimly lit, and split into cubicles. Raquel went inside the second one to her left, so Portia joined her. She didn't know what to do, but she didn't want to prolong it, so she took the liberty of unzipping her own dress. It fell below her waist, and she stood in front of Raquel in a sage colored satin and lace bra.

Raquel stood there and watched her for a second, and then

she came closer, and massaged her breasts. Portia had never been touched by a woman that way, so she was nervous. She took a deep breath, and tried to relax.

Raquel's touch was gentle. She reached around, and un-hooked her bra, and she whispered for Portia to have a seat. Portia sat down on the burgundy chaise lounge behind her, and Raquel knelt between her legs. She was still fully clothed.

She took both of Portia's jugs in her hands, and finger rolled her nipples until they stiffened. When they stuck out like twin peaks, she leaned in and licked them one at a time. Portia could-n't front. Her tongue felt delightful. Raquel squeezed her tities together, and sucked them simultaneously. Portia leaned back and enjoyed it, and her breathing got heavier.

True to her word, all Raquel did was lick and kiss on her breasts. And she was good at it. Portia was pretty sure the crotch of her panties was wet. She started moaning, but she caught herself. It really felt good.

Portia's baby was only about three months old. She wasn't breastfeeding anymore, but she was still lactating a little. But if anything was coming out, it must have been sweet, because Raquel was working on them bad boys like Hershey Kisses. Portia was practically trembling. She felt like she was having an orgasm. She couldn't believe it.

Portia was breathing heavy, so Raquel could tell she had en-joyed herself. She smiled, and got up. She said, "Thank you very much. That was great." After that, she just disappeared.

Portia was glad she left, because it would've been really awk-ward having to talk to her after that. Exactly what would she have said to her? She put her bra back on, and zipped up her dress, and she just sat there thinking for a second.

Portia felt funny. She hoped that shit didn't make her a les-bian. She had really enjoyed the breast play. But that didn't make her gay, did it? Portia thought about Jay, and she felt guilty. Had she been unfaithful to her husband? Was what she had done considered cheating?

Those two Cosmopolitans Portia drank helped her justify everything. All she did was have a little fun. And it was research for her book. Nobody would ever find out.

Portia got up, and went downstairs. She wondered what Fatima was up to. She took her cell phone out of her purse, and tried calling her, but she got her voicemail. Portia decided to go look for her, but she had to use the bathroom first.

When Portia got to the bathroom, she was lucky. Fatima was right in there. But what she was doing caused Portia to do a serious double take. She couldn't believe her eyes, but she saw Fatima plain as day. She wasn't even trying to hide. She was bent over, snorting cocaine from a bunch of lines spread out on a mirrored glass tray. When Portia saw that shit, she felt like crying. What the fuck was Tima doing to herself? She was out of her mind.

Portia had a little baby to take care of at home, so she and Fatima hadn't really been hanging out much lately. So she had no idea what that girl was up to. Portia knew she'd been partying a whole lot, but she hadn't known it was that serious.

Fatima didn't even see her come in. Portia went on to use the bathroom, and came back out when she was done, and washed her hands. That's when Fatima noticed her. She smiled at her brightly. "What up, P? Where the hell you been, girl?"

Portia guessed she was done getting high, because there was another girl bent over that mirrored tray now. Portia didn't even let Fatima know she had seen her, because that wasn't the time, or place for a confrontation. Fatima was grown, and she already knew what that shit did to you. And she also knew what it could lead to. If she wanted to be stupid, that was on her.

The more Portia thought about how dumb she was, she got more and more pissed off. She copped an attitude, and told Fatima she was ready to go. Fatima looked at her funny, and asked her what had happened. Portia told her nothing happened. She said she was just ready to go.

Just then, Charlene walked up to them. She had been in that little cocaine circle too, so Portia had few words for her. She was probably the bad influence that introduced Tima to that shit. All those new bitches she hung around had her doing some crazy shit. Fatima was a stupid, weak bitch, and she was being a follower.

Portia asked Fatima if she was ready to go, and she just

walked off without saying goodbye to Charlene. Fatima apologized to Charlene for their abrupt departure, and she made up an excuse about Portia not feeling well.

Charlene told Fatima not to sweat it. They hadn't come there together, and she wasn't quite ready to break out yet. Charlene said she was having too much fun to leave.

On the way home, Portia acted like everything was okay. She'd called herself helping Tima by removing her from that environment. She cared about her friend, even if she was stupid.

Portia's little encounter with Raquel was on her mind hard body. She had to tell somebody, so she told Tima, and swore her to secrecy. Fatima just laughed at her, and said it was really no big deal. Portia told her that, afterwards, she had felt mad funny. Like everybody was watching her.

Fatima figured that was the reason she was in such a hurry to leave. She told Portia that married life had really turned her into a big square. Portia just smiled, and she told Fatima she had fun, but that lifestyle wasn't for her anymore. She said she had some juicy stuff to write about, though. She had learned about all kinds of sexual behavior. Then Portia added that Jay was definitely getting some pussy when she got home, because she was horny as hell. She couldn't front, that Raquel could suck some tities.

CHAPTER FOURTEEN

Khalil paced the floor of his basement apartment angrily. He had been trying to contact Laila all day. He wondered why she wasn't taking his calls. His first assumption was that she was laid up with that nigga.

Khalil hated that nigga Cas. He didn't know what the fuck he had done to his wife to make her turn on him the way she had, but it seemed he had Laila pretty brainwashed. Probably just from buying her shit, because he had all that money.

Khalil was bitter, and filled with resentment. He had cleaned up his act after he heard about Laila's accident, and tried to stand by her side and be the husband she needed. But he had been told in not so many words that his services were no longer needed. And she wondered why he was getting high.

She didn't want to have anything to do with him. When he talked to her last, and asked her if she loved him, she said, "I love you the way God says love you." What the fuck did that mean? It sounded like she meant she didn't have any feelings for him.

Khalil had gotten so frustrated by Laila's constant request for a divorce, he had started smoking heavy again. He had tried to stay clean. He had spent a few weeks in a rehab, and the whole nine. It was Laila's fault that he had slipped again. Every fucking time he spoke to her, she kept saying, "When are you going to sign the divorce papers? When are you going to sign the divorce papers?"

Khalil had contested the divorce, and wasn't signing shit. Laila had destroyed their marriage, and now she wanted out. Well, he wanted to work it out.

"You fuckin' cripple, wheelchair bitch! You fucked up everything Laila! Everything! You destroyed our family!" Khalil swung at the air, and punched like it was Laila's face. He was blind with fury. He wished that bitch was in front of him. He would have beaten the shit out of her.

Khalil was spazzing out because he hated Laila for messing everything up between them. She should've just been a little more patient with him. As soon as shit got a little rough, she took the kids and bailed. He couldn't stand that fucking bitch.

In his selfishness, he forgot how patient Laila had been with him, especially when he'd first got hooked on that shit. He forgot how he'd abandoned her, and their two daughters for drugs. He forgot how he hadn't even stood by her side after the death of their baby daughter, Pebbles. And he barely kept up with the activities of his only living child in the world, Macy, because he was so busy stressing Laila. When he called, he hardly even asked what Macy was doing.

Khalil was typical, with his "Temporary Male Amnesia". Unfortunately, T.M.A. was a common condition. Some men had a way of shifting all the responsibility of a breakup on the woman in the relationship, and they completely forgot about all the fucked up shit they did.

For Khalil, it was easier to blame Laila and Cas for his marriage failing. He wasn't taking any of the responsibility for anything that had gone wrong between them. He felt like killing that nigga, Cas. He could vividly imagine dumping bullets in that nigga's torso. He had fucked around on sacred territory. That nigga stole his family, and that was some personal shit worth killing for.

Khalil was beyond salty. He was low, and his pride was hurt. He had lost the two fistfights he had with Cas, but the next time they met, he would be the last man standing.

$$\$\$\$\$\$$

Jay and Cas were at their Manhattan office a little later than usual. They had been going over some paperwork, and getting some legal advice from their business manager. At this point in their lives, both men had more money than they could spend. There were only so many diamonds and cars a dude could buy.

Fortunately, Jay and Cas were no longer in that state of mind. They were both on some grown man stuff, and interested in stuff like returns on investments, and capital gains instead. They socialized with dudes that owned investment firms, and yachts, and vacationed in places like the South of France. Their lives were good.

But with the Feds on their tails trying to draw up a case against them, Jay and Cas had been looking for new, and clever ways to hide their money. They were getting it done slowly but surely, transferring only moderate amounts at a time so it wouldn't look any more suspicious than their normal account activities. They knew the pigs were smart, so they tried to be smarter.

Their latest venture was with some much respected alliances they had recently acquired. Jay and Cas' new friends were Men of the Cloth. They were clergy, with respected and accredited non-profit charitable organizations, dedicated to empowering economically challenged African nations. The mission of the non-profits was to enable the countries' growth, by building schools and hospitals, and creating jobs to stimulate their economy.

Jay and Cas could dump millions of dollars into this cause, and disguise their money in the process. The catch was that none of those hospitals, or school buildings would ever be completely finished. The greater portion of the donations was recycled back to the donors in the form of certified checks in fifty thousand dollar increments. Long story short, Jay and Cas would get all of their money back, less ten percent, plus whatever else they found it in their hearts to "give back". They were depositing the certified checks in offshore accounts.

Just then, Jay's cell phone rang, and he saw it was a number with a 910 area code. He wondered who was calling him from North Carolina. He answered, and discovered that it was Ysatis, Humble's little shorty. Jay smiled when he thought about his little homie. Humble was a good little dude, may he rest in peace. He was Jay's protégé.

Jay hadn't heard from Ysatis in a long time. The last time he'd spoken to her, she'd called to let him know that she and her mother were settled down south. He remembered the way they were introduced. When Humble was killed, they had put out a reward for the culprit, and Ysatis had come forth, and given up her slime ball, douche bag of a brother, Nasty Neal. Brief recollections of the way she told them her brother had often raped, and molested her crossed Jay's mind.

He greeted Ysatis amiably, and asked her what was good. She told him she'd been okay, and then she expressed the fact that she wanted to come back up top to finish school. She said her mother had passed away a few months ago, and she saw no reason to remain in the south. She said she was flying to New York that Sunday. Jay told her to contact him when she arrived.

After they hung up, Jay thought about the way he, Cas, and Wise, God bless the dead, had made that creep, Nasty Neal, disappear without a trace. That slime ass nigga Hop was with them too. Hop's true colors had been revealed later, when he tried to set them up that time when Jay got shot in the face, but he got what he deserved too. And those Scumbag niggas who'd tried to rob them got theirs too.

Wise had been killed in a gun battle that escalated from that beef. Jay swallowed hard at his memory. He missed the hell out of that dude. He was still struggling with the fact that he was departed from them. It wasn't easy. It really wasn't. They had a lot of years in, and shared some good times.

$$\$\$\$\$\$$

Ysatis landed in New York three days later. She called Jay, and asked him to pick her up from the airport. Jay was tied up, and thought about sending a car for her, but on the strength of Humble, he delegated a few tasks to his assistant, and headed for LaGuardia Airport.

When Jay got to the airport arrival section, Ysatis was waiting by the curb just as she'd said she'd be. She had certainly grown up. And Jay had to admit she looked well, like that myth about the air down south being better for you was true.

Ysatis was pretty, slim, and caramel complexioned, with a button nose. She had her hair pulled back in a ponytail, so she looked even younger than she was. When Jay pulled up, she smiled brightly. It was gray and drizzling outside, but Ysatis' presence sort of livened up the atmosphere. Jay parked, and got out of the car. She greeted him jovially, and they hugged. He got good vibes from her.

Jay opened the passenger door for Ysatis, and she climbed on in. He popped the trunk of his Bentley, and threw in her suitcase. As he walked around the car to get back under the wheel, the raindrops grew heavier and faster, so he quickened his step.

Once settled inside the coupe, Jay grinned over at Ysatis. He sort of felt like an older brother. It was good to see her. Probably because she made him think of Humble. She was Humble's girl at one point, so Jay just felt obligated to look out for her. He told Ysatis to fasten her seatbelt, and he strapped himself in, and pulled off.

Jay expressed his sympathy once more for the passing of her mother, and then he asked her what she had been up to. Ysatis was a real chatterbox. She gave Jay a detailed description of her life down south during the past two years. She said she had completed a couple of years at NC State, gotten her driver's license, purchased a nice car, and then wrecked it.

He laughed, and asked her where she was staying. She said she was staying with a friend. Ysatis asked him if he minded stopping to get something to eat before he dropped her off. Jay was hungry himself, so he stopped at a nice diner in Queens. They got some grub, and Jay dropped her off in Brooklyn an hour later.

He called her every couple of days to check on her, to make sure she was alright.

Two weeks into her stay, Ysatis called Jay and told him she had been robbed by her homegirl's conniving older brother. She said the dude stole her whole three thousand dollar stash. She told Jay that when she told her friend what her brother did, she flipped on her, and said she didn't believe he had taken her money. She said she trusted her brother, and told her to leave if she didn't. Ysatis told Jay she had to get out of there fast, before she winded up going to jail for hurting somebody. Then she confessed to him that she was now penniless.

Jay being the thoughtful guy that he was, he told her to stay put. He was just leaving a meeting with his attorney in Manhattan when she called, so he was free for a while. He retrieved his Bentley from the parking lot, and hit the Brooklyn Bridge to go pick up Ysatis.

When he got there, she was still a little upset. Her feelings were hurt, and she was pissed that her money had been stolen. Jay told her she shouldn't have been traveling with that kind of cash in the first place. He took her to The Marriott downtown, and booked her a suite, and he told her to relax for a few days. Before he left, he gave her some pocket money, and told her to call him if she needed anything.

Jay was loaded, so it was nothing for him to get Ysatis a room at The Marriott. That was like chump change. He had frequented far more expensive and exquisite hotels. But to Ysatis, his putting her up in The Marriott was a big deal. She knew Jay had money, but she thought that was really nice of him. She beamed in delight. And she ordered room service that evening.

A few days later, Jay stopped by to check on Ysatis. He had paid for the suite for a week, so he asked her what her plans were. She kept it real, and told Jay she didn't have a clue, but said she really wanted to transfer to a college in New York. She said she just had to figure out a way to finance it. She told him she had financial aid, but she knew school in New York would be considerably more expensive than the university she'd been attending down south.

Jay was always one to support education, so he told her that he was willing to sponsor the portion of tuition and board her financial aid wouldn't cover. Ysatis asked him to what extent, and Jay told her to go for the best. Ysatis grinned, and said she'd always had her eye on NYU. Or perhaps Columbia University. She said she was a year away from completing the requirements for her bachelor's degree, and then she wanted to further her education. New York had some of the finest graduate schools in the country.

Jay agreed. Seeing how enthused Ysatis was about staying in New York, and finishing school, he was compelled to assist her.

Jay had a heart of gold, and wanted to help solve her problems. Food and shelter were the single most important elements of survival, so he just wanted to make sure she ate, and had a decent place to stay while she went to school.

Jay thought about putting her up in one of his apartments, but he didn't really have any vacancies that suited her. The only apartment he had available was a three bedroom, and that was too much space for Ysatis alone.

The more Jay thought about it, he didn't think it would have been a good idea to move her into one of his cribs anyway. That probably wouldn't sit well with Portia. She'd be thinking some other shit if she found out, and it wasn't even like that. He just liked helping people. Jay knew he couldn't take his money with him when he died, so he might as well do something good with it now. He paid up the hotel suite for the remainder of the month, and told Ysatis to be searching for a crib.

Ysatis tried not to be picky, so she found something modest in Crown Heights, located on St. Marks Street. It was a small one bedroom apartment, but it was cozy. She appreciated Jay's generosity, but she didn't want to be a burden. The way she saw it, her education was more important. She would live just about anywhere she could while she finished school. When she got her degree, she knew she'd be able to afford a better lifestyle.

The cost of living in New York was so high, that little apartment cost a thousand dollars a month. And she had to pay her own utilities. Ysatis told Jay she would be able to pay her utilities because she had a little monthly income from the house she owned, and rented out down south to a woman with the government subsidized rent assistance program, Section-8. Ysatis said the house was paid for already, so all she had to do was pay the property taxes once a year. She said her tenant paid her own water bill and light bill, and there was no gas bill because the stove and heating system were all electric.

Jay didn't even see the apartment Ysatis chose. He just gave her eight thousand dollars to do whatever she needed to do. Ysatis told him she went to Ikea, and furnished her whole apartment, and said it was real cozy. Jay was just happy that he could help.

$$$$$

Portia had decided to not make a big deal over her discovery of Fatima's cocaine use. She didn't want to blow it up, so she told herself that Fatima would see the light and realize how stupid doing coke was, and leave that shit alone.

But contraire to Portia's wishes, Fatima's "party girl" phase worsened. Girlfriend was out of control. Over the past few weeks, she'd been hosting these wild parties at her house, and letting Cheyenne plan the guest list. To say the least, her address was becoming well known, and Portia suspected that some freaky activity went on at her house.

Fatima, Portia, and Laila didn't live far apart, but Fatima refrained from telling them about her parties. Laila was homebound for the most part, and Portia had acted so scary the night they went to that swing party, so Fatima didn't think they were ready to learn about her "other" extracurricular activities.

Another thing Fatima hadn't told her girls was that she was running through money like it was going out of style. She had been spending at least seventy or eighty grand a week, just on partying, and supplying all the get-high for the group of leeches that were Cheyenne's friends. They snorted so much coke, it was like they had vacuum cleaners for noses.

Fatima hadn't seen her daughter in weeks. She spent most of her days drunk, and coked out lately. She'd initially starting snorting powder just to curb her appetite, so she could lose a few pounds. When she was on that shit, she didn't even think about eating. She was about thirty pounds slimmer now, but she had developed an addiction that was really getting out of control.

Even her mother had noticed a change in her. A few times she had called her house, and total strangers answered Fatima's phone. So Doris had taken the liberty of paying her daughter a visit that night. When she had arrived, she was shocked to see how many houseguests Fatima had. She was also surprised to see that she had dark circles under her eyes. Doris was no fool. Those circles implied drug use. And Fatima was losing so much weight.

Fatima's mama got in her ass, and the truth hurt. She got upset, and didn't want to hear any lecturing, but Doris told Fatima that if she didn't get her shit together, she was going to take custody of her daughter. Her goal wasn't to hurt Fatima, she was just exercising tough love. She figured that if she threatened her with taking Falynn, then Fatima would get it together.

CHAPTER FIFTEEN

Portia had been on her treadmill for the last hour, going hard, trying to get in a few miles before the baby woke up. Ten pounds slimmer, she was feeling good about herself. Jay loved the weight she'd put on, but she didn't like having that little roll around her belly.

Portia had a lot on her mind to walk off. She let a few weeks pass without taking any action, but she was so distraught by the notion of Fatima throwing her life away, she was moved to pay her foolish ass a visit. The way she was carrying on didn't make any sense. Even her mother knew she was fucking with that shit. Mrs. Doris had called Portia the day before. She sounded all flustered, and asked her to try and talk some sense into her daughter. And Portia certainly had plans to.

She told Jay she was going out for a little while, and headed for Fatima's. When she got over Fatima's house, her lesbo girlfriend answered the door. Cheyenne was wearing a white bikini top, a pair of white, way too small shorts that could've easily fit Falynn, and silver flip-flops. Her shorts were all up in her crotch, and you could tell her nasty ass didn't have on any underwear. Portia couldn't stand that hoe.

Cheyenne said hi to her, but Portia didn't speak. There was no point in being phony. That bitch could take it how she wanted to take it. She had no business answering Fatima's door anyway. Portia was disgusted.

She didn't return Cheyenne's greeting, but she was curt with the words she did choose to address her with. "Won't you go put on some clothes? Every time I come over here, you parading around half dressed, lookin' all stink. Them shorts are all stuck up in your funky behind. You need to go wash, and put on some damn drawers."

Cheyenne placed her hand on her hip, and teased Portia.

"Ooohh, you're so sexy when you're angry. Come on Portia, let me calm you down."

She flicked her tongue out at Portia, and said, "Allow me to suck on those big tits. I'll make you feel even better than Raquel did. You naughty, dirty, little girl, you." She licked her lips, and stuck her tongue out at Portia provocatively again.

Portia was shocked. She just stood there in disbelief for a second. That bitch was talking to her like she knew her, or something. And where had she gotten her information? It had to be Fatima. Portia couldn't believe she told that bitch her business.

Seeing Portia's reaction, Cheyenne smirked, and started going in. "Don't look so surprised, Portia. I know you get down. I know what happened at that party, sistah. Somebody got their tities sucked. By a girl." She winked her eye, and turned around and walked away like she really did something.

Portia couldn't believe that bitch had just disrespected her that way. How could Fatima run her mouth like that? And what was Cheyenne doing in her fucking business anyway? That bitch was out of her mind if she thought she was getting away with that. Portia had a response for all that slick shit she just said. Definitely.

Just then, Fatima came downstairs looking all giddy, and shit. She was lazy with satisfaction from Cheyenne's tongue, and also feeling good from the two lines of coke she'd just snorted. She wondered what was up with the surprise visit, but she greeted her homegirl gleefully. "P, what up, babygirl? To what do I owe the pleasure?"

Portia wasn't smiling. Fatima saw that she had this sour look on her face, but she was shocked as hell to see her run up on Cheyenne, and grab her by the neck. Then Portia just started beating the shit out of her.

Fatima yelled, "Oh shit!" She couldn't believe it. Portia was fucking Cheyenne up. Cheyenne tried to fight back, but she didn't really have any hand skills. Fatima half expected her to bust some karate moves or something, since she was Chinese. Then she remembered Cheyenne said she grew up in Long Island. She wasn't from the 'hood like they were, and it showed.

Fatima ran over there, and yelled, "Portia! Stop it!"

Callie heard Fatima yelling, so she ran out of her bedroom, and watched the drama from atop the stairs. She wasn't getting involved, but she wasn't about to miss out on the action either. Portia was really fucking Fatima's girlfriend up.

Portia didn't even hear Fatima screaming. She was busy was chastising Cheyenne, and pounding on her. She knocked that bitch down on the floor, and then she stomped her, and punched her in the face repeatedly. She got tired of bending down, and started kicking the shit out of her.

Cheyenne tried, but her strength was no match for Portia's. Fatima tried to stop her homegirl from whipping on her girl toy. Cheyenne wouldn't do her any good with a busted lip. Fatima tried to break it up, but she could see that Portia was pissed. She wondered what Cheyenne had done to upset her so badly. When she finally managed to subdue Portia, she asked her what was up. "Portia, my God, what happened?"

Portia wanted to make sure that bitch didn't come out her face again, so she spat another warning at Cheyenne. "I been wanting to bust yo' ass for a while, bitch, so that ass whipping was a long time in the making. You think I just beat the shit outta you just now, bitch. If you ever disrespect me again, I'll fuckin' kill you! That's my word! You do not know me!"

Then Portia turned to Fatima. She snapped, "You wanna know why this bitch just got her ass beat? 'Cause you ran ya' fuckin' mouth, and told her my fuckin' business. That's why! This hoe came at me sideways, like she know me! And fuck you too, Fatima! Fuck both of ya'll dyke bitches!"

Portia was so tight, she forgot the reason she came in the first place. She spun around on her heels, and bounced. Fatima had some nerve, boy. She wished she hadn't told her shit.

Fatima watched Portia storm away. She jumped in her car, and sped off. Damn, she was really mad. Fatima had just been chitchatting with Cheyenne when she leaked that incident. It wasn't even that serious. It was no big deal to her, but she knew that was major to Portia. She was sorry she'd repeated her secret. She should've just kept her lips zipped.

Fatima knew she was dead wrong for telling Portia's business, but she turned to Cheyenne and barked on her. "Did you have to run your fuckin' mouth? That's why Portia jumped on yo' ass! But don't worry, I won't tell you nothin' else!"

Cheyenne just sulked, and held her eye. Portia had given her a pretty mean shiner. It was getting bigger by the second, and it hurt so bad it was throbbing. That fucking bitch. Cheyenne didn't say anything, but she decided she wasn't taking that lying down. That shit wasn't over.

Cheyenne looked so pitiful standing there holding her eye, Fatima went to the kitchen and got an ice tray from the freezer, and a hand towel, and she made her an icepack. She walked back out to Cheyenne, and handed it to her. She looked a mess. Her top was torn halfway off, her hair was a mess, and her eye was swollen completely shut.

Cheyenne took the icepack, and stormed away. She had no words for Fatima. She hadn't helped her when her violent friend attacked her, so she was going to pay for that shit too.

Callie went back to her room, and kept her mouth shut. She had left her cell phone on the nightstand, and Smoke was due to call any second. She couldn't wait to tell him about the fight she had just witnessed. When she told him about Fatima's little Asian girlfriend before, he told her to make her an ally if she could. Callie didn't know about that though. She wanted to be the only woman Smoke associated with.

$$$$$

Three days later, Casino drove Laila to the hospital to have the baby. She was almost two weeks overdue, so her doctor had decided it was time. They were going to induce her labor that afternoon.

Later that day, she was given a C-section, and she gave birth at 3:23 P.M. on July 11, 2008. Portia had been at the hospital with her all day. She and Cas had nervously awaited, and then witnessed the Caesarean birth of him and Laila's little girl. The baby was six pounds and nine ounces, and she was a beauty.

Laila was in a lot of pain after that C-section. She was doped up, and not really in mommy mode. Cas and Portia understood. They saw what she had just been through with their own two eyes. The doctor had actually cut her open, and removed the baby, and then stitched her back up. It was amazing.

Laila was too weak to hold the baby, but Cas took up all her slack. He was so proud of his little princess. He had a little girl now, and he couldn't have been happier. And she was so pretty. Cas felt complete. He already had a handsome seven year old son, and now he had a little baby girl. Casino loved his kids more than anything else in the world.

Portia got a chance to hold the baby too. She was overjoyed that she had a little niece so beautiful. She was perfect, and so precious. Portia stood with Cas when he spoke to the doctor about the baby's condition. By the grace of God, she was completely healthy. The only thing they had to be concerned about was the fact that she had Neonatal Jaundice, which was a yellowish discoloration of the skin and whites of the eyes. The doctor told them not to be alarmed, because that was a common condition for newborn babies. The baby just had to stay in the hospital for a few days, and lay under this special blue light for a certain amount of time everyday, and she would be cured.

Cas told Portia he and Laila hadn't decided on a name as of yet. He said he had a name he liked, and asked her for her opinion. He wanted to name his daughter "Skye". Portia thought "Skye" was pretty, but she told him he should run it by Laila first, before they officially put it on the birth certificate. Cas laughed, and agreed with her.

He thanked Portia for being there. She and Laila were the best of friends, and he loved that about them. He knew his man Jay would've been there too, but he was home with him and Portia's baby. He had stayed home with the kids, so Portia could go and see about Laila.

Portia stuck around until visiting hours were over, and the hospital security guard asked her to leave. Before she left, she promised Laila she would be there the next day to sit with her. She told her she would bring Macy up there too.

The kids were in school when Laila went to the hospital that morning.   Portia had called Macy's cell phone during lunchtime, and told her to take the school bus to her house, because her mother was in the hospital. And then Portia called home, and gave her the number to the phone in Laila's hospital room. When Macy got the number, she called Laila's room phone a trillion times to see how she, and her new little sister were doing.

Thinking about Macy made Laila smile. She knew her daughter couldn't wait to see that baby. The thought of that was still weird. Laila still found it hard to accept the fact that she had another child.

Portia kissed her friend goodbye and got ready to leave, but she stopped, and stared at Laila for a second. Portia asked her if she was alright. Laila told her she was okay, except for that painful cut from the C-section. Her exact words were, "that shit hurt like a mothafucka".

Portia laughed, and told Cas and Laila she loved them, and she said goodnight. She was glad Cas was staying overnight. She knew firsthand that the first few days after having a baby weren't easy. And she hadn't even had a c-section, so she could just imagine. Luckily, Laila wouldn't be in the hospital long. The doctor had told them she would be released in about three or four days.

Portia waved at Laila and Cas one last time, and headed on to the elevator. She smiled at the security guard, and ignored his complaints. He kept saying that visiting hours were over five minutes ago.

Portia's mind drifted to Fatima. She had called her several times during the course of the day, but she got no answer on her house phone, or her cell phone. Portia had left her four messages. She couldn't believe Fatima hadn't come to the hospital to see about Laila. Portia didn't make a big deal out of it though. She just prayed nothing was wrong. She and Tima hadn't spoken since Portia stormed out of her house that day she beat up Cheyenne.

When Laila had asked Portia where Fatima was, she told her the truth. She had no idea. Portia hadn't told her about Fatima's snorting coke yet. Laila had been too far into her pregnancy for that type of news. Laila loved Fatima like a sister, so she would've worried about her a lot. Especially after what she had been through with Khalil smoking that shit.

Portia drove on home to her family. She missed her husband, and her babies. She wondered what her little Trixie was up to. Was she sleeping, or awake? Portia called home to check and see. Jay answered, and told her the baby was in his arms that very second, playing helicopter. Portia laughed, and told her man she was on her way.

When she hung up, she was still grinning. Jay had that baby so spoiled, it didn't make any sense. As soon as Trixie saw her daddy coming, she got excited and started bouncing up and down. She got mad hype when she saw Jay, and also when she saw a bottle. Her little cute chubby self just loved to eat.

Portia got home about ten minutes later. Jay was feeding the baby, and Jazmin was in front of the TV watching a "Sponge Bob Square Pants" DVD. That, and "Max and Ruby" were the only cartoons she sat completely still to watch. Jay said Jayquan and Macy were upstairs in his bedroom, on his computer logged onto MySpace.

Portia kissed her husband and babies, and she went upstairs to change, and get comfortable. She stuck her head in Lil' Jay's room to see how he and Macy were doing, and Macy bombarded her with questions about who the new baby looked like. Portia laughed, and filled her in as best she could. She told her she would get a chance to see her sister in the morning. Jayquan asked if he could miss school the following day to go to the hospital too. Portia told him to ask his father first.

Portia went and got comfortable, and she slipped on some slippers, and went back downstairs with Jay. She smiled at him fondly. He looked so sexy when he was in daddy mode. She winked at him, and licked her lips. Jay caught the flirtation she threw at him, and knew what it was. He was getting some that night. After the kids went to sleep.

And sure enough, after they tucked Jazz in bed, and put the baby down for the night, Portia and Jay had a quickie. It was short, but sweet, and when it was over, they were both sticky.

After they were done sexing, Portia went to the bathroom

and cleaned up. She brought back a hot soapy rag, and she wiped Rocky off so Jay wouldn't wake up with him stuck to his leg. Jay was dozing off already. Portia snuggled up under him, and they cuddled until he was fast asleep.

Portia couldn't sleep, so she thumbed through the cable channels, while Jay snored lightly in her ear. She kept on thinking about Fatima. It wasn't like her to not show up when Laila was having her baby. Something had to be wrong.

She got up, and tried calling Tima again. She was still getting no answer. It was after two A.M. now, so Portia began to really worry. She was sorry she had stormed out on Fatima days ago, and not kept up with what she was up to. Portia knew she wasn't in the right state of mind lately.

She thought about their dear friend, Simone, and the way she had killed herself. Simone's phone had just rang out the same way when Portia had been calling to check on her. And when she finally went over her house to make sure she was okay, it was too late. Simone was already dead.

Portia got scared, and panicked at the thought. She knew she wouldn't be able to sleep until she contacted Fatima. She slipped on a pair of jeans, and a tee shirt, and put on her black Gucci sneakers. She ran downstairs, and grabbed the keys to the black Mercedes. Portia unlocked the gun cabinet and retrieved her gun, and she stuck it in her black Gucci Pelham bag. Jay had her under strict orders to always carry one. She relocked the gun cabinet, and exited the side door to the garage.

After she closed the door, Portia reset the alarm keypad. She wasn't taking any chances, especially while her family was asleep. She got inside the car, and used her remote to open the garage door, and she headed for Fatima's. Portia looked in her rearview mirror to make sure the automatic garage door had shut.

As Portia drove along, she told herself there was no reason to worry, because Fatima was okay. She wondered exactly what her excuse for being M.I.A. would be. It better good, whatever it was.

When Portia got to Fatima's house, she was shocked at what she saw. The driveway was packed, and there were even more cars parked at crazy angles all over her front lawn. There was music coming from inside the house, and it was absolutely too loud for that neighborhood at that time of night. Portia parked in one of the only empty spaces left, and got out of her car. What the hell was going on? Why the hell was Fatima having a wild party like this, and at her house?

When Portia got inside, it was even worse than she thought. The first thing she noticed was that Fatima was an equal opportunity hostess. There were people of all nationalities, and walks of life in there. There were blacks, whites, Asians, and Arabs. There were hip-hoppers, punk rockers, yuppies, and Portia even saw a few gothic folks. The party was diverse, but they all apparently had one thing in common. They were into heavy drugs. Everybody was either doing something, or looked like they had just finished doing something.

There were strangers everywhere. People were lounging, drinking liquor, doing drugs, and a few were even making out. Why was Fatima hosting this shit at her house? Portia didn't recognize a soul. And she had a feeling Fatima didn't know half of those damn people herself.

Portia really disapproved. She didn't think it was a sin for Fatima to succumb to her wild side every now and then, because everybody already knew she had one. But she was crazy for having that type of gathering at her home. She had broken one of the most important rules in life. You weren't supposed to shit where you eat at, and sleep at.

Portia scanned the room, and she finally located her pitiful friend. To her horror, that dumb ass girl was passed out on the sofa. A big ass, wild, crazy soiree was going on in her damn house, and she was asleep dead in the middle of it. Portia just shook her head. She was disgusted with Fatima. It seemed like she was going through her second childhood. That fool was growing dumber instead of wiser.

Portia hurried over, and shook her awake. Fatima barely opened her eyes. She was real groggy, and out of it. She just mumbled something.

Portia wanted to slap her pathetic ass. She couldn't believe the way she was just babbling incoherently. She shook her again, harder this time. "Tima, it's me, Portia. Wake up! Get up, and take a look around. Look at what's goin' on in your house! Fatima! Get up, and tell all these people to leave! You can't be no hostess in this condition. Look at yourself! You're out of it! Come on, be real."

Fatima looked like she wasn't registering her words. It was like she was stuck, or something. Portia looked closer, and she noticed her eyes were rolling around in her head. She got scared, and wondered exactly what Tima was on. It couldn't have been coke. Wasn't that supposed to keep you wide awake?

Fatima had to have taken something else. Maybe she'd taken some kind of powerful pills, like OxyContin, or something. Portia hoped it wasn't heroin, or LSD. The way she looked, there was no telling what she had been into.

Fatima was so out of it, Portia got scared. She had to clear that house out. It was time for those mothafuckas to get the hell out of there. She really believed Fatima needed some medical attention. If she was in her right state of mind, there was no way she would've just been laying there like that, while all those people fucked up her house.

Portia ran and turned the stereo off. She yelled at the top of her lungs, "The party's over! Everybody out!"

A lot of people got up and started to leave, but some of them just looked at Portia like she was crazy. Like they weren't going to listen to her. Portia looked around, and nodded at the ass-draggers' reluctance. Challenging her, were they? She had something for their asses. She reached in her Gucci bag for her gun.

Portia pulled out a chrome .380, and tried it one more time. "I said everybody get the fuck out!" She cocked the gun, and pointed it towards the ceiling.

"Everybody out! Now!" Portia pulled the trigger, and let off a shot. Boom! That gunfire was loud as hell, so the rest of those bastards scrambled for the front door.

Everybody bounced, except for Cheyenne. And she looked like she had no intentions on leaving. She just eyeballed Portia, and headed upstairs.

Portia looked at that hoe like she was crazy. "Excuse me, didn't I just say "everybody out"? That means you too. Get out, bitch! You ain't shit but a bad influence on Tima. The fuckin' devil in disguise! She wasn't like this before your no-good ass came around. You outta here, bitch! Get the fuck out!"

Cheyenne narrowed her eyes, and just stared at Portia for a second, like she was thinking about testing her. She looked over at Fatima for some support, but she saw that she was out of it.

Portia pointed her gun at Cheyenne, and said, "I never liked yo' ass. I wanna do this anyway, you fuckin' hoe. I done already busted yo' ass the other day. Now gimme a reason to pop you, bitch! I will put some lead in yo' funky ass! That's my mothafuckin' word!"

Cheyenne didn't call her bluff. The look in Portia's eyes told her she wasn't afraid to shoot her, so she took heed. She was nonchalant about it. She looked back at Portia, and rolled her eyes. But that bitch exited the premises just like she was told.

Portia followed her to the door, and said, "And don't come back! Your welcome is worn out, bitch!" She slammed the door, and locked it behind her.

Portia couldn't stand Cheyenne. She could see right through her. That bitch was nothing but a leech. She kept Fatima's head clouded up with booze, coke, orgasms, and God knew what else, while she was busy spending up all her fucking money. If Fatima was too blind to see that, then Portia had to be her eyes.

She hurried back over there to her pathetic friend. "Tima, look at you. Come on, we goin' to the hospital." She tried to pull Fatima up from the couch.

Fatima heard Portia, but she was too fucked up to respond. Portia kept pulling her, and said, "Come on, girl! You're heavy, shit!"

She managed to get Fatima to her feet, and outside to her car. Getting her inside the car was another struggle. Portia was out of breath when she jumped under the wheel.

She drove to the hospital as fast as she could, constantly talking to Fatima to try to keep her alert. When she pulled up in front of the emergency room, she jumped out the car, and ran to get help. Portia kept it real, and told them her friend outside in the car was on something, and kept passing out.

A few emergency workers rushed outside with a stretcher, and they took Fatima inside the E.R. They quickly scooted her in the back to do whatever they had to do.

They wouldn't let Portia come back there, so she waited out front for four hours while they pumped Fatima's stomach, and ran all these tests on her. It turned out she had a bad reaction from mixing alcohol, and barbiturates. They said she would be fine, but it was a good thing Portia had brought her to the hospital when she did.

About six o'clock, Portia was finally allowed to see Fatima. That fool admitted that she had taken some pills somebody gave her, and she said didn't even know what they were. She admitted that was irresponsible, and dumb of her, and she promised Portia she would be more careful from then on. Portia just listened, and saved her lecture for the ride home. She was just glad her ass was alright.

About seven that morning, the doctor released Fatima, and they left for home.

On the way home, Portia was cranky and tired from being up all night, and she wasn't in the mood to sugarcoat anything. She told Fatima off. She said, "Fatima, you gotta do better, sis. This shit don't make no sense. What if you had killed yourself? Suppose you never woke up. I mean, damn. You're too old to be wildin' like this. You got a daughter, and you got too much money now to be doin' stupid shit like hosting drug parties, and mess."

Fatima's response was, "Well you know what they say, P. Mo' money, mo' problems. I don't know what to tell you. I'm just not happy."

Portia was tired of that played out self-pity role of hers. She just said, "But you're searching for happiness in the wrong places. You won't find it in drugs, boo. Learn to find happiness within, and in your child."

Portia thought about something, and paused. After a few seconds, she continued. "And if you wanna freak off, then take your ass to Jamaica, to one of those freaky resorts like Hedonism, or something. Enough with the "live-in lover" shit. That chick Cheyenne ain't no good for you. I'm not judging what you do, but come on, Tima. You have a reputation to protect."

Fatima didn't argue with Portia. She didn't say another word.

When they got back to Fatima's house, Portia walked her inside. She looked around at the big mess the partygoers had left, and shook her head. She was not about to help clean up that mess. Fuck that, she was going home. She had a baby to take care of. Once Fatima got some rest, she could handle that on her own. She would probably just call a cleaning company anyway.

Portia told Fatima to go lie down for a little while. Before she left, she asked her if she needed anything.

Fatima started crying. She said, "Portia, I am so sorry. Please don't leave me here by myself."

Portia sighed at her pitiful friend. She felt sorry for her. She asked, "Where's Callie?"

Fatima wiped her eyes. "Oh yeah, I forgot. She's upstairs. So I ain't here by myself, P. Go on home, girl. I'll be okay. Thanks for everything."

Portia had been so caught up in seeing about Fatima, she had forgotten all about Laila having the baby. All of a sudden she remembered, and said, "Oh, by the way, Miss M.I.A. Laila had a girl today."

Fatima covered her mouth with her hands, and said, "Oh my God! I gotta go back to the hospital, and see the baby. Is Lay okay? Why you ain't say somthin' while we were just at the hospital?"

Portia shook her head. "She's not at that hospital. Bitch, just go to bed right now. We'll go see her later on. Come on and lock your door. I'm out."

Fatima smiled, and said, "You better put that fuckin' gun away when you get home. Don't fuck around and shoot nobody, bitch." She followed behind Portia to lock her door. It had been a long night.

When Portia got back home, she made herself a cup of hot chamomile tea to help herself relax. Fatima had gotten on her last nerve, but she was glad she was okay. She didn't want to lose anymore friends.

Portia went downstairs in her office. She checked her email, and then she went online to Gucci.com, and ordered Jayquan and Macy these Gucci sneakers they wanted, and a new bag from their latest Hysteria collection for herself.

While she was submitting her credit card information, Jay came downstairs. He caught her off guard, and scared the mess out of her.

He said, "Hey, Kit Kat. What's wrong? Where the hell you been?"

"Over Tima house." Portia rolled her eyes. "She had some issues."

Jay could tell she didn't really want to talk about it, so he didn't press. He just said, "Well, relax, Ma. I can tell you're worrying about something."

Jay knew her well. Portia just smiled at him, and said, "I'm good, boo."

She was tempted to tell him she was at the hospital all night with Fatima, but she didn't want him judging her friends. She was ashamed of the fact that her girl even went through that. Portia knew Jay wasn't a judgmental person, but that was easier said than done. She hadn't even told him about the time she beat up Cheyenne, because she didn't want him to know Fatima was messing around with women, let alone drugs.

Jay told Portia to go get some rest. She was feeling it now, so she told him that was a good idea. She printed out the receipt from her Gucci purchase, and shut the computer down.

Portia got up and stretched, and she asked Jay for a piggyback ride upstairs. He just looked at her, and laughed. She told him she was serious.

Jay shook his head. P was crazy, but that was his baby. He turned around and stooped down low, so she could get on his back, and he carried his queen upstairs. Portia giggled like a little kid the whole time, with her silly self.

CHAPTER SIXTEEN

Laila and Cas' baby was born healthy, and she was doing fine. Cas had named their daughter "Skye". She had Cas' last name, and she was gorgeous. She was perfect, and looked just like a little doll. But for some reason, Laila wouldn't hold her. She flat out refused to.

Portia had never seen anything like it. She knew Laila had been a great mother her first two rounds, so it was really odd that she wasn't bonding with her baby. Cas was doing his part, and also trying to take up Laila's slack, but there was only so much a father could do. That baby needed her mother. The newborn stage was the most vulnerable state of a child's life. But Laila wouldn't even hold the baby when she cried.

Cas wondered what had happened. He couldn't understand how she had suddenly turned so cold. Her behavior was just unnatural.

Laila had become a bitch to everyone, shunning all of their efforts and attempts to get through to her. She had also developed this crazy defense mechanism. She didn't want to hear a word anybody had to say about anything.

Cas was so concerned, and so on edge, he took the baby to Portia every time he had business to take care of. The baby was so small, he didn't trust anyone else with her yet. It was sad, but he couldn't depend on Laila to nurture her.

Cas was patient, because his mother and Portia kept on saying that Laila just had a bad case of Postpartum Blues. Cas had made it a point to talk to the doctor after each of his children were born. He'd asked questions, so he knew that Postpartum Blues was indeed a real condition that some women went through after childbirth. But to his understanding, it should've only lasted about two weeks. Laila had been acting that way for about two months now. It was really serious.

Cas fought with Laila to go to the doctor to get checked out, but she refused. After three more weeks went by with no change, he decided that he wasn't taking no for an answer. The following Monday morning, he insisted that she get her behind ready so they could go to the doctor.

A few hours later, Laila was diagnosed with Postpartum Depression. This was a condition far more extreme than Postpartum Blues. The doctor explained to her and Cas in depth what was going on with her body. Laila's bitterness about being unable to walk had caused her to develop a severe psychosis.

The doctor told them that Laila's hormones were involved as well, so there was no quick fix for her condition. Cas was surprised to learn all that. The complex way God had created the female species was really amazing.

Laila's doctor said there was no cure for Postpartum Depression, and only time would tell if she would get better. He prescribed therapy, lots of rest, love, and a thirty day supply of anti-depressant pills.

Laila had sat through the entire doctor visit emotionless, and she acted the same way on the ride home. Cas didn't say much to her, because her responses were so limited. She acted like he was getting on her nerves.

Portia stuck by her dear friend throughout it all. She never once complained about watching Laila's baby. She kept Skye so much it was like she had two babies of her own. It felt like she had twins, because the babies were only three and a half months apart.

But Portia managed to hold it down. Macy stayed over and helped out sometimes too. Having two babies in the house was a twenty-four hour job. And the girls were always on two different schedules. If one of them would sleep through the night, the other would wake up crying.

Eventually, it became a bit overwhelming. Portia started to get a little exhausted. Macy had a life of her own, so she couldn't help out all the time. She had to go to school, and she also needed time to study. So Portia thoroughly screened a few candidates, and she hired a nanny to help her out.

Weeks went by, and everybody just tiptoed around Laila.

Late one night, Cas tried to talk to her again. He wanted nothing more than to reason with her, but she took everything he said and twisted it around. She got all emotional and screamed at him, and then she told him to just leave her the fuck alone.

Cas didn't feel like arguing. He wasn't with all that. He was just trying to get through to her, but Laila threw some serious pop shots at him. She even told him that since it was him who had made the decision to have the baby, it was him who should take care of it.

The last thing she said to Cas in their argument was, "As a matter of fact, since you wanna be such a "family man", go back to Kira and your family. What you gon' do with me? I can't even fuckin' walk. I'm helpless! So just go 'head. You gon' walk away sooner or later, so leave now, Cas. Leave me the fuck alone!"

Cas looked at Laila like she was crazy. She was straight bugging. He had no words for her after that. What the fuck was she talking about, go back to Kira. He left Kira for her. And he had been by her side through her whole ordeal, thick and thin.

Laila pissed him off so bad after she said that, he just walked out of the room. He would've left the house if his baby wasn't there. Macy was there, but she was already asleep. It was eleven o'clock at night, and she had school the following morning. He didn't want to stick her with the responsibility of babysitting. That was he and Laila's child.

Cas said another prayer that things would get better, and he went to the nursery to check on Skye. She was still peacefully asleep, so he went downstairs. He and Laila didn't say anything to each other for a while. He was tired of kissing her ass. He knew she was going through something right now, but she was really being impossible.

A little while later, Portia called to see how they were doing. Cas needed to vent, so he told her how her homegirl was bugging. He told Portia he was going to take care of his baby, but he had little words for Laila. As soon as he said that, he heard Skye crying on the baby monitor. He told Portia he had to go check on her, so he would talk to her later.

While Cas was checking on the baby, Portia was stepping in her shoes. She was going over there to talk to Laila. She told Jay she had just talked to Cas, and he told her Laila was tripping hard. When she told him she was going over there, he didn't protest. They were all like family.

When Portia got to Cas and Laila's, she greeted Cas with a sisterly kiss to the cheek. He had the baby in his arms when he answered the door, so she played with Skye for a minute. Portia asked Cas if she could have a word with Laila alone.

He made a face, and motioned like she was upstairs. Then he shrugged, and shook his head. He looked like he was through. Portia knew Laila was really pushing him to the limit. She had to talk some sense into her, before she blew it. Cas was a good dude.

Portia headed upstairs to play "Oprah". But she was sick of being everybody's counselor. She needed a rock too. Her two best friends were both bugging. Fatima was strung out on a self-pity trip, and Laila was really no different. She had been wallowing in self-pity ever since she had that baby, and enough was enough.

Portia walked in her room, and she was sitting up in bed watching television. Portia said, "what up" to her, and got to the point. She was straight up with Laila. "Sis, you need to pull yourself together, and get out of this funk you're in. You gotta get pass this, babygirl. It's time. Now."

Laila just rolled her eyes, and rudely picked up the remote and turned up the volume of the show she was watching. She was clearly in stubborn mode. She was lounging around in her pajamas, and didn't feel like being bothered.

Laila wasn't trying anymore. She had just given up. She hadn't even been doing her physical therapy anymore. She'd just quit for a little while at first, until the stitches from her C-section healed up. But now they were healed, and she'd yet to continue her therapy. She had been in a rut since she gave birth. Laila hadn't told anyone, but she hated herself. She felt like her existence was pointless, and her baby deserved better.

Portia was determined to get through to her friend that night. She walked over and shut the TV off, and stood in front of it.

"Laila, talk to me! What is going on with you?"

Laila finally spoke, and her words were soaked with venom. "Go home and mind your fuckin' business!"

Portia was shocked, but she said, "You are my fuckin' business, bitch! You're like a sister to me. We're family, Laila! And I ain't leavin' 'til you tell me what's going on!"

Laila's stubborn ass wouldn't give in. Portia was completely out of ammo, so she ran downstairs and got the baby from Cas. He handed Skye over without a word. He knew where Portia was going, and he didn't interfere. He was praying she got through to Laila too.

When Portia got upstairs, she walked back in Laila's room, and held the baby out to her. "Laila, look at your little cub. Isn't she precious? This baby is absolutely beautiful. You can't deny that, right, Lay?"

Portia carefully held the baby, and she moved her back and forth in front of Laila like she was dancing. Portia started singing "Isn't She Lovely", by Stevie Wonder. "Isn't she lovely? Isn't she wonderful? Isn't she special?..."

Laila turned her head, and refused to look. Portia was getting on her nerves. She was on the verge of punching that bitch in the face. She was lucky she had the baby in her arms.

Portia put Skye right in Laila's face, and said, "Look, Laila. This is your baby. A perfect, little angel faced blessing, straight from the mighty hands of God."

Laila wouldn't say a word. She kept her head turned, and her eyes closed.

Portia was persistent. "Here, hold the baby, Lay. Hold her. Come on, Laila. She's yours. Hold her."

Laila wasn't buying it. Portia couldn't believe it. She said, "At least look at her! She's beautiful. And she's yours! Open your eyes and look at her, damn it!"

Laila wouldn't budge. All of a sudden she flipped, and snapped at Portia. "Get out! Get the fuck outta my house, bitch! Get out!"

Portia wasn't going for it. She didn't care what she said. Enough was enough. "Laila, this is your baby! How can you not look at her? How can you not hold her? You're her mother, for God's sake! What is with you?"

Laila stuck to her guns. She would not look at the baby. But Portia could tell she was getting to her, because tears started rolling down her face. She laughed bitterly, and then she turned around and looked directly at Portia. She didn't bother to wipe away her tears when she spoke.

"Alright, bitch! You want the truth? Let's see if you can fuckin' handle it. Here you go. I'm convinced that God hates me. He took away my mother and father when I was still a child. He took my baby Pebbles away from me not even two years ago, and now I'm a paraplegic. I'm never gonna walk again. So take this baby, and get out. 'Cause I can't do nothin' for her. I can't even breastfeed her, with all this medicine and shit they got me on. I can't do shit! I'm nothing, Portia. So I can't be a mother, okay? I'm nothing! I can't fuckin' walk!"

Portia started crying, and pleaded with her. "Laila, please! Don't say that! You are gonna walk again. You are! You hear me, girl? You gotta have faith. You have to believe that you can, Lay!"

Laila looked at her like she was stupid, and said, "Girl, are you fuckin' slow? I don't have no feeling in my legs. None. I'm finished in this town, Portia. Accept that now, and save yourself some grief. I wish I would've died in that car accident. I'd rather be dead than live like this. I ain't nothin' but a fuckin' cripple." After that, Laila broke down and started crying like a baby.

She was breaking Portia's heart, but Portia had to be strong for her. "Don't say that, Laila. Please don't say that. Let's thank God that you're alive. And it's only your legs that have no feeling. That means there's only half of you that we gotta get back in commission."

Laila stopped crying, and shook her head. "Unbelievable. Un-fucking-believable. You just don't get it. Good night, Portia. Good night. Please just leave."

Laila just wanted to wallow in self-pity. Portia was getting on her nerves. She'd been minding her own miserable business, and she had come in and upset her. She knew Portia meant well, but she wished everybody would just leave her alone. She started crying again. She was just mad as hell.

She yelled, "I hate all ya'll mothafuckas! Why didn't you just let them give me a fuckin' abortion?!"

Even after that, Portia wouldn't give up. She couldn't. She knew Laila had a heart. She was a good person, and a great mother. She stuck that baby right in her arms.

Laila resisted at first, but once she looked into her little girl's eyes, she couldn't fight it anymore. The baby had Cas' eyes, and her nose and lips. Laila broke down, and started sobbing uncontrollably. She felt absolutely horrible. She had to be the worse mother in the whole wide world. Everybody probably thought she was some type of hell demon for the way she had treated her baby. Especially Casino.

Portia was right, Skye was beautiful. She had these bright eyes that were just filled with wisdom, like she'd been here before. And she had a head full of silky curly hair. Somebody had put a cute little pink barrette in the top and made a little pigtail puff. It looked so cute. Laila wondered if Cas or Macy did that. She smiled.

Laila was overjoyed. Her heart swelled with overflowing love for her baby. It was that exact moment that she unconsciously shed her psychosis. She smiled at Portia through teary eyes. Portia was a true friend. Laila was glad she had forced the baby on her. She had achieved what not even a licensed therapist with a Ph.D. could do. She had helped her bond with her baby. That was what friends were for.

Now Laila felt inspired to fight. She had good people in her life that loved her, and children who depended on her. She couldn't give up. She reached for Portia's hand.

Portia took Laila's hand, and gave it a squeeze. She stood there for a few minutes and watched her cuddle her baby. She was moved to tears, but thank God, they were tears of joy this time. Portia leaned over and kissed her friend on the forehead, and then she kissed the baby. Her work there was done. She told Laila to call her later, and she left and went downstairs.

Cas was sitting at the foot of the stairs waiting for Portia. The last thing he had heard was Laila screaming "I hate all ya'll mothafuckas. Why didn't you just let them give me an abortion?" So he was pretty sure Portia had failed in her attempt to make her bond with the baby, just as he had so many times. He didn't even feel he had to ask what happened.

He looked up and noticed that Portia didn't have the baby in her arms, and he looked surprised. "P, where's the baby?"

Portia grinned, and pointed upstairs. Before she knew it, Cas came over and gave her a big bear hug. He picked her up, and swung her around and around. Portia just cracked up. She loved it. Cas was like her big brother. She loved him to death. They had been through so much together. She was glad she could be a ray of sunshine in his life. She knew it hadn't been easy for him.

Cas was a real dude. He had stood tall, and never left Laila's side, and Portia really respected him for that. Laila had herself a prize. That brother was a man.

$$$$$

Ysatis hadn't been living in her apartment for two whole months before somebody broke in. The first thing she did was call Jay. She told him that her crib had been burglarized. She lived on the ground floor, and the thief broke the lock on the window gate, and came inside. She said they had marched right out the front door with her stuff.

Jay asked Ysatis if she'd called the police. She told him she did, and they came and made a report. Jay told her to sit tight that night. It was late, so he told her he would assist her the following day.

After they hung up, Jay called Casino's mother. He needed an apartment in a safe neighborhood A.S.A.P. Ysatis was a young, single woman living in NYC. There was a lot going on in the rotten apple, and she was the perfect candidate for some creep to take advantage of. If something were to happen to her, he didn't want it on his conscience.

Cas' mother, who Jay affectionately referred to as Ms. B, was a successful real estate broker who had been in the business for over thirty years. Ms. B. was glad to hear from Jay. She told him she had two lovely duplex apartments in Manhattan, over by Central Park West. She said they were huge one bedroom units, located in a fancy, high-rise building, with round the clock security, a doorman, and the whole nine. She said there was even a gym located in the building, and the view was awesome.

Jay told her that sounded okay to him. Ms. B told him the rent was six thousand dollars a month, and the landlord required one year paid in advance at the lease signing. Jay told her he'd have a check for her in the morning, plus whatever her commission was.

Ms. B laughed, and told him she would waive the commission that time, because she owned the building.

Jay laughed. He wasn't even surprised. She had taught him and Cas the real estate game. He joked, "I should've known you were the landlord. Ms. B stand for "Big things". It ain't no secret that you're loaded, Ma Moneybags."

Ms. B chuckled, and jived along with Jay. "You already know. You got-damn right, baby. I am loaded. Mostly because of guys like you. And I ought to charge you more than that, just for having the audacity to ask me to find an apartment for your little mistress."

Ms. B laughed, but Jay knew she was serious. She had the wrong idea. He wasn't messing with Ysatis. She was like a little sister to him, so he cleared that up immediately. "Nah! It's not like that, Ms. B. For real." He explained to her that the apartment was for a friend, who he was just looking out for.

Ms. B said, "Honey, that's what they all say." She laughed, and told Jay she was just kidding. After that, she asked about his family, and how everybody was doing.

Jay told her everyone was well. He hoped she believed him about the apartment being for a friend. He thanked her again, and told her he would call her in the morning.

Ms. B was mad cool. And she was a classy lady. She was the reason Jay and Cas had gotten into the real estate market in the first place. She had told them way back in the early nineties, while they were still young bucks, that the market in New York City was going to bubble.

Around that time, due to the increasing crime rate, a lot of black homeowners in Brooklyn were selling their houses, and moving down south. When Ms. B saw that Jay and Cas were getting money, she had sat them down, and told them to play smart and invest their dirty money into something that would feed them for the rest of their lives. She told them that if they made the right investments, they would eventually be wealthy, and possibly set for life. And she had been completely right.

Back then, the bulk of their fellow hustlers that were getting money in that era blew their dough on cars and jewelry, but Jay and his good homie Cas had put their money into property. And they had later schooled young Wise, and he had done the same thing.

Jay remembered when they took Wise under their wings like it was yesterday. Wise had been a little dude, only about sixteen, telling him and Cas he liked their style, and wanted to roll with them. There was just something about the way he carried himself. And then one day, they witnessed him smack the shit out of this dude who was like twenty years old, which was their age at the time. The dude had a loud mouth. He kept yapping about all the shit he would do to a young punk ass nigga like Wise. The funny thing was, Wise slapped him silly, and he didn't do shit. Especially after Cas told him to fall back.

Jay and Cas had been so impressed with the amount of heart Wise had, that day they adopted him as their little homie. They gave him some work, but their relationship wasn't just that of employer and employee. Over time he became like a real brother to them.

And real estate had certainly helped them achieve their goals. Wise was gone now, but he definitely got a chance to touch it before he left. He died rich. Jay smiled proudly at the memory. He really missed his dude. Damn. Fucking with those houses was what had made them millionaires first, even before all the music shit. Jay would always be grateful to Ms. B. for that.

Jay thought about Ysatis. It was fucked up when a person's home front was violated. Especially a single woman like her. But she would soon have a safe haven. Jay just wanted to look out for her on the strength of Humble. That was the least he could do. And it wasn't any trouble to him. There hadn't been any strenuous activity involved. He had simply made a phone call, and was cutting a check the following day.

The next morning, Jay's schedule was full. Some things came up at the last minute, so he didn't have time to help Ysatis relocate. Instead, he sent two big dudes from Street Life's security team over her crib, with a van to assist her with the move to her new luxury apartment.

In just hours, Ysatis was safely moved into her ritzy mid-town apartment. To her delight, it was also lavishly furnished. Ysatis' lifestyle changed immediately. She was elated. That was no doubt the best place she had ever lived.

The weeks that followed, Ysatis got settled in. She was more comfortable, and felt much safer in her new place. She was living like a queen. Jay hadn't been over to see it yet, but he financed it, and that was all that mattered.

She tried not to bother Jay that much, but when she did call him, he took care of whatever she needed. Usually through a third party, but who was she to complain? He always got somebody to take care of it, but it was all good. At least he did call her on a regular basis.

Ysatis liked Jay's style. He was as big-time as big-time could get. After a while, she began to mistake the brotherly affection and generosity that he showered on her for something else. It could've easily been argued that she was still messed up in the head from her older brother, Neal, sexually abusing her as a child, and unconsciously drawn to Jay because he treated her like a little sister. Or it could've been the old "young girl searching for a daddy figure" theory. And Jay was also a man of stature, wealth, and power, so that helped influence her crush too. But whatever the reasons, she developed a real "thing" for Jay.

And it got really bad. She began to fantasize about making love to him. She would fall asleep at night touching herself, and thinking of him. As time passed, it got worse and worse. She was curious, and felt she had to do something about it.

One day Ysatis decided she couldn't take it anymore. She knew Jay was a busy man. He was usually all business, and very family oriented the rest of the time. It seemed like the only time he showed interest in her was when she called, and told him something was wrong with her.

She figured the only way she was going to get close to him was if she played the damsel in distress role, so she decided to wear that out. Ysatis called Jay, and told him she had an emergency she couldn't discuss over the telephone. She made it sound so urgent, Jay promised to come by that evening, after he left the office.

Ysatis hung up the phone, and did a ballerina jump. She was glad he was coming. Jay was her knight in shining armor. He had saved her before, when him and his crew had removed her sick, perverse older brother from her life, who'd sexually abused her through her entire childhood. And now Jay was financing the greater part of her college education, and paying all her bills.

She had a part-time job, but her measly paycheck was no where near big enough to cover her expenses. Jay was basically her sole provider, and she appreciated it. She looked around at her lavish apartment. He had really gone all out. So didn't that make her his mistress? She felt indebted to him, and wanted badly to please him.

Just thinking about Jay made Ysatis tingle down there. She spent endless nights touching herself, and fantasizing about him. The feelings she had for him were a little more severe than a crush. She had fallen in love with him.

Ysatis wanted Jay so bad it was driving her mad. She suppressed her pent up sexual desires by throwing herself into her schoolwork, but she lived for his phone calls. Every time she spoke to him, all he did was ask her the same three questions. "What up?", "You ayight?", and "How's school?" But unbeknownst to Jay, the sound of his voice made her weak, so she cherished those brief conversations.

About two hours later, Jay showed up at her apartment. He looked so good, she swore she felt faint. Jay was a good looking dude, but it was his swagger that put the icing on the cake. His presence was just strong. The way he shook and moved, even a total stranger could tell he was a powerful man. He took her breath away, so Ysatis breathed deep, and tried to relax before she let him in.

When Jay walked in, she greeted him with a warm hug. Jay

noticed that hug was a little tighter and closer than usual, but he overlooked it. It could've just been him, so he didn't make it out to be more than it was. He felt a little awkward, but he asked her how she was doing. She said she was fine, and he asked how school was coming along. She said everything was good, and told him finals were coming up.

Ysatis looked nice. He could tell she had just gotten her hair done. Jay thought about telling her, but he didn't want to give her the impression that he was checking her out. He decided against complimenting her. Instead, he asked her, "So, what's wrong?"

Ysatis looked confused for a second. She said, "Huh?"

Jay said, "On the phone, you said you had a problem. Remember?"

She made a face, like her memory was jarred, and then she smiled, and waved her hand. "Oh, it was nothing. It sort of worked itself out. Thank goodness."

Ysatis changed the subject. She grabbed his hand, and said, "Oh yeah, Jay! You haven't even seen my place yet. Come on, let me give you a tour. Don't you wanna see your "tax dollars" in action?"

Jay grinned, and followed her. It felt good to help somebody. He had the money, and Ysatis was a good kid. The further he stepped into the crib, the more impressed he was. And when he went upstairs, that was it. Ms. B wasn't playing. That joint was nice for real. It made him feel good to be able to expose Ysatis to the finer things in life. He figured she'd become accustomed to living a certain way, and that would make her strive hard in life to maintain it.

Jay told her the apartment was nice, and asked her how she liked living like a princess. She said it was great, but she just got a little lonely sometimes. She said after all she had gone through with people stealing from her lately, she chose not to have any friends over. She said if her friends saw the way she was living, they would get the wrong impression and think she had money she didn't have. She said she didn't need any more "friend-nemies".

Jay understood that. He was a little surprised that she was

so wise at her age. He knew she'd been forced to grow up fast, but he was glad she'd grown up smart too. Jay knew firsthand how so-called friends could hate on you, and become your enemies as well.

Ysatis offered Jay a drink. He laughed, and told her she was barely old enough to drink herself. She told him she'd be twenty-one in a few months, and believed that was legal enough. She said she wouldn't allow him to leave without sharing a toast with her.

Ysatis poured two shots of Hennessy, and stared admiringly at Jay while he downed his. She even found the way he drank from a glass to be sexy.

Ysatis refilled Jay's glass, and got a little bold. She batted her eyes, and said, "I'm glad you came by. I really missed you. It's nice to see you, Jay."

Jay peeped a little flirtation in her eyes when she said that. Or was it just his imagination? He hoped so, because that wasn't a good look. An alarm went off in his head, but he figured it was nothing. She was just being young.

Ysatis kept on. "But I'm sure you never get lonely, being a man in your position, and all. You probably have tons of important friends, and throw great parties all the time, that I bet all the A-listers show up for."

Jay laughed, and shook his head. He preferred not to live that type of "industry" lifestyle. He said, "I don't party much anymore. You don't know who to trust, so it gets lonely at the top."

Ysatis smiled at him, and said, "A man with a heart as big as yours should never be lonely."

Those were kind words. That comment forced Jay to smile. He knew he should have been getting on home, but since she said she was lonely, he figured he'd sit with her for a minute. He knew the poor kid didn't have any family left, so he felt sorry for her. He couldn't imagine life without his family.

Ysatis refilled Jay's glass one more time, and asked him to excuse her for a minute. She said she was going to put on her slippers because her shoes were uncomfortable. She threw him the television remote, and disappeared.

Jay sat there and flipped through channels, while he downed another shot of Henny. He called downstairs to his driver, and told him he'd be out in a little while. He had taken a car because he'd known parking would be scarce.

Ysatis returned, and she had gotten comfortable alright. She had changed her shoes, and her clothes too. She had on a pair of pink slippers, but they were the high heeled sexy kind, with fur on the toe. And she was wearing a short, pink satin robe.

Jay didn't comment, but he thought her attire was inappropriate. But she was in her house, he reasoned, so she could dress as she pleased.

Ysatis sat down on the sofa opposite Jay, and nonchalantly asked him, "So, what are we watching?"

She was referring to the TV, but Jay was watching her at the time. He didn't know she had such nice legs. He felt ashamed at the thought, and decided it was time to break out. It was obvious she wanted to unwind, so he needed to give her some privacy.

Jay stood up, and stretched. He faked a yawn, and said, "Well, I guess I better be goin' home. I'm a little tired. It's been a long day."

When she saw him get ready to leave, Ysatis panicked. She had rehearsed that moment too many times in her head to just let him walk away like that. She stood up, and said, "Wait! Don't go yet. Please."

Jay looked at her like he was sort of confused, and didn't respond.

Ysatis knew time wasn't on her side, so she had to do something drastic. If she wanted to keep him there, she had to let him know where she was coming from. Desperate to get her message across, she went for broke. She took a deep breath, and tugged on the belt on her robe. It opened, and she let it fall to the floor. She placed her hands on her hips and eyed Jay sexily, to make sure he knew what it was.

Jay just stood there looking at her like she was crazy, so Ysatis got a little nervous. Why wasn't he drooling yet? She'd been under the impression that her nakedness would have made him lose control, but it appeared to have no effect on him. Now she figured she had to do more. She knew Jay sort of looked at her like a little sister, but she had to show him that she was a big girl.

Jay couldn't deny that she had a nice body, but he acted unimpressed. He was cool, calm, and collect. "Ysatis, what are you doing?"

Ysatis didn't know what to say. She just shrugged, and said, "Nothin'. I just wanna thank you for all you've done for me." She walked closer towards him.

Jay looked aggravated. She was try'na play him like some creepy old man. He shook his head. "Nah, shorty. I'm not like that. You don't owe me nothin'. It ain't even that serious."

Ysatis didn't want to hear that. She wanted him so bad, she could feel him inside of her. She pleaded with him through goo-goo eyes, and spoke seductively. "But I wanna thank you. So please just let me." She started touching Jay, and rubbing on his chest.

Jay pushed her back off him. "Chill, shorty! Nah!"

Ysatis would not be deterred. She grabbed Jay's hand, and placed it on her left breast, and she massaged him over the pants. She wanted him to make love to her, and would stop at nothing until he did so.

Jay snatched his hand back, and pushed her. "Yo, what the hell is wrong with you? I'm out."

Ysatis cooed, "There's nothin' wrong wit' me. I just like you. Please don't go, boo." She approached him again.

Jay couldn't believe the way she was behaving. She was coming on mad strong. He resisted her advances, and pushed her away again. But he couldn't front, his dick was hard. He tried to will his erection down. It was time for him to go.

Ysatis wouldn't quit. She was rubbing on his crotch, and kept on trying to kiss him on the neck. She murmured softly in his ear, "Hold me, Jay. Please, just hold me..."

Those sexy pleas broke down Jay's resistance. His brain told him not to comply, but his dick had a mind of its own. Temptation overruled all reasoning. At least for the moment. He placed his hands around her tiny waist, and traced the small of her back. Her skin was soft.

Ysatis stepped closer into his embrace. It felt so good being in his arms, she felt faint. She laid her head on Jay's shoulder, and exhaled. He was such a man. She believed she really loved him. He had to be the one. Look at the way he treated her. No one had ever been so kind. With that in mind, Ysatis wanted desperately to cater to Jay, and show him a little appreciation.

She didn't say a word. She just looked in his eyes to show him she meant what she was about to do. She wanted to treat him like a king. She wanted to love him. She sank to her knees, and unfastened his belt buckle. He didn't protest, so she knew that was what he wanted. Ysatis knew Jay was older than her, so she really had to please him like a woman. Like his woman. That's what she wanted to be. His woman. So she had to leave her mark, and make him come back to her. She freed him from his boxers.

When Jay's manhood sprang out, Ysatis gasped. He was even larger than she had anticipated. She stroked it adoringly, and then she placed its grandeur in her mouth. Ysatis put everything she had into that blowjob. She was determined to win him over. She knew he had a wife, but she wanted him to leave home and move in with her. She was tired of staying in that big apartment by herself.

Poor Ysatis was young, and gullible. She actually believed she had a chance. Like Jay would consider abandoning everything he had for her. She didn't have a whole lot of experience with men, so she didn't know it was possible for them to appreciate you when their dick was hard, and then disregard you afterwards. She would learn that from Jay, a lot sooner than she knew.

Jay stroked the back of her head, and made her feel beautiful while his dick was down her throat. He had his eyes closed, like he was living in a dream. Ysatis looked up at him, and just knew she had won him over. She was so happy and proud. He was playing in her hair like the head she was giving him was unbelievable. Encouraged by this, she sped up her rhythm.

All of a sudden he groaned, and thrust himself in and out of her mouth with more force. Ysatis hung in there like a champ.

That was the moment she was waiting for. She knew he was about to cum. She kept her eyes on the prize, and her jaws on his dick. Jay would definitely be hers if she swallowed. That was what real women did, wasn't it? That would show him how serious she was.

Jay came, and then he caught his breath. After he relieved himself down Ysatis' throat, he definitely felt some emotions. But contrary to what she believed, love wasn't one of them. Jay was extremely displeased with himself. He actually felt like he'd taken advantage of her, so he was overcome with guilt and shame.

Ysatis stood up and grinned at him all dreamy eyed, and then she asked him if he wanted to spend the night with her. Jay felt so bad he didn't even want to be around her. He quickly put his dick away, and mumbled that he had to go.

He didn't look at her. He just made a beeline straight for the door. Ysatis yelled after him that he had left his cell phone on the coffee table. That was the only reason he looked back.

Jay turned back around to get his phone, and he remembered his manners. He told Ysatis he would give her a call the following day. He'd forgotten how delicate a girl could be when it came to stuff like that. He didn't want to hurt her feelings. Truthfully, his issues were more with himself than with her. She wasn't the first young girl to throw herself at him, so he should've just turned her down, and gone home. He felt horrible about what had just happened.

Ysatis smiled, and walked him to the door. She was disappointed, but she hugged him, and told him she'd be waiting for his call. Jay didn't comment, but he knew she'd be waiting a long time. He was glad her rent was paid up for a while. He left Ysatis' house with intentions to stay away from her. He had a feeling he fucked up.

On the elevator ride down to the lobby, Jay got a call on his phone from his little princess, Jazz. He knew she was calling to find out when he was coming home. She was a real daddy's girl. She was always asking for him, so Portia had taught her how to call him on speed dial. All she had to do was press "1" on the phone, and oftentimes she did.

For the first time in his life, Jay sent his daughter's call to voicemail. He felt bad, but he needed a minute to get his head together. At the moment, he was feeling too low to talk. He'd give her a call when he got in the car.

Outside, Jay sat in the back of his limo, and contemplated his next move. He felt so guilty, it was hard to go home and face Portia and the kids. He directed the driver to take him to an upscale Irish bar in Midtown, called Shelley's Lounge. It was a down low spot, and that was good for a dude like him. Jay liked to keep a low profile, so he usually avoided mostly Black populated spots. Unless it was business related, and he was promoting, or something.

When he got there, Jay went in and had a drink, while he sorted out his thoughts. He called his wife and told her he'd be home late, and then he intentionally stayed out until he thought everyone was asleep. He figured he'd go home and just sleep off his guilt, and the following day he wouldn't feel so bad. He thought about confiding in Cas, but didn't even want him to know what a creep he'd been for taking advantage of Ysatis like that. That wasn't even like him.

CHAPTER SEVENTEEN

That weekend, Jazmin wanted to see Falynn, so Portia had personally gone to Fatima's parents' house in Brooklyn, and picked up Falynn so she could spend the night with them. Jazmin had been begging to see her best buddy for weeks. Her and Fay just loved each other. It was too cute.

And both of those little girls loved to sing. On Saturday evening, Portia had the television on the VH1-Soul channel, and Solange Knowles' "I Decided" video came on. Jazz and Fay almost broke their necks running to the TV. They loved that song. They were even imitating the choreography. Unbelievably, they had the dance steps down to a tee, and knew all the words. They caught on fast. Those little chicklets were adorable. Portia just laughed.

Jay was cracking up too. He couldn't believe those kids. They were dead serious. You should've seen the looks on their faces. He looked at Portia, and grinned. He said, "Yo, P, I see dollar signs!"

Portia laughed, and said, "I know that's right, boo!" She knew Jay was serious. But who knew what the future held. Those kids never ceased to amaze her. Her and Jay had house full that weekend. On top of their three brats, Fatima's daughter, and Laila's girls were staying over that weekend as well.

$$$$$

That same day, Kira had decided to go over Jay and Portia's house. She loaded up her son in her new Aston Martin, and they went to pay her brother a visit. That would give her little man, Jahseim, an opportunity to play with his first cousins. He'd been asking about Jayquan, Jazmin, and the new baby, Trixie, a lot. Despite what was going on between her and Jay,

Kira wanted their kids to grow up close.

Kira also wanted to talk some business with Jay. She was seriously thinking about terminating her contract with Street Life Entertainment, and she wanted to discuss it with him first. She and Casino were divorced now, and she wasn't sure if she was comfortable with her career in his hands. As far as she was concerned, she and Cas were enemies. Kira's decision to leave Street Life was also fueled by the fact that one of their rival record labels had offered her a nice deal.

When Kira popped up out of the blue, Portia answered the door. Kira could see the surprise in her face. They'd seen each other not too long ago, but Kira hadn't visited their house since she and Laila had that big fight. She had gotten pissed off at Jay, so she threw a rock and broke the window, and drove off. That was over a year ago.

Portia smiled, and greeted her sister-in-law and nephew jovially. She grabbed Jahseim and hugged him, and gave him a big kiss. He was such a handsome little dude. He was eight years old now, and that boy was getting big. And he was the spitting image of Cas. Portia could tell he was going to be a real heartbreaker when he grew up.

Portia was glad to see them, but she didn't know how to take Kira. Sometimes she acted real funny towards her. Portia knew that was only because Cas was with Laila, so she just ignored it. Whatever Kira's beef was, it wasn't her fault. She hadn't been the matchmaker that put Cas and Laila together. They had discovered each other on their own.

Kira was unpredictable, so Portia was unsure of the type of mood she was in. She told her Jay was up in the rec section, and offered them something to drink. They both said they were okay. Kira told Portia she had lost all her baby weight, and looked good.

Portia just smiled, and thanked her. She didn't say anything, but Kira's timing couldn't have been worse. Portia was babysitting for Laila and Cas that night. They had gone out to dinner. Their darling little Skye was upstairs, asleep in the crib right next to her baby, Trixie. Portia believed that Jahseim had the right to know he had a little sister, but it wasn't her and Jay's place to break the news to him.

Jahseim ran off to find his big cousin, Jayquan, and Portia walked Kira to the second floor where Jay was. After that, she went upstairs to check on the kids.

Jahseim ran to his Uncle Jay first, and hugged him. Jay hugged him back, and gave him a noogie on the head, and then he gave his little nephew a pound. He couldn't believe how tall he was getting. That boy looked just like his daddy. He asked Jay where Jayquan was, and Jay told him he was upstairs in his room. Lil' Jah broke out, and ran upstairs without another word. Jay laughed. He knew Jayquan was like Jah's big brother.

When Jazmin saw her cousin, Jahseim, she punched him in the arm, and called him ugly. He pushed her back, and called her a stupid dummy. They loved each other, but they fought like that all the time. Jazz pushed him back, and she ran downstairs to find Kira. She loved her auntie. When Jazmin left, Jahseim started picking with Falynn.

When Jazmin got to the rec section and saw Kira, she ran and jumped in her arms. She was so excited. And she couldn't wait to show her auntie her new sister. Jazz kept tugging on her, so Kira told her they would go upstairs as soon as she finished talking to her daddy.

Jazz was hype. Kira hadn't been there a good ten minutes before she grabbed her hand again, and demanded she go upstairs with her to see the "babies". Kira heard Jazz say, "Auntie Kira, let's go see the babies", but she figured her plural usage was just a cute mistake. She agreed to go see the baby with her niece.

When Jay watched Kira follow Jazz upstairs, he knew drama would soon follow. He headed upstairs behind them. It wouldn't be fair to leave Portia on the hot seat when Kira started asking questions.

Kira looked back at Jay following her and Jazmin upstairs, and she smiled. It was really good to see her big brother. He looked really well. And she missed the kids too. They were family, and really should've been spending more time together. Their mother was always saying they didn't act like sister and brother anymore.

Kira couldn't front, she'd been taking what she'd been going through with Cas out on Jay. She made up her mind that instant to change that. It was time to extend an olive branch to her big brother.

When Jay got to the top of the stairs, Kira turned around and gave him a big hug. She told him she loved him, and apologized for acting like such a bitch to him because of Cas. Kira even rethought the reason she had come. Maybe she was moving too fast with her decision to leave Street Life. She had sold a lot of records there, and she knew Jay and Cas were responsible for her success more than anybody. They had pushed her shit hard body. They made her a star, and she would always be grateful for that.

That hug from Kira stirred some feelings in Jay. It had always been important to him that she adored him. That was part of the reason he'd spoiled his baby sister so much in the past. Their father wasn't around, so he had helped raise that girl.

Jay was glad his sister had made up with him, but he'd never been angry at her in the first place. It wasn't him who'd been acting shady. He hadn't been harboring any hard feelings. That had been her acting crazy. He loved his little sister, and didn't want to see her hurt, so knowing she was about to find out such unwelcome news really bothered him.

Kira walked in the baby's nursery behind Jazz smiling from ear to ear. Portia had decorated the room so pretty. She looked in the crib at her little niece. She was so cute. But Kira was surprised to see another baby laying in the crib with Patrice. She wondered whose child that was. She went over to get a closer look.

Kira didn't make any inferences yet. She just said, "That's a cute baby."

Portia and Jay glanced at each other. Kira noticed the little secret look they shared, and she wanted to know what that was about. She played it cool, but she'd never been the type to bite her tongue. She came right out and asked who the child belonged to. "Whose baby is this, ya'll?"

They didn't say anything. Neither of them was prepared to tell Kira about Cas and Laila's lovechild. And it wasn't really their place to.

Kira turned around and faced them, and she asked again. "Whose pretty little baby is this?"

Portia said it casually, like it was no big deal. "Oh, she's Laila's."

Kira stiffened. You could've knocked her over with a feather, but she acted indifferent. "Oh. What's her name?"

Portia said, "Skye." She didn't really want to have that conversation, but she knew Kira. It wasn't over.

Kira pretended to admire the baby, but she secretly examined her features to see who she looked like. "Skye, huh? That's pretty."

Tired of beating around the bush, she came right out and asked, "Is Cas the father of this baby?"

She looked directly at Jay after she asked that. Portia could pussyfoot around all she wanted to, but her brother better not lie to her. Kira kept her emotions intact, and waited for an answer.

Jay looked away, and just sort of shrugged his shoulders. He didn't want to get into all of that. He wasn't the person she should be questioning.

Kira looked at Jay avoiding eye contact with her, and shook her head. And Portia was pretending to be busy, brushing imaginary lint off her shirt. Kira was no idiot. She couldn't look at her either. Her so-called brother and sister in-law both looked like they were hiding something, so she knew that baby was Cas'. Kira was tight as hell, but she didn't say another word. She kept her cool, and decided to break out.

She knew she could be a real loose cannon when she flipped, so she didn't let it out. The way she felt, if she got started there would be no turning back. And to think, she had come over there to make amends. But now she felt betrayed by Jay, and his wife. Jay was some kind of brother. And Cas messing around with that cripple bitch Laila was probably what Portia's trifling ass wanted all along. That was her fucking homegirl.

The words "Fuck ya'll mothafuckas" were right on the tip of

her tongue, but Kira just turned around and left.

Jay watched his sister do an about-face and walk out, and he felt horrible. She looked like she was mad as hell. He followed her downstairs, and he calmly told Kira to leave Jahseim at his house for the rest of the weekend. He didn't say anything, but he figured that would give her time to get her head together. He knew she was hurt by the news.

Jahseim wanted to stay anyway, so Kira agreed to let him stay the night with his uncle. She kissed her son, Falynn, and her niece, Jazmin, and she headed outside to her car. Kira had managed to keep it icy thus far, but when she got in her whip and locked the doors, she let her tears fall free. And there were plenty. She was deeply hurt about that baby. She knew it was over between her and Casino, but their divorce had just been finalized. That meant he made that baby while he was still married to her. That was real fucked up.

Cas was a no-good, two-timing bastard from hell. Kira didn't know what she was going to do, but she definitely wasn't taking that shit lying down. She was crushed, to say the least. The news about that baby was really killing her, and someone was going to pay for her pain.

She couldn't wait to confront that no-good mothafucka Cas. She hated him for that shit. She might even step to that bitch Laila again. They had already fought one time before, so they could definitely get it poppin' again. That was nothing. As a matter of fact, they had fought right there at Jay's house.

Kira remembered Laila was in a wheelchair now, so she ruled out the option of punching her in the face. Still aghast, she started up her car and drove off. It was difficult to drive, because that big pill she had swallowed was still stuck in her chest.

$$\$\$\$\$\$$

The following morning, Khalil went to the corner store to purchase a pack of cigarettes. He picked up a newspaper too, and slid Poppy behind the counter a ten dollar bill. He got his change, which was just coins, because cigarettes were priced so high in New York City. Afterwards, he headed across the street to the Spanish restaurant on the corner.

Khalil ordered a cup of coffee and a toasted bagel, and he sat down and thumbed through his newspaper while he ate. He happened to come across a write-up about Street Life Entertainment. That was them niggas Jay and Cas' record company. Khalil hated that dude Cas, and he wasn't too fond of Jay either, but he was interested nonetheless.

As Khalil read the article, his smile grew wider and wider. It looked like them niggas were about to go down. To his delight, the paper said their whole enterprise was under federal investigation. They were allegedly linked to the organization of a Colombian drug lord named Manuel Saldano. The reporter cited them to be residents of the prestigious Marquis County in New Jersey.

Khalil smirked to himself. Now he knew where Laila was living. She had been hiding out, but the truth had a way of coming to the light. Khalil drove an inconspicuous looking hoopty, so he thought about driving out there to Jersey. He wanted to find his wife. And this time he wasn't letting anyone get in the way. He patted the .38 revolver in his inside jacket pocket for reassurance. He'd been carrying the gun ever since he and Cas had their last run-in.

Khalil felt an immediate power surge. With that gun, even Superman didn't have shit on him. He was going to take Laila back from Cas, even if he had to bust her in her head, and drag her ass to his car like a caveman. Fuck that, she was his wife.

Khalil looked at the article again, and his hopes rose. If all went well, Pretty Boy Cas would be going away for a long time. In shackles. Khalil leaned back in his seat, and thought of a way to make sure that happened.

$$$$$

The second day Falynn stayed over, she kept telling Portia she wanted her mommy. Portia called Fatima on both her house and cell phones four times that day, and got no answer on either. At first, she gave Fatima the benefit of a doubt. But as time went on, she just assumed that Fatima was "partying" again.

Portia got pissed off. She should've known Fatima was lying when she told her she was going to get her shit together. That was nothing but that old addict talk. Now she knew why Tima hadn't been calling lately. She probably couldn't face her.

Fatima's drug use had Portia so worried, she couldn't keep it to herself anymore. She saw her friend on a path to self destruction, and she couldn't just stand by and let it happen. She needed help to help Fatima. She couldn't seem to get through to her by herself. Homegirl needed a serious intervention, and that was all there was to it.

Portia opened up and talked to Jay about it that night. She told him she had been reluctant to put her girl's business out there, but she was scared for Fatima. Jay was surprised to learn Fatima was abusing drugs the way Portia described. That wasn't like her. He understood the seriousness of the matter, and promised to get on it ASAP. He saw how worried Portia was. It upset him to know too.

Jay made a call to Cas, and pulled his coat about the situation. Cas was unhappy about the news as well, and agreed that something had to be done. They agreed to go have a talk with Fatima the following day.

After that, Cas told Jay that Jahseim had called him from over there, and asked if everything was okay. Jay told him about Kira seeing the baby, and getting upset, and told him he'd suggested she leave Jah with him for a few days.

Cas didn't have any beef with that. Jay was his son's uncle, and he loved him like he was his own. Portia loved him to death too. And so did the kids, so Cas knew he was alright. Jah was with family.

Cas told Jay he'd had a talk with Jahseim about his new little sister a few days after she was born, so he already knew about the baby. He admitted that he'd asked him not to tell his mother yet. Cas said he couldn't think of a way to tell Kira about it himself, and wasn't sure if he felt like he was obligated to.

Jay understood where he was coming from. And now he understood why Jahseim had handled the news so well. Nobody had actually broken the news to him, but Jay knew he overheard his mother talking about it. Regardless of what, Jahseim acted like he loved the baby. He played with her, and asked if he could hold her.

Jay told Cas he would see him the next day, and they said goodnight. Cas then asked to speak to his son.

The next morning, Jay and Cas knocked on Fatima's door around eleven. It was an unannounced, surprise visit. When she came to the door, they apologized for popping up on her, and told her they needed to talk to her about a few concerns they had.

Fatima wasn't mad they came, but she regretted the fact that her house was a complete mess. There was evidence of the party she had last night everywhere, so she wished they had called first. She wasn't exactly prepared for company, but nonetheless, she opened the door and invited them in.

After they all greeted each other, Jay and Cas had a seat. Neither of then bothered to comment on the messy condition the house was in. They just got to the point of their visit. They told Fatima they didn't mean to offend her, but they had gotten word that she'd been carrying on inappropriately, and they wanted to take preventive measures before things got out of hand.

Fatima couldn't believe they had come at her like that. She was dumbfounded at first. The truth hurt, and it really put her on defense. She crossed her arms, and rolled her eyes. Portia was a snitch ass bitch. She was gonna bark on her ass when they left. How dare she cross her like that, and tell Jay and Cas her business?

Fatima sat there with her arms crossed, and her mouth poked out like a scolded child. She didn't know who they thought they were, telling her what to do. The way she had been carrying on was none of their damn business.

Deep down inside, she knew they were only concerned because they cared. She was the widow of their dearly departed homie, but they weren't only concerned on the strength of Wise. They were all like family. They had been through a lot together. And those two dudes had never held back on her. Not once. Not even when she'd demanded a detailed description of the way Wise was killed. They told her every detail.

Jay and Cas didn't let on that they knew about her drug use, but Fatima knew they knew. Especially when Cas said, "Partying doesn't really make the pain go away. It only numbs it temporarily."

That statement struck some type of chord in her. He had described what she was doing to a tee. She had really been trying to numb the pain. Despite her attempt at nonchalance, Fatima's eyes watered up. She looked down, because she didn't want them to see her cry. She didn't want to appear any more pitiful than they already thought she was.

Jay and Cas both felt bad that she was crying. It was obvious that she was still hurting over losing Wise, and also from whatever other issues she was dealing with. They hated that they even had to have that conversation, but it was very necessary. They had seen that shit destroy too many pretty girls, and they weren't about to stand by and act indifferent.

They had mad love for Fatima. She was a part of their inner circle, and Jay and Cas both shared an unspoken, but understood zero tolerance policy for weaknesses. And most importantly, they knew Wise would've wanted them to intervene. Jay went and sat next to her on the sofa, and Cas got up to go find her some tissue.

When he returned from the bathroom, Jay had his arm around Fatima, and she was crying on his shoulder. Cas felt sorry for her. Damn, women were so emotional.

In effort to lighten up the mood, Cas told her they had good news. He said he and Jay wanted to send her on a "vacation" to an exquisite "resort". He told her she'd be able to rest, relax, and get herself together, and he said there would be people there she could talk to. He told Fatima he believed she should except the all-expense-paid, exotic getaway, so that she'd come home feeling refreshed, like a totally new person.

Fatima knew Cas was talking about going to a rehab. She didn't know whether to be offended, or thank him and Jay. She knew she had to get it together, but did they think that little of her? Wow, they wanted her to go to a rehab. She voiced her disinterest. "Thanks, I appreciate the offer, but I don't know about that one, ya'll."

Seeing that Fatima was hesitant, Jay added, "It's a discreet place in Honolulu. Go have some fun in the sun, and nobody will even know who you are."

He reached in his back pocket, and handed her some papers. "This is a five-star resort. Here are some brochures. Look these over, and you can check it out online."

Fatima reluctantly took the brochures. She wasn't interested, but she didn't want to be rude. She glimpsed at the pictures on the front. The photos of the beach did look inviting. But she sat the brochures down on the coffee table, just to let them know she wasn't with it. She didn't need to go to no rehab. She could work on herself. She had willpower, so she could get clean on her own.

Fatima said, "Thanks. I really appreciate ya'll going through all this trouble for me, but I think I'll pass. Don't get me wrong, I could use a vacation. But just not now. No offense, okay?"

Jay and Cas said there was none taken, and they told her their offer would still be on the table if she changed her mind. They each hugged Fatima, and Jay told her to quit being such a stranger. He said she didn't even come around anymore.

Fatima promised to stay in contact with everyone more often. Just then, her doorbell rang. She remembered she had called her cleaning company and scheduled an early afternoon cleaning. She told Jay and Cas she was expecting two girls from the agency. She said it was time to clean up house, in more ways than one.

They told her they had to be going anyway. Fatima walked them to the door, and thanked them for coming to see about her. When she opened the door, there were two non-English speaking Ecuadorian women waiting out front with their supplies. She told Jay and Cas she would see them later, and let the housekeepers in.

After Jay and Cas drove off in Cas' Rolls Royce Phantom, they both decided they would give Fatima the benefit of a doubt. But they agreed that, if she couldn't get it together on her own, she was going in that rehab, be it voluntarily or forced. They both hoped it wouldn't have to come to that.

After Jay and Cas left, Fatima sat there and waited for Guadeloupe and Penelope to finish cleaning, and she took a look at her life. Realization slowly dawned on her, and common sense told her that enough was enough. Her fucking life was in shambles. She was on cocaine heavy, and she'd been popping a lot of pills lately. Even after the bad experience she had, when Portia took her to the hospital. But now she was taking Percoset, which she knew was still highly addictive. She had actually gone to the doctor and lied about having severe pain, just to get prescription refills.

It hurt her to admit it, but she really had a drug problem. She needed help. She really did. Jay, Cas, Portia, and her parents were all right. Fatima couldn't believe she had allowed herself to get hooked like that. That wasn't even typical of her character. She had to get clean. Seriously. But could she really do it on her own? Fatima weighed her options. Maybe she did need to go to a rehab, or something.

Fatima decided to at least read the brochures. To her surprise, they were actually pretty impressive. One of them read:

Welcome to Renaissance Honolulu, the only treatment center directly on the beach! Renaissance Honolulu's facilities provide beautiful, serene atmospheres for our clients. Situated on its own private beach, our extended care residence boasts magnificent views and the gentle sound of the surf. Each day the residents enjoy gourmet meals and engaging treatment activities...

Each guest has a choice of his own villa, which are all 2400 square foot beauties, either nestled in the Honolulu Hills, or on our very own private beach. The villas in the hills are magnificently landscaped with trees and vegetation. The pool, outdoor Jacuzzi, and our nearby waterfall offer breathtaking sunrises and sunsets. The beach villas offer a beachside paradise with a beautifully landscaped yard, including a swimming pool and Jacuzzi, overlooking the ocean...

Another brochure contained details about their different

treatment methods, and wellness and recovery programs, like holistic and spiritual therapy, music and art therapy, aquatic therapy, and adventure therapy. According to the brochures, their goal was to heal the mind, body, and spirit. They said they implemented yoga, meditation, and massage in their recovery programs as well.

Fatima sat there in her recliner thinking about how bad she needed a healing. She wondered if they could fix her wounded soul. She pondered the notion until she dozed off.

CHAPTER EIGHTEEN

Later that afternoon, Jay and Cas drove to Manhattan for a meeting with their associates. Cas was under the wheel, and he noticed that Jay's phone was ringing like crazy. But for whatever reasons, he wasn't answering. He had put it on vibrate, but Cas still heard it going off. He didn't bother to question Jay about who the caller was, but it was obvious that they weren't on his "favorites" list.

Jay was huffing and puffing like he was real aggravated. He said, "I'ma change my fuckin' number, man."

Cas just kept on driving. He wasn't a nosy dude, but Jay was like his brother. He couldn't help but be concerned, so he glanced over at him and asked, "Who pissed you off, son?"

Jay hesitated for a second. A part of him didn't want Cas to know how he got down, but his bro had worse dirt on him than infidelity. He could disclose anything to Cas. Jay knew he could trust him. They had murdered niggas together, and kept their mouths shut.

Jay sighed, and said, "Man, this chick keep on calling me... I don't know what the fuck to tell her. I ain't mean... Yo, son... I don't know..."

Cas looked puzzled. Jay wasn't being clear with him. He was having trouble with his words, so whatever he was trying to say must've been difficult. In order to lighten the mood, Cas joked with him. He impersonated Dave Chapelle, and said, "Man, what the fuck are you talkin' about?"

Jay looked at him, and just laughed. Cas was a fool, but he was right. He'd spoken, but he hadn't said shit. Jay cut out the lollygagging, and gave it to his main man straight. He told Cas about everything, from the way he'd been paying Ysatis' tuition, and leasing her apartment, to the way things got out of hand when she went down on him. Jay told Cas he broke out on her right after that. He said that was the last time he spoke to her, and he felt bad.

When he finished talking, Cas was quiet for a second. What was he supposed to say? Jay was a dude. None of them were perfect. He was a little surprised, but he wasn't about to judge him. Jay had never judged him, or acted any kind of way towards him because of something he had done. Not even when he'd found out he got his little sister pregnant years ago, when he first came home from being locked up. Jay didn't appreciate the news but he had kept it one hundred with him, and remained his main man regardless.

Cas just told Jay, "Man, shit happens. But the way you're ignoring her, and not answering the phone, that makes bitches act stupid, son. You know what they say about a woman scorned. You should just talk to her, and tell her what it is. Tell her what happened shouldn't have, so she should move on and find somebody her own age. She's too young, trust me. You don't even need the headache."

Jay nodded in agreement. He knew Cas had learned that age thing from Kira.

After those words of wisdom, Cas changed the subject. He told Jay about this new healthy and delicious organic soy smoothie he had created. He said it was loaded with nutrients and antioxidants. He called it his "Cas-matic Cleansing Coolata", and he broke the ingredients down to a science. Everything from the ginseng, six different types of organic berries, and fat free soymilk he used, to the wheat germ sprinkles and sprig of mint he garnished it with. He offered to fix one for Jay later, at no expense.

Jay accepted his right hand's offer, and laughed. He guessed that organic smoothie was Cas' version of comfort food. He was attempting to make him feel better. But that smoothie did sound good, so he wanted to try one.

Cas was a health food fanatic, and he worked out regularly. He believed the body was a precious temple, and always treated his that way. He didn't eat red meat, and believed that people who did really abused their colon.

Jay took good care of himself, but he wasn't quite as anal as

Cas was about the food and stuff. He watched what he ate, but enjoyed an occasional hotdog or steak. And he worked out, but not as much as he should. He made a mental note to step his game up a little bit. Jay too believed his body was precious. That was the main reason he wasn't into drugs. He and Cas both had a drink every now and then, but that was as far as it went.

$$$$$

Meanwhile, Ysatis sat in her apartment holding the phone. She was distraught over the way Jay had been handling her. She needed to talk to him. She loved him. He didn't understand. She was head over heels, and he wouldn't even answer his phone. She realized Jay didn't think much of her. Something had to be done to change that.

$$$$$

Laila had resumed her physical therapy fulltime. She had just finished with her session that afternoon, so she told her team she would see them the following day. After she locked the door behind them, she called her attorney for an update on the progress of her divorce proceedings. She was disappointed to learn that Khalil still detested the divorce.

Khalil was really making Laila dislike him. She felt horrible living in sin the way she was. She and that asshole were separated, but they were still under vows. She wasn't in a rush to marry Cas, but she hated living in sin. And it wasn't fair to Cas. He and Kira were already divorced. He had come correct, and she was still tangled up in her mess.

Laila wanted to honor God's laws. She needed Him to bless her too bad. In the back of her mind, she believed that she'd have a better chance of walking if she cleaned up her slate, and got right with God in every aspect. As much pain as she had in her life, it was like God was angry with her. She didn't know what she'd done to piss Him off so bad, but she wanted to live right.

If Khalil would sign the divorce papers, she would no longer be committing adultery. That would be one less sin. Then hopefully God would pardon her, and let her walk again.

Laila had gone through a period of lost faith, and she had been upset with God for allowing things to be the way they were. But she had been praying a lot lately, and God had renewed her faith. She realized that without Him in her life, she would never walk again. Faith was all she had.

Laila was so upset with Khalil for making her have to live in sin, she called his mother's house to speak to him. That bastard answered the phone, and she patiently asked him what the hold up was.

Khalil told her he didn't like the way she was pressuring him, and said he wasn't ready to sign yet. Laila tried to be civil with him. She asked him what would make him ready. He had the nerve to say, "Laila, let's try again."

Laila refrained from telling him how bad what he just said disgusted her. Instead, she just told him that wasn't a good idea. Khalil got salty after that, and told her if she wanted to get rid of him that fucking bad, she better make it worth his while.

Laila said, "Is that what you want, money? I will pay you to sign the papers, Khalil. Just sign 'em."

Khalil told her he would get back to her, and hung up the phone. He wasn't as dumb as everybody thought he was.

The following day, he hired an attorney, who just happened to be a bigger slime ball than Khalil. He dug up every thing on Laila. He found out about her new house in Jersey, and even told Khalil she was waiting on a big settlement from her insurance company, from the car accident she was involved in.

The lawyer told Khalil that since Laila had come into all of this while they were still married, he was legally entitled to half. He said he could even sue Laila for alimony, because he was unemployed at the time, and she made more money. And she was the one with all the health insurance, and other benefits on their family. He told him he was even entitled to part of her disability check.

Khalil turned into a real asshole when he got this information. If Laila wanted to play hardball like that, he would drag her ass into court and demand his share of her new property and money. And whatever the hell else she had. She obviously didn't know who she was fucking with.

A week later, Laila got the list of demands and conditions from Khalil's attorney, and she screwed up her face in disgust. That mothafucka was pitiful. He had stooped to a new low.

She called him, and asked him what type of pathetic slime ball he had become. She told him to just let go, because the shit he was doing was sad. He said, "Whatever", like he didn't give a fuck, so she told him she would just see his black ass in court, because she'd be damned if she was giving his sorry ass anything.

After that, Laila asked him if he even cared what his daughter thought of him. She told him he must've not had any pride at all. He was trying to strong-arm her out of money to support his lazy ass, and she was in a wheelchair, and taking care of his child alone. And she never asked him for one cent.

Laila talked it all over with Cas that night, and he was very unhappy about the situation. He was disgusted with that dude. He didn't appreciate him trying to milk Laila like that. Cas toyed with the idea of making him sleep with the fishes. That would be a quick fix for the situation.

Laila must've known what he was thinking, because she asked him not to get involved. She said she didn't want things to get out of hand.

Cas told her he would stay out of it, and he announced that he had to go pick up his son. That was his weekend with Jahseim, so they would be staying at his place. Out of respect for Jahseim, he didn't stay at Laila's when he got him.

Laila understood, and didn't have any beef with that. They both knew things would be different after she was divorced. She even hated that Macy saw what was going on. But Macy was older than Jahseim. And she was mature enough to understand what had happened between her parents. Macy knew her daddy was weak, so she wasn't even mad at Laila for moving on.

But Jahseim was only seven years old, and his mother was really playing the victim role. After Laila was divorced, Cas would sit him down and explain that he had a new girlfriend.

Laila was fond of Jahseim. They got along fine so far, so she didn't want to upset him. It wouldn't be good to let him see her in the bed with his daddy. She knew how children were. They wanted their mommies and daddies to be together.

$$$$$

That news about Cas' new baby still had Kira sick. But she was slick too. She waited until it was his weekend to come get Jahseim before she blew it up. He came over to pick up their son, and as soon as he pulled up, she confronted him about that baby.

Kira had prepared herself for his denial, but to her surprise, Cas just looked at her and said, "Yeah, that's my daughter. Why?"

She was thrown off by his frank response. He didn't even try to deny it. It was like he was proud. Kira wasn't going for that shit. She looked at him like he was ignorant. He must've been bugging, talking to her like that.

Kira said, "Wow. You bastard. We were still married, Cas! That's some foul ass shit! I see how you carryin' yours now." She shook her head, like she couldn't believe him.

Cas knew she was hurt, but he kept a stone face. Kira hadn't thrown him off guard. Jay had already told him she knew about the baby. He hadn't meant to hurt her, and truthfully, he felt real bad about it. But if he displayed emotions, that would show weakness. Kira was too much of a drama queen for that. She would only try to take advantage of the situation, and get more extra. Cas didn't know what to say. So for lack of the proper words, he didn't respond.

Kira kept on shooting at him. "So you ain't got shit to say? Come on, nothin'?"

Cas sighed. He wasn't the bad guy. He put his left hand in his pocket, and shrugged. "Look, it is what it is."

Kira screwed up her face. The most important question was

on the tip of her tongue, so she said, "Were you fucking that bitch the whole time we were married?"

Cas said, "No."

That made Kira feel a tiny bit better, but she kept on torturing herself. She needed to know the truth. "So, you really love her, huh?"

Cas was getting impatient. He didn't like the way she was questioning him. "Why?"

Kira shrugged. "I just wanna know."

Cas wasn't about to lie to her. He'd never been a liar. And he'd never been the type to tell a chick what she wanted to hear either. So he just pleaded the fifth, and didn't answer her.

Kira just stared at him. She knew Cas. She wasn't about to get any answers out of him. Not about something he didn't want to talk about. But he hadn't denied it, so that was sort of an admission. He was in love with that bitch.

Kira contemplated her next move, but at the moment she was at a loss. Cas was acting like he couldn't care less. She was hurt that he didn't give a damn, so she had to leave an impression on him.

She said, "I hope you don't think I'ma take this laying down, nigga. Because I'm not. You crossed the wrong chick, Cas. Word up. And I mean what I say. Remember nigga, payback is a bitch." Kira spun around on her twelve hundred dollar Guiseppe Zanotti open toes, and walked inside the house.

Cas watched Kira storm away, and resisted the urge to call her back. For some reason he wanted to tell her he was sorry. Not that he should feel bad, because she had been fucking around on him with that young nigga, Vee. But Cas was old fashioned in a sense, and he took the marriage vow extremely serious. He really hadn't meant to get Laila pregnant. Not that fast.

But everything happened for a reason, and he wasn't going to deny any of his children. Ever. His only regret was the fact that the baby had been conceived before he and Kira's divorce was finalized. They were divorced when the baby was born, but he could understand Kira's beef about the timing.

Cas looked up, and saw his son coming out of the house. He

smiled at his little man, and put his other worries and concerns on a backburner immediately. He loved his son with all of his heart. Jahseim was growing up fast, and he was a smart little dude. He had sense enough to know when he and Kira were on the outs.

Cas tried to be cool with Kira around their son, but she didn't know how to be docile. Cas hated involving Jahseim in their disagreements, but Kira was so childish sometimes. She liked to argue in front of him, and say things he shouldn't even hear at his age. He shouldn't be worrying about grown folks stuff.

Jahseim already knew he had a little sister. Cas had a talk with him when she was born, and he explained to him that wouldn't affect their relationship. Kira seemed to think otherwise. But Cas made sure his son knew he loved him, regardless of whatever was going on between them.

Cas hugged his boy, and gave him a noogie. Jahseim laughed, and wiggled out of his embrace. He said, "Pop, I told you I'm gettin' too big to be still gettin' noogies."

He put up his hands to box, and said. "Come on, old man. Let me see what you got."

Cas laughed at his little offspring's display of heart. He said, "Oh, word? You try'na get tough, son?"

Jahseim stuck out his little chest, and said, "I was born tough. You already know." He threw the first punch, and kept his guards up, just like his daddy taught him.

Cas playfully slap boxed with his son, impressed that he was using the blocking skills he had taught him. His boy was nice with the hands. Jah was right, he was born tough. It was in his blood.

Cas downplayed a lot of stuff from his past to his son, because he didn't want him to grow up glorifying street life. So Jah didn't even know the extent of his father's reputation in the streets for putting fools on their ass. Killa' Cas was notorious for knocking dudes out. He had always been gifted with the hands, so the apple didn't fall far from the tree.

When they were done, Casino grinned proudly at his boy. He had let him win the last round. After he declared Jahseim the victor, they both hopped in the truck. You should've seen the look on that kid's face. He was really feeling his little self.

Casino made sure his son was safely strapped in his seatbelt. After he put his on, he pulled off. In his side mirror, he saw Kira staring at him angrily, with her arms crossed. She looked so pissed off, there were daggers shooting from her eyes.

Cas didn't know what to tell her. The baby was here now. She just had to get over it. But she was sure acting like she was scorned.

$$$$$

Meanwhile, there was another scorned lover across town. Khalil was sitting in his basement apartment, flipping through the old photo albums his moms had. She had pictures of he and Laila's wedding, and pictures of his daughters when they were little girls.

Khalil wiped a tear from the corner of his eye, and wondered how he had blown it. He had such a beautiful family. He couldn't believe what a fuck up he had become. No wonder Laila didn't want him. If he were her, he wouldn't want him either. He definitely had a weakness. He could finally admit it, but he couldn't seem to get pass it.

He was still angry that Laila had moved on. He had upset her by hiring an attorney to go after her finances, but he had only done that to retaliate because she wanted a divorce so bad. It wasn't about the money. All he really wanted was another chance. He told himself that if Laila took him back, he would get his shit together, and keep it there. But if she continued to pursue that divorce mess, he would make it as hard for her as he could.

$$$$$

A little voice in the back of Jay's head told him he should've just talked to Ysatis on the phone, and told her what it was like Cas suggested. But she'd been leaving him these sad messages, telling him how emotionally broke down she was over him, and he just felt real sorry for her. So he tried to be Mr. Nice Guy, and go over and apologize to her in person.

Jay went over to her apartment to tell her he had made a terrible mistake, and he thought it would be a good idea if they just swept it under a rug. He said he wasn't tripping, and promised her he would continue to pay for everything he'd originally agreed to pay for, until she finished school. He told her that right now in her life, her education was most important. He told her he would call to check on her. After that, he left.

Ysatis was glad to see Jay, but she didn't like the way he brushed her off. What was he talking about? She had feelings for him already, so it was too late to sweep it under a rug. She knew she had messed up by calling him so much, and leaving those pathetic messages, but she had really been desperate. He'd probably thought she was crazy, or something. But she needed to see him.

Ysatis was wide open. She knew Jay had been avoiding her, and that made her want him even more. Jay had gotten under her skin so much, it was ridiculous. She was obsessed with him, but the approach she had taken wasn't working. She thought he would've ran over there, and rescued her from the misery she'd suffered by not having him around.

He didn't, but at least he was speaking to her again. She didn't want to mess that up. Ysatis decided to fall back, and try another angle. She wanted Jay in her life, and would stop at nothing to get him. She wanted to fuck with him. She knew she could give him what he needed.

Ysatis stopped calling Jay for a few days. She used the time to put together what she believed to be a master plan. But in order to pull it off, she had to play a mind game on him, and make him believe she was over him.

She didn't call Jay for two whole weeks. And he didn't call to see about her either. Ysatis fought the urge to reach out to him. The way she figured, the long-term benefits of it all would be worth it.

CHAPTER NINETEEN

Kira got up early the next morning, and completed her forty five minute pilates workout. Afterwards, she followed with thirty minutes of cardio, and then she hit the shower.

When Kira got out the shower, she walked around nude, and air dried. Before she got dressed, she trimmed her pubic hairs, and called Jay to ask about her studio schedule. They were in the process of making arrangements to record her upcoming album.

Jay answered the phone, and they shot the breezed for a minute. Since they were having a friendly conversation, she took the opportunity to pick her brother's brain about his homie Cas. That whole "baby" situation was eating at her so bad, she couldn't even sleep.

Kira casually switched the topic to Casino. She told Jay she thinking about going out that night, because her son was with him that weekend. After that she said, "Jay, you know ya' man Cas is about to tie the knot again. Don't you think he's moving a little fast?"

Jay laughed, and said, "What? Cas ain't 'bout to tie no knot. Where'd you get that from?" He just shook his head.

Kira said, "Son, I'm tellin' you. Yes he is."

"No he's not", Jay said firmly. "Laila's not even divorced yet." He regretted saying that as soon as it came out of his mouth. He'd forgotten who he was talking to. What the hell was wrong with him?

Just as Jay predicted, Kira made a big deal about that. She said, "What? So how the fuck Cas know that's really his baby."

Jay just sighed. "Oh boy, here we go", he thought.

Always talking slick, she said, "Cas let a bitch trap him like that? That nigga ain't as smart as I gave him credit for."

Jay knew it hadn't gone down like that, but he didn't even

bother to explain. Kira would just twist everything he said around. He just wanted out of that conversation. He didn't even want to get into all of that. He'd already said too much. Jay made up a quick excuse to get off the phone.

After Jay hung up, Kira just sat there holding the phone for a second. She couldn't fucking believe it. Her intentions were to be nosy, but she had no idea Laila was still married. That bastard Cas had broke his neck to divorce her, and the bitch he left her for wasn't even divorced yet. Kira wished she hadn't even signed the papers. She should've held out for more. She should've taken him for everything he had.

Kira was salty. She was mad at Cas, and everyone who had advised her to sign those divorce papers. Jay, her sister Laurie, and even her mother had all said, "Just go ahead and sign the papers, girl." They all thought her ten million dollar settlement was beyond fair.

Kira couldn't front, Cas had made sure she and Jahseim were alright. She got the house, and way more money than she needed. And he put even more in a trust for their son. But she still felt cheated. She wanted revenge.

When Cas brought Jahseim home that Sunday evening, Kira opened the door and hugged her son tightly. She missed her little prince. She kissed him on the forehead, and rubbed his head affectionately, and then she told him she had a surprise for him. She told Jahseim to go on inside and put away his things. Her son was her sunshine. She didn't know what she'd do without him in her life.

Jahseim was grinning at Kira like he missed her too. He and his mother were close.

Cas couldn't help but smile at the display of affection between his son and baby mother. He kissed his son on the forehead, and told him he would see him the following weekend. He watched his little man go inside, and he turned back around to Kira. She was no longer smiling. Now she had this constipated look on her face. He wondered what she was uptight about now.

Kira made sure Jahseim went upstairs, and then she screwed up her face at Cas. She told him he was pitiful for messing around with a married woman like that. She told him he was absolutely no type of role model for her son. She said she wondered how he could teach Jahseim to be a respectable man if he was living like that. She hinted that she should keep him away from him for a while, since his ethics were questionable.

Cas addressed Kira's little indirect threat immediately, before she could even finish talking. They weren't about to start playing those type of games. How dare she even insinuate some shit like that? The thought of her trying to keep his son away from him angered Cas so much, he didn't even care how his next words came out.

"Yo, let me stop you right there. You'll float in the fuckin' river before I let you keep my son away from me. I really hope you understand that."

Kira just looked at him for a second. He hadn't yelled at her. Cas never raised his voice to get his point across. But there was no doubt in her mind he meant what he said. She didn't read any remorse in his face either. He kept it real icy. And he didn't even try to soften up his words. She thought about coming back with a counter threat, but she fell back.

Kira knew when to back off. She didn't say anything, but inside she was having a pity party for herself. She knew Cas loved his son, but damn. How could he threaten her life like that? He really didn't love her anymore. Would he really fucking kill her? How could he even say that? Did he hate her that much?

Kira didn't stop to think that she was making Cas hate her. She was being a total bitch. Perhaps she wanted him to hate her as much as she hated him for leaving her. That shit was crazy. They had a real love/hate thing for real. She still loved him, but she also hated that mothafucka for what he did to her.

Kira was emotional, and a bit selfish in that she forgot about the fact that she had cheated on Cas first, with the rapper Young Vee. And she had flaunted it in Cas' face by flirting with Vee in public. But now she made herself the victim, like she was a battered spouse.

Cas didn't say another word. He just broke out. Just like that.

Kira just stood there, and she broke down in tears. She hated

Casino. She wanted him to pay for the way she was hurting. She wanted him to feel double her pain. She was a woman scorned, and she wanted that bastard to feel her fury.

The following day, Kira was still heated. She was appalled that Cas loved Laila enough to treat her that way, so she put on her thinking cap, and tried to devise a foolproof plan.

That afternoon, Kira dropped her son off at her sister, Laurie's house, so she could put her plan into effect. Her next stop was Avis Car Rentals, to pick up the rental she had reserved. She wanted an inconspicuous looking vehicle, so she chose a black Toyota Camry with little chrome on it.

Kira usually drove her pink Porsche, her red BMW 750, or the silver Aston Martin V8 Vantage she copped with part of her divorce settlement, so she knew there was no way anyone would suspect she was driving a Camry. That just wasn't her style.

The windows were tinted, but her gut told her she should still put on the disguise she brought along. Before she drove off the lot, she opened her Chloe bag, and pulled out a stylish auburn streaked wig, and a pair of dark charcoal tinted Chanel shades. Kira fixed her wig in the mirror, and she chuckled at herself. She had to admit though, she didn't look bad.

She sat there until she dialed her brother on the phone. When Jay answered, he sounded a little under the weather. Kira asked how he was doing, and he said he wasn't feeling so great at the moment. He said his stomach had been upset all day, and he had the bubble gut. Kira told him that was way too much information, and called him a "stankin' booty ass lil' boy". Jay just laughed.

Kira casually threw in an inquiry about Cas, and her brother informed her that he was over at his place. If Jay had the runs, she knew Cas would more than likely be traveling solo. That would be a big plus for her.

Kira drove right over there, and she late waited Cas at the end of Jay's road for about an hour. When she saw Casino coming out of Jay's long, winding driveway, she waited a few seconds, and then she started up her car, and followed him. She was careful to keep a safe distance behind, because she knew Cas was always on point. She prayed he wouldn't notice her tailing him.

Kira followed her ex-husband around for the remainder of the day. After Cas left Jay's house, he went to the City. First he stopped at Street Life's headquarters, and then he left his office, and headed to another tall skyscraper in Manhattan. After that, he went to a seafood restaurant. Kira realized it was dinnertime.

She got curious, and went inside to see who Cas was dining with. She walked right pass him, but Cas didn't recognize her. The wig, shades, and Oscar de la Renta trench coat she had on had served their purpose.

To Kira's surprise, he was eating alone, and talking business on his cell phone the whole time. She took advantage of the free time, and ordered herself a seafood salad to go. She'd been so busy following Cas, she hadn't eaten all day.

When he was done eating, Casino's next stop was the radio station, Hot 97. She figured he was probably going to drop off some new music, and do some promoting for the new clothing label he and Jay had in the works. Kira was pretty sure he had her new single with him. She expected to hear it bumping on the radio soon, probably by the following day.

When Cas came out of Hot 97, he went back to his office for a few hours. At around ten o'clock that night, he headed back to Jersey. Kira was two cars behind him. After they went through the Lincoln Tunnel and came out in New Jersey, she stayed close on him. She was glad he was driving a Lamborghini, because she could single out his taillights in the night traffic.

Cas' last stop was a house Kira didn't recognize. From the way he parked in the driveway, she had the feeling he would be staying there for a while. The house was pretty nice. That sure didn't look like the condo he was supposed to be living in. That had to be where his bitch Laila, and his bastard child lived.

Kira sat outside in her rental, and waited for three hours. She had to see if he was coming back out, and going home. At close to two AM, the lights in the windows went out. Cas was obviously spending the night. Or did he live there?

Kira blurted out, "Oh hell to the no!" She was so angry, she started to march across the street and bang on that damn door. She couldn't believe him. She hated Casino. He was a foul ass dude.

She took a deep breath, because the pain in her chest spread up to her throat. Kira reminded herself that she and Cas were divorced now, so she had no grounds. She finally decided to take her behind home. But she would not take that shit lying down.

She drove off, and headed for her house. She had better things to do with her time than follow that scheming motha-fucka Cas around. She would be back, and next time it wouldn't be a friendly visit either. On her way home, Kira flirted with the idea of getting revenge.

Needless to say, she spent the remainder of the week in a heavy fog. Seeing Cas go home to Laila with her own two eyes had put a new perspective on things for her. Laila had officially won, and that was a hard pill to swallow. Kira wouldn't admit it to anyone, but she stayed up all night long crying, and she'd been drinking heavily as well.

But during her downtime, she had concocted some twisted ideas to get Cas back. She just had to wait until the time was right.

$$\$\$\$\$\$$$

That weekend was Cas' turn with his son. On Friday, he went and picked Jahseim up as usual.

After Cas and her son left, Kira decided to make her move. She knew Cas stayed at his place when their son was with him. To her knowledge, he never took Jahseim over Laila's house. So Kira knew that was a good time to strike. She spent the day drinking, and convincing herself that what she planned to do was justifiable.

Later that night, when she had pumped herself up, Kira dressed in a black Roberto Cavalli tee-shirt, and black Cavalli skinny jeans, and then she slipped on her black Chanel sneakers. After she was dressed, she glanced in the mirror and chuckled. She was drunk, but she noted what a stylish, and smooth criminal she made.

She still had the black Toyota Camry she'd rented. She had carefully parked it behind the house, so Cas wouldn't see it in the garage when he came over. Kira stuck a book of matches in her left pocket, and she went outside and loaded the trunk with a red five gallon can of gasoline, that was usually reserved for the riding lawnmower the landscaper used to cut the grass on her estate.

She got in the car, and started her up, and she drove over to the house Cas' new family resided in. That bitch Laila thought she had won, but Kira would see about that. The fat lady hadn't sung yet.

On the way there, she told herself the action she was about to take was necessary. That bitch Laila had fucked up her whole world. Her life would be better if she wasn't around. As far as Kira was concerned, that town wasn't big enough for both of them.

And how dare Cas move that bitch so close to her. Their houses were only about twenty miles apart. Kira sipped on another shot of expensive tequila, and drove on. The alcohol only made her mission clearer. Her motive made complete sense to her. That bitch Laila was her opponent, and her goal was to destroy her.

When Kira got to the house, she parked a few houses down, on the side of the road. She looked up at the windows of the houses up and down the street, and most of the lights were out. That was a sign that most folks were asleep.

She popped the trunk, and got out the car as quietly as she could, careful not to slam the car door. She took the gas can out of the trunk, and softly closed it, and then she crept over to Laila's.

Kira tiptoed around to the back of the house. She prayed there were no dogs on the premises. She hadn't really thought about that one. Lucky for her, she made it back there without any canine encounters. She figured there was less of a chance of being seen at the back of the house, so she opted to start the fire back there.

Kira walked up to the house, and opened the gas can. She

poured gasoline around the base of the house, and then tossed a good bit on the back door. That property was a symbol of direct disrespect, so she wanted it to burn.

Kira got a little theatrical. She struck a match, and said, "Hast la vista, mothafuckas." She dropped the burning match, and the fuel lit ablaze.

"Good riddance", she said. When that house burned down, she would be rid of all the bad memories. Fuck Cas, his bitch, and that baby!

Kira was fucked up, but those shooting flames began to sober her up. She'd obviously been unaware of the seriousness of her actions. She just torched a home in the middle of the night, when all of the occupants were probably asleep. There was a possibility she might really kill somebody.

Kira panicked, and grabbed the gas can. She thought about ringing the doorbell to alert Laila about the fire, but she would incriminate herself that way. Kira just ran to her car. She looked back at the fire. It was spreading a lot faster than she had anticipated. She felt bad now. God had changed her heart, but it was too late for second thoughts.

She quickly jumped in her car, and threw the gas can right in the backseat. Before she drove off, she dialed 911, and reported the blaze to the fire department. Kira pretended to be a concerned passerby, and remained anonymous. After she called for help, she felt better about leaving the scene.

Kira put the car in drive, and when she pulled off, gasoline spilled all over everything. "Damn", she cursed aloud. In her haste, she'd forgotten to close the gas can. Now everything smelled like gas. If the police were to stop her, she'd be in a world of trouble. It wouldn't be hard to tie her to the crime at all. She had to figure out a way to get that gasoline out of that rental before she took it back. Kira said a quick prayer, and she sped home as cautiously as she could.

$$\$\$\$\$\$$

A few hours earlier, Laila had spoken to Cas on the phone, and said goodnight. He told her him and Jahseim were playing a video game, so they didn't talk long. Macy was spending the night at her girlfriend's house, and the baby was asleep, so Laila told Cas she was going to get some rest. Sometimes the baby woke up in the middle of the night, and she didn't want to be cranky.

Laila told Cas she and Skye were fine, and there was no need for him to check on them again that night. She told him she would speak to him in the morning. She didn't like to interfere with Cas' time with his son. After they hung up, she looked over at her little sleeping beauty to make sure she was breathing okay.

Satisfied that Skye was fine, she laid back on her pillow, and drifted off to sleep. Laila was so tired because she had spent long hours with her physical therapy team earlier that day. That's why she fell out so quick.

At three a.m. when the fire started, Laila was in a deep sleep. She heard the smoke alarm going off, and thought she was dreaming. She yawned and stretched, and lazily opened her eyes.

Oh shit, she smelled smoke! She sat up quickly, and realized the house was on fire. Laila panicked, and grabbed her cell phone from the nightstand, and pressed 2. She had Cas on speed dial, ironically, in case of an emergency.

What the hell was she doing? She knew Cas couldn't get there fast enough to help her. Laila sat there afraid for about two seconds, and then she had a flashback from the car accident she had, that left her paralyzed. She remembered being trapped upside down in her burning Lexus. Those flames were so hot, at the time she hadn't been sure if she was going to make it.

Realization dawned on Laila, and jolted her. Time wasn't on her side! She got up, and got in her wheelchair as fast as she could. Her cell phone fell on the floor, and she didn't bother trying to pick it up. She had to move! Immediately! She wasn't about to get burned up in no damn fire. She'd cheated death before, and she wasn't dying this time either. She had children to live for.

The baby was still asleep in her crib, right next to Laila's bed. She quickly wrapped Skye up in her blanket. Lord, she had to get her baby out of there. She was more concerned with saving Skye's life than hers. Laila just wanted to get downstairs. They had to get out of there. She could only move so fast, so every second mattered.

In her haste, Laila completely forgot she had called Cas. When his phone rang, it was after three AM. He looked at the caller ID, and saw that it was Laila. He said hello, but he didn't get a response. Cas knew something had to be wrong. He jumped up out of bed, and he dialed 911 while he got dressed.

When Cas stepped in his jeans, it occurred to him that his boy was asleep in the next room. He couldn't leave his son alone. He ran in Jahseim's bedroom, and quickly got him up. He told Jahseim to get dressed fast. Afterwards, they both hurried to the car. Jahseim didn't ask any questions. He had sense enough to know that whatever they were rushing for at that time of night had to be real important.

When they were both safely strapped in their seatbelts, Casino sped off in his Maserati. Less than three minutes had passed since Laila called. Along the way, he prayed everything was okay.

$$$$$

A few miles away, Laila was desperately pioneering her escape. She was praying for the safety of her child the entire time. She thought about the way she had regretted being pregnant, and having Skye, and how she'd refused to look at her, or hold her when she was first born. The thought made her feel so bad, she started praying out loud. "God, I am so sorry. Please don't let anything happen to my baby! Get us outta this house safe, Lord! Please!"

Laila managed to get to the electric chair lift, and they made it downstairs. It was darker, and smokier down there. Laila looked over and saw flames shooting through the kitchen. She was horrified. The whole back of the house was ablaze, and the fire was spreading quickly.

Laila held her baby close to her, and headed for the front door. She had that electric wheelchair on high-speed, moving as quickly as she could. All she could think about was her baby's lungs filling up with that deadly smoke. She could barely breathe herself. And she couldn't see either. Her eyes were burning bad as hell from all that thick black smoke.

Skye was hollering at the top of her lungs. Poor baby. She didn't know what was going on, but Laila took her crying to be a good sign. That meant she was still breathing. Laila looked back, and saw the blaze coming toward them fast. It was like something in a movie. Her living room was fifty by eighty square feet big, and Laila thought she knew every inch of it. But under those conditions, she felt like a total stranger in there. Lord, she was getting faint. They had to get out of there.

Laila thought it was her imagination when she felt her wheelchair slowdown a little, but then it came to an abrupt stop. She was so scared, she damn near had a heart attack. All that smoke in the house must've caused some type of malfunction in the operating board.

Laila panicked. Dear God, she had to make it over to the door. There was still about fifteen more feet to go. The average person could have easily sprinted to the front door and been home free, but Laila couldn't walk, so she was caught in a life or death situation. She had never been so scared in her whole life. It was so hot in there, and she couldn't see. Would she and her baby get burned up beyond recognition? Were they about to die?

Laila prayed for strength from God, and she decided if they had to go, she would die trying. Suddenly, she didn't hear her baby crying anymore. That was the factor that motivated her to dive out of that wheelchair. When Laila hit the floor, she held Skye in one arm, and used the other to drag them across the floor. The task was grueling. It required so much effort, she groaned, but God gave Laila the strength.

The natural reaction of trying to escape death caused Laila to unconsciously attempt to crawl. A second later, she could've sworn she felt some twitching in her knees. Then it got stronger. Dear God, she could feel her legs!

Laila was able to crawl a little bit, and that helped her get to

the door a lot quicker. She didn't even stop to think of what
an accomplishment she had just made. She didn't have time.
She had to save her baby.

Laila made it to the door, and kneeled at the foot of the door
panting. It wasn't over yet. She still had to make it outside.
She reached up, and unlocked the door. With what felt like the
last breath she had in her body, she turned the knob, and
crawled out of that burning house to her and her child's safety.

Laila was grateful to God they'd escaped, but it took so much
out of her, she laid there panting for a second. But she couldn't
rest yet. She was too worried about her baby. She rolled over
to see about Skye.

Laila hit the baby on the back two times, and she started hollering again. Laila breathed a heavy sigh of relief. God was so
good. She was thankful, but exhausted beyond her imagination. She was on the verge of passing out right there on the
front steps, but her baby crying in the crook of her arm kept
her mindful.

That fire was moving like crazy. Now the flames had reached
the top floor as well. Unbeknownst to Laila, when she opened
the front door, the oxygen in the air she let in gave the fire more
fuel. It was burning out of control.

Just then, Cas pulled up. When he saw the fire, his heart fell.
He prayed his girl and baby were okay, and he told Jahseim to
stay in the car. Cas jumped out, and ran to the house. He
couldn't believe it was just burning like that.

Cas could see the flames shooting through the house. He
thought Laila and Skye were in there, so he was willing to put
his life on the line to rescue them. He had to get them out of
there.

As soon as he climbed the steps to run in the house, he saw
Laila and the baby sprawled out on the concrete. When their
eyes met, he would never forget the look she gave him. Cas had
never felt so needed. He scooped both of them up in his arms,
and quickly raced away from the house.

Cas was met by a small swarm of concerned neighbors, who
had come out to be of assistance. Two ladies assured him that
help was on the way, and someone produced a blanket. He put

Laila and the baby down on the lawn, and wrapped it around them.

Laila looked weak. Cas prayed her and Skye were okay. He hoped they hadn't inhaled too much smoke. Smoke could be deadlier than fire. He wondered if they needed mouth to mouth resuscitation, or something? Casino proceeded to check their vitals. He had taken a CPR class before, so he knew what he was doing.

Just then, he heard loud sirens. The fire department had arrived. A neighbor ran over and summoned the EMT, and told them about Laila and the baby, and they moved quickly to assist them. The firefighters moved quickly to put out the blaze too.

Laila and Skye were whisked away in an ambulance. Cas thanked the neighbors, and then he jumped in his car, and he and Jahseim followed the ambulance. He left the fire department to battle the fire on their own. He would find out the details later. At the time, he didn't care about the house. Not as much as he cared about making sure his family was alright.

CHAPTER TWENTY

After Kira torched Laila's house, the days that followed, she was extremely paranoid. She kept on imagining the police knocking at her door, and arresting her for setting that house on fire. She had learned from her brother that Laila and the baby were okay. Jahseim had updated her as well.

Kira would never forget the way her son had informed her about Cas' baby being involved in the fire. When Cas had dropped him off, he rushed in the house and said, "Mommy! My little sister almost got killed in a big fire. But thank God, she's okay."

When Kira had heard those words come from his mouth, she felt even more horrible. She had been so immature, she hadn't even thought about it that way. That baby was her son's sister.

Now that it was over, she was glad Laila and the baby were okay. Kira knew she made a stupid decision, and she was sorry. Talk about "sour grapes". She'd heard the house was burned up pretty bad. Damn, she really played herself. She just hoped everything would blow over, and get back to normal. She had an album to record, and so far she only had about two singles done.

Jay had made a comment about Kira bullshitting around, and she knew he was right. She had been busy focusing on a way to break up Cas and Laila, and she had only wasted her damn time. Jay mentioned that Laila and her kids were staying with him and Portia for a little while. Kira knew that, the type of guy Cas was, he would relocate her fast. So her burning that house down was really pointless.

Kira's conscience was eating at her so much, she decided to get low for a few days. She called and arranged a quick Caribbean getaway. She lied to Jay and her mother, and told them she was going away so she could do some writing for her album.

Kira left Jahseim with her mom, and she lied about where she was going for some reason. She told everyone she was going to Jamaica, but she booked a villa in the Turks and Caicos Islands for a week. She had to get her mind right.

Kira knew she hadn't done all she could've to make sure they couldn't trace her to that house burning. If they came to question her, she didn't even have an alibi. If she could have turned back time, she would have done things a lot smarter. Hell, she wouldn't have even gone through with it.

$$\$\$\$\$\$$$

After Laila's house burned down, her, Macy, and the baby went to stay with Portia and Jay for while. Just about everything in the house was destroyed by smoke, or fire damage. Miraculously, they were able to salvage the lovely, huge painting Jay had given her of her dearly departed daughter, Pebbles, portrayed as an angel. The painting needed to be cleaned, and reframed, but it was intact.

A few days later, the fire department closed their investigation of the incident. They ruled arson as the cause of the fire. They said a flammable substance, gasoline in that case, had been poured around the base on the rear of the house, and lit afire.

When they discovered that crime was involved, they updated the police. The fire chief assured Cas and Laila that they would work closely with the police department, to make sure whoever was responsible would be caught.

When they were informed that someone had set the fire, Cas and Laila were equally shocked. They both wondered who could've done such a thing. Cas didn't say anything, but he planed to make the culprit pay. Who the fuck would set the house on fire? And in the middle of the night? They could've killed Laila, and his baby.

Laila was even more aghast than Casino, because it was her who was actually inside the house when it happened. Her, and her baby. Laila thought about Khalil, but to her knowledge, he didn't know where she lived.

Cas didn't say anything, but he thought about Kira. But as far as he knew, she didn't know where Laila's house was either.

Cas and Laila talked about it, and he asked her if she wanted to have her house rebuilt, or move to a new location. She told him she was leaning towards moving. It didn't sit well with her that someone had done that intentionally. She wouldn't feel safe there anymore. She hinted about moving back to her house in Brooklyn, so she wouldn't be a bother.

When Laila said that, Cas made a mental note to have his mother start searching for a mansion to put her and the kids in. As matter of fact, he needed his moms to find somewhere for "them" and the kids to live. Enough of the games. They were moving in together officially this time.

They had only been hesitant because that nigga Khalil didn't want to give Laila a divorce. Cas decided to go speak to that chump. If he had been there with Laila that night, he could've protected her. They were all moving somewhere safe now.

Cas didn't know about Kira's plan to break him and Laila up yet, but it had only backfired. Now he was too worried to leave Laila alone. He promised her that he would have her relocated in a new house, as soon as humanly possible.

Cas wanted to do it right. As far as he was concerned, his son was the only person he needed approval from. The only reason he hadn't been at home with Laila that night was because he hadn't been real with his son yet, and told him Laila was his wifey. Jahseim was a mature little dude. He'd questioned Cas in the car the night of the fire, but he just ducked most of his questions. He owed his son an explanation.

Jay told Cas that Jahseim was staying at Mama Mitchell's for a few days. He said his sister had gone out of town for a few days. According to Jay, Kira was in Jamaica "writing".

That was good news. Cas wanted her to get that album done too. Even if they were on the outs personally. She was a Street Life artist, so they still had a business relationship. Time was money, and there was a lot riding on it.

That evening, Casino went and had a man to man talk with his son. Cas aired everything out. He explained to Jahseim that he and Laila were a couple now, and would be living together soon in the new house he was shopping for. Jah actually thought that was a good idea. He said that way Cas could watch the baby better. He said he didn't want anyone else to try to kill his sister.

Cas hugged him tight, and told him not to worry. He assured him that he wouldn't allow anything to happen to any of his babies, including him, ever again. Jahseim made a little face. He didn't like to be called a baby.

Cas laughed, and told him that he would have his own bedroom in the new house. And a game room, and everything else he wanted. He was so proud of him. He had so much sense. He was only eight years old, but he was a smart little dude.

$$\$\$\$\$\$$

When Portia and Jay learned about the fire, they opened up their home to Laila and her family immediately. It worked out good, because they still had the equipment they had installed when Laila was staying with them, when she first came home from the hospital. Portia did her best to make sure Laila and her girls were comfortable during their stay.

Once again, Laila was grateful to have such a great best friend. She and Portia had been through a lot, but girlfriend was definitely real. Now, Fatima was a different story. She didn't know what was up with that chick lately. Laila just hadn't heard from her. She knew for a fact that Portia had called Fatima, and told her about her house burning down. Laila didn't expect her to do anything about it, but a kind word or two would've sufficed. They were supposed to be girls.

Now that Laila was staying with her, Portia had started leaking information. She claimed she hadn't said anything before because she hadn't wanted Laila to be worrying about Fatima's crazy ass. Now she admitted Fatima was fucking around with some heavy narcotics.

When Laila heard that, everything made sense. Fatima certainly hadn't been herself lately. Now she knew why she'd been acting funny. Laila's first reaction was to want to help her friend.

Portia told Laila she'd done just about everything there was to get Fatima some help, but homegirl was content to wallow in her misery. Laila asked Portia to come with her to Fatima's house the next day. She had to try to talk some sense into her.

Portia tried calling Fatima again, and this timed she actually picked up. She sounded liked she was drunk. To Portia's surprise, she agreed to meet them for lunch the following day. She just hoped Fatima remembered.

Laila smiled at the news about Fatima meeting them the next day. Her and her girls hadn't been in touch like they used to. They went back too far for that. They had been each other's strength in the past, and they should continue to do so. If Fatima was weak, they had to be her rock.

Laila was experiencing sort of a renewed sense of faith, so she was feeling positive about life. God was working for her. He had shone his mercy on her, and she was blessed. Laila had a little secret.

That fire in her house was ill-timed, and luckily, no one was seriously hurt. But ironically, there was actually cause for celebration. Laila was on the road to walking again. As her doctor had explained, sometimes it took one trauma to undo another.

At the time of crisis, her nerves had reacted to her fear, and allowed her to crawl. The doctor had used some type of fancy medical terminology, but Laila preferred to call it an act of God. Now she could take a few steps, with the help of a walker. According to her therapists, she was making great progress.

Laila had kept her accomplishment a secret from Cas, and all her friends so far. She didn't want anyone to know yet, because she didn't want their expectations of her to be so high. She still had some inerasable doubts in the back of her mind. But her faith was stronger.

$$\$\$\$\$\$$

Those fire investigators were on point. They called Laila the next morning, and informed her that they had discovered footprints that came from a women's size nine Chanel sneaker. They asked if the footprints belonged to her, or anyone she knew. Laila told them she hadn't had any company lately, and she was wheelchair bound, and unable to walk around her property freely, so the footprints didn't belong to her. Besides, she wore a size seven. And so did Macy.

Laila had a bad feeling about who it was, but she played dumb to the investigator, and didn't volunteer any information. They were the authorities. It was their job to solve the crime, not hers.

When they hung up, Laila called Cas, and told him what the investigator had said about the footprint discovery. Casino didn't comment, but he knew Kira wore a size nine. And Chanel was one of her favorite designers.

He knew damn well Kira didn't do no shit like that. Was she crazy? Before he reacted, he decided to go talk to Jay in person. Cas told Laila he would see her in a little while. When he hung up, he grabbed his car keys, and headed for Jay's crib.

About ten minutes later, he rang the bell. Jay was surprised to see Cas so early in the morning, but he didn't question him. He just opened the door, and let him in. Cas gave him a pound, and then he gave him the news about the sneaker prints found at the crime scene.

At first, Jay didn't say anything. He was sort of in denial. He didn't think his sister would do something like that. And Kira wasn't the only chick in the world with size nine feet. Portia wore a size nine also, and she had Chanel sneakers too. He voiced his reasoning aloud to Cas.

Cas was a pretty logical person, so he agreed with Jay that there was a chance that Kira wasn't guilty. But he suggested Jay talk to his little siste,r and find out what was what.

Jay agreed that a sit-down with Kira was in order. He didn't say anything yet, but if she did do it, maybe they could deal with it in-house some sort of way. Arson was a serous crime. That shit could put Kira's ass away for a while. She was still in Jamaica, and due to return any day now. Jay wanted to be the first person she spoke to when she got back.

Unfortunately, the crime had already been solved. The following Tuesday, when Kira got back home, they already had a warrant for her arrest. She was picked up that same afternoon for questioning.

Kira was apparently one of America's dumbest criminals. She had done so many things wrong, all of the evidence pointed back to her. They even knew about the rental car she had used.

Kira was thoroughly interrogated, but she didn't panic, and talk. She was scared to death, but she told the police she wanted to see her lawyer first. She demanded the phone call she knew she was entitled to, and she got in touch with her brother. She knew Jay would get her an attorney down there immediately.

When Jay got the call from his little sister saying she was in jail, he told her to sit tight, and keep her mouth shut, and he'd be right down there. Jay called Cas, and told him Kira had been arrested. He asked him to keep it on the hush.

Cas told him he didn't even have to ask him that. He sounded like he really felt bad about it. He agreed that the first thing Kira needed was a lawyer. Cas told Jay to keep him posted when he got down there.

Jay called their lawyer, Solly, and he found Kira the right attorney in minutes. After that, Jay told Portia what happened. As soon as she heard, she got ready to go down to the precinct with him.

A few hours later, they managed to spring Kira on $100,000 bail. Jay didn't press Kira for any answers in front of Portia, because he knew she'd clam up. He dropped Portia off at the house, and told her he was taking his sister home. Portia didn't object. Them two needed to talk.

Portia had to hold her tongue the whole ride. She'd started to tell Kira how much she didn't appreciate the immature, life threatening stunt she'd pulled. Laila and Skye were like her sister and niece, and she could've killed them.

Kira was Jay's sister, so Portia would let him deal with her. She knew Jay disapproved of what she had done just as much as she did.

On the way to Kira's house, Jay told her she'd better start talking, or he was leaving her on stuck. He had to know exactly what they were up against.

Kira was quiet for a minute, but she knew there was no point in lying to her brother about anything. He was one of the only people in the world she could trust to make sure she was okay.

She opened up, and told Jay how she had rented a car and followed Cas, and then witnessed him going home to that house he'd bought for Laila. She told Jay she was so hurt and jealous, she got drunk, and decided to torch it. Kira told Jay how she'd had second thoughts, and called 911 before she'd left the scene.

The police were using that as evidence against her too. The first 911 call had come from her cell phone. She had really trapped herself off.

Kira realized the seriousness of the situation. She could get a lot of time. She really regretted doing what she did. She begged Jay to talk to Cas, and have Portia try to talk to Laila. She wanted her to know how sorry she was. She said she was even prepared to pay Laila, if there was a way she could avoid jail time. She told Jay she couldn't do a bid. She had her career, and she had to raise her son.

When Kira mentioned her son, Jay told her she could've been responsible for the deaths of a mother and her baby. She dropped her head when he said that, and took a moment to respond.

Kira said, "Yo, son, I'm really sorry. Damn."

Jay told his sister she'd better do some serious praying. He could tell she was shook up and scared, so he didn't lecture her too bad. He would leave that up to their mother. He hadn't told her yet, because he didn't like his mother worrying. But he was going to make sure she knew how crazy her daughter was. Maybe their moms could talk some sense into her. Kira had done something real stupid, and she could throw away her whole career behind it.

When Jay got back home, he talked to Cas and Portia about the proposition Kira had made. She was willing to pay her way out of trouble, if she could.

Cas had already decided he would talk to Laila, and see what she wanted to do. Kira was stupid, but she was his son's mother. He didn't really want to see her in jail, if he could help it. And she was his artist as well. He hated what had happened, but he wasn't going to be the one to pressure Laila into anything. Portia was the person to talk to her about something like that. Coming from him, it would seem coerced.

That night, Portia spoke to her friend, and surprisingly, Laila said she was willing to accept a payoff. She said she didn't really want Kira's son to be motherless, while she did time. But she said the offer better be worth it, because Kira could've killed her.

Jay informed Kira's lawyer that Laila didn't want to press charges, so he took that to the D.A. The D.A. wanted to play hard-nosed. She refused to drop the charges that the state had against Kira. She wanted to make an example out of her, so the next person wouldn't think about doing anything like that. And the fact that Kira was a well-known rapper made it worse. She had it in for celebrities.

As hard as Jay and Cas had worked to keep everything under wraps, the story was leaked to the press, and Street Life Entertainment's name was in headlines again. The story was portrayed in many ways. One newspaper's headline read, "Rap Diva Kira Makes It HOT". It was more negative press, but the controversy it stirred up contributed to record sales nonetheless.

The gossip pushed Kira's single to popularity, and it was number one on the charts before they knew it. But that increased the district attorney's unwillingness to give her a break even more. She said she was tired of rappers and celebrities thinking they were above the law.

Another factor in the case was the insurance company. They were reluctant to pay to repair of the damage on the house, so they were pushing for the criminal charges to stick on Kira as well. The insurance company's lawyers had done their homework, and they knew Kira was a rather successful artist, so they wanted her to be liable for the damages.

Jay tried to protect Kira by saying he would pay out of pocket for the repairs. That kept the insurance company from getting further involved. The bad news was that now the D.A. wanted to charge Kira with attempted murder. She said she was going all the way.

Cas couldn't believe Kira had tried to kill Laila, and his baby.

He was so through with her, he felt like kicking her stupid ass. But he still put up money out of his own pocket to try to help keep her out of prison.

He wasn't condoning what she had done, but he didn't want his son to be unhappy. She was lucky she was his son's mother. He would do anything for his son.

Cas didn't want Jahseim's progress to be hindered by his mother's imprisonment. His son was a little man now. He was smart, and he had a lot of sense. He was very proud of his little dude.

Kira acted so stupid. He couldn't stand that broad sometimes. After that fire incident, he didn't know what level she would stoop to. He had been contemplating taking his son, and raising him himself anyway, but he didn't want it to happen like that.

Cas didn't want her dumb ass to go to jail, so he helped her out financially. He knew money got things done. If the right palms were greased, some of those do-good mothafuckas would look the other way. Rich white people did bad stuff, and got away with it all the time.

CHAPTER TWENTY ONE

Jay glanced up at the sky as he exited his office building. It looked like it was about to rain. Street Life headquarters was located right in the heart if the city, so there was never much sun amongst the tall buildings anyway. But that day it was particularly dark. For some reason, the heavy clouds looming around made Jay feel like something was about to happen.

He had been in the city taking care of business all day, and was finally about to be out of there. What a relief. He'd had two meetings that day, with some important people about some significant issues pertaining to Street Life's future operations.

Cas had just called him to find out how things had gone on his end. Jay told him all went well, and told him his assistant should have updated him by now. Cas told him he'd already been emailed a full report, but he wanted to hear it from the horse's mouth. Jay told him he had everything under control.

Jay knew the only reason Casino wasn't there was because he and Laila were in Jersey, looking at a property he was thinking of purchasing. Jay understood the importance of putting family first, so he had no beef with that. He and Cas were partners, so they were supposed to hold each other down. They'd been cronies for almost three decades.

The chauffer opened the door for Jay, and he got in the back of his hired car. He yawned, and stretched. The leather chair was a little cold, so he asked his driver to put the heat on low, and warm up his seat. He was feeling a little tired. He hadn't slept well the past few nights.

That was one of the reasons Jay hadn't drove into the city that day. He didn't have the energy to waste dealing with the traffic. He was just glad he was able to go home. Jay looked over at the fully stocked bar in the back of the limo, and thought about fixing himself a shot of Hennessy. He decided against it, because he hadn't eaten yet.

Jay yawned again. He hadn't been resting like he should. There was a lot going on lately, especially with Kira's pending case, and all. It was still hard for him to believe his baby sister had done something so stupid, and cruel. He really had it up to here with Kira's stunts and tantrums. That one could've cost somebody their life. And she knew there was a baby in that house too. That was the part Jay didn't get. He didn't know what to make of Kira's psychotic antics, but he was about to wash his hands.

It was always something with that girl. But this was by far the most foolish thing she had ever done. He just thanked God that Laila and the baby were okay. She and the kids were still staying with him and Portia, but Cas was relocating them into a new house soon.

As the driver maneuvered through Manhattan, Jay stared out the back window at the busy pedestrians. New Yorkers stayed on the go. For some reason, Ysatis crossed his mind. He wondered how she was doing. He thought about giving her a call. He hadn't checked on that girl in about a month, he felt a little bad about that. Jay dialed her number, and she picked up on the third ring.

It had been more than four weeks since Ysatis had heard from Jay last. Ironically, she was almost at her breaking point, and about to call him anyway. She was thrilled that he finally called to check on her. Ysatis thanked her lucky stars, but she played it super cool, and gave him the impression that she had other things going on. She actually even switched over to the other line, and kept him on hold for a whole minute. Jay waited patiently until she switched back over, and then she told him she was sorry, but she'd been talking to her "boyfriend" on the other line when he beeped in.

Jay was relieved that Ysatis seemed to be over that school girl crush she had on him. That eased his guilty conscience about not checking on her. He was glad she seemed okay. He thought of Ysatis sort of like a little sister, and he was genuinely concerned about her wellbeing.

Even though Jay hadn't been in touch, he'd still been looking out for her. He had set her up in a nice crib, and was still paying for her education, so it wasn't like he just left her for dead. Ysatis was just a kid to him, and she didn't have anybody.

Jay's stomach started growling, and that was a clear indication to him that he needed sustenance. He asked Ysatis if she had eaten yet. She said she was sort of hungry, so Jay told her he would pick her up in a few minutes. He told her he'd call her when he got downstairs, and he hung up.

Jay directed his driver to her address. He didn't see any harm in grabbing a bite to eat. Ysatis was a good girl. She had just gotten a little confused that day. Jay was just glad that shit was behind them.

When he pulled up outside, he called Ysatis, and told her to come on out.

After Ysatis hung up, she grabbed a jacket, and hurried on down to Jay. When she got outside, she was a bit surprised to see a limousine waiting for her. The driver opened the door for her, and she got in and sat next to Jay. Ysatis almost melted, but she was so cool he couldn't tell. The driver got back in, and he headed to their destination.

Jay often took a hired car when he visited Manhattan, because parking was so scarce. It was nothing fancy, or out of the ordinary for him. But when Ysatis stepped in that black stretch limo, she was cheesing from ear to ear. Homegirl felt like royalty. She and Jay were both dressed in jeans, but they may as well have been wearing ballroom attire. That evening was more special to Ysatis than the prom she had never attended.

Jay directed his driver to a sports bar in mid-town, called Richie's. It was a popular spot, with mostly Caucasian attendees. He chose Richie's because it wasn't too fancy. He had seen the way Ysatis was grinning in the limo, so he didn't want to give her any more "red carpet" impressions. But they had good food at Richie's too, and he could glimpse at the game as well.

When they got to the sports bar, they were seated in a booth. A minute later, a waitress came and took their order. Ysatis ordered Buffalo wings and mozzarella sticks, and Jay decided on a grilled chicken Caesar salad. They also ordered two drinks.

Ciroc on the rocks, and a margarita.

While they waited on their food, they chitchatted about the election, amongst other things. Ysatis told Jay she was a volunteer for the Barack Obama democratic campaign. Jay thought that was great. He and his man, Cas, had donated a lot of money to the cause, because it was certainly positive.

It would be enormous to have a young, black president. Especially one as cool as Senator Obama. Jay really liked what that dude stood for. With the economy in such dire straits, the country was in need of change. Senator Obama definitely had his vote.

Their food and drinks came, and they continued their discussion. The conversation was pretty interesting. Jay loved to talk politics, so he pointed out some key issues he disagreed with Obama's opponent, John McCain on, and ordered them another round. Ysatis was only halfway through her first margarita, but he was finished his drink, so he didn't want to be rude.

Jay kept up with world news, but he was surprised that Ysatis was up on such important issues at her age. She told him she was so caught up in this election, she'd decided to change her major from journalism, to political science the following semester. She said she would minor in journalism instead. Jay told her that was a good look, if that was her passion.

He and Ysatis hung out for about another hour, and then Jay glanced at his Rolex. It was almost midnight, so it was time for them to be going. He had to get home to his family, and she had a class in the morning. Ysatis begged him to have one more drink with her. Jay gave in, and ordered another round.

About thirty minutes later, they headed outside to the limo. Jay told the driver to drop Ysatis off at home first. Ysatis acted like she could hold her liquor pretty good at the sports bar, but in the car, she admitted she was feeling it.

When they pulled up in front of her building, she asked Jay to walk her upstairs. There was always a doorman on duty at the ritzy high-rise building twenty-four hours, seven days a week, but it wasn't exactly their job to see tipsy tenants to their front door. So Jay got out and went with Ysatis, to make sure she got home safe.

After they got off the elevator, and walked down the hall to her apartment, Ysatis unlocked her door, and asked him to come in. Jay hesitated, but he followed her inside. He had to take a leak. He asked her if she minded if he used her bathroom, and Ysatis told him to go right ahead.

Jay hurried to the bathroom to take a whiz. He shut the door, and unzipped his pants, and proceeded to relieve himself. The next thing he knew, she opened the door, and walked right in on him!

Ysatis placed her hand over her mouth, like she was shocked. She said, "Oh my goodness! Jay, I'm sorry! I'm so fucked up, I forgot you were in here!"

Jay made a face, and said, "Come on, you forgot that fast?" He couldn't believe Ysatis. She was full of shit.

He shook his head at her, and turned away, and tried to urinate with a little privacy. He'd been drinking, so a lot was coming out. He tried to squeeze out the last few drops of urine fast, because she was standing there just staring at his shit.

Ysatis got real bold. She said, "While we're on the subject... " She eyeballed his penis and licked her lips, and then she continued. "Don't we have some unfinished business?" She prayed her seduction would be successful this time.

A warning bell went off in Jay's head. Damn, Hot Mama was at it again. And he couldn't front, her come-on made him nervous. Why did she have to start with that shit? He was done urinating, so he flushed the toilet, and he turned away from her to put his dick away before he addressed her. He was a little tipsy, but he still knew better. It was time to go.

Jay turned back around and faced her, and he found his voice. "Look... You need to get ready for school in the morning. Goodnight, Ysatis." He started to walk right pass her.

Ysatis stood her ground. She couldn't let him leave. She blocked the bathroom doorway, and pleaded with him softly. "No, Jay! Please don't go. I just want you to stay for a little while." She looked him right in the eyes when she said that.

Before Jay could respond, she took off her shirt. She wasn't wearing a bra.

Jay shook his head again. That crazy ass girl was just standing there topless. But to his dismay, his soldier stood up at attention. Jay silently cursed his erection. Damn, what the fuck was wrong with his dick? He played it cool, and pushed her out of the way.

Ysatis looked down and saw the front of his pants rise, and she smiled like she had struck gold. She could see that he was feeling her. It was working. She stepped in closer, and traced her French manicured nails across Jay's chest. With the other hand, she reached in her back pocket, and pulled out a special condom. She held the little black and gold package up, and twirled it around enticingly. She murmured, "We had a good time tonight, Jay. Let's put the icing on the cake."

She wrapped her arms around his neck, and whispered in his ear. "N.S.A. baby. No strings attached. I promise. Just hold me. Please?"

Her tities were so perky. And she kept rubbing them against him. Jay found himself wondering if she had been braless all night. Normally he would've listened to that little voice in the back of his head, but his better judgment was clouded by all that Ciroc vodka he drank. And not to mention lust.

Nah, he couldn't do that. He was married. Jay thought about Portia. He loved her, and would no doubt be with her for the rest of his life. She held him down, and she was a good mother to his children. And Portia had some good pussy too. She kept his sexual appetite well-fed. So what the fuck was he doing?

Ysatis started kissing on his neck, and the devil started talking to Jay. He told him that he was a man, and entitled to a little trim on the side every now and then. It had been a long time since he had sampled something different. Years, actually. He took good care of his family, and he had his shit together. So what harm would a quick nut on the side do? Jay toyed with the idea of beating that real quick before he went home, and his hands unconsciously found Ysatis' tities.

When Jay started rubbing her breasts, she almost yelled out, "Yippee!" The ball was in her court. Ysatis finally exhaled. She stood there for a few seconds, while he massaged her nipples into erect peaks. She ran her hands along Jay's back and shoulders, and caressed him. She wanted him so bad.

Ysatis backed up, and peeled off her Antik Denim jeans. She stepped out of her pants, and stood there in hot pink, lace boylegs.

After he saw those sexy lace panties, all the blood in Jay's brain went south, straight to the veins in his stiff dick. All logic flew out the window. He wanted to fuck her. Right then and there. She had a condom, so it was okay. And it was a Magnum too. That was his favorite brand, when he used to be out there. He could slip in and out of that pussy fast, and protected by a comfortable shield.

Ysatis peeped the appreciative onceover Jay gave her. It looked like it was going down. Damn, now she wanted to please him more than ever. She sank to her knees in front of him.

Jay couldn't resist. Fuck it. He unzipped his pants and freed himself, and she worked on his pipe like a professional plumber. That shit felt good. It crossed his mind that she could have gotten so good by doing mad dudes. Ysatis seemed like a good girl, but he really should've put that rubber on before she gave him that blowjob.

Jay was surprised at himself. He didn't usually play with his health. He was a married man, who shouldn't be taking such chances. He knew he could still mess around and catch something, just by getting his dick sucked.

But damn, Ysatis was going in on that blowjob. She licked Jay's joint like a lollipop, and his breathing got heavier. The head was on point, but now he wanted to beat. He wanted to sample that pussy. Just one time.

He took the condom from Ysatis, and tore it open. He stopped her from pleasuring him, and rolled the Magnum on. It had really been a while since he'd used one of those things. He turned down a lot of pussy.

Jay told himself he could walk away right then, and turn Ysatis down too. If he wanted to. A fraction of him was guilt ridden, but not enough to quit. He decided to just make it quick.

Ysatis stood up. Jay didn't want to look at her face, so he turned her around and bent her over the sink. She arched her back, and spread her legs. She seemed real eager to receive him. Jay held her by the waist, and slid inside her. She cried out softly.

He couldn't even front, that pussy was good. He reached down beneath her, and fondled her breasts. Her nipples were hard, and they stiffened even more under his touch. Damn, her pussy was real wet.

After only about thirty strokes, Jay felt himself about to cum. He knew that was fast, but he wasn't trying to impress Ysatis, or satisfy her. He sped up his rhythm, and let it go. After he came, he pulled out, and caught his breath. That was some real selfish fucking, but he didn't mean any harm. He just didn't want Ysatis to catch feelings, and make the sex out to be more than it was.

After Jay ejaculated, Ysatis smiled to herself. She didn't have an orgasm, but she was satisfied that she'd been able to satisfy him. If that made any sense. She was also satisfied by the sense of accomplishment she felt. If all went well, she and Jay would be seeing a lot more of each other.

Jay flushed the condom, and he reluctantly asked Ysatis if she was okay. He expected her to tell him she wasn't satisfied by his wack ass, one minute sex. But she grinned, and said she was good.

Jay told her he had a good time as well, because it seemed like the right thing to say. He didn't want to make her feel slutted, or cheap, but he had to get going. As far as he was concerned, he had given her what she wanted. He wasn't about to stay there and romance her, or cuddle, so he hoped she wouldn't trip.

When Jay told her he had to get home, Ysatis said she understood. She said she knew what it was, so she wasn't offended that he had to rush off. Not this time. Jay told her to get some rest, and promised to call and check on her the following day. They hugged before he left, and then he made his exit. She just smiled the whole time.

That dreamy eyed smile Ysatis had on her face gave Jay a bad

feeling. As he sat in the back of his limo on the way home, he
leaned his head back and closed his eyes for a minute. A part
of him regretted having sex with Ysatis. He just hoped things
wouldn't get out of hand.

Jay glanced at his Rolex. It was almost two A.M. He hoped
Portia would be asleep by the time he got home. He didn't
even know if he could face her right now.

Meanwhile, Portia was at home still wide awake. In fact, she
was sipping on expensive red wine, listening to slow jams on
the surround sound, and soaking in their marble Jacuzzi. The
water was nice and hot. Portia had also been puffing on a little
weed, so she was pretty mellowed out.

Portia was the only adult in the house at the time, and she
was in total relax mode. Jay wasn't home yet. And Laila had
gone with Cas to look at some houses earlier, and then she had
called a little later to tell Portia she was staying out overnight.
Portia had told her to go ahead, and get some dick. Laila just
laughed, and told her she was silly.

Portia told her girl not to worry about the kids. She didn't
mind babysitting. It wasn't a problem keeping her children anyway, because Macy looked after her little sister, Skye, like she
was hers. Portia didn't even have to bathe her, or change her.
Macy helped out a lot with her little one, Trixie, too.

All of the kids were asleep now, from oldest to youngest.
Macy, Jayquan, Jazmin, Trixie, and Skye. Now Portia was just
waiting on her hubby wubby to come home. Jay was in for a
treat that night. She was horny as hell. Her period had been
on all week, so it had been a few days for both of them.

Portia leaned her head back, and sang along with one of her
favorite soul oldies, by Aretha Franklin. "I'm givin' him something he can feel...To let him know - this love is real..."

Jay got home about a half hour later. Portia smelled good,
felt good from the blunt and wine she had indulged in, and she
was ready to love him good too. She met her man at the front
door. She was looking real sexy. She had her hair pinned up,
and she was wearing a black satin chemise, with no panties, and
black silver studded Dsquared2 stilettos.

Jay loved when she didn't wear any panties, so Portia just knew it was about to be on and popping. But she got the disappointment of her life. Jay acted like he wasn't even interested. Hell, he barely looked at her. He just glimpsed her way when he came through the door, and said, "What up, Ma? I'm surprised you're still up."

After that, he headed straight for the stairs. Jay yawned, and then he looked back over his shoulder. He said, "I'ma take a shower, and go to bed, P. I'm so tired, it's a damn shame."

Portia just stood there in disbelief. The nerve of him. She just stood there for a second, and watched him walk up the stairs. She didn't say anything, but that was sort of a blow to her ego. She was hurt, but more confused. That was the first time Jay had ever turned down an opportunity to have sex with her, since they'd been together. Ever. That was damn near ten years. Could he really be that tired?

Portia gave Jay the benefit of a doubt. He had been a little stretched out lately. He had a lot on his plate. Her husband was a very busy man. And he was human. Nobody wanted to have sex all the time. And then there was the possibility of the federal investigation he and Cas had been given a hands up on coming down on Street Life at any time, so he had to be a little stressed.

But then again, Jay used sex to combat his stress. She knew that much about him. Portia's woman's intuition told her something was up. She knew her man. There was just something about the way he'd acted. And he wouldn't really look at her. And she was looking real good. What was that about? Her gut told her Jay had been out fucking around.

When the reality of the situation hit Portia, she became enraged. And then she felt sick. Had that mothafucka gone upstairs to shower off another woman's scent? Had he violated her like that?

Portia took a deep breath, and got her shit together. Determined to get to the bottom of things, she marched upstairs to question Mr. Mitchell about his whereabouts that evening.

Jay didn't dig the third degree Portia gave him when he got out the shower, but he answered her questions just to ease her mind. He obviously couldn't tell the truth about where he had just come from, so he made up something and told her she was bugging. Then he slipped on his boxers, and a pair of pajama pants, and got in the bed.

Portia wasn't an idiot. Jay had this snappiness in his tone, and she knew that was just a sign of guilt. She'd never gotten that from him, but she'd seen that same attitude from dudes she was involved with in the past, when she caught them cheating on her. Unexplainable defensive behavior.

The last words Jay said to her that night were, "Look, Ma, I got a real bad headache, and I don't feel like talkin'. I'll see you in the morning. Good night, P. Love you." After that, he closed his eyes.

Jay pretended to fall asleep immediately, but he really just laid there with his eyes closed, wondering how Portia knew him so well. He usually loved that about her, but that night it ticked him off. Even though he knew he was guilty.

Portia still had suspicions, but she let Jay off the hook so he could get some rest. Actually, she just let him believe everything was cool. She was no fool. It wasn't over. Not by a long shot.

Portia took off her sexy heels, and chemise, and she slipped on an oversized tee shirt, and a pair of comfy slippers. She decided to go downstairs to her office and just surf the net for whatever, until she got sleepy. She had a lot on her mind.

She and Jay had been together for a long time, and he hadn't cheated on her since they'd been married. Not to her knowledge. There had been one incident with this bitch named Tiffany, who had called his cell phone years ago. But Jay swore their dealings had occurred before they tied the knot, so Portia had given him a pass for that one.

She was no angel when she met him either. She used to dance, but he had pardoned her for all of that. And ever since they'd been together, she had been faithful to him. She hadn't even thought of messing around.

Women were insecure and delicate creatures by nature, so Portia asked herself if it was her fault. She unconsciously ran over a mental checklist, to make sure she was on her job. She worked out and lost the baby weight from both her pregnancies, she kept Jay satisfied in bed, she kept herself up, she never openly defied him in front of the children, she was his personal cheerleader and ego booster to make sure he always felt like a man, she kept the house clean, she took care of the kids, and she cooked, and did whatever else she could to make her husband happy. What the hell was wrong with men? Was it true that they were never satisfied?

Portia remembered some of the last words of advice her mother had given her the last time she'd visited her. Laila and Fatima had stayed overnight at her house that time too. They had discussed her friends' marital problems, and then Patricia had told Portia that her thing seemed to be together, but she said, "Babygirl, no relationship is beyond tests."

Portia knew that was absolutely true, but she didn't want to jump off the deep end yet. She didn't even have any proof. All she could do was take Jay's word. She was getting herself all worked up, over possibly nothing. She decided to give her husband the benefit of a doubt. Jay was a good man, and he had never lied to her before.

CHAPTER TWENTY TWO

The next day, Fatima slept real late. When she opened her eyes, it was night time again. She sat up, and looked out the window in disbelief. How long had she been out? Damn, what day was it?

She reached over and got the cordless phone from the nightstand, and checked the caller ID. She saw that Portia and Laila had called her a ton of times, and there were a few calls from other so-called friends as well.

Fatima grabbed the remote, and turned on the TV. She was right in time to see presidential candidate, Senator Barack Obama's democratic nomination expectance speech. She turned up the volume. Fatima tried to keep up with politics, when she was sober.

Obama gave a hell of a speech. Fatima was intrigued, and proud. She prayed that intelligent, eloquent black man would be the next president of the United States. The 2008 election was historical.

After the speech was done, an ABC correspondent said, "There you have it, folks. A moment in history. Once again, tonight being the anniversary of Dr. King's famous "I Have A Dream" speech, given forty five years ago... Tonight, Thursday, August 28, marking the end of a historical democratic convention..."

Fatima sat up in bed. "Wait a minute", she said aloud. Did that reporter just say it was Thursday? Fatima couldn't believe it. She picked up her cell phone, and checked the date. Wow, it was true. It was Thursday. That meant she had been out for two days. The last time she remembered being awake was Tuesday night, at the party she'd hosted. She didn't even really know how she made it to her bedroom.

Fatima felt ashamed. She needed to slow down a little. That

didn't make any sense. She looked at the record-breaking audience at the democratic convention on TV. A lot of them were waving Obama/Change signs and banners. Fatima realized that she needed a change in her life as well. But beyond politics. She needed a change within. She didn't know what had become of her, but she didn't feel good about herself.

The world was on the verge of change, and there she was, getting high and sleeping for two whole days. That was her contribution to the cause. That was ridiculous. She had to get her life together. She kept on saying that, but she wasn't walking the walk. She got up to take a shower. She was just waking up, and it was almost bedtime. That felt strange.

When she got out of the shower, Fatima went downstairs to find something to eat. She walked pass Callie's bedroom, and saw that her door was shut. She figured she was probably asleep. Fatima felt lonely.

Downstairs, it looked like a tornado had been through her house. It was an absolute mess. She would deal with that in the morning. Fatima decided to call Portia's house to see what her and Laila were up to.

While Fatima fixed herself a sandwich, she called her homegirls. Portia acted like she couldn't believe she'd called. Laila got on another phone in the house, and they gave her the full business.

Fatima didn't even offer a rebuttal. They were absolutely right. They hadn't heard from her, or seen her lately. She told them she missed them too, believe it or not.

When Laila told her about the huge, lovely, six-bedroom house she and Cas would be moving into soon, Fatima was ecstatic. They all agreed to meet for dinner that week, so they could celebrate.

They talked on the phone that night for close to two hours. After they hung up, Fatima thought about snorting a few lines. But she didn't give in. She actually rolled herself a blunt, and did a little reading. She wished she had just stuck to smoking weed. It never gave her any problems. A lot came along with all that new shit she had tried.

Fatima thought about her daughter, and felt guilty. She hadn't spoken to Fay since Monday. She swore to herself that the following day, she was going over her parents' house to get her. She needed to spend some time with her.

She thought about the way Laila had got all quiet after she asked her where Falynn was, and she'd told her she was staying with her mom and dad. Fatima knew her girlfriends were skeptical about her parenting skills. Especially Portia. She didn't appreciate it, but she knew their scrutiny was due to her recent erratic behavior.

Fatima vowed to herself that she would get back in touch with her daughter, and be a good mother. She told herself that wasn't just another empty promise.

Upstairs, Callie was in her bedroom laying down, thinking about the telephone conversation she'd just had with her baby, Smoke. He told her that he was short on his time, and would be released a little sooner than she thought.

That night he'd urged her to have certain things lined up for him when he touched ground, and he was specific too. He told Callie she had been on that job long enough to have milked the cow, so most importantly, he needed a car. Preferably a European model. He also said she better have a crib, and at least a hundred grand in cash when he touched.

Callie laid there thinking of a way to compensate the lack of funds, shelter, and transportation she had for her man when he got out. She had been staying with Fatima, but she'd only managed to steal a little jewelry here and there. Smoke wanted the big take.

Just as he'd ordered, she had stole Fatima's driver's license, social security card, birth certificate, and even a checkbook that matched the bank account number she had. She had lifted the license right from her wallet. She had just lucked up and came downstairs one morning, and seen Fatima passed out on the couch. Her purse was sitting on the end table next to her. Callie took one of her major credit cards that day too. There were so many, she doubted she would miss it.

Callied had found Fatima's social security card and birth certificate one day when she was searching through her room. She also found bank statements, so she scribbled down the account numbers. When she saw the balances, her eyes grew big as full moons. Fatima was loaded.

Callie knew she had the means to do some real damage to her pockets. But a part of her was really grateful that Fatima had trusted her enough to open up her home to her. She'd let her drive her car, and she had told her she was welcome to everything she had. Fatima really had a good heart.

Portia had been generous too. She had given Callie money on like four different occasions, ranging anywhere from one to five thousand dollars at a time. Portia was the one who'd sent her the money to get up there in the first place. She even took her shopping. Callie knew those girls were looking out for her on the strength of her dead sister, Simone. They had been Simone's best friends when she was alive, and that was the reason they trusted her.

That night Smoke asked about Jay and Casino too, the guys Portia and Laila went with. They were also the owners of that record label Fatima's dead husband, Wise, had been signed to, Street Life Entertainment. Callie told Smoke the truth, which was she barely ever saw those dudes. She told him she'd been playing the "good girl" role, so she always declined her sister's friends' invitations to hang out. She always said she was tired, or just acted like a homebody.

Callie didn't know what Smoke was up to, but she just wanted to play her part well. She knew she had to produce fast because, as nice as her sister's friends had been to her, disappointing her man was not an option. He was getting ready to come home, so something had to give.

$$$$$

After she burned Laila's house down, Kira paid out a lot of money trying to get out of trouble. But she was disappointed to learn that she was still going to jail. The D.A. wouldn't give in. She wanted something. But Lucky for Kira, she only had to do a year. After what she was facing, she was relieved.

Knowing she had to go in soon, Kira decided to get off her butt and work hard. That was something she just hadn't been doing. She did some modeling, and she got her ass back in the studio, and recorded two albums' worth of material. She also did three music videos. Kira was used to a certain lifestyle, and she didn't want to fall off. She went hard during her free time, so when the time came to go do that year bid, she would have a little money stacked.

The day finally came for Kira's sentence to start. They had a little party for her the night before, but she ended it early so she could get up in the morning and have breakfast with her son, and her mother.

That afternoon, Jay and Kira's attorney took her to turn herself in. Before they left, she hugged her brother and cried. Jay told her to chuck it up. He assured her that time would go by fast.

While Kira was in prison, she heard her songs on the radio. But she couldn't properly promote her album behind bars. Jay and Cas did what they could to keep sales boosted. At first, the prison controversy kept the album abuzz. But as time went along, the second single wasn't doing so well. As a result, the album's sales were going disappointingly mediocre, at least compared to Kira's last two albums.

Kira just sort of sat in her cell depressed for a few weeks, but she took that to be a lesson from God. She had been taking her blessings for granted, and now she regretted not being smarter.

While she was away, Jay, Laurie, and her mother came to visit her, and they took turns bringing her son up there. That was the hardest part about the whole thing. Having to look Jahseim in his face, and admit she had messed up. Her little man acted like he forgave her for leaving him out there. She thanked God he didn't have to fend for himself. He had her family, and of course, his father.

Cas was a stand up dude. He visited her too, to make sure she was alright. They had a pretty decent conversation too, mostly about their son. Kira apologized to Cas, and she sent her apologies to Laila and the baby again as well. She meant it from the heart. What she had done was stupid, and she didn't expect to be forgiven, but she really wanted them to know she was sorry.

Cas told her Laila wasn't harboring any hard feelings. He said she was doing okay. Before he left, they hugged, and he told Kira to hold her head. Then he joked with her. He nodded to a lesbian couple a few tables over, and said, "Yo, be on point in here, K. Don't come home turned out."

Kira saw that he was referring the butch with the fade. She made a face at him, and said, "What? Please! You crazy? Cas, these bitches don't want it. You already know!"

Cas laughed. Kira had always thought she was tough, even when she was young. He told her that if she needed anything, not to hesitate to call.

For some reason, Kira knew he meant that. She smiled and waved at him, and she headed back in to be strip searched. She hated being in the system, but it would be over soon. She only had eight more months to go.

$$$$$

Portia's mind hadn't been totally at ease since that night Jay had come home acting all strange. Her gut told her he had been up to something, but she had no proof. She just left it alone, and things were pretty normal between her and Jay for the most part.

One afternoon, Portia was in her office doing some bookkeeping, and printing out some UPS labels for some packages she had to ship. When she was done, she decided to glimpse over the bank accounts, because she had a dispute with the phone company. They claimed they didn't get a payment that she was sure she'd mailed them. The dispute was over three hundred dollars. Repaying it wouldn't put her in the poorhouse, but it was the principle. She had to find a copy of the check.

Portia logged into their bank's secure website, and she looked over their online bank statements from the past few months. As she glanced over the images of canceled checks, one in particular caught her eye. It was a check written out to New York University, in Jay's handwriting, for the amount of thirty four thousand dollars.

Portia paused for a second. She tried for the life of her to pinpoint a person they knew who was a student at NYU. While she thought about it, she looked for similar transactions. She found two more checks that were written over the past year. Together, the three checks totaled $87,000. That was a hefty amount of money, so Portia was concerned. Come on, that was her family's finances.

She raised an eyebrow in suspense. She had given Jay the benefit of a doubt, but now she had to start digging. Portia printed out a copy of each check for her records. She looked at the checks closer, and she realized there was a number written on each one. It was the same number, so it must've been the student's I.D. number, or something.

Portia hoped she hadn't discovered what she thought she had. A hundred questions ran through her mind. Who was the student at NYU? Was Jay paying some stripper's way through school, or something? Was he some bitch's sugar daddy now? If that was true, then Jay had slipped. He had fucked up big time.

Just that past Thursday, Portia had seen an episode of "Cheaters", the television show that busted unfaithful beaus on camera, and she had flirted with the notion of spying on Jay. She didn't want to go all public with her business like the people on the show, but she'd thought about hiring a private investigator to follow Jay, just to see if they could dig up any dirt on him. Now Portia saw that it was really necessary.

After she located a copy of the three hundred dollar check she needed to back up her dispute with the phone company, Portia exited the online banking site, and used to internet to do a little research. She found a female owned private investigation company, called Confidential Inc. Their site boasted that they had the best, most undercover, predominately female staff of investigators in the country. They claimed they went anywhere to get results.

Portia jotted down the phone number, and called them up. After a brief telephone interview, she was told they could help her. The lady on the phone gave her an appointment for 9:45

the next morning, and said she had to come in and sign an agreement, and give them a deposit. She told Portia that they billed hourly, but the initial payment would cover the basics. She said anything extra would be discussed as it came up.

The next morning Portia had an early appointment, so she got the kids up, and out for school. Driving them would've slowed her down, so Jayquan and Jazz rode the school bus that day. They weren't thrilled about that, but they were good sports. Portia made sure they ate breakfast before they left.

After she saw them off, Portia got herself and her baby ready. Jay was still asleep, so she shook him and told him they were going to the doctor. He was so tired because he came in late the night before. He told her he was in the studio with a new act. Cas had dropped him off last night, so she knew they were together.

Portia put Trixie's car seat in Jay's Bentley, and they drove to the city. She had a funny feeling in her stomach the whole time. She prayed the trip would be a waste of time. She really wanted to regret hiring those folks. She prayed they wouldn't catch Jay doing anything out of the ordinary.

Portia paid for parking, and got out the baby's stroller. After she strapped her baby in safely, they headed to the high-rise building Confidential Inc. was located in. Portia had put together a folder with the copies of the checks she found, and a photo of Jay inside. She wanted to move things along as fast as possible. Not knowing the truth was tormenting her.

Upstairs on the nineteenth floor, Portia sat with Hailey Breiland, the agency's founder. Hailey was youthful looking, deeply suntanned blonde. She told Portia she was a former detective, retired for seven years now. She said she had retired young because she'd been shot in her chest in the line of duty. She told Portia that her luck had worsened shortly after that, when her daughter was kidnapped. She said that was what had inspired her to form her private investigation company, and now she dedicated her life to helping bring closure to folks who needed answers.

Portia asked Hailey if her daughter was returned to her safe, and she shook her head sadly. That reminded Portia of Laila's situation when she lost Pebbles. Her eyes almost watered up. Damn, that was sad.

Portia unconsciously gave her baby a little squeeze, and kissed her on her forehead. She would go crazy if something were to happen to her. Trixie was sitting on her lap being a good girl. She acted like she knew her mommy was taking care of some important business.

Hailey also told Portia she was divorced, and on her second marriage, because her first husband had a thing for nineteen year old brunettes. That being said, she and Portia bonded instantly.

Portia told her she suspected her husband was having an affair, with a younger woman, whose college education she believed he was paying for. She showed Hailey the copies of the checks, and handed her Jay's photo.

Hailey assured her that Confidential Inc. specialized in results, and told her she would have her answers soon. She gave Portia a detailed description of the measures that would be taken to record her husband's activity.

Portia was satisfied, so she signed the contract, and wrote her company a five thousand dollar check. Hailey thanked her, and told her she was putting one of her best girls, Natalie Pratt, on the job. She said they would contact her if they needed any further information. Portia thanked her for her time.

The days that followed, Portia tried to act normal. She even had sex with Jay, so he wouldn't notice anything different. But she wasn't really being fake. She loved him. She loved him so much, that a part of her was in denial. She wanted to be wrong about him messing around.

Portia told herself that she was just being fair. Jay was on trial, and he was innocent, until proven guilty. But the verdict would be in soon.

$$$$$

A few days later, Ysatis called Jay, and he answered the phone like an idiot. He felt kind of bad about the way he ran out on her after he'd beat. He didn't want her to feel like he'd just used her for sex that night, so he asked if she wanted to grab a bite to eat. He was hungry anyway, so it was no big deal. Jay didn't know it at the time, but that was a bad idea.

That night they had sex was the last time he'd seen her, so he called himself just making a friendly visit. He had already promised himself that under no circumstances was he ever going to have sex with Ysatis again. So they were just going to eat, and that was it.

When his driver got to Ysatis' crib, Jay told him he would be right back. He got out to go upstairs and take a leak. It was a pretty nice night out. Ysatis' building was right by Central Park, and even at that time of evening, there were lots of folks out bike riding. So when Jay got out the car, he didn't pay any attention to the woman on his left, who appeared to be fumbling with a faulty tire on her bicycle.

Dressed in full biking gear, with a helmet and kneepads, Private Investigator Natalie Pratt was on the job. She was a pale, freckled, redhead in her late twenties. She wore glasses, and had her hair pulled back into a ponytail. Natalie was cleverly disguised as an average New York City cyclist, and she was taking pictures of Jay, and he didn't even notice.

Natalie had a hi-tech digital camera built right in the spotlight of her helmet, and the spectacles she wore were specially designed too. They had high powered optical lenses, so she could zoom in on targets hundreds of feet away. She could snap a photograph, and store the image with a simple tap to the side of her glasses' frame.

A few minutes later, Natalie got her best photos. Jay and Ysatis came out of the building, and they climbed into the black limousine waiting out front. She zoomed in on the couple, and pretended to scratch her temple. Click, click.

Jay acted like a gentleman, and waited for Ysatis to get in the car first. Natalie smiled to herself. Click, click. Click, click. She got a great photo of him with his hand on the small of her back.

When the car pulled off, Natalie jumped on her bicycle, and tailed them to a sports bar a few blocks away. There was no dress code inside, so she chained her bike safely to a pole, and went in there behind them. Natalie kept on her helmet, and was able to get a few good shots of the couple dining.

After they were done, she got on her bicycle again, and followed the limo back to the same address. Jay didn't go inside that time. She shot photos of the young lady exiting the limo, and entering the building alone.

Natalie glanced at her watch. It was almost midnight, and time for her to call it a night. She headed home to her midtown apartment, eager to download the photos she had taken, and show them to her client.

Five days after she'd hired them, the P.I. called Portia and asked her to come in for an update. To Portia's dismay, when she got there, it was all about shit she didn't want to hear.

Portia had been right about that number that was written on all the checks Jay wrote to NYU. That was a student I.D. number. According to the records at NYU's student admissions' office, that student was a girl named Ysatis Martin, and her mailing address was the same address of the building Jay had been photographed going in, and coming out of.

And on top of that, when they did a search to find out who the apartment was leased to, the paper trail led to Jay. The money had come from his account. That bastard was paying for a Central Park apartment. For a bitch!

Portia's blood began to boil. Her blood pressure must've really shot up, because she felt lightheaded. She just kept flipping through the photos of Jay with that damn girl, who he was paying tuition for. That son of a bitch!

Portia saw them laughing and eating, but she still couldn't prove they were having sex. The P.I. told her that, on that particular occasion, he hadn't been alone with Ysatis long enough to have had intercourse. But if he wasn't fucking her, then why was he paying her rent, and her tuition?

Portia was driving herself crazy. She didn't know whether to just assume it was true, and accept it, or have faith in her husband. But that would be living in denial, and she was no fucking airhead.

Portia thought about going over there to confront that bitch herself. She had the address now, so there was nothing stopping her. Or should she just ask Jay, and rely on him to be honest?

   She decided to talk to her homegirls about it first, to see what they thought. She thanked Natalie and Hailey for their hard work. They assured Portia they were still on the job, and told her they would be in touch. Portia left the office with a heavy heart.

CHAPTER TWENTY THREE

Laila was at Portia's house, in her bedroom on the phone, in another heated argument with her deadbeat husband. She was trying not to speak loud, so Jay or Portia wouldn't overhear her. That shit was really embarrassing. She hated imposing on their privacy as it was, so she didn't want to be in their house yelling like she was crazy.

She was completely annoyed with all the stupid shit Khalil was on the phone talking about. He was wasting her time. She had a lot to do that day. She was preparing to move into her new house, and she didn't want to converse with the asshole responsible for taking joy out of it.

Laila had simply wanted her divorce to be final before she and Cas officially moved in together. Was that too much to ask for? To be allowed to lead a respectable life. Khalil was a spiteful ass bastard. He knew it was over between them. He just didn't want her to be happy. She was really starting to hate him.

Laila was fed up, so she came out hard on his ass. She said, "Khalil, why don't you move on? It's over between us. Forever. So you better take this money, and move on! Please. Just sign the papers, nigga. Or we'll just be in court forever, 'cause I ain't giving you nothin' else. Fuck that! I'm sick of you, you fuckin' leach! A hundred grand! Take it, or leave it, mothafucka!"

Khalil was vexed. He said, "What? Are you outta your mind, bitch? That's chump change! You think you and that mo'fucka gon' just ride off into the sunset, and be happy? Is you stupid? I'll kill that nigga first! Don't be stupid, Laila! You gon' fuck around and get ya' man wig piece pushed back. And yours! Then ya'll can rest in peace together. In the graveyard!"

Laila frowned at the phone in disgust, like it was Khalil in person. He was talking real reckless, and she was about to get off the phone with his ignorant ass. But before she hung up, she checked that nigga. "You ig'nant ass, black fool. You better watch your mouth, and be careful what you say, 'cause you don't know who you fuckin' with."

Khalil retorted, "Bitch, fuck you and that nigga! I'll smoke his bitch ass!"

Laila just sighed. "Ayight, you disrespectful mothafucka. Don't say I didn't warn you." After that, she just hung up on that asshole.

Laila didn't plan on telling Cas about the threats Khalil had just made on their lives. She didn't know what had gotten into him, but he was a real "phone thug" that day. Laila brushed it off, but only because she took Khalil's threats to be idle. She didn't believe he had the heart to kill her, or Cas. She was more concerned about Cas killing him if he found out what he said.

Laila knew Cas wouldn't take those threats lightly. If he found out, Khalil's ass would come up missing, or something. That fool was being an asshole, but he was still her children's father. She didn't want him to get killed, or anything. He had clearly underestimated Cas' character, and capabilities.

And Laila didn't want Cas to get in any trouble either. She knew what he was capable of. That's why she had told Khalil that was her final offer. She prayed he would take it, and go on about his business.

Unbeknownst to Laila, Cas had come over a few minutes before she hung up the phone. He'd been standing outside her bedroom door, and he caught the end of her conversation. But he didn't blow it up. He waited a minute after she got off the phone, and then he knocked on the door.

Cas and Laila went out to dinner that night, and he was sort of quiet. Laila didn't pry, but she could tell there was something on his mind. She didn't know he had overheard part of her telephone conversation, and knew Khalil had been talking greasy, and stressing her out. Cas was very angered and perturbed by this. It was really eating at him that someone, particularly Laila's crackhead, deadbeat husband, was standing in the way of his lady's happiness.

That nigga Khalil wouldn't sign the divorce papers, and Laila had qualms about them moving in together while she was still married. Cas could understand that. She had a teenage daughter, so what type of example would that set for her?

Casino made up his mind to step in, and rectify the situation. He didn't want to kill Khalil. He just planned to "convince" him to sign the papers. That scumbag was holding out for more money, and enough was enough.

Cas didn't like dudes who took advantage of women, especially a woman he was in a relationship with, that they both wanted to make honest. Laila was going to be his next wife. It was real with her, and he'd be less than a man if he let a bozo like Khalil stand in the way of that.

That dude was totally expendable to Cas. He didn't give a fuck about his existence. Only on the strength of Macy was he even still breathing. But he kept on testing him. Casino didn't like to be tested.

The next day, he decided it couldn't wait. Cas didn't want to alarm Jay, because he wasn't really sure how it would pan out. He didn't even want Jay to know the extent he was willing to go to get Khalil to sign those papers.

Cas didn't want to involve Jay. He had enough stuff of his own to worry about. Jay didn't need to be getting caught up in his relationship mess, so he summoned some other homies to roll with him. One of them was a dude named Andrew, who they called "Handy Andy" in the 'hood, because like a handyman, he was known for putting that work in. The other dude was called Eighty, because it was known that his robbery weapon of choice was a .380.

Cas knew the men he chose were standup cats, because both of their track records reflected that. He knew Eighty had stuck up a few dudes, but he didn't judge a person for what they did, as long as they didn't do it to him. When Cas called them with the financially rewarding proposition, they both took the bait without even asking any questions.

He picked the two of them up in Bedford-Stuyvesant, out in Brooklyn. After they got in the car, they rolled around The Stuy with Cas in an inconspicuous looking, gray '02 Maxima, with black tint. Cas knew Khalil would never expect him to show up in something like that. He wanted to catch that nigga with his pants down. That dude was a real thorn in his side. He was standing in the way of his family's happiness, and Cas was fed up.

He thought about just taking that lame to Manuel's meat house, and offing him, but he was Macy's father. Cas was fond of Laila's daughter, and he didn't want the blood of her pops to be on his hands.

After about forty minutes of riding through the neighborhood, Cas lucked up and spotted that clown. Khalil was just about to turn the corner of his block. Cas knew he lived with his moms, so he wanted to catch him before he got in front of his house. The timing was perfect. It was just getting dark outside, and they were sitting at a red light. Cas pointed Khalil out, and told his goons to hop out, and grab him. He told them to try not to hurt him.

Handy Andy and Eighty moved swift and quick. Both of them were pretty trigger happy for the most part, but they respected Cas' wishes to get the dude in the car unharmed.

Khalil had been drinking a few beers, so he was a little off point. He was preoccupied with thoughts of the stewed chicken and rice he had seen his moms preparing, before he'd left the house a few hours ago. He saw the gray colored Maxima sitting at the light, but he didn't think twice about it. It never occurred to him that his demise could possibly be waiting inside that car.

When the two thugs got out the car, and approached him, Khalil looked behind him to see if they were heading for somebody else. Then he noticed the looks on their faces. They were both mean mugging him something serious. They approached him on either side, and grabbed him. "Get the fuck in the car, nigga", one of them commanded.

Khalil dropped his weight, and struggled with them, but his resistance was unsuccessful. The men lifted him off his feet, and shoved him in the car head first. Khalil opened his mouth to yell, but one them shoved a big ass .380 in his face.

He kept his mouth shut after that. Now he regretted the fact that he had sold that old .38 revolver he had. He had gotten two hundred bucks for it, but now he realized it was priceless.

The men who'd grabbed him sandwiched him in the back seat, and the driver pulled off.

Everybody was quiet for a minute. The driver was the first to speak. He addressed the henchmen first. He said, "Good job, fellas. That wasn't too messy."

Khalil recognized the voice. It was that nigga, Cas! Laila's new man. All kinds of stuff ran through Khalil's mind. Did they come to kill him this time? Laila had that nigga open. She must've been sucking his dick good. That was why he kept on getting in their business. Laila was his fucking wife. Didn't he get it?

Khalil didn't say these words aloud, because he knew the ball wasn't exactly in his court. He had to play it cool. He asked Cas what he wanted. "Man, what's this about?"

Cas glanced at him in the mirror, and grinned. "Come on, man. You already know."

Khalil didn't reply. Cas just kept driving, and he didn't speak anymore. Eighty and Handy Andy were equally quiet in the back. They were following Casino's lead. That was his show. They had no idea what that shit was about, and neither of them cared. They were only concerned with their proceeds, and nothing else.

Cas drove uptown, to a creepy looking section of the Bronx. He drove through dark streets and alleys, and didn't say a word.

Khalil was shitting bricks by now. He was sure they were going to kill him, and leave his body in a back alley, for the rats and cats to eat his remains. And he would rot there, until some kid chasing a roll away ball discovered him, and somebody finally called the police. By the time they notified his mother, his body would probably decayed and unrecognizable, calling for a closed casket. He wondered if Macy would even show up for his funeral. She probably didn't think too highly of him right about then, and he couldn't blame her. Khalil was on the verge of begging for his life, and promising Cas he'd leave Laila alone.

But he had pride. He decided that if he had to die, he would die with honor. He kept his mouth shut, until he saw what that nigga Cas had to say.

Cas pulled up in an abandoned lot that epitomized the term "concrete burial ground". He shut off the car, and only then did he speak again. "Listen carefully, because I won't repeat this. Laila wants a divorce, but you don't. If you die, she wins. Everybody wins. End of story. You decide."

Khalil didn't respond. They all sat there quiet, in the dark. After a few seconds, he heard the sound of Cas cocking his gun. And it sounded like a big gun. Khalil's heart rate quickened. He wished he'd taken the final offer Laila had given him a few days ago. Now he could die penniless.

Cas gave him one more chance. "So what's it gonna be? I got shit to do, man." He said that to indicate that he would kill him, and continue his evening without a second thought.

Khalil got the message. He tried to talk his way out of it. "Hey, look man. I never said I wasn't gonna sign. I just told her I needed a little more "persuasion", if you know what I mean." He laughed nervously.

Cas reached in his jacket pocket, and pulled out a certified check for a hundred grand. He handed him the envelope, and said, "That's Laila's final offer. Take it, and live. Or leave it, and die."

The choice was clear. Khalil looked at the check, and said, "I'll take it."

Cas pulled a manila folder from under the sun visor. He took out the divorce papers, and handed them to Khalil. He also passed him an ink pen. "Sign by each x", he commanded.

Khalil's hand was shaking so bad, he could barely write. He finally managed to get it right, and he breathed a sigh of relief when he was done. He thought about the fact that they could still kill him, but he figured Cas would've already done it if he planned to. And he would've never given him that check. Laila wouldn't have needed his signature if he was dead.

Cas took the papers, and looked them over to make sure he signed them right. He couldn't stand that slime ball Khalil, but he had a good heart. He dug in his pocket, and peeled off two c-notes, so the nigga could get home. He gave him the bread, and said, "Go home, man. Get a cab, and beat it."

Cas told Eighty and Handy Andy to let him out the backseat.

Eighty got out, and stood there ice grilling Khalil until he broke out. He was tight that he hadn't been able to at least snuff that nigga. He had looked forward to torturing that dude. He could've put in some work, but he was disappointed.

Handy Andy just laughed at Eighty, and shook his head. He hopped in the front, in the passenger seat. Unlike Eighty's violence thirsty ass, he was perfectly content with the easy bread they had just earned with Killah Cas. Eighty got back in the back, and Cas pulled off.

When they got back to Brooklyn, true to his word, Cas pieced his accomplices off, and thanked his mans for holding him down. A small part of him felt good that he had gotten duke to sign those papers without having to break any of his bones. But another small part of him had been looking forward to that, so that nigga was lucky.

Now Cas was in a good mood. He drove back to Jersey, and went over Jay's house. When Portia let him in, he greeted her with a kiss to the cheek, and played with the babies for a minute. They were downstairs playing in Jazz's portable playpen. He threw them up in the air one by one, and made them laugh for a while.

Portia told him Laila had gone upstairs to take a shower, so he went up there, and tapped on her door.

Laila figured that was Cas at the door. She knew his knock. He came in, and handed her a manila envelope, without saying a word. She opened it up, and realized that he had just presented her with the papers that would unblock their happiness.

When Laila saw Khalil's signatures, she just grinned. She told Cas she didn't even want to know how he got it done. But that fool had talked all that "over my dead body" stuff so much, Laila just had to know one thing. "Is he still alive?"

Casino laughed, and told her he was fine. He told Laila no violence had occurred. He said he had simply used his persuasive powers.

Laila laughed, and hugged him. She loved her man. She told him she was ready to pick out her new furniture now. Cas just laughed.

$$$$$

Portia had been walking around for a few days debating with herself about her findings. She was trying to wait and see if the P.I. would get back to her with some type of proof that a sexual relationship existed between Jay and that bitch, and she was driving herself insane.

Portia was embarrassed by the fact that Jay could be cheating on her. To her, that was sort of an indication that she couldn't please her husband. But she decided it was time to talk to her friends. She knew Laila and Fatima wouldn't judge her.

Portia told Laila she had to talk to her about something, and then she called Fatima, and asked her over.

They all got together that night, and sat in Portia's office with the door shut. Portia showed them the photos first, and then she told them she'd hired a P.I. to follow Jay. Then she told them about how Jay had been paying the rent and tuition of the girl in question. After she confided in her girls, Portia felt better.

Her best friends passed the photos back and forth, and both of them were quiet for a minute. It was hard to believe Jay had done something like that. He had always been such a good guy. They didn't want to act naïve, but if they hadn't seen the photos with their own two eyes, they probably would've told Portia she was wrong about him cheating.

Portia told them the P.I. said Jay hadn't stayed at that bitch's apartment long enough to have sex that night, so they advised her to wait it out, and not make a move until she had proof. They both knew she had a good husband. Portia and Jay were the perfect couple. Laila and Fatima both wondered what the hell Jay was doing.

A few minutes later, Fatima got a call on her cell phone. She excused herself, and walked off to have her conversation in private.

About fifteen minutes later, she came back in the office all teary-eyed. When they asked her what was wrong, she told them she just got off the phone with her mother, and she had got on her about Falynn. Tima was clearly upset, but Portia gathered she was feeling more guilt than anything.

Fatima said her mother was trying to register Falynn for kindergarten next fall, in school by her house. She said Doris had insulted her by insinuating that she wasn't the best choice of guardian for Falynn. Fatima was real offended, and she went on and on about how she was going to show her mother she was wrong, and make her eat those words.

Fatima started crying, and kept saying she was a good mother, like she needed assurance. She told them she was going to get her daughter back from Doris, and get on her job.

Portia and Laila listened to her, and offered her shoulders to cry on. Portia didn't say anything, because Tima was so down, but she hoped she meant it that time. She did need to get her shit together. She never had her daughter, and Portia couldn't understand that. She needed a break every now and then herself, but Fatima had been on vacation from her responsibilities for months.

Portia listened to her vent, but she was preoccupied with her own misery. She wanted to talk more about her findings with Jay. They hadn't discussed it as much as she wanted to, but she didn't want to tune Fatima out, or overshadow Laila's excitement about her and Cas' new house. She put her problems on a backburner, so she could be there for her friends.

When Fatima was done wallowing in self-pity, Laila made an announcement. She told them Cas had miraculously gotten Khalil to sign the divorce papers, so she was officially free. When Portia and Fatima heard that, they were both pleased. They all agreed to go out to eat at Sergio's that weekend to celebrate.

Laila was finally divorced. Talk about good riddance. That was such great news, Portia broke out some top shelf champagne she had in the fridge. They popped a bottle of Ace of Spades, and shared a toast to Laila's good fortune, and her and Cas' bright future. Laila was so caught up in the spirit of good news, she almost revealed her secret. But she thought about it, and decided to wait until she was walking a little better to tell them.

That Friday evening, Portia and Laila met up at Sergio's

Bistro first. Portia had driven there from home. Laila had spent the day with Cas at their new house making preparations, so she arrived in a hired car. It was raining outside, so the two of them hurried inside the restaurant together, and they got a table for three.

While they waited on Fatima to get there, Laila told Portia all about the interior decorators she and Cas had interviewed that morning. She said Cas had hired the one of her choice, to work with her to furnish the house. She told Portia the house was so big, she dared not to attempt to decorate it by herself. Portia said she totally understood. She had hired someone when she and Jay first moved into their home too, and then again when they'd redecorated last year.

Fatima finally showed up, and she was wearing these big ass, dark Chanel shades. It was a cloudy and rainy evening out, so to Portia, it looked like she'd been doing something she had no business doing.

Portia smelled liquor on her breath when she hugged her, so she made a face. "Girl, it's pouring outside, so what's with the shades?"

Fatima nonchalantly replied, "Oh, I got bags under my eyes. I was up kinda late, 'cause..."

Portia didn't even want to hear it, so she just cut her off. "Oh. And where's Falynn?"

"Still at my parent's house."

Portia didn't say anything. She just made a face. Fatima had wasted all that damn time telling them all that crap about how much she was ready for a change. She was just so full of shit. She had just talked their ears off about the turnaround she claimed she was making in her life, and about how she was going to be a better mother. It was all bullshit. She was just a typical fucking fiend, and Portia was fed up with her.

Fatima put her hand on her hip, and said, "Oh boy. Here you go judging me again. I hate when you do that shit."

She rolled her eyes, and kept on. "Portia, you swear you're so fuckin' perfect, wit' your do-good ass. Miss Fuckin' Do-good. Don't worry about where my child at. Worry about your own life, bitch."

Portia just looked at Fatima like she was stupid. Where the hell did that come from? She remained calm, and said, "You know what, I'm not even gon' entertain you, and your nonsense. Ain't nobody judging you. That's your guilty conscience, 'cause you know you ain't on your job. And I'm not perfect, bitch. I just handle mines, and take care of my fuckin' kids."

Laila tried to intervene, because she saw where it was going. Damn, they hadn't even eaten yet. Before her friends got loud, she said, "Come on, ya'll. Chill."

Fatima ignored Laila. She wasn't trying to hear that. She leaned across the table, and stuck her finger in Portia's face. She spat, "You need to worry about your own shit! You ain't Mary Poppins, bitch! You always runnin' around wit' your nose in other people shit! That's why Jay fuckin' the shit out that lil' young girl. 'Cause you ain't on your job! Mind your own fuckin' business, bitch!"

Portia was so stunned by Fatima's comment about her marriage, her jaw dropped for a second. She couldn't believe that bitch had said some shit like that. That was a low blow, and it hurt. She thought of an equally painful statement to come back with, and brought out the big guns. She snarled, "You fuckin' pitiful ass, drug head dyke! You need to go yo' ass to rehab, you Amy Winehouse, crackhead bitch!"

Now Fatima's mouth hung open. She couldn't believe Portia had gone there. That was fucked up. Was that all she thought of her? She didn't really have anything worse to come back with. That was a pretty venomous insult Portia had hurled at her. But she had something for her condescending, Miss Goody Two Shoes ass.

Fatima said, "You fake bitch." She smirked, and shook her head. "Well, I'm not the only dyke at this table. Am I, Portia? Since you wanna dry snitch, then what about you, and your little breast play incident with Raquel? Laila, did you know about that?

That was the ultimate. As dark skinned as Portia was, she must've turned beet red. You could've knocked her over with a feather. She scoffed, "You dirty bitch. Fuck you!"

Fatima said, "No, bitch. Fuck you." She got fed up, and got up and reached across the table, and mushed Portia in the face.

Portia jumped up. "Bitch, now I know you on drugs!" She couldn't believe that slut put her hands on her. Now she had to open up a can of whip ass on her.

Portia jumped across that table, and pounced Fatima out. After that four piece, her drunk ass didn't know what hit her. But she fought back. Fatima came back swinging, but Portia blocked most of her wild hits, and tapped her on the jaw.

Fatima stumbled, but she recovered. Frustrated that Portia was winning the fight, she charged at her, and clawed at her face. Portia pried her hands from her eyes, and countered with a jab and an uppercut.

Laila just sat there in her wheelchair, unable to do much to stop her two best friends from killing each other. It looked like they were really fighting to the death. Those bitches were going pound for pound, and blow for blow. The onlookers in the restaurant were staring at the battle like they had ringside seats.

Laila could see that her friends were both filled with some seriously misdirected anger, but she commanded them to stop acting like fools in front of all those damn white people. She did all she could to make their asses quit fighting. Everything except get up.

Portia and Fatima didn't know about her secret yet. She was walking a little, but she wasn't getting around good enough to break up no fight. Laila didn't want to risk getting hurt. She was finally making progress, and wasn't going to let her childish friends' incongruous behavior set her back. She didn't need anymore bumps in her road.

Fatima had four drinks, and snorted three lines of coke before she came. Her sobriety and fighting ability were definitely affected, or at least she could've argued so. Anyhow, Portia got her down on the floor in a headlock, and then she put her in a sleeper hold. When it came to self-defense, Jay had taught her a lot. Fatima shouldn't have fucked with her.

Fatima struggled wildly, but with Portia's knee in her back, and arms wrapped around her neck, she couldn't do much. "Bitch, get off me", she demanded. "Get the fuck off me!" She was tired, and breathing real heavy.

Portia was out of breath too. She said, "See, that's what you get for actin' stupid. You hit me first! You need to grow the fuck up, bitch! We're in our fuckin' thirties now."

Fatima was mad, and she was huffing and puffing. But she knew Portia was right. They were grown women, with children. And they had been best friends since they were thirteen. That was twenty long years. Now Fatima felt like an ass.

She calmed down, and surrendered. "Ayight, P. You got it. Let me up."

Portia looked down at her with surprise. She had really expected more resistance, so she was hesitant. "You sure? 'Cause I do not wanna fight you, Tima."

Fatima said, "Real talk. Word to God, P. Just get up. You're hurting my back."

Now Portia felt bad. She said, "Sorry." She let her homegirl go, and got up, and then she extended her hand to help Fatima up too.

Fatima reached for her hand, and got up. She said, "My bad, P. I just got a lotta shit on my mind. My mother talkin' 'bout she gon' take me to court. She's try'na take Falynn away from me."

Portia just looked at her. Now she understood why she was so touchy.

Fatima said, "Don't look at me like that, P. I already know. I gotta get my shit together. Real talk."

Laila said, "Well, knowing is half the battle. So that's what's up, babygirl."

Fatima just nodded. She did know. Now she just had to do something about it.

The restaurant manager had been notified by a waitress about the scuffle, so he came out to address the situation. He was a prim and proper looking gentleman, in a dark three piece suit. When he came over to their table, he introduced himself and addressed them politely, but he was stern. He expressed great unhappiness about being informed of what he referred to as a "common bar fight".

He said he refrained from having them removed from the

premises by security because he recognized them, and knew they were regular patrons, whom he'd never had a problem with. And then he asked them if they wouldn't mind respecting the integrity of the five star dining establishment, and conducting themselves in an orderly fashion, like ladies.

Laila apologized, and assured him that everything was under control. Portia told him they were cool, and ready to order. She said she needed a drink. Fatima said she seconded that.

After their waitress came and took their order, Portia and Fatima went to the ladies room together to fix their hair. They got a few stares, but it didn't really bother them. When people noticed they were unfazed, most of them continued their dining experiences.

Portia and Fatima looked at each other in the mirror, and laughed it all off. That was the good thing about being true blue friends. Even after a knockdown drag-out fight, the realness and love was unconditional. They made sure their appearances were up to par, and they headed back out to their table, and had a seat.

While the friends dined, they made light of the fight, and moved on to discuss a few lighter, more comical topics. But there was still a little sadness looming about, because everyone had underlying issues in their lives. Issues they would love to fix for each other, but just couldn't.

Portia had fears that her spouse was involved with a younger woman, Fatima was struggling with a serious drug habit, and Laila was literally trying to get back on her feet. But they all still managed to be there for one another in someway.

Fatima and Portia promised Laila they would come check out the new six bedroom mini-mansion she and Cas were moving into. Laila was so excited. She told them it was three times the size of her last house. Both of them were really happy for her.

After they were done eating and drinking, they all hugged, and agreed to keep in touch more often. When they left the restaurant, Fatima rode off in her Bentley, and Laila rode home with Portia in her Benz.

$$$$$

After Fatima left the restaurant, she went home, and sat in the dark on the sofa. Even though she and Portia had made up, the fact still remained that she had a serious problem. Fatima knew it was all on her to make it better, but she had a little pity party for herself.

She was forlorn beyond her imagination. She just felt so alone, and wished she had somebody to love her. She didn't want the lifestyle she had adopted anymore. She wanted to live right, and be a role model for her daughter. Enough was enough. She had to quit smoking those damn cigarettes too. Portia was absolutely right. That wasn't her. All the drugs, alcohol, and nicotine she was putting in her body, she was probably killing herself. Was she crazy?

Fatima broke down, and cried about everything in her life she wished she could change. Her number one wish was to have Wise back in her life. It was like a piece of her was missing, and she had this huge empty void in her soul. It tormented her on a daily basis, and she knew that was part of the reason she'd been popping pills, doing coke, and drinking so much the past year.

Fatima knew she'd been using Wise' death as a crutch for her addiction, and she had to get on. It was time for her to get some help. Admitting that was painful for her, but that truth was self-evident.

Callie came downstairs to go to the kitchen for something to drink, and she heard Fatima crying. She turned on the light, and asked her what was wrong. Fatima needed a shoulder to cry on, so she spilled her heart. She even kept it real and told Callie she was thinking of going away for a couple of weeks, to get herself together. She said she felt like she had hit a record low, and it was time to do something to take back her life.

Callie seemed so sincere. Fatima was so touched by her concern, she had an idea. She didn't want to put her out while she was gone, especially knowing she had no where to go, so she asked Callie if she'd mind house-sitting for her while she was away.

Fatima knew Callie lived a quiet life, so she wouldn't have any wild parties, or anything. She couldn't even get her to socialize at the gatherings she had. Callie just locked herself in her room every time. All she did was go to work, and come back home. Fatima thought about it, and she knew she had made the right decision.

Callie looked at Fatima earnestly, and said, "I'd be a little nervous here in this big house all alone, but if you need me to, then I will. And I'll do whatever else I can to help. You've done so much for me, Fatima. I couldn't say no to you about anything."

Fatima smiled, and thanked her. Callie could tell she ate it all up. She casually asked her, "So, when are you leaving?"

Fatima made up her mind right there on the spot, so there was no turning back. She said, "Next week."

Callie hugged her, and said, "Don't worry, girl. You'll be fine."

Fatima squeezed her hand. She appreciated the support.

Callie stayed in character, but inside she was ecstatic. The timing couldn't have been more perfect. Smoke was coming home the following week.

CHAPTER TWENTY FOUR

When Portia woke up the next morning, she thought about the fight she had with Fatima. She was glad they squashed it, but she kept on hearing her homegirl's words. Fatima had said, "That's why Jay fuckin' the shut out that lil' young girl. 'Cause you ain't on your job!" That mess got Portia tight every time she thought about it.

Fatima's words had stung, but Portia's beef was with Jay, not her. It was him who had put her in the position to be ridiculed like that. And she was handling that shit a little too well. Portia decided to go over to the address the P.I. had given her. She wanted to talk to that bitch, Ysatis, and tell her she better stay the fuck away from her husband.

Portia got up and got ready, and she woke up Laila, and told her she had to make a run. Laila agreed to look after the kids for her, since Jay wasn't home. He and Cas had pulled an all-nighter in the studio.

It was Saturday morning, so all the kids were still asleep, including the babies. Laila had an appointment with her therapy team at four, so Portia promised to be back by then.

She had called for a hired car right before she got in the shower, so she could just go to the city and back, without having to worry about parking. A black Town Car arrived about fifteen minutes later, and Portia headed on out. She hadn't told Laila where she was going, only because she would've probably tried to talk her out of it.

When Portia got to the address of the building, she told her driver she wouldn't be long. He was being paid well for a roundtrip, so he didn't care. Portia got out the car, and walked up to the building.

It was pretty classy. There was a burgundy uniformed doorman at the entrance, and he asked Portia if he could be of assistance. She lied, and told him she had come to visit her dear friend, Ysatis, in apartment 15-B. She told him she was expecting her, and thanked him for his concern. She hurried pass him to catch an open elevator.

When she got off the elevator at the fifteenth floor, she walked up to the apartment door. She paused, and took a deep breath, and she rang the bell. Portia heard footsteps come to the door, so she waited patiently for the person on the other side to answer. She guessed they were looking at her through the peephole. She rang the doorbell again.

Finally, the door opened up, just a crack. Portia couldn't see the face, but a woman's voice said, "Umm... May I help you?"

Portia tried to get a good look at her, but it was kind of dark inside the house. But she had seen her in the photos the private investigator had given her, so she knew she wasn't a bad looking girl. From the portion of her silhouette Portia could make out, she appeared to be a lot slimmer than she would have thought Jay preferred.

The girl must've got impatient. She asked Portia if she could help her again.

Portia said, "Ysatis, I'm Portia. I need to speak to you about my husband, Jay."

When Ysatis heard that, she started to slam the door. Portia pushed the door, and stuck her foot in the gap just in time. She said, "Wait! I just wanna talk to you for a minute!" She shoved the door harder, and tried to get inside. Damn, the chain lock was on.

Ysatis was pushing the door with all her might, trying to close it. She was convinced that Portia was crazy. She probably had a gun, or something. There was no way she was letting her in. Her heart was racing with fear. She said, "Miss, get away from my door, before I call the police!"

After she threatened her with the police, Portia calmed down, and tried to keep the situation under control. She said, "Listen, Ysatis. I didn't come here for that. I just want to ask you a few questions. Are you screwing my husband?"

Ysatis ignored the question, and wouldn't cooperate. She wasn't talking to Portia. She knew Jay wouldn't approve of that, and she didn't want to anyway. She wasn't stupid. He was paying her rent, and her tuition. She had no business communicating with his wife. All she said was, "I don't know what you're talking about. Go away!"

She was trying to play with her intelligence. Portia got offended. She shoved that door as hard as she could, and tried to break the damn chain. "Bitch, open this door!"

Luckily for Ysatis, the lock didn't give. She warned Portia again. "You'd better get away from my door. If you don't leave, I'm calling the police!" She took out her cell phone, and dialed 911.

Portia saw that bitch was calling the cops on her. Damn, she didn't come over there to get arrested. She just wanted to find out the truth. She decided to break out. Jay was the one she should've approached anyway.

Before Portia left, she gave Ysatis some food for thought. She was firm, and said, "If you think I'm crazy, you a hundred percent right. Bitch, if you don't stay the fuck away from my husband, I'll fuckin' kill you. Remember, I know where the fuck you live. And that ain't a threat, it's a promise." She stopped pushing the door, and walked away.

Ysatis slammed the door shut, and locked it fast. She heard the 911 operator ask where the emergency was, but she just hung up. She was just glad Portia left.

As Portia walked away, a concerned neighbor opened his apartment door, and stuck his head in the hallway. He was a balding, middle aged, white guy, and he looked like a real stiff. Portia was so angry with the way things had turned out, she looked at him and said, "For your information, sir, there's a whore living in the apartment right across from you. In number 15-B." The neighbor looked shocked.

After that, Portia knocked on random apartment doors on her way to the elevator. Every time somebody answered, she informed them about their slut for a neighbor. She kept repeating, "Are you aware that there's a prostitute living in this building? Right on your floor! In apartment number 15-B!"

Ysatis heard Portia in the hallway yelling those horrible things about her, and she was completely embarrassed. She wanted to run behind her and make her shut up, but her fear outweighed her humiliation. For all she knew, Portia could be packing.

Ysatis stood there with her heart pounding for a few seconds. Jay's wife was really crazy. She had threatened her life. When she calmed down a little, the first thing she did was call him to let him know his wife came over there wilding.

On the elevator, Portia got back in character. She was too cool for that shit. She moved like a boss. When she got to the lobby, she pranced out of that building with dignity. She felt low inside, but she was not about to cry in front of all those white people. The way that bitch had avoided her questions, Portia knew she was guilty. Jay was fucking her.

When Portia got outside, she looked around at her surroundings. Central Park, huh? Jay had really gone all out. He put his little mistress in an expensive area. Trick Daddy had splurged that time. That girl must've been sucking and fucking him really good. Portia got back in her hired car, and directed the driver back to her house in Jersey.

Jay was still at the studio, so he was busy when Ysatis called him. He started to not answer the phone. But when he found out the reason she called, he was glad he did. He couldn't believe what she told him. He didn't get emotional, but he asked her exactly what she had told Portia. Ysatis assured him that she hadn't said a word about anything. He told her to stay in the house, and not answer the door if she came back.

When Jay hung up the phone, he paced the floor for a few minutes. He knew he had no grounds, but he was tight. What the fuck was Portia snooping around, knocking on people's doors for? He had to think of a way to get out of that one.

He came up with a story, and prayed it would work. He was just going to tell Portia that Ysatis was a new artist, who he and Cas were in the process of signing. At the time, that was all he had. He just hoped she believed it.

$$$$$

Portia spent the bulk of the day crying. She didn't even tell anyone about her visit to the Central Park apartment of her husband's mistress, probably because it made her look desperate. And she was ashamed to tell Laila and Fatima that Jay was guilty. She didn't even want to talk about it. Not yet.

After Laila left for therapy, Macy and Jayquan looked after the little ones, while Portia holed up in her office and pretended she was writing. But she was actually in there crying. She wondered how a chick not even old enough to legally purchase alcohol, was woman enough to win the adoration, and financial support of her husband. A bitch with nothing to offer him, except for sex.

Portia was disappointed. Disappointed in Jay, disappointed in love, but primarily disappointed in herself. How had she become naïve enough to believe there was such a thing as a faithful man? The lifestyle she'd lived before she settled down with Jay had taught her early on how weak and adulterous men were. What had made her believe she was so special?

When she was an exotic dancer, she had witnessed firsthand the way some married men carried on. Some of the shit she'd seen was unbelievable. Stuff like married men eating strange women out in public, and then returning home to their wives like everything was normal. Women they knew were employed in the sex industry at that.

Portia realized she had put too much trust in Jay. He was just a man. She guessed she had given him too much credit. But still, the thought of him being inside another woman made her sick.

Portia had already made up her mind. She couldn't hold it back any longer. She planned on confronting Jay when he got home. She kept on looking at those photos, and comparing herself to Ysatis. She wasn't insecure, but she couldn't help it. It felt like she had something she didn't. Portia couldn't deny that she was pretty, but she didn't see anything special about her. Jay had risked it all. She wondered if it would be worth it to his black ass.

The part that really hurt the most was the fact that the girl was so young. Did that mean Jay was into young girls? Did her body turn him off? Or was she just old news? Maybe she

should just take it as a sign from God. Eventually, Jay was probably going to leave her and the children for a younger woman.
That made so much sense to Portia, she convinced herself it was
true. It happened to women across the world everyday. What
the hell made her so special?

Portia cried her heart out about the harsh reality of Jay leaving her for a younger woman, and she decided she would be the
one to go first. She wouldn't give him the satisfaction of abandoning her first. He wasn't about to make her look like a fool.

She was leaving him, before he abandoned her. Men didn't
change. His messing with younger women would more than
likely become a pattern. It would only be a matter of time before he felt like the grass on the other side was greener. Or in
his case, felt like the ass was greener.

It wasn't easy to just walk away, but Portia knew she had to
teach Jay a lesson. He had to learn not to take her for granted.
He used to be the perfect husband, but he obviously thought
it was okay to slip now. Or had the nigga been creeping all
along? Portia wasn't sure, but she believed she would have
known in her heart. She would've felt it, like she did now. Her
husband was slipping away from her. What happened to her
marriage? What had she done wrong?

Jay got in around eleven that night. He had been up for two
days, so he was dog-tired. He kissed Portia, and smacked her
on the ass, and asked her to fix him something to eat. He tried
to act regular, so she wouldn't know he already knew about her
going over Ysatis' crib. He wanted to see what she had to say
first.

Jay couldn't front, he was nervous as hell. He didn't know
how shit was going to play out, but when she brought it up, he
was sticking to his story. To his surprise, Portia made him two
nice turkey breast sandwiches, and didn't say anything about
Ysatis that night. She actually told him to get some rest, and
went down to her office.

She stayed down there late. After Jay took a shower, he went
down there to say goodnight. And he wanted to feel out her
vibe before he laid down and closed his eyes. Portia said she
was writing, so she would see him in the morning. He gave her

a kiss on the forehead, and went on to bed. He noticed how
Portia tensed up when he got close to her, so he knew she was
uptight. He wondered if it was safe for him to go to sleep that
night. Maybe she was being too cool about it.

There were two reasons why Portia changed her mind about
confronting Jay that night. Number one, she saw how tired he
was. She wanted him to be well rested and focused when she
blew him up. And two, she planned on leaving right after she
aired it out, and she didn't want to leave that time of night. She
wanted to make sure her babies got a good night's sleep.

Jay didn't sleep so well. He woke up early Sunday morning,
and he noticed that Portia hadn't even come to bed. She
must've slept on the couch, or in a guest bedroom. Jay knew
that wasn't a good sign. He got up and showered, and got
dressed, and he thought of an excuse to get out of the house.
He usually stayed home on Sundays, to spend time with his
family, but he had a feeling he should stay away from Portia that
day. Jay peeked in on his children. They were all still sleeping,
so he went downstairs to the kitchen for some orange juice.

Downstairs, he saw Portia sitting at the dining room table,
going through some kind of paperwork. She was dressed kind
of early too. Jay said good morning, and asked her what was
up. She just shrugged, and said, "Nothing."

She was acting weird, but she still hadn't said anything. Jay
went on in the kitchen, and poured himself a glass of juice. He
sat on a stool at the island counter, and thumbed through some
mail that was on the countertop.

While Jay was sitting in the kitchen, Portia walked in there,
and dropped a manila folder on the countertop in front of him.
It contained the photos of him and Ysatis. She crossed her
arms like she was the U.S. Attorney General, and looked at Jay
expectantly.

Jay looked at her like he was puzzled, and opened the folder.
When he saw the first photo, his heart skipped a beat. Oh shit!
If Portia had gone that far, how much did she know? Jay
thumbed through the pictures over and over, stalling for time
to get his words together. It was clear that his wife had done
her homework, so whatever he came with had to be good.

He realized that the cockamamie story he had come up with wouldn't quite suffice. Especially after he saw the shots of him and Ysatis dining, and exiting her building. He could see from the outfit he was wearing, those photos had been taken the last time he'd seen her.

Portia stood there watching Jay looking all stupid, and going through the pictures. He was caught red-handed, so she guessed there wasn't much he could say. But she wanted some type of response, so she tapped her fingernails on the table loudly. "Well? What's this about, Jay?"

Jay was cool when he spoke. "Yo, what's with the detective shit, P? If you wanna know somethin', then ask me. Don't be hidin' in mothafuckin' bushes, takin' pictures and shit."

Portia made a face. She liked his nerve. Typical man. That mothafucka was trying to use reverse psychology on her. Portia wasn't going for it. She folded her arms again, and just looked at him.

He sighed, and said, "Look, it's not what you think, Ma."

Portia asked, "So what is it then?"

Jay kept a straight face. "She's a singer. An artist that we might sign." Damn, that lie didn't even sound convincing to him.

Portia nodded, and kept on. "So if she's an artist, what business do you have coming out of her house?" "P, it's not like that. Trust me. That was strictly business." Jay looked at her sincerely, and nodded.

Portia was dying to let him know the extent of her findings, but she held back for a minute, to see if he would tell her the truth. "So she's an artist, and that's it? You sure, Jay?"

Jay nodded earnestly. Portia just looked at him. She wished she could believe him. She asked the one question that would determine if he was guilty, or not. "So how long have you known her?"

Jay said the first thing that came to his mind. "I just met her a few weeks ago, P. That's my word."

Portia bit her lip. Jay was a lying, guilty, no-good bastard. He was fucking that bitch. Portia was crushed. She felt like she needed oxygen. She just shook her head sadly. "A few

weeks ago, huh? And that's your word. You lied right to my
face, Jay. Wow."

She fought back the tears. He wasn't even worth it. Portia
flipped, and turned it up on that nigga. "You fuckin' lying Pin-
nochio piece of shit! Your little mistress' name is Ysatis Martin.
She's twenty years old, and a fulltime student at NYU. Her tuition has been financed by you for the past year, and she leases
an apartment on Central Park West, which you paid for, Trick
Daddy. You lying son of a bitch!"

Portia shook her head at Jay in disgust. "You send your
bitches to school, huh? What the fuck are you, The United
Negro College Fund for hoes? A twenty year old, Jay? I see
you like 'em young."

Jay was just silent. He was giving her the opportunity to
vent. Whatever he said at that point would be the wrong thing.
Damn, he was an idiot. He should've told Portia about Ysatis
when she first moved back to New York. He had never even
mentioned her. He should've told Portia back when she was
Humble's girlfriend, and they took care of her brother, Neal,
for molesting her. If he told her how it all happened now, she
wouldn't believe him. Everything had started out innocent,
but now it looked like he had some type of hidden agenda. He
couldn't fault Portia for thinking Ysatis was his mistress.

Portia continued. "What, baby? Am I too old for you know?
I guess I'd better quit while I'm ahead. I don't know how long
you've been fuckin' around on me, but now you fucked up. You
broke the eleventh commandment, boo. You got caught."

Portia paused for a few seconds. She was so angry she was
shaking. She couldn't believe he was cheating on her. She
reached over and slapped fire out of Jay.

Jay jumped. Damn, she slapped him hard! That shit almost
made water come out his eyes, but he didn't even respond. Portia was the only person who could get away with that.

She started up again. "Negro, let me tell you somethin'. I
ain't no poo-put bitch! You got it all twisted, baby. Trust me.
You really gambled on the wrong shit this time. I'm leaving
you for this, Jay."

Jay's shoulder's stiffened. He didn't want to hear that bullshit. She wasn't leaving him and going anywhere. He voiced his disagreement. "Nah, Ma. I'm tellin' you, you're wrong about this. Come on, it ain't even that serious."

"It ain't that serious? Wow." Portia laughed bitterly, and shook her head. "Say some stupid shit like that again, and I'll pick up somethin' and bust yo' fuckin' head open, nigga!" She looked at Jay like she dared him.

Jay didn't respond to that, because he knew she was upset. He just said, "Look, P, I'll just talk to you later. When you calm down."

Portia just shook her head at him, and she walked away. She went upstairs to pack her shit. Fuck Jay. He was nothing but a lying piece of shit.

Jay just acted nonchalant. He believed Portia would calm down after a while, and then he would convince her that there was nothing going on. He just went in the living room, and pretended he was watching the election coverage on the big screen. But he saw Portia actually start bringing stuff downstairs, so he got alarmed. She had a suitcase!

Jay got up, and tried to stop her. He had to think of something fast. All he could come up with was, "Oh, it's like that, P? You don't trust me? I trust you with everything. You got access to all my fuckin' bank accounts, and my money, and shit. Everything! So why would I start holding back on you now? I told you I ain't mess with that girl!"

Portia dropped the bag she was carrying, and screamed, "Nigga, I don't need shit from you! I got my own bank account, and my own money! Maybe not as much as you got, but I ain't no broke ass chick!"

Jay sucked his teeth impatiently. "P, cut it out. What's mine is yours, and you know that. Now, I told you I ain't mess wit' that fuckin' girl. We went out to eat a burger, and that's all!"

Portia made a face at him, and clenched her fists. He just wouldn't stop lying. She picked up her suitcase.

Jay saw that she wasn't listening to him, so he got frustrated. "What do you want me to say? I'll call her right now, and she can tell you herself."

Portia looked at him like he was crazy. "After you done al-

ready briefed her on what to say, and what lies to tell me? I
don't think so."

Jay said, "Kit Kat, please. I'm telling you the truth. I'm
sorry, but that's what it is."

Portia was quiet for a second, and then she just said, "No,
you ain't sorry. But you will be." After that, she didn't have
anymore words for him. She went outside, and loaded up her
car.

Portia had thought about waking up Trixie and Jazmin, and
taking them with her, but she decided to leave them with their
father. That would be good for Jay's ass. He needed some
down time.

Jay was standing at the front door watching her, with this
angry look on his face. Portia walked back over there, and addressed him calmly. But she told him like it was.

Her last words were, "I'm glad I learned about all the extracurricular time you got on your hands to fuck around. I'm
usually home all day with the kids, so I never have any free time.
So now, you can use your free time keep your children, Jay.
Let's see how you make time to go fuck around when you gotta
watch the kids! Tell my children I love them, and I will call
them later."

Portia spun around on her heels, and burned it up. Jay
fucked up when he cheated on her. She would show him what
a bad decision he had made. That bastard was really going to
miss her.

She hopped in her Benz, and drove off. Before Portia got to
the end of their winding driveway, Jay was calling her cell
phone. She ignored his call, and continued driving. She started
to go over Fatima's, but she decided to check into a hotel instead. She had a lot of crying to get out of her system, and she
needed to do it alone.

She wished her mother was still living. Patty Cake would
know what she should do. Portia couldn't believe her world
was falling apart so quickly. A part of her wanted to go back
home, and believe Jay would never cheat on her again. But she
had to have zero tolerance for something like that. If she let
him get away with it the first time, he would keep on cheating

on her.

Portia wiped away the tears that were falling from her eyes. Why was it that men always had to fuck everything up? She guessed she had just given Jay too much credit. He was just like all the rest of them. They all thought with their stupid assed dicks.

Back at the house, Jay sat with his head in his hands, wondering why he had just let Portia walk out on him. At first, he figured she needed a little space. He had tried to play all macho, but he wondered where she had gone. And she had left the kids with him.

Deep down inside, Jay knew that part of the reason he hadn't protested about her leaving was because he knew she'd be back soon. He knew she couldn't stay away from the kids. The kind of mother Portia was, she wouldn't leave her children for long. Jay loved his kids, but he hoped they were the security he needed to bring her back home. Hopefully before nightfall.

A few hours later, Portia sat in a huge, ritzy hotel suite all alone. She had smoked a little weed, and was sorting her thoughts out. She had to make a decision. Could she really leave her husband? Especially over some damn chicken head. But Jay must've had some strong feeling for her if he was paying her rent and tuition. Portia mulled it over, and she knew that bitch Ysatis would be happy if she left Jay. She wouldn't give that hoe the satisfaction.

"But that nigga cheated on you, girl", she told herself aloud. "So he has to pay for that."

Saying it out loud made Portia know what had to be done. She had to make Jay pay. He had to feel it. She wasn't going to condone him cheating on her. She didn't give a fuck how wealthy that mothafucka was. She would go to jail for the "big one" before she let him do that to her. She would kill his black ass.

Portia stayed in her suite all day. She ordered room service, which she only half ate, and then she stayed up pretty late that night watching Dave Chapelle, and some other shows she liked. Jay called her cell phone a zillion times, but she ignored his calls. Fatima and Laila called a lot too, probably to make sure she was alright. Portia didn't even answer her phone. She just didn't feel like explaining herself.

Portia also got a call from her cousin Melanie, whom she hadn't heard from in a while. She let that call go to voicemail as well. She would call her back another time, just to make sure she was okay.

At about four a.m., Portia tried to get some rest. She knew it wouldn't be the best rest, but she had to sleep a little bit. She laid in bed, and thought about her children. She could hear her baby cooing, and imagined Trixie blowing bubbles the adorable way she had started doing. Then she could see Jazmin pacing the floor, and demanding to know where she was, just like she did when her daddy was late. And Portia was certain Lil' Jay had wanted to know why she wasn't there to cook Sunday dinner. She smiled at the thought of her little angels, and realized that breaking up her family was going to be a lot harder than she thought.

Portia cursed out loud. "Shit!" She really hated Jay's ass right about then. He had put her in a fucked up position, and she was tight. She missed her kids. She doubted that she would be able to function without them.

Unable to sleep yet, she got up and turned on the lamp on the nightstand by her bed. She opened the drawer, and found a Bible, a notepad, and a pen inside. Portia had a poet's soul, and emotions inspired her to write sometimes. Good and bad emotions. She grabbed the pen and pad, and sat down and put some words she had in her head on paper. She scribbled,

To my FORMER husband Jay,

Over the years, you've inspired me to write a lot of things. Now, since you're such old news, my latest dedication to you came out in the form of an old school rap. When you read these dope lyrics, please imagine me wearing a Kangol, with a big ass gold rope chain around my neck. Here it goes:

Fuck you, bitch ass nigga

Fool, you lucky I ain't pull the trigger
Yeah, you had a chick goin', but hey, go figure
Guess you rather run around with hoes and gold diggers

Can't believe you made a move so trife
The shit really hurts man, cuts like a knife
At one point I was happy just to be your wife
But now nigga, you better stay the fuck outta my life!

As of today, Mr. Jay Mitchell, you are hereby declared official "Black History".

Fuck off Asshole,
Your Ex-wife, P

When Portia was done, she folded the letter up, and put it in a long envelope. She wrote their home address on the front, and didn't bother to write a return address on it. She would mail it later that day.

Portia climbed back in bed, but sleep still didn't come easy. She thought writing that letter would've been her closure, but it obviously wasn't that easy. She said another prayer, and fell into a troubled sleep.

CHAPTER TWENTY FIVE

The next morning, Fatima called and woke Portia up at around nine. She said she was sorry for calling her so early, but she wanted to make sure she was okay. Portia told her what happened, but she told her girl she was good.

Fatima paused, and then she told Portia she understood her need to get away. She said she had been up all night thinking, and she had decided to go to Hawaii, to that "resort" Jay and Cas had offered to send her too. Portia told her she was happy she had made that choice, but she told her she should call Jay about that herself. She told her they weren't talking.

Fatima asked her just how long she planned on running away. Portia told her she didn't want to talk about it, so she left it alone. They agreed to talk to each other later that day. Before they hung up, Portia told her she was proud of her, and told her to be strong. Fatima told her to be strong too. She knew Portia wasn't doing so great. God bless Wise, she remembered being crushed about him cheating on her, the same way her girl was. Whether she admitted it, or not.

After she got off the phone with Portia, Fatima called Jay. She didn't let on that she knew Portia had left him, because she didn't want to be all up in their business. She was sure he already felt bad enough without her chastising him. She just let Jay know she was ready to take him and Cas up on that offer, if it was still on the table. She told him she was ready to go to rehab.

Jay told her that was good news. He said he would arrange a flight for her as soon as possible, if she was ready. Fatima told him it was now, or never. Jay told her he was proud of her. He promised Fatima he would call her back with details.

After they hung up, Jay smiled to himself at the thought of Fatima finally seeking some help. He was glad she wanted to

get herself together. He said a silent prayer for a positive turnaround in his life as well.

$$$$$

True to their word, Jay and Cas booked Fatima first-class ac-
commodations at the five-star Renaissance Honolulu. She left
for Hawaii two days later. Fatima felt good knowing she'd left
Callie in charge of her house while she was gone. She could
relax, and not have to worry about going home to find out
she'd been robbed, or something. She was glad she had somebody she could trust. Fatima was confident she had made the
right decision.

When she got to Hawaii, she was immediately overcome with
the beauty of the atmosphere. She had been quite a few places,
but that was her first time visiting there. It was absolutely
breathtaking.

Fatima had opted for a beachside villa, so every morning she
woke up and stepped on her terrace, and watched the sunrise
over the ocean. That was how she began each day she was there.
After that came thirty minutes of yoga and exercise, and a well-
balanced breakfast. Then her days were filled with full body
massages, spa treatments, meditation, holistic therapy, sun-
bathing, and last but not least, support group meetings.

Fatima slept with her terrace doors open every night, so she
got lots of well needed rest, under a pleasant ocean breeze. It
was an experience she definitely needed in her life at that point.
She started feeling real good about herself. Fatima was in the
process of self renewal, and she planned to emerge completely
rejuvenated.

$$$$$

Meanwhile, Portia was on her third day being M.I.A. She
was still in her hotel suite hiding out. She had called to check
on her babies, so she knew they were okay. She'd started feeling
guilty about being away from them, but she knew she left them
in good hands with their father. Jay wouldn't ever allow any

harm to come to them, so she wasn't tripping. But she did miss her little ones.

When Portia called, Jay had taken the phone from Jayquan. He said he got her letter, and he didn't find the little "old school rap" she wrote him amusing. And then he demanded to know where she was. Portia just sucked her teeth, and told him not to worry about it, and then she hung up.

She had done some soul searching over the last few days, and she made up her mind to go stay at her mother's house for a while. She hadn't been back there since right after Patty Cake had passed away. She paid the taxes and utilities as they were due, but she hadn't felt strong enough to go back yet. She guessed she had needed a reason to face it sooner or later anyway.

After Jay cheated with Ysatis, that was the place she would seek refuge. Portia thought about remodeling the house. The bedrooms first, for her children. She was really grateful she had that house. It was all hers, and she had enough space for her and her kids to be comfortable.

She made up her mind. She was moving back to Brooklyn. That was her hometown anyway. Fuck Jay. He was the one who cheated, so she didn't need his ass.

Who was she kidding? She did need Jay. He completed her. But she had to show him she meant business. He could not fuck around on her. Her heart couldn't stand it. She could barely even breathe.

Tears clouded Portia's vision once again. She just couldn't seem to shut off the waterworks. Damn Jay for doing this to her. She got it together, and got ready to drive to Brooklyn. She had to force herself back into civilization, so the trip would be good for her.

On the way there, Portia thumbed through the radio stations, and she came across a country station playing Tammy Winnette's old classic hit, "Stand By Your Man". "Stand by your man. Let the world know you love him..."

She left the radio tuned there, and thought about Jay. She had done that. She had stood by him. Through it all. So how dare he betray her the way he had? That no-good bastard. Why did men always have to mess everything up? They said all men cheated, but she wasn't the type of woman to go for that bullshit.

When Portia got to her inherited house in Brooklyn, the first thing she noticed when she got out the car was the "For Sale" sign on the house next door. That was where her neighbor, Ms. Hattie, used to live. The house looked sort of abandoned now, so she wondered where she and her family had moved to. She hoped they were all okay.

Portia opened the gate to the front yard of her house, and took a deep breath. there were lots of dead leaves on the ground, so the yard needed to be swept. But other than that, it was home. She stood at the foot of the steps, and a thousand memories flashed through her mind. She remembered running up and down those stairs playing when she was a child, despite her mother's warnings about falling down and breaking her neck. She had taken a few spills out there too. That was when her father was still alive. He was usually the one that bandaged up her knees, when she ran inside screaming and crying.

Portia remembered playing hopscotch, and double-dutch in front of her house when she was a kid too, and other games like "freeze tag", "red light-green light 1-2-3", and "hot peas and butter". Those were some of the most fun times of her life.

Then she grew a little older, and met Laila, Fatima, and Simone, God bless the dead. That was when the good times really began. Portia could remember them all sitting outside on her steps in the summertime all night, until the break of day. They used to just be chilling, and bugging out, and all the dudes from the corner used to come and holler at them.

Dudes always showed their clique love and respect. They were the cool chicks. They even used to stash their guns and packs for them sometimes, so they wouldn't be dirty if the police jumped out on them. The fellows looked out for them with money in exchange, and supplied them with all the weed they could smoke. The guys were just their homeboys, but they were still boys. Portia, Laila, Fatima, and Simone were all pretty girls, so one of them was always getting hit on. All of them probably creeped off once or twice, but it was all love.

Portia thought about the time she and Simone had lost their virginity the same day, when they were fifteen. They had done it with these two cousins, named Hasaan and Nashawn. Afterwards, they went in the hotel bathroom, and compared notes. Then they had snuck back in Portia's house, and pretended they'd been home all night.

They didn't get busted that time, but there'd been an occasion when they had. Patty Cake had surprised them all one night, when they snuck in from a party. She'd been waiting in Portia's bedroom, hiding in the closet. She saw them sneak in, and get ready for bed. She blew their asses up too. As a result, Portia got grounded for three weeks.

Portia smiled at the memories, and she headed around to the ground floor entrance. She could feel her mama's spirit before she even opened the door. She turned her key in the lock, and walked on inside. Everything was just as she'd left it.

It had been a while since she'd been there. She had left everything just the way her mother left it when she went in the hospital that last time. Portia was melancholy at first. But the more she looked around, she was overcome with joy. There were so many memories there. Every nook of the house was filled with sweet memories. Things were a little dusty, but it was definitely home.

She walked upstairs to Pat's bedroom, and looked at the hundreds of perfume bottles on her dresser. Her mother had every top shelf designer scent you could name, from Alfred Sung, to Yves Saint Laurent. Portia opened her walk-in closet, and thumbed through her wardrobe. She glanced at Pat's bad ass suits, blouses, dresses, and hats. She had everything organized, and color coded. Her shoes were the same way. Patricia Lane was truly a diva.

Portia smiled, and walked around the room. It even still smelled the same. She stepped into Pat's huge closet again, and sniffed her clothing. She sighed, and whispered, "Oh God. Mommy, I miss you so much."

She had a seat on her mama's bed, and then she laid across it for a second. She could still smell her on the pillows and linen. Portia wrapped herself up in the cover, and closed her eyes. It was almost like her mama was hugging her. She laid there for a while, and she dozed off before she knew it.

She woke up about an hour later, and she felt stronger for some reason. She knew she had to keep on, no matter what. That day marked the start of a new beginning. She needed to find herself. Portia didn't appreciate the fact that she didn't feel whole without Jay.

She loved him, but now she realized she had built everything around him. She had put his needs before hers. She had even risked her freedom for Jay. She could've gotten life in prison if she had got caught with all those hot ass guns in her bag at the hospital that time.

And Jay wasn't even guaranteed to her. Life was clearly not the fairytale she'd been pretending to live in. Her family wasn't perfect. Jay wasn't promised to her. He could leave her for somebody else. Or God forbid, he could be snatched away from her, just like Fatima had lost Wise. Or they could wind up divorced, like Laila and Khalil had.

Her homegirls had probably believed they would be with their husbands forever too. Portia realized she had been a little naïve. She had to get stronger. Life had taught her that nothing lasted forever, so she had to apply that concept to everything.

Ironically, Jay had always tried to make her stronger. He didn't know just how tough she would be from then on. He had created a monster.

Portia was no idiot. She knew her husband was a good catch, and would probably always be targeted by some other woman. Jay had swagger, and women flocked to that. But she had to be able to trust that he would resist the temptation. He used to, so what had happened that time?

Portia was thinking too much. It was too quiet in the house, so she went downstairs to turn on some music. Music was good for the soul. She came across her mother's old gospel collection. She fished through it, and found songs she remembered listening to with her mother and grandmother when she was a child.

Portia popped in a gospel CD of classic oldies, and one of

her favorite songs played first. "Better Than Blessed", by Candi
Staton. Portia sang along, and reminisced. "I'm blessed- better
than blessed, thank you Lord. I'm blessed -better than blessed,
praise the Lord... I may not have houses and wealth, and I may
not have all my strength and health. But I'm blessed- better
than blessed - thank the Lord..."

Next, a soul stirring song called "Where is Your Faith?" came
on. Portia hummed along, and cried. The time on earth was
precious. She was really touched by that music. It reminded
her of her mother so much. Pat used to play gospel every single
Sunday she was alive. Even the few times she didn't make it to
church.

Portia knew she had to start taking her children to church
more often. Her mother had given her words of wisdom before
she passed. She said, "Raise them with God, Portia. The way
I raised you."

Portia smiled at memories of her trucking to Sunday school
as a child early Sunday mornings. She remembered when her
Sunday school teacher, Deacon Jamison, had given the pupils
who'd correctly memorized the entire 23rd Psalm five bucks a
piece. She had run to her parents proudly, and bragged about
knowing that bible verse. She'd been such an innocent child
back then. Her daddy used to make her recite that bible verse
every time their family had visitors.

Portia still knew that verse it. She said it aloud. "The Lord
is my shepherd, I shall not want. He maketh me lie in green
pastures, he leadeth me beside still waters. He restoreth my
soul... Sure goodness and mercy shall follow me all the days of
my life..." Portia knew that those religious teachings she had
received as a child were the reason God had kept her, and spared
her life when she was caught up earning her living as an exotic
dancer, and doing "privates". And she wasn't going to kid herself. She knew she needed God now too. She needed Him
more than anything. That was the only way to get through the
adversity she currently had going on in her life. She made up
her mind. Her and her children were going to church. Her
mother's church, where her Aunt Gracie preached.

Portia thought about one of the last conversations she had

with her mother. God rest her soul, Patricia had said "No relationship is beyond tests." She had thought she had her thing on a string, but now she saw that her mama was right. If that "Ysatis" incident wasn't a test of her marriage, then what was?

But Jay had picked the wrong way to test her. He had done the ultimate. When Portia thought about him sexing another woman, her insides cringed. It made her literally sick. And it made her want to cut his dick off. Real talk.

$$$$$

Down in Honolulu, Hawaii, Fatima was busy basking in the sun. She called all her loved ones that afternoon, and told them she was fine. She kept it real, and told them she was going through a physical, mental, and spiritual healing process, and it was soothing to her soul.

Fatima had taken on sort of a bohemian role while she was there. Most days her attire consisted of a long, batik print spa dress, over a bathing suit, and tan leather flip-flops. She bought those dresses in just about every color. And she let her hair air-dry, and wore it naturally curly, and usually tied it back in a scarf that matched her dress. That completed her neo-earthy look.

She was healthy, and happy as ever. The "vacation" had certainly done her some good. Fatima knew that a part of her would remain in Hawaii, because the island was so beautiful it had stolen her heart. She hated to leave, but she told her friends she would be home soon.

$$$$$

Back at Fatima's house, Callie and Smoke lay intertwined on the bed in the guestroom she occupied at Fatima's house. They just finished having mind-blowing sex, so Callie was all giddy, and basking in the afterglow of their lovemaking. Smoke was smoking a cigarette.

Callie had picked him up from jail just hours before. They had come back to the house to fuck, relax, and figure out their next move. He was finally home, and they had a lot of catching up to do.

Smoke had been impressed when Callie pulled up in Fatima's big boy Mercedes. She confessed that it wasn't theirs, so he laughed, and told her they were copping black and white "his" and "hers" joints just like it. When they got to the house, he was even more impressed when he saw where she'd been staying. He could smell money all up in there. He would've been telling a lie if he said he'd ever stepped foot in a house that damn bad. That shit was like a mansion. He could tell that bitch Fatima was holding.

Smoke was always about business. Now that he'd gotten his nuts out of the sand, he wanted to know how big the take was. He came right out and asked, "So, how much we get outta this broad so far? What it's lookin' like, Ma?"

Callie tensed up a little, but she took a deep breath, and tried to relax. It was hard to tell him the truth, but she just came out and admitted that she didn't have any real money yet. After she said it, the disappointed look on his face made her feel like she wasn't even worthy of him.

She was eager to please him somehow, so she reached in her nightstand drawer, and pulled out a plastic zip-lock bag filled with Fatima's social security card, birth certificate, and all the other stuff she did have.

Smoke took the zip-lock bag, and examined its contents, and his frown turned into a smile. And it grew bigger with each item he looked over. When he looked at Fatima's bank statements, he yelled, "Hot damn! Ma, that's what the fuck I'm talkin' 'bout. That's what's up! We gon' clean this bitch out!"

Callie smiled, but she was a little confused. Smoke could see that she didn't understand, so he was patient with her. He explained that they were going to take a trip out of town, because in some states, you only needed a birth certificate and social security card to get an official I.D. card. He told her that after she got a photo I.D. in Fatima's name, she could "be her", and make bank withdrawals, credit card purchases, and even be able to sign for them to cop some foreign whips.

Callie was skeptical. She had doubts about being able to walk in a bank, and just take out someone's money, but Smoke

told her she had all they needed. Most banks only asked for
two pieces of I.D. when making a withdrawal. He said she
would have the new identification she was getting when they
went out of town, and the major credit card she had stolen from
Fatima's wallet. He was pretty thrilled about the whole thing.

Smoke made the decision that they would leave town the following day. They ordered a pizza, and after they ate, they spent
the remainder of the night fucking all over the house. They
fucked on Fatima's dining room table, in the kitchen, on the
patio, and even outside by the pool. When Smoke was cumming, he shot off in the water. And just about anywhere else
he thought was disrespectful.

The following morning, the corrupt couple got ready to hit
the road. Callie didn't want Fatima to come home and panic
when she saw she was gone, so she left her a note. She and
Smoke left around noon.

The note she left said, "Welcome home! I had a little emergency, but I'll be back next week. Thanks for everything, Love
Callie."

$$$$$

About two weeks later, Jay was down in an illegal, afterhours
gambling spot. It was located in some basement in Harlem,
and it was somewhere he probably had no business at. He had
been bored and lonely, so he had basically gone just to get out
of the house. But so far, his luck down there had been just like
his marriage was lately. Bad.

They had a dude at the front, searching people before they
came in. Before Jay was patted down, he was honest, and told
the security dude he was holding. The dude felt the two guns
in his waist, and his first thought was that Jay was there to rob
the joint.

Jay sensed his hesitation, and flashed a bankroll on him. He
wasn't fronting. He just wanted duke to know he wasn't thirsty.
Jay peeled off five crisp hundreds, and slid it to him, and he was
allowed to enter the joint with his two trademark guns.

Jay wouldn't have gone down there without his guns, so he

appreciated scrams looking out like that. But he didn't know how many other dudes in there had paid him to let them bring their blickers inside too. So he didn't plan on dropping his guard while he was down there.

Jay ventured into the back room for a few minutes, where the strippers were. There was this girl in a tiny neon green bikini dancing on a makeshift stage. This young dude stood by, and watched her dance. He was visually drunk, and rowdy as hell.

The girl's breasts bulged out of her top, and threatened to escape the flimsy straps at any moment. She got in his face, and said, "I know you gon' look out for me. Right, boo?"

The guy sized her up, and said, "Hell yeah, ma. Lay down, and close your eyes. Do some freaky shit for me, and I'ma make it rain on you, shorty. That's my word." He flashed a wad of cash, and hit her with the "sincere" face, and a reassuring nod.

The girl's eyes lit up. She ate that bullshit up like cotton candy. The dude suppressed his laughter. She was so stupid and greedy, it was unbelievable. He planned to teach her money hungry, conniving ass a lesson.

When she got down on the floor, he made it rain on her all right. He tossed pennies and nickels at her by the handful, throwing them with force. The coins struck her all about the face and body.

The coins stung, and bruised her skin. When the girl realized that she was being disrespectfully pelted with coins, she winced, and jumped up and tried to dodge the barrage. She yelled, "Nigga, what the fuck you doin'?"

He said, "You want money? Here, bitch! Take it!" He threw even more coins at her. Nickels, pennies, and dimes. He laughed, and yelled, "Fuck you, bitch!"

Jay felt sorry for the girl, but he didn't stick around to see anymore. It was unfortunate that she had been disrespected that way, but he minded his business. That was the bouncers in the joint's responsibility, not his.

He should've minded his business when it came to Ysatis. He had tried to help her, and winded up having his wife bail on him as a result. He wasn't ever getting involved and helping another damsel in distress as long as he lived. When you helped a chick, she thought of you as some fucking knight in shining armor, and then shit got all twisted.

Jay headed back to the room on the side, where the high rollers were. It wasn't long before he had lost just about all the cash he had on him. Jay hated losing, so he contemplated making a run, to go get some more money.

While he was thinking about it, just as he thought, somebody had to test him that night. This dude he didn't know started mean mugging him, trying to start a face war.

Jay didn't know what his problem was, but he didn't do the face fighting thing. He didn't see the point in it. But he took that dude's expression to be a sign of disrespect, so his killer instinct kicked in. Immediately, he mentally set up the scenario he would use to slaughter him outside.

That was a classic example of why Jay had no business in there. He didn't want to have to murder somebody's son that night. That was why it was good to be married. It gave you an excuse to go home early. If you weren't around the bullshit, you didn't get in it.

The dude must've sensed that he was dangerous, because he relaxed, and kept it on a hop. That nigga didn't really want it. But Jay still didn't sleep on him. He didn't sleep on anybody. It was time for him to go anyway. He couldn't believe it was already five A.M. He needed to go home, and crash.

Jay hated sleeping alone. That was why he'd been hanging out so late some nights. Luckily, Laila had offered to keep an eye on the kids for him that night. But she was moving out later that week. The renovations and interior decorating would be complete in a few days, so she and Cas were finally moving into their new home. Jay thought it was great that things were working out for them. At least somebody would be happy.

He thought about his estranged wife. He was really fed up with Portia's shit. Enough was enough. He missed his wife. It was time for her to come home. Jay knew he had messed up, but he would make it up to her. If she gave him the chance. Portia wouldn't even answer her phone when he called her.

Another slap in the face was the fact that he knew she had been over Cas and Laila's new crib, which was only about fifteen minutes away from their house. He knew she was mad, but that was foul. She could've at least stopped by to see the kids. That chick was wilding.

Jay knew where she was. In Brooklyn, at the house her mother left her. He decided that after he went home and got some rest, he was going to BK to see what the hell that girl was up to. Fuck that, she was his wife.

$$\$\$\$\$\$$

Later that evening, Jay drove to Brooklyn. Along the way, he rehearsed exactly what he would say to Portia when he saw her. He couldn't front, he was mad nervous. He couldn't believe Portia had him under pressure like that. But he would never admit it to anyone.

When he got to where she was staying in Bed-Stuy, he parked his Bentley, and went over his lines one more time. Jay sat there for a few seconds, and got up his nerve, and then he got out, and rang the doorbell.

When Portia heard the bell, she went to the door. When she saw it was Jay, she sort of frowned. What the hell was he doing there? A part of her was happy to see him, but she opened the door with a frown on her face. It was nothing like the smile she used to always have for him before. And she was intentionally rude. Instead of saying hello, Portia said, "Jay, what are you doing here?"

Jay was thrown off by her snappiness. She made him feel like a straight sucker, so he got on defense. All that shit he'd rehearsed in the car was out the window. He wasn't telling her he missed her now. He wasn't some fucking lame, so his response to her question was curt. He said, "I just came to see when you comin' home." Jay quickly added, "Because of the kids."

Now she wouldn't think he was begging her to come home because he missed her. He was fed up with Portia's shit. He didn't come over there to kiss her ass. In a demanding tone, he asked her, "What the fuck are you doin' over here anyway?"

Portia crossed her arms, and looked Jay right in his eyes.

"Didn't you hear what Barack Obama said? It's time for a change. I'm gettin' me back. I lost myself catering to you. So the little stunt you pulled just reminded me to put me first."

Jay didn't want to hear that shit. He got impatient, and said, "Yeah, but you have kids. They come first. Remember?"

Portia smirked at his selfish ass. She liked his nerve. She said, "Yeah, I do have kids. And I miss my babies too. In fact, you wanna know what I've been over here doin'? For your information, I haven't just been bullshitting. I'm getting the house ready for my children to move in. Come on in, and have a look around."

Jay didn't reply to her nonsense, but he walked inside the house. Portia kept on testing him. As he looked around, he fondly remembered his mother-in-law. Pat was a good woman. God bless her soul. He really hoped she was resting in peace. It was sad that she was gone.

Jay reluctantly followed Portia upstairs. He had the feeling he wouldn't be pleased with what he saw.

When she showed him the bedrooms upstairs, he was speechless. In one of the rooms, there was a brand new twin sized bedroom set, with a Sponge Bob comforter on the bed. That was obviously supposed to be Jazmin's room. Jay knew Sponge Bob Square Pants was the only show she sat still long enough to watch.

The bedroom in the middle was a little smaller, but there was a brand new crib in there. Elmo from Sesame Street was Trixie's favorite television character, and his presence was all up in that room. There were Sesame Street decals all over the walls, and the crib dressing, the curtains, and the lamp were the same Elmo-based theme.

The last room he looked in was the biggest. It was empty, and he could see that Portia was still painting in there. She had chosen a nice light blue color.

Portia knew Jay was wondering who the room belonged to, so she went on and told him. "This room is for my son, Jayquan, who is welcome to come and stay with me and his sisters anytime he wants. His new furniture will be delivered tomorrow morning. I ordered him a really nice, custom-made bedroom set, so it took a little time to get ready."

Portia could see that Jay had the dumb face. She was glad he was looking all constipated. Good for his ass. She continued rubbing it in. "And if you're wondering where my room is, it will be downstairs. I've decided to leave my mother's bedroom untouched. I'm hiring a contractor to open up the den and the parlor downstairs, and convert the space into a master bedroom and bathroom. Just for your information. Not that you should care, or anything."

Jay didn't even respond. He was too hurt at the time. And there was a big lump in his throat. It was blocking his speech.

Portia could tell he was upset. She had intended to piss him off. She had to show him she wasn't playing. She spoke to him again. "Look Jay, the only reason I showed you the kids' rooms is because I'm sure you're concerned where they'll be living. I just wanted you to know they'll be okay. There's a little less space here, but it's a comfortable and loving environment, so they'll get used to it. And by the way, I checked out the schools here, and their records are pretty decent."

Portia said, "So... Is there anything else you wanna know?"

She gave Jay the opportunity to talk, but he didn't say anything. After a minute, she said, "I don't mean to be rude, but I have some painting to finish. Jayquan's furniture is coming early in the morning, and I want the paint to be completely dry."

Jay dropped his head. He was low. He hadn't realized Portia was so serious about not coming back home. He had thought she was just trying to teach him a lesson, but it looked like she really meant business. She was not planning on coming home anytime soon.

Jay wasn't a bitch, but he sort of felt like crying. Damn, he felt low. Portia made him feel real small. But he deserved it. He knew he did. Shit just got blown all out of proportion.

Portia could tell he was hurt, but so the fuck was she. She re-loaded, and started shooting at him again. She said, "Oh yeah, about the reason you came. You know, the kids. I'll call your mother, and ask her if she'd mind watching them for a few days, if your children are too much of a burden on you. I thought about it before, but I wanted to spare your mother the disappointment of me informing her that I needed a babysitter, because I moved out, and am desperately trying to prepare a decent place for me and her grandkids to live, because her son cheated on me with a little twenty year old girl, that he sent to college. Oh yeah, and paid her rent." She eyed him, and dared him to respond.

Jay was a powerful man. He was well respected. He gave out orders all day, but that indirect tongue lashing made him feel like a scolded little boy. He didn't even know what to say to that. He just snapped, "You don't gotta call my mother. Don't bother. My kids are fine."

Jay shoved his hands in his pockets. He was about to break out. Fuck that shit. Who the fuck was she talking to like that? He was no lame. He asked her one thing before he left. "Yo, you need anything?"

Portia wanted to tell him she needed him to be good to her, and be careful with her heart, and love her like she loved him. But instead, she just looked at him with an emotionless expression on her face, and said, "Just look after my children for a few days."

Jay nodded. That was automatic. He didn't bother to remind her that they were his children too. He took care of his, and she knew that.

Portia said, "Other than that, I don't need anything you have. Thank God. Good bye, Jay."

Jay did an about-face, and he got the hell out of there. A part of him regretted even coming. He felt like a real chump, but he should've known it was too soon. Portia was still mad. Very mad.

He got back in his Bentley, and pulled off. He wanted to curse, and call her all kinds of bitches, but he knew everything that happened was his fault. He prayed she would get over it soon. He was really down over this shit. And now she was talking about taking away his children.

He would have to see about that. If Portia didn't come around soon, he would have to drag her ass to court. Jay loved his children more than anything in the world, and he wasn't about to miss being involved in their lives because of Portia's stupid bullshit. No matter how justifiable it was.

After Jay left, Portia was thinking too much, so she turned the radio on. Seeing him had brought back too many feelings and emotions. She tuned in to 98.7 Kiss FM, and one of her favorite old hits was playing. "I'm Not Your Super Woman." That was her jam back in the days. When they were in the eighth grade, her and her girls had written down all the lyrics, and memorized them. Portia sung along with the record.

"I'm not your super woman. I'm not the kind of girl that you can let down- and think that every thing is okay. Boy, I am only human... and this girl needs more than occasional hearts as a token of love from you to me..."

For some reason, Portia just started crying. She couldn't even sing the words. She felt like fucking strangling Jay. She wasn't super woman, but she was as close to perfect as he would get. To hell with that trifling asshole. The thought of him up in some other bitch's pussy nauseated her.

Portia was mad. She had sacrificed a lot for Jay. She had been acting like a fucking housewife lately. She was no damn desperate housewife. But she'd been so busy taking care of Jay and her family, she barely had time to take care of her business.

When she got pregnant with Trixie, she had informed her agent, Penelope, that after she had her baby, she was taking a year off to bond with her. Portia had postponed the book tour they had planned. And Penelope had secured her a spot speaking on the independent film panel at the Worldwide Film Festival, and she hadn't even attended.

Portia knew she had been seriously neglecting her writing career, her publishing company, and the film company she and Jay had. Fatima hadn't been on top of things either, because she was dealing with her own demons. Sinclair-Lane Publishing was sort of at a standstill.

They were selling a few books, but nothing compared to what they could be doing if they went hard. They had created a buzz, so they had an audience. Between all three of Portia's titles, they had independently sold over 150,000 books so far. But if they had stayed in it, it could've been even better. And people were eagerly awaiting Portia's fourth book.

She had to get her mind right, and get back on top of her business. God willing, Fatima would come home from Hawaii on the right track, and they could get it popping. Portia had been content, because Jay's money was so long, she never had to worry about anything. But there was no guarantee that Jay would always take care of her. That type of thing happened to the first wives of wealthy men all the time.

But it wasn't just about that. She wanted to leave her children a legacy too. At the time, everything was uncertain. There was an economic crisis going on across the country. It was all over the news. So it wasn't the time to sit home, and depend on a man. She should be hustling, and putting money away for her children's future.

Portia decided she wasn't giving up on her dreams. She would rather give up on love. If she had invested all the time and energy she put into loving Jay into her work, she would've probably been a renowned author, and filmmaker by now. But she put everything she had into love, and her investment didn't pay off the way she deserved.

CHAPTER TWENTY SIX

Fatima came home about three days later, and she looked great. She felt great too. She was renewed, and felt whole for the first time since Wise died. Fatima had regained physical and mental strength, and she'd also strengthened her relationship with God. Being on that beautiful island reminded her of God's ability to create greatness. She too was one of His creations, so she would never abuse her body the way she had again.

More than anything, Fatima missed her daughter. She had promised herself, and God, that she was going to be a better mother. After she was done unpacking, she was going to her parent's house to get her baby. And then she and Fay were going out somewhere.

Fatima decided to take her princess to see a live show. The Wiggles were at Madison Square Garden, so Fatima called Telecharge, and got four of the best seats she could buy. Falynn loved The Wiggles, and Portia's daughter, Jazmin, loved them too. She bought a ticket for Portia as well. She was in Brooklyn, close to where Fatima's parents' house was, so she could scoop her up when she picked up Falynn.

She called Portia, and told her to be ready when she and the kids came through. Portia sounded happy to hear from her, and even happier that Fatima had tickets to take Jazz and Fay to see The Wiggles. After that, Fatima called Jay, and asked him if she could pick up Jazmin. He said okay, and promised her Jazz would be ready when she got there.

After they hung up, she started unpacking. She thought about the warm greeting Jay had given her on the phone, and smiled. He told her it was good to have her back. She had thanked him again for sponsoring her "vacation", but he said it was nothing. Fatima told him she'd be there to get Jazz in an hour.

After she spoke to Jay, she called Casino, and thanked him too. Cas greeted her with equal enthusiasm. He said he was happy she had returned from Honolulu feeling as good as she sounded. He was genuine, and told her to never hesitate to ask him for anything she needed.

Fatima thanked him again, and she told him she would be by soon with a housewarming gift for him and Laila. Cas told her that wasn't necessary, and said she was welcome anytime. When they hung up, they were both smiling.

As Fatima unpacked, she wondered where Callie was. She hadn't been able to get her on the phone the past few days. Not even on her cell phone. Maybe she had moved on. Fatima would've preferred that she'd waited until she got back, but from what she could see, her house was okay.

When Fatima went downstairs to the kitchen, she found a note from Callie. It said she had some type of emergency, and would be back soon. When she went back upstairs, she looked in Callie's bedroom. Some of her clothes were still hanging in the closet, so it did look like she was coming back. Fatima didn't notice anything strange, so she went on about her business.

Fatima picked out an adorable little Christian Dior outfit for her daughter to wear. She would take it with her, and change Fay's clothes when she got to Brooklyn. And that day she could also wear the diamond earrings her daddy bought her. Falynn liked to play rough, so she was only allowed to wear them on special occasions. Fatima didn't want her to lose them. Fay had lost a lot of earrings.

When Fatima looked in her jewelry box, she didn't see her baby's earrings. She looked everywhere, but she could not find those earrings. She just had a funny feeling. It seemed like somebody had been going through her stuff. Or was she bugging? She looked through all her drawers, and her jewelry box for Falynn's earrings one more time. Those were her first diamonds, and they were a gift from Wise.

And where the hell was her husband's Rolex? She treasured that watch. Wise had been wearing it when he was shot. But now it was missing. Fatima couldn't help but wonder if Callie had anything to do with her not being able to find her things. She didn't want to believe that was possible, but where the fuck was her shit? She kept her things in certain places, so she knew she wasn't crazy.

The fact that she couldn't find that jewelry really bothered Fatima. Hopefully, she had just misplaced it, and it would resurface in the house somewhere. But she knew there was a good chance that somebody could have stolen it.

Fatima didn't have time to brood over the issue right then. She had to pick up the kids, so they could get to the show on time. But she definitely planned on questioning Miss Callie when she returned from wherever she was.

$$$$$

Cas and Laila had moved into their new home, and they were just settling. It had taken a few weeks longer for them to move in, because Cas had thoughtfully decided to have a small elevator installed. There were a lot of stairs in the house, so that made it easier on Laila. Finally, everything was done in the house, except for a few personal touches she planned to add.

Laila was still fighting hard to walk, but she was inspired by the progress she was making. Her dream was to be able to walk around freely in her big, bad ass, new house. Especially in the fabulous kitchen she had.

The interior decorator they'd hired had interviewed her and Cas individually, and he had combined both of their ideas. He created the warmest, most comfortable environment Laila could've ever wished for. Everything was just so "her". She finally had her own luxurious space. It was elegant, but the décor was also homey.

Cas had the painting of her late daughter, Pebbles, restored, and mounted on the wall. It was one of the first things you saw when you walked in the house. That painting was a gift from Jay, so Laila thought about him. She'd felt bad about leaving him at the house, when Portia had left him all alone with the kids.

Laila understood what Portia was going through, so she wasn't talking bad about her homegirl. She didn't have a problem with looking after her children. Portia just needed some time to herself. Laila would never forget how Portia took care of Macy for her, when she was in the hospital, and couldn't. And then she also took care of Skye for Laila, when she had all those psychological issues, and wouldn't.

Portia was a real friend. And so was Jay. He had never once hesitated to open up his home to Laila and her family, in her various times of need. She had asked Jay if he needed her to stick around a little longer, to help him out, but he assured her that he and the kids were fine. Laila just felt so sorry for him. Even if he'd messed up, he was a good dude.

And Jay was a great father. He hired a thoroughly screened babysitter to look after the kids when he couldn't, but he took them with him whenever he could. And Cas told her Jay had been going home early everyday to look after them.

Laila didn't want to get involved in him and Portia's spats, so she didn't bother to lecture Jay on the perils of infidelity. She could tell that brother was already feeling it. He came by the house to visit her and Cas, and he looked like he was so sad.

Laila went to check on her brownstone in Brooklyn last Tuesday, and she made it a point to go see about Portia while she was out there. She had tried to talk Portia into going back home, but girlfriend was stuck on teaching Jay a lesson. She told Laila she was remodeling, so the kids could come and live with her out there.

Laila hadn't pressured her, but she went home and leaked that info to Cas. After that, he even went to Portia's house, and tried to talk to her one day. He had suggested that she go home, for the sake of the children, but Portia was stubborn. She flat out refused.

Laila knew that time healed wounds, so she just continued to pray for her friends' marriage. Absence made the heart grow fonder, so she hoped Portia's disappearing act would work. Laila wanted her to go back to her husband, but she understood where her girl was coming from. She was a woman too. She knew how bad it hurt to be taken for granted by someone you loved.

To hear Portia tell it, Jay hadn't just cheated. He really had a mistress, whose rent and tuition he'd been paying, and the whole nine. And Portia said the girl was a lot younger. He was actually taking care of her, like a sugar daddy, or something. That was some heavy stuff. Laila didn't act any way to Jay, but she knew how her girl felt.

$$\$\$\$\$\$$

About ten days later, Callie had yet to return. Fatima tried calling her again, but now her cell phone was disconnected. Now she was completely convinced that Callie was the one who'd stolen her missing jewelry, so that was good riddance as far as she was concerned. Fatima had even noticed a few more pieces missing, her chunky diamond bracelet Wise had bought her for one. That bitch Callie was foul.

That afternoon, Fatima got her previous month's bank statement in the mail. When she opened it, she couldn't believe it. She just blurted out, "What? Get the fuck outta here!"

She knew she had fucked up a lot of money partying and getting high. Probably well over a few hundred grand. She hadn't been on top of things the way she should've, but there was absolutely no way she had run through more than two million fucking dollars. Oh hell no! Somebody was stealing her damn money!

Just then, the telephone rang. Ironically, it was a call from her bank. It was the manager herself. She notified Fatima that there had been strange activity on her account, and said she was calling to verify a few things. She asked Fatima if she'd been traveling cross-country the last few weeks, and she told her no. She'd gone to Honolulu, but Jay and Cas had financed that entire trip.

The bank manager asked Fatima if she was aware of the excessive spending going on across the country. She said, according to their records, she had supposedly made close to a million dollars in withdrawals over the past two weeks, at banks located in Pennsylvania, all the way to Nevada.

Fatima told the woman she didn't know what she was talking about. She asked her to freeze her accounts, and she ordered an investigation. The manager viewed her account activity while they were on the phone, and read some of the charges off to her. Fatima's checkbook had obviously been stolen too, because a lot of money had also been transferred by checks written, and deposited into other accounts.

Out of everything, Fatima was most surprised to learn that she had just "purchased" a brand new Mercedes Benz, with a check written out for eighty thousand dollars, payable to "Wesson's Mercedes Dealership". She was totally shocked, but she had every intention on getting to the bottom of that shit.

The bank manager told her that identity theft was a federal crime, and suggested she notify the police immediately. She assured her that she would work closely with her, and the proper authorities, to straighten it all out. She also suggested that Fatima review her credit card statements accurately, to see if any of her other accounts had been tampered with as well. Fatima hadn't even thought about that. She thanked the lady for informing her, and they agreed to be in touch.

When they hung up, Fatima located a stack of unopened mail she had, and singled out her credit card statements. When she opened the first one, she was horrified. There were lots of charges she didn't recognize. Damn, it didn't stop. Another one of the statements had even more of the same.

Fatima was fed up. She called and put a fraud alert on her credit profile with all three Credit Reporting Agencies, TransUnion, Equifax, and Experian. After that, she began calling her credit card companies to dispute the extraneous charges. They informed her that she needed an official police report in order for them to investigate the charges.

Fatima got in her car, and took a ride down to the local police station. She didn't like associating with the law, but things were getting out of control. She had to get the police involved.

She parked outside the precinct, and went in and explained that she was a victim of identity theft. A middle-aged, brunette officer took her statement. She told Fatima that she could come and get a copy of the police report in two business days, if she brought in a fifteen dollar money order.

When Fatima finally picked up the police report, she faxed it to the credit card companies, so they could get the ball rolling. There was no way she was paying for all that stuff she didn't even purchase. Fatima was a valued customer, so they worked closely with her to get to the bottom of things. And so did the police.

It wasn't long before she got a phone call. The credit card company notified her that someone had checked into a lavish hotel in L.A. under her name. They gave her the hotel address, and the suite number.

That same day, she got a call from her bank saying someone in Los Angeles had just tried to purchase another Mercedes in her name, but they'd refused to honor the check this time, because they had frozen her account as she'd wished. They told Fatima they had contacted the dealership, and learned that the person had then paid for the car with cash, and drove off the lot.

Fatima thanked them for calling. Now she had a lead. Culprit Callie was in L.A. She realized that she had let the devil in her house. It was bad enough Callie had stolen her baby's teardrop diamond earrings, and her dead husband's Rolex. But she took it to a whole new level when she stole Fatima's identity. And to make matters worse, the reports kept coming in. American Express informed Fatima about almost a hundred and fifty thousand dollars worth of charges in clothing alone, all purchased in boutiques in L.A.

Fatima called her and Wise' accountant, and the lawyer in charge of her estate, to let them know the situation. She had to make sure they were on top of things from then on. In her heart, she knew that mess would have never happened if she hadn't been getting high. She had not been on top of her business.

After she got off the phone with her attorney, Fatima called her best friends to let them know just how bad Callie had snaked her. She told them that bitch was in Los Angeles, still spending her money.

Portia and Laila were both really pissed. It was hard to believe that Callie was the sister of their true blue homegirl, Simone. Simone would never have gotten down that way. They all wondered how they could even have the same blood. That bitch Callie was foul.

Laila was just settling in her house, and she still couldn't travel freely, so Portia offered to go over there with Fatima. They decided to hop on the first thing smoking the next day. They both just had to arrange childcare for their little ones.

Falynn had been staying back home with Fatima, so she asked her parents to mind her for a couple of days. Her parents agreed. Portia had just moved her daughters to Brooklyn with her, so she called her mother-in-law, and asked her to look after them for a few days. Mama Mitchell agreed as well.

Before they booked a flight, Fatima reminded Portia that they had connections. At first, Portia ran that "I don't want nothing from Jay while we're split up" bull crap, but she gave in with little persuasion. That being said, they called up Ralph McGregor, the company pilot, and arranged a flight to California early the next morning.

Just as Portia hoped, Ralph respected the fact that they were the wives, and didn't ask any questions. Or so she thought. Ralph valued his position, and liked his salary, so he called Jay and Cas first, to make sure it was okay.

When they got the call, neither of them objected. They both just wondered what Portia and Fatima were up to. Especially Jay.

Portia and Fatima decided to take some protection, just in case. Their guns were licensed and registered. And they were flying on a private plane, so they could take them with them. Times like that, it was good to be married to money.

Fatima didn't tell Portia, but she called Jay and Cas that night. She talked to them, and told them she and Portia were going to L.A. to confront Callie for stealing her shit. At first, they'd insisted on sending someone with them. Fatima told them they were taking their guns with them, so they would be okay.

After that, Jay and Cas insisted on making sure they had

someone to look out for them when they got out there, and they wouldn't take no for an answer. They asked Fatima to disclose the itinerary, and hotel location, and they made a call to some of their West Coast cohorts to get the women some protection.

Jay had a lot of concerns, so he thought about forbidding Portia to go. But he knew Fatima was her friend, so she wouldn't be trying to hear that. She probably wouldn't have listened to him anyway. Not while she was angry at him.

CHAPTER TWENTY SEVEN

Fatima and Portia arrived in L.A. early the following afternoon. The palm trees were welcoming, but they were both tired from their early morning flight. They checked in at the five star Westin hotel, into a two-bedroom suite. Once they got settled, the first thing they did was take a nap.

A few hours later, the girls woke up feeling refreshed. Portia showered, and got dressed first. Fatima was in the shower when Portia heard a knock on the door. She looked through the peephole, and saw two young dudes that looked like straight gangbangers. Portia immediately sensed danger. They were probably with Callie! But how had they gotten wind of their arrival?

Instead of answering the door, Portia quietly put on the chain lock. And then she ran and got her gun. Then she ran to the bathroom, and flung open the door, and she informed Fatima about their would-be attackers.

"Tima! Yo, it's some niggas at the door, and they look like they some gangstas, and shit. I don't know who the fuck they are, but girl, I got my shit, and I'ma pop one of these mo'fuckas if they came over here try'na start some... "

Fatima slid open the shower door, and stuck her head out. To Portia's surprise, she was grinning. She said, "Those are our friends, P. Don't worry."

When Fatima noticed Portia holding her gun up like Malcolm X in the famous "By Any Means Necessary" portrait, she started cracking up.

Portia looked at her like she was crazy. She said, "What the hell are you laughing at, and what you mean "those are our friends"?

Tima took a second to gather herself from her laughing fit before she continued. "Oh my God. Girl, you are funny. Just open the door, and let 'em in, P. Trust me. I'll be out in a second."

Portia just looked at her, and shook her head. She went back out front to let the dudes inside. She peeked out the peephole, and saw they were still standing there patiently. Portia was wearing black Taverniti jeans, a hoodie, and Louis Vuitton sneakers with the red bottom. Before she opened the door, she made sure her gun was on safety, and tucked it in her waist, under her hoodie.

Fuck that, her and Fatima weren't from out there. L.A. wasn't their turf, and it was better to be careful than sorry. In the words of her deceased homegirl, Simone, "It was better to have it and not need it, than to need it and not have it." Portia wasn't taking any chances. She was going home to her babies alive.

She opened the door, and got a good look at them. They were both handsome dudes. One of them had on a navy blue plaid shirt, and the other had on a blue and black lumberjack jacket. Both wore dark blue Levi's, and Chuck Taylor All-Stars. With all that blue they had on, Portia assumed they were gang affiliated.

The dudes removed their baseball caps, and greeted her respectfully. The taller, slimmer one was brown skinned, and he had soft, wavy hair that was parted down the middle, and braided into two cornrows. He said, "What up, Miss? You must be Portia. I'm Five, and this here is Vino." He pointed to his friend, who extended his hand for a handshake.

Vino was dark skinned, and just a little shorter, with attractive broad shoulders, and nicely shaped up, spinning waves. Portia shook both of their hands. They had their navy blue flags on display, and something about their eyes said they were real killers, but they were both gentlemen. Truthfully, she had grown up around worse where she came from, so she wasn't afraid. Portia wondered how they knew her name, but she said, "What up, fellas? How ya'll doin'?"

Vino answered first. "We're fine, thank you. Our big homies, Jay and Cas, asked us to look out for ya'll during ya'll stay out here. Mind if we come in?"

Portia smiled. Jay and Cas. She should've known. She opened the door for the fellows to enter. They came in, and she offered them a seat.

Before he sat down, Five said, "I'm not being nosy, but where's Fatima? The big homies didn't think you two should be going anywhere unescorted."

Portia laughed, and shook her head. "Nah, she's in the back getting dressed."

Both men nodded. Vino sniffed the air, obviously smelling the weed they had been smoking. He looked at Portia, and asked, "Ya'll smoke?"

She laughed again, and nodded. "Yeah. Ya'll?"

He nodded, and said, "I do." He looked over at his man Five, and said, "But he don't."

Vino went in his pocket, and took out a small plastic bag. He handed it to Portia, and said, "That's you."

Portia took the bag, and opened it up. It was about a half ounce of some potent stuff. She didn't see any seeds, and it had a good smell to it. She thanked him, and asked how much she owed him for it.

Vino looked offended, and shook his head. Portia thanked him again.

Just then, Fatima came out the back, and greeted their new friends with a smile. "Hey fellas! How ya'll doin'?"

Both of them stood up like gentlemen, and shook her hand. Fatima could tell they were young thugs, but they had manners. This quality in them impressed her. And they were both cuties too. She smiled, and asked their names. After they were all formerly introduced, she sat down and chitchatted with them,

Portia sat down to roll up, but she quickly got back up, and removed the gun from her waist. She placed it on the coffee table in front of her, and proceeded to split open a grape flavored Dutch Master. She had this serious look on her face, and everybody just started laughing at her. She hadn't meant to be humorous, but she guessed the way she put the gat on the table to twist up the blunt was comical to them.

When she was done rolling up, she sparked up, and the three smokers rotated the blunt. Five flipped through TV channels

while they got mellow. After they were done smoking, they all
decided to stay in, and order room service. They were in the
hotel right across the boulevard from where Callie, and whoever
she was with were staying, so they wanted to be on the low as
much as possible. Until it was time to make their move.

Jay and Cas had already given Vino and Five the rundown,
so they already knew what it was. Their instructions were simple. Protect the women at all times, and at all costs while they
were on their coast. In exchange, upon the ladies' safe arrival
back east, they would be compensated with fifteen thousand
dollars apiece. Vino and Five knew from the past that the big
homies were good for it, so they were cool with those terms.

After they all ate, they discussed their strategy. The time to
approach was nearing. Fatima was the most anxious of the
bunch, and nobody could fault her for it. She was the one
who'd been ripped off, so it was real personal.

$$$$$

In the five star hotel directly across the street, Callie and her
guest, her long time beau, Smoke, were just finishing up some
heated late afternoon fucking. Things were so good lately, they
had been celebrating nonstop. They had money, two fine cars,
the most expensive clothing, champagne for days, and every single thing else they needed to get by. The two of them had been
holed up in their luxurious suite for two whole days. Their next
stop was Mexico, but Smoke had a little business to tend to
first.

He wouldn't let Callie in on it yet, because he felt like discussing it might cause some type of jinx. He had something
lined up through a dude he'd been incarcerated with. Smoke
was no idiot. He had enough bread to get by, but he wasn't
under the impression that they were set for life like Callie was.
The cost of living was cheaper in Mexico, but the land and setup
he had in mind would still be costly.

Smoke's plan was to invest in some top of the line heroin.
He already had some workers lined up, and he was on his way
to meet a possible new connect. They weren't going to make

any transactions that day, but they had agreed to meet, just to feel each other out. If all went well, Smoke would just be driving back and forth across the border, picking up pesos ever so often. That was his long-term plan to finance his new lifestyle.

Callie told Smoke that, while he was gone, she was going to ride out, and find a beauty parlor that specialized in black hair. Smoke had her under the impression that they were going to get married as soon as they touched ground in Mexico, so she wanted to look her best when they left the next day.

$$$$$

When Portia and Fatima got ready to approach Callie, their Crip homies went along to assist. They didn't say much, but they certainly made a statement, with their ice grills, and navy blue flags on display in their left back pockets. Fatima had requested they find her a baseball bat, and she carried it with her.

They late waited Callie outside the hotel for about two hours, and finally, Fatima saw her driving up. She was all alone. They couldn't believe it. Homegirl was straight stunting, and profiling in a white drop top Benz. She had her music turned up, and was bobbing her head to the sounds of that rapper, Young Berg's hit, "You Give Me the Business."

Fatima noted that she was pretty comfortable, and off point for a bitch who'd bitten off the fingers of the hand that fed her. She must've not been aware of the laws of karma.

Callie tossed her bouncy, freshly set hair over her shoulder. She had her Chanel glasses on, looking all cool, and fronting hard in her new drop top. She was swaying to the beat of the song, and singing along with the hook. "You give me the business, give me the business... If you know exactly what I wanna do. Then I'ma give the business to you... Baby I'ma give the business to you..."

Fatima crept up, and approached her on the left, just as she was about to turn into the hotel for valet parking. Callie was singing the perfect song. She had really given Fatima the business. But now she was about to get the business back, full blast. Fatima yelled, "Bitch, get out the car!"

When Callie saw Fatima, her face looked like she saw Jesus Christ in sequined nipple pasties, and tap shoes. She opened her mouth to protest, but before she could respond, Fatima swung the baseball bat and busted the windshield.

After the glass shattered, she dropped the bat and sneered, "Now that's the business, bitch!" She mushed Callie in the face, and then she snatched her up out the driver's seat like she was a rag doll. Fatima was so angry, she didn't know her own strength. She had been working out lately, or it could've been the fact that she was sexually backed up. Wherever the energy came from, she beat the dog shit out that bitch.

Callie didn't even bother to deny the accusations Fatima hurled at her with each blow. She couldn't do much anyway. Especially with Portia standing there looking at her like she would blast her if she hit Fatima back. Callie remembered the time Portia had shot up in the air to clear out one of Fatima's wild parties, so she knew that bitch carried a gun. And, oh shit, they had some hard looking niggas with them too.

Portia didn't have to jump in, and beat up Callie. Fatima had that covered pretty well. Portia played an even smarter role. While Fatima was beating Callie's ass, she made sure she got her purse out the car. She opened it up quickly, and removed the hotel key, and her wallet. She stuck the hotel key in her back pocket.

As soon as Portia opened the wallet, she saw a Pennsylvania driver's license with Fatima's name, but Callie's photo on it. That dirty, lowdown bitch. Portia took out the cash, which was around two grand in c-notes. The wallet had illegal credit cards in it too, so that was evidence against that conniving bitch. When the police confiscated the car, it would fall into the right hands. It was good that Callie had that phony driver's license in Fatima's name. It would support Tima's claim to the police on the spot.

Just like they figured, someone called the cops. The rollers showed up three cars deep. Portia tossed Fatima the wallet, and told her it was Callie's, and she and the fellows nonchalantly broke out before the cops got out of their cars. Vino and Five didn't do pigs anymore than Portia did. They had guns on them too, and they'd all had some bad experiences with the police.

The cops who showed up at the scene were no-nonsense, and impartial. They didn't bother listening to anybody's story. They locked Fatima and Callie up. But Fatima wasn't worried about it. She had made sure she brought along her police report detailing Callie's identity theft, and legitimate documents and I.D. confirming who she was. She handed that over to the police, along with Callie's wallet full of phony stuff impersonating her.

And she wasn't mad Portia walked away and left her. That was what she was supposed to do. There was no point in both of them getting arrested. Fatima knew Portia would be down to the station to get her as soon as possible.

Portia, Five, and Vino nonchalantly went inside Callie's hotel while the police were outside arresting her and Fatima. The fraud investigators at the credit card company had given Fatima the hotel, and the exact number of the suite Callie had checked in, so they went straight to it.

When Portia stuck the key card into the door, the little light turned green, and it clicked open with ease. Five and Vino entered first with their guns drawn, just to make sure the coast was clear. Satisfied that no one else was in the room, they all entered quietly. After a quick search through the room, Portia found a big ass duffel bag full of money hiding in the closet. It was under like fifty bags of brand new designer clothing. There was so much cash in the bag, she could hardly lift it.

She went through a few of the bags of clothes, and she realized there had to be a man with Callie, because a lot of the stuff was for a male who wore a size thirty six pants. It was some nice ass stuff too. She wondered where the dude was.

Portia informed Vino and Five of her discovery. She asked them their pants sizes, and they both said thirty six. She emptied another big suitcase she found in the closet, and stuffed it with as many items as she could. That stuff rightfully belonged to Fatima. She had paid for it, so they could have that couture male clothing.

Portia looked for a way to take it all with them, but her instinct told her not to bother with anymore. Plus, it was evidence against Callie that the police needed to find when they raided the room. There was plenty stuff left in there for them to charge her with.

Vino took the bag of money, and carried it for Portia, and she passed the suitcase full of clothes to Five. They all knew they needed to move fast, before the police, or whoever the dude with Callie was showed up. They shut the room door behind them, and left as quickly as they had come.

$$$$$

While all this was going on, Smoke was on his way back to the hotel. His meeting had gone well. It looked like his plan was going to work. He and his newly established connect were scheduled to make the deal the following morning. All he needed was two hundred of the seven hundred grand they had stashed at the hotel.

He was lost in emotion, thinking about his newly acquired riches that made it all possible. Every time he thought about all those stacks of money, hidden in a duffel bag in the closet of the hotel suite he and Callie were occupying, he was giddy with happiness. They were on their way to Mexico the very next morning, to live like a king and a queen. Shorty had done well, so she deserved his heart.

Callie was a fast learner, and under his guidance, she had pulled off a master take. With all the money, clothing, and cars they had, the job had netted them well over one million dollars. Not bad at all. Especially since no one had been hurt. That was the great thing about it. There hadn't been any bloodshed, or mayhem associated with this job. Smoke really knew how to pick 'em. At the stop light, he popped his collar, and brushed his shoulders off. He was the mastermind behind the come up, so he deserved a pat on the back.

It was Callie who had executed the plan, but he'd given her all the plays. She'd stolen the social security card and birth certificate like he told her, so she was able to get her own driver's license in that broad, Fatima's name, when they stopped in

Pennsylvania. So when they'd purchased the two black and white Mercedes Benzes, the dealership had no reason to dispute anything, since Callie had a legitimate driver's license stating she was Fatima Sinclair-Page.

Shit had really been sweet on their cross-country drive. They had a good run. They'd picked up at least fifty thousand dollars cash from banks in every state they'd stopped in. Smoke smiled to himself at the thought of all the dead presidents he had in his possession. It was all he could do to keep from hopping out at the light, and dancing a little two-step jig.

Smoke turned the corner of Sunset Boulevard, and drove up just in time. He thought he was bugging at first, but he saw the police placing handcuffs on Callie. And she had blood on her face. "Oh shit", he cursed aloud. What the fuck had happened so fast?

Smoke was a seasoned criminal, so he didn't panic. He got low in his seat, and drove on by, gradually increasing his speed until he passed all the heat. He was relieved when the light turned green just in time. At first, he was concerned that the flashy, black, chromed out Mercedes he was driving might attract attention, but he realized he was downtown L.A. There were no raggedy cars around. Every vehicle was flashy.

He cursed again when he thought about all that money he had stashed in the hotel suite. He would double back later, and check it out. He knew shit was hot, but he had to figure out a way. There was too much bread at stake. Smoke felt literally sick when he thought about the odds. The possibility of seven hundred grand just being snatched away from him was pretty strong. It was too unlikely that the room hadn't been searched. They probably found that fucking money already. Damn! Fuck that, he still had to go back and check. Anything was possible.

$$$$$

The police couldn't really charge Fatima with much, because the car was registered in her name. She had destroyed her own property, so she only got a slap on the wrist for disturbing the peace. It was just a summons, and required no jail time.

Callie on the other hand, was in bad shape. She had a long list of charges, and her crimes were federal. She had been caught with phony I.D. with Fatima's name on it, and that was all they needed to pin all the charges on her. She literally got caught holding the bag.

Callie was a trooper, to an extent. She didn't mouth a word about Smoke to the authorities. She was detained on federal charges, and was told she'd be charged in all of the states she had committed fraud in. That was about twenty states, so she could kiss her black ass goodbye. Unless Smoke had some type of master plan, like she was depending on.

After Portia picked Fatima up from jail, they all went back to the suite and chilled out. They must've joked about the way Fatima had put that baseball bat through that windshield, and snatched Callie out that car for a whole hour. Five and Vino told them they were some crazy ass chicks, and said they could roll with them any day.

About two hours later, Fatima winked at Portia, and told her and Vino goodnight. She headed for the back, and Five got up and followed her. Portia didn't recall exactly when the romance had transpired between them two, but she could not believe it. Fatima's hot ass was going to fuck him!

Portia held back her laugh. That damn girl was crazy. She knew it had been an eternity since she had some dick, so she certainly didn't judge her. And Five was a young dime. Vino was too.

Portia understood how Fatima felt, because she couldn't front, she felt some type of attraction to Vino. And she could tell it was mutual. But she was married to his "big homie", Jay. She and Jay were split up at the time, but she couldn't play herself like that. Could she? Lord knows, she was tempted. There was something about that young boy.

Portia thought about it. She hadn't had any in a while. But even outside of the physical attraction, Vino was just easy to talk to. The more they talked, she found herself opening up to him for some reason. She even told him about her separation from her husband, and about the way Jay had cheated on her as well.

Vino didn't talk against Jay. Not one word. In fact, he told Portia that Jay had to love her, if he'd gone to those lengths to protect her. He said when he spoke to Jay, he was adamantly concerned about her safety, and that was the reason him and Five were there.

Portia smiled. She knew Jay cared about her. Vino was right. The young man was wise beyond his years. She liked Vino. She liked the way he carried himself. He acted like such a man. He was warm and receptive, and when he told her everything would be okay, it sounded so sincere. It felt like he really cared about her.

Portia hadn't had a lot of male company lately, so she knew she was a tad vulnerable at the time. But he was just so mature. It was hard to believe he'd only been on this earth the twenty five years he'd confessed to.

Vino told her a lot about his self that night too. Portia found out that his real name was Vincent, and he was the youngest, and only living son out of three born to his single, churchgoing mother in South Central. He was heavy into the music thing, and he and Five had their own production company. They did beats, and they had a couple of artists they were trying to put out. He said they'd had pretty decent local success, but were looking for ways to expand.

Portia figured that was the way Jay and Cas knew him and Five, through the music. They must've produced some tracks for them, or something. Portia didn't ask Vino how he knew Jay, because she didn't want to keep talking about him. Instead, she told Vino she was proud of the way he was aspiring to be successful. It seemed like he was focused.

Vino said he was no angel, but he wasn't trying to wind up dead in the streets, like his older brothers had. When he said that, he really touched Portia's heart.

Portia was curious, so she asked him if he and Five were Crips. Vino was honest with her. He said he was a wild kid once, but he didn't bang anymore. He explained to her that where he was from, affiliation was a lifetime thing, so he wore his colors proud, just like Snoop Dog, Lil' Wayne, and a lot of other dudes did. He said he had a lot of little homies still banging, but they looked at him and Five as inspiration to leave that shit alone, and get money.

Portia was really into the whole "Obama for President" thing. Even though Jay and Cas had contributed a million dollars, she had sent in her own separate donation of a thousand dollars to the campaign. She asked Vino if he was voting, and he said yes. He told her he was a proud democrat, who was voting for Barack Obama on November 4th. He said it was time for a change. After that, Portia found him even sexier.

Vino admitted to never being much into politics before the '08 presidential election, but he said the notion of possibly having a black president was so powerful, he was proud. Portia agreed with him that it was awesome. She'd been following the election closely, and she was praying that Senator Obama won.

It seemed like everyone was down for the cause. Change was necessary. Everything was a big mess. The country was at war in Iraq, the economy was fucked up, and the judicial system was grossly biased. Under the Bush administration, everything was fucked up. It was definitely time for something different.

It was getting late, but they were so immersed in their conversation, they didn't notice the time. Portia and Vino smoked another el, and continued to converse. Vino wondered if it was his imagination, but it seemed like she was inching a little closer to him. He felt like she was throwing him signals. He was a little confused. Did she want him to beat that?

He definitely wouldn't have minded, but she was the big homie's wife. And he was being paid well to look out for her. And quiet as kept, he and Five had some major negotiations on the table with Jay and Cas. They had the capabilities to help them go to the next level. They were making global moves. Portia was sexy as hell, but a pretty piece of ass wasn't worth risking their deal.

But damn, he knew it was good. He could tell by the way she walked. Portia was the kind of woman he planned to wife one day. She had brains, class, ass, pizzazz, her own cash, and just the right hint of street. That was the epitome of the perfect wife. Not that he was ready to settle down. Vino was strictly on a paper chase right now.

Portia didn't know why, but she was feeling very attracted
to Vino. She just wanted some sort of body contact, so she pretended she was cold, and snuggled up under him for "heat".
Being the gentleman that he was, when she told him she was
cold, Vino wrapped his arms around Portia to keep her warm.
He told himself that it was no big deal, but he knew there was
a little more to it than that. He dug her, and couldn't deny the
sexual tension between the two of them.

But Vino restrained himself. Although little did he know, a
part of Portia was praying he would make the first move. She
thought about Fatima back there getting wore out by Five, and
she got a little envious. Portia knew that morally, she couldn't
really do what Fatima did, because Fatima's husband had
passed away. Unlike her, she was no longer bound by her wedding vows.

Portia thought about the reason she had left Jay in the first
place. He had messed around on her with that damn young
girl. That was when she realized that having sex with Vino
would be the perfect payback. She sort of felt like she owed
Jay. He needed a taste of his own medicine. She wondered
how he would feel if he knew she slept with a younger man.

Portia felt like Jay's little affair validated the adultery she was
contemplating. She made up her mind. If Vino made the first
move, baby boy was gonna get it. But only if he made the first
move. She couldn't look like some whore, or skeeze.

He never tried anything, so nothing happened that night.
Except a little innocent cuddling. Vino wouldn't touch her.
And Portia knew what it was. He was a decent dude, who
didn't want to take advantage of her vulnerability. And he was
also morally obligated to Jay. That was honorable, so she could-
n't even be mad at that. It was a sign of genuine respect. But
him not touching her just made her want his fine, young ass
more.

Portia fell asleep in Vino's arms. Both of them were fully
clothed. In the morning, him and Five left around nine.

Fatima was glowing from all the "bomb ass sex" she kept on
talking about. Portia told her she was hating a little bit. She
couldn't help it. She was lonely. She'd enjoyed the comfort of

being in Vino's arms, but she desired more. A lot more.

She and Fatima had one more day left in L.A. They were flying out the next morning. Since the mission they'd gone for was already accomplished, they spent the whole afternoon shopping in designer boutiques. They hit up everything, from Armani to Zanotti.

Portia had her own plastic, but she used the Black card Jay gave her. He was footing the bill for all of her expenses. That was the least that bastard could do. She loved him, but she was still angry, and in dire need of something to make her feel better. She spent a lot of Jay's money that afternoon, but needless to say, she thought about Vino most of the day. There was just something about him.

When they were done shopping, Portia and Fatima sat down at a posh restaurant for a late lunch. They both ordered a roasted garlic chicken and spinach Panini, and Fatima gave her another recount of her hot sex with Five the night before. She told Portia that at first, she'd been under the impression that "Five" stood for the number of bodies he had, but now she knew it stood for "make a bitch cum Five fuckin' times!"

Portia laughed. She was so stupid. Next, Fatima described his penis size, shape, and color, and she told Portia it curved just a little to the right. When she talked about the sex, she kept on fanning herself, and shaking her head. That dick must've been the truth.

Portia sat there staring at her food, and rearranging what was left on her plate. She wondered if she could be honest with her homegirl. She and Fatima were close again lately, they way they used to be. Portia decided she would tell her. What the hell. Fatima was like her sister. Tired of debating with herself, she just blurted out, "Tima, I think I like Vino."

Portia expected her to look surprised, but Fatima kept cool, and kept eating. She looked at her, and said, "Bitch, I knew you wanted to fuck him."

Portia looked shocked, and demanded, "How?"

Fatima grinned. "Because last night, when I got up to pee, I peaked at ya'll. Ya'll was sleep, but you was allover that nigga. I was like, "Damn, did they fuck?"

Portia had to laugh. "Hell no! You crazy? But girl, I ain't gon' front. I wanted to. For real! Tima, you know that's my type of nigga. A broad shouldered, chocolate dime, with those pretty ass waves. Ooh!"

Fatima laughed, and said, "You know what's funny? You just described Jay too. Why don't you just go home, and fuck your husband."

Portia sucked her teeth. She said, "No! Jay's ass is on ice right now. And you know that, Tima."

Fatima shrugged nonchalantly. "So fuck Vino. Fuck him tonight, girl. You know what they say. What Jay don't know won't hurt him. That's my bro, and he's a good dude, but like the old saying goes, "what's good for the goose, is good for the gander!""

Portia said, "Word! But then again, two wrongs don't make a right."

Fatima countered with, "But what goes around, comes around."

Portia grabbed her head, and laughed. "Okay! Enough of the clichés."

Fatima said, "I know, right?" She laughed. "Nah, but I'm serious, P. Fuck that. Do you, Ma-ma. You know your secret would be safe with me. They could pluck out my eyeballs, and then my toenails one by one, and even cut off a limb. I'd never tell. I swear." She dramatically saluted Portia after her pledge, and looked solemn for a second.

Portia laughed, and said, "You are so fuckin' stupid."

Fatima said, "But I'm serious. Call Vino. For real. That would give me an excuse to get with Five again tonight. Girl, that boy can eat some pussy. And the nigga can fuck too!"

Portia laughed. "Bitch, you just ain't had no dick in eons. That's why yo' ass is so dick-matized. Gary Coleman probably would've tore that pussy up."

Fatima cracked up. Portia was joking with her, but at the same time pondering whether or not she should call Vino. Maybe she should flip a coin. She just had so many doubts.

She said, "Fatima, how can I cheat on Jay? I've never done that. Even after what he did to me, that shit would be hard."

332   Dollar Outta Fifteen Cent - Part III

Fatima understood. For some reason, she felt compelled to tell Portia a story she had never shared with her, or Laila, because she had been too embarrassed. She told her how Wise had come home early one day, and caught her out by the pool getting eaten out, by this girl she'd met at an adult toy party, named Raven.

Portia couldn't help but laugh. Fatima went on to explain that she hadn't been getting what she needed from her husband, so she had crept around a little bit. But only because he had crept around on her so much. She said Portia was right, two wrongs didn't make a right, but her affair had somehow made the pain a little more bearable. She said she felt like she'd gotten even with Wise.

Fatima told Portia that she'd take that beat down and choke-smack he gave her all over again, because that day he learned how she felt when he cheated on her. She told Portia she was human, so she should do whatever she had to do to get over it, because as much as she kept fronting, she knew she was still hurting over Jay cheating on her. That was the main reason she couldn't go back to him yet.

Portia laughed like hell when she pictured a wild-eyed, gun yielding Wise chasing Fatima's girlfriend out the house. God bless his soul, Wise was a funny dude. Fatima was crazy too, but real friends didn't judge each other. But on a serious note, her homegirl had said a mouthful. Portia appreciated the advice.

When they got back to their hotel suite, Fatima called Five, and casually inquired about Vino for Portia. Luckily, they were together. Fatima invited them to come through later, and chill. He told her they would see them in a few hours, after they handled some business.

Portia was so nervous, she damn near smoked a whole blunt before they came. Fatima fixed her a drink, and told her to be easy. She had to laugh, because she hadn't seen her girl that on edge about a guy since high school.

The boys showed up at around eleven, and they all greeted casually. Fatima gave Five a little kiss on the lips that made him blush. Too thuggish to be caught blushing, he quickly caught himself.

Portia gave Vino a big smile. As nervous as she had been, she was happy to see him. She took his hand, and squeezed it, and she asked him what he'd been up to that day.

A little while later, Tima and Five disappeared again. That was when Portia decided to be bold, and make the first move that night. She invited Vino into the other bedroom in their suite. He looked sort of surprised, but he accepted the invitation, and followed her. She lied, and told him she preferred to watch television in there, because she had noticed there were more channels on that TV.

Vino went for the bull crap she shot him. He knew that was just a nonchalant approach to get him in the bedroom, but it was better than what he would've came up with. He laughed to himself. She was subtle. He liked that. He liked her style.

He followed Portia, and stared at her abundant ass swaying in front of him, and he became erect. Vino told himself it was mind over matter. If anything jumped off, he wouldn't be the one to initiate it. He had to be a hundred percent clear that was what she wanted. There was too much at stake.

As soon as they got in the bedroom, Portia closed the door, and wrapped her arms around his neck. Vino hugged her back, and squeezed her. She felt so good in his arms. He palmed her fat ass. It was real soft, just like he'd imagined.

Portia's breathing got heavier. She needed the affection. She wanted to make the moment last. And she wanted more. She saw that Vino was a little hesitant, so she got the ball rolling by helping him out of his shirt. Afterwards, she ran her hands along his chest and shoulders. He was sexy.

Vino followed her lead, and helped her out of her shirt as well. And then out of her pants. And then out of her bra, and thong. Portia stood in front of him naked, and he caressed her body. Her skin was like silk. Damn. He didn't usually do that to girls, but he wanted to taste that. He wanted to give her something to smile about. He picked her up, and laid her spread-eagled on the queen-sized bed.

To Portia's surprise, he went down on her. And even better, he knew what he was doing. She didn't realize how much she'd missed getting her pussy eaten. The boy was good. He knew the imperativeness of focusing on the clitoris. He had her moaning and groaning. All Portia kept hearing in her head was the hook to rapper, Shana's song, "I Was Gettin' Some Head." He didn't stop until he was sure she was pleased.

Vino could tell Portia was cumming, because she wrapped her thighs around his neck, and started trembling. After he was done orally pleasuring her, he came up for air, and got ready to hit that.

Portia had her own condoms. She had gotten two from Fatima, but it was nice to see him pull out his own. She liked the fact that he was a condom carrier. That was a big plus. He rolled on the rubber, and then he entered her nice and slow. They both sort of gasped.

Vino was so overcome with the feeling, he was lost for a second. During the first few strokes, he struggled to find his rhythm. That stuff was sweeter than saccharine. He almost came that quick.

Portia relaxed her muscles, and let him lead. She hated to admit it, but she knew a part of her was only fucking him to pay Jay back for cheating on her. But baby boy was starting to hit her spot, so that was some sweet revenge.

Vino's dick was nice and thick, and just a little shorter than Jay's. Maybe an inch. But that was cool with Portia. He still had more than enough to fill her up. And his loving was experienced. The boy had a hell of a deep stroke. Damn. Vino was great in bed. He rocked her world, and her universe.

Portia had her eyes closed. She was caught up. She caressed his back and buttocks, and pulled him deeper inside of her. Before it was over, she moaned and called out his name, over and over. She must've had like three orgasms.

That pussy was so good, Vino just wanted to wallow in it all night. He breathed hard in her ear, and groaned. Portia had grade "A". She had that "good-good." And that thing was sopping wet. When he came, he bit into the pillow to keep from yelling out.

That was argumentatively the best box Vino had ever had. But he decided to keep that observation to himself. He didn't want Portia to think she had him open. He dug her, but they both knew what it was. It was just a one night stand.

After they were done sexing, Portia laid in his arms for a while. The moment was too sweet to disturb. They'd just had fantastic, safe, bell ringing sex, so cuddling just seemed appropriate. She needed to feel loved, and beautiful, and he gave her that. Portia leaned over, and planted a kiss on his cheek. That was her way of saying thank you. Vino just blushed.

Portia and Vino got up, and showered together. Afterwards, they just talked, until they fell asleep in each other's arms.

The next morning, Portia and Fatima's flight was leaving early, so they packed, and got ready to head to the airport. The trip to L.A. had been exciting, and rewarding. The ladies were going back home with a bag full of Fatima's recovered stolen money, all the bad ass, new season clothes they had shopped for, and fond memories they would still share when they were both old and gray. They each had a little secret that would get them through many a stressful day in the futures. Something to smile about.

Five and Vino took them to the airport, and hung around until they saw them on their plane, just as they were instructed. Before they departed, Portia and Fatima hugged their younger lovers, and thanked them for looking out for them during their stay. It was time to say goodbye. They had all exchanged numbers, so they agreed to keep in touch.

After the jet took off, Vino and Five called Jay and Casino to let them know the girls were on the way. Each of them had fond memories too. They had enjoyed the time they spent with the ladies very much. More than either of them would ever let on to the big homies.

When asked how they wanted their money, Vino and Five agreed to wait until they saw each other in Atlanta, at the BET awards in a couple of weeks. BET was doing a tribute to Wise' memory, and he had also been nominated for two awards. Jay and Cas were going down on his behalf. So were Wise' mother, Fatima, and his daughter.

CHAPTER TWENTY EIGHT

Jay was in his office, leaned back in his leather executive chair, with his feet up on his desk. He gazed out over the city lights. His office was pretty high up, so he had an awesome view of the New York City skyline from the window.

He thought about his homie, Wise. He and Cas had just returned from the BET awards in ATL the past weekend. BET's tribute to Wise was real nice, and he had won one of the two awards he'd been nominated for. Rose, Fatima, and Falynn had gone up there on the stage with them to accept it on his behalf. Jay was sure Wise was smiling down on them all proudly.

While he and Cas were down in Atlanta, they had seen their little homies Five and Vino, and given them the fifteen grand a piece they'd promised them to look after Portia and Fatima out in L.A. After the awards, they'd all hung out together. Jay's nephew, Dave, and their man, Moe too. And they'd had a pretty good time. After they'd put in appearances at the after-party, they hit up a few afterhours spots, where there was gambling and girls. Most of them had focused more on the gambling than on the strippers. Jay had lost around a hundred gees, but he still had a good time.

Jay was at the office later than usual that night, simply because he didn't want to go home. He figured, "go home for what?" He had a big, bad ass house, but there was nobody there. Even his little man Jayquan had abandoned him that weekend. He had gone to stay the weekend at his Uncle Cas and Auntie Laila's new crib, so he could chill with Macy. Jay didn't protest, because he knew how close Jayquan and Macy were.

He didn't want to be alone. And he didn't want to go home. Without Portia and his kids, his house wasn't a home. Jay was feeling real driddy. And he was lonely. He knew he could've snapped his fingers, and there would've been females lined up to pleasure him in every way he imagined. But that wasn't where his heart was. He wanted his wife back.

Portia had been back from L.A. for a few weeks now, and she still wasn't fucking with him. She had made her point. She wasn't playing. He got it. For the billionth time since that shit had occurred, Jay wished he could've turned back time. He kept hearing the lyrics to that old song in his head, "Ain't No Sunshine When She Gone."

Jay was bored. He needed to do something to occupy his time. He had just called Cas a few minutes ago, but he said he was in for the night with Laila and the kids. Jay wasn't even mad at that. He knew Cas had his hands full, because he had his little man, Jahseim, with him too.

Times like this, Jay really missed his crimie, Wise. Just then, his cell phone rang. He picked it up quickly, hoping it was Portia. He looked at the caller ID, and saw that it was Ysatis. Annoyed, he just pressed "ignore", and sent it to voicemail. If that day was like any other that week, she'd keep on calling back. And then, when she realized he wouldn't answer, she'd block her number, and call again.

Jay wasn't being mean, but he didn't like explaining himself. He had told Ysatis to fall back, but she didn't get it. She kept on calling him, and asking why. He just didn't want to be bothered, and that was it. She had caused enough trouble. Even though he knew no one had forced him to take the bait.

And to make matters worse, she kept leaving messages saying she was in love with him, and shit. He was a fucking idiot. He had forgotten how vulnerable a woman could be. Especially a young girl. Right about then, Jay really wished Ysatis would've just stayed her ass down south.

He felt incomplete without Portia. His life sucked. He knew he had to get her back. He just had to figure out a way how, and pray that time healed wounds. The lyrics of a song Jay liked, "Lost Without You", by Robin Thicke came to mind.

"I'm lost without you - can't help myself. How does it feel - to know that I love you baby. Lost without you..."

He would never admit it to Portia, but he felt like he was lost without her. He knew now that she was his better half, and it took her leaving him to really realize that.

$$$$$

Not far across town, Ysatis was distraught. She was upset that Jay wasn't taking her calls. She kept getting his voicemail. She had left tons of messages, but she had received no response from him thus far.

She had to figure out something, because he had obviously cut her off, probably to please his wife. If she couldn't get to Jay to show him how much she loved him, there was no way she could break that bond. But she had to find a way. She needed him.

$$$$$

As Cas changed his baby's pamper, he thought about his man, Jay. He didn't sound so well when he'd called a minute ago. Cas was worried about that dude. Jay wouldn't admit it, but he was going through it since his wife had left.

The baby fell asleep in Cas' arms. On his way upstairs to lay Skye down in her nursery, he passed the kitchen, and saw Macy washing the dishes. She was also flicking suds on Jayquan and Jahseim. The boys had been picking with her all day. Cas laughed to himself. Those kids were so silly.

Laila was down in their theatre, relaxing and watching a movie. She had cooked a big meal earlier, and fed their whole tribe. Cas laid Skye down for her nap, and he went to tell Laila he was going out for a while, to check on Jay.

Laila thought Cas was staying in that evening. He'd promised to watch a movie with her, but when he told her he was going to see about Jay, Laila didn't protest. She was worried about Jay too. She told Cas to tell the kids to join her for a movie, when they were done cleaning up the kitchen.

Cas double-checked the baby monitor in the nursery, to make sure they could hear Skye downstairs, if she woke up crying. He gave out hugs and noogies, and told the kids he'd be back a little later, after he hollered at Jay.

Jayquan told him he was glad he was going to check on his
Pops, because he wasn't himself lately. Cas told him not to
worry, because his father would be fine. Cas reminded Macy
to check on Skye, and she promised him she would look after
her baby sister. Cas thanked her, and then he kissed Laila, and
told her not to wait up, because he was pretty sure he'd be getting home late.

Outside in the car, Cas called Jay, and told him he was coming out to hang for a little while. Jay told him he didn't have
to come out, but he sounded glad when he insisted. They
agreed to meet up at their man Wings' sports bar in the city.

Cas was in a good mood, because Laila's condition was
changing for the better. But on the other hand, he felt for his
main man. He and Jay hadn't been out in a while, so they
needed to hang out. He had to get his boy up out of the
dumps. Jay was in a real slump about Portia leaving him. Cas
really felt bad for him, so he couldn't leave him hanging like
that. The man was going through it.

When Cas pulled up at Wings' well lit up establishment,
which was cleverly named "Wings", Jay was waiting outside for
him. He hopped out his Aston Martin, and let a uniformed
young boy valet park it. He looked like the type that might
take a fine vehicle like his for a test drive on the low, so Cas told
him to take care of it. The dude just smiled, and said, "Nah,
man. I'ma park it right now."

Cas laughed, and gave him a hundred dollar tip. The little
dude was trying to earn an honest living, and he respected that.
He looked over, and saw Jay standing on the sidewalk, with one
hand in his pocket. If Cas knew his homie well, he had his hand
on his gun. He knew the routine. Hell, he was strapped too.

He walked over, and gave Jay a pound, and the two friends
headed to the front of the long line. The host at the front recognized them, and they were immediately escorted to the VIP
section.

Inside the club, Jay and Cas sought out the proprietor. But
they didn't see their homie Wings yet. As they walked in VIP,
they were met by a sea of familiar faces. Some of them were

some well respected and notable individuals, from celebrity ac-
tors and artists, to industry executives, and professional ball
players. As they made their way to their table, Jay and Cas gave
out pounds, and waved to the folks they were most familiar
with.

Wings always had a good crowd, but it was kind of packed
up in that joint that night, probably because it was the weekend.
And despite the fact that there were topless dancers employed
there, there were a considerable amount of women present. It
was a classy midtown cabaret, usually frequented by predominantly males, but it looked like the chicks had come out in numbers that night.

When they settled in VIP, Cas tipped one of the scantily clad
waitresses, and told her to go let her boss know he and Jay were
there. Then he ordered their first round of drinks. Two double
shots of Hennessy, straight. As soon as their drinks came,
Wings appeared. He greeted them each warmly, with a hearty
pound, and a man hug. It was obvious that he was glad to see
them, and they felt the same way. They hadn't seen each other
since Wise had passed away.

Wings joined them at their table, and they reminisced, and
caught up on old times. That dude was a real comedian. He
had Cas and Jay laughing. Wings ordered them another round
of drinks, and asked if they wanted something to eat, on the
house. Cas said he had already eaten, but Jay ordered some of
Wings' popular "beer battered buffalo wings", to see what all
the hype was about.

Casino and Jay had barely been there for thirty minutes, before someone sent them over a bottle of Cristal, along with the
message "Long time no see" scribbled on a napkin. The waitress who brought it over pointed to another table across the
room. Some light skinned dude sitting there greeted them with
a raised glass.

The dude was smiling like he really knew them, but Cas and
Jay remained on point. They didn't like to get too friendly with
dudes, especially after all the shit they had been through. There
was undoubtedly something familiar about duke's face, but neither of them could call it. The thing they noticed most was

that he had on way too much jewelry. So much it was corny.
His earrings were as big as a female's.

The guy realized they didn't recognize him, so he stood up,
and made his way towards them. He never took the grin off
his face while he approached them, but neither Jay or Casino
felt comfortable returning the smile. Not until they knew what
his angle was. Both of them were armed, and had easy access
to their pistols.

Jay placed the face first, so he told Cas, "Yo, that's lil' Lite,
who pulled our coat when them niggas Miz and Wayne-o ran
up in my crib. Remember that night, son?"

Cas nodded. How could he forget it? Lite had been waiting
outside Jay's house in a getaway car. When they pulled up, he
had alerted Jay, Cas, and Wise about his mans plans to rob Jay.
Cas had stayed outside and kept an eye on Lite, while Jay and
Wise crept inside Jay's house though the back door. He'd
heard shots fired inside, and later learned that Jay caught that
slime ball nigga Wayne-o right in the middle of raping Portia,
and blew his brains out.

Wise had shot that other coward, Miz, and chased him out
the house. When he came running out, Cas was waiting in the
driver's seat of their getaway car. When Miz jumped in the passenger seat, he urged who he thought was his man Lite to drive
off fast, but Cas had bodied that creep on the spot.

Lite had hid in the back of the van the whole time his so-
called best friend was murdered. That little dude was so scared,
he pissed on himself. Only because he had informed them
about the robbery when they pulled up, Cas had given him a
pass, and told him to get out of town.

Lite came and gave each of them a pound. Jay and Cas
greeted him with friendly slaps on the back, and asked him how
he'd been. Lite was an alright kid, considering. He didn't have
to warn them about Jay's home invasion like that. But he was
lucky he did. There weren't any hard feelings now, at least not
on their part.

But neither of them would ever really trust that dude. Cas
would never sleep on a man he had pulled a gun on before. And
Lite was a part of a group of losers who'd plotted to rob Jay.

And Portia got raped in the process, whether he had anything to do with that part, or not. They hadn't seen Lite since.

But Jay and Cas were in an alright mood. They sat back amused, and watched Lite attempt to impress them. He snapped his fingers, and ordered a nearby waitress to bring them some champagne glasses. He said he wanted to crack a bottle with them for old time's sake. They got his drift. The little dude wanted to let them know he was touching paper too. Neither of them was on that flossing shit, but they allowed him his little moment to stunt.

Jay and Casino had a drink with Lite, and it seemed to make his day. They sat and conversed about the latest going on in the old community, mostly about who was dead now, or locked up. None of them lived in the 'hood anymore, but they all got wind of what went on from contacts.

Lite was leaking too much info. That dude talked too much. In just minutes, he told them he was set up in the south, with operations spanning from North Carolina, down to ATL. He told them he was striving to become the king down there. He said he was getting money the fast and illegal way, but he had ambitions of venturing in the music business sooner or later, similar to the way they had. He gave it up, and told them he looked up to them, and was inspired by their accomplishments.

Cas told Lite he was just blowing smoke up their asses, and the three of them laughed. Lite said that wasn't the case, he just respected dudes that were about it. He said they actually walked the walk, and he was just happy to see a couple of dudes that made it. They were from the same place he was from, and they were a living example that success was obtainable.

Jay and Cas were both humble, so they didn't show it, but it was nice to hear those words from a young brother. They appreciated the revere, but they informed Lite that all that glittered wasn't gold. They let him know there was a flipside to every coin, and everything had a price.

Wings came back over to see how they were. Jay and Cas told him they were good. Lite noted that Wings showed Jay and Cas a lot of love, and he got offended that he hadn't treated him equally. He felt like Wings overlooked him like he was a sucker. It was bad enough that he had slipped a dude five hundred dollars for his VIP table, and then seen Jay and Casino get ushered right in, on some red carpet shit. He bet they didn't even have to wait on line outside, but he did.

Just then, a couple of dancers walked up, and eyed them all sexily. They asked if they could give them "the royal star treatment". Jay nor Cas was interested in getting a table dance. Neither of them was really into that stuff anymore. Not at the moment anyhow, so they politely declined.

Lite, on the other hand, was still a sucker for a fat ass. He straightened his back, to make sure they noticed his diamond flooded chain and medallion. Lite knew he stood out, and he could tell them bitches recognized. He was "that nigga".

He licked his lips, and nodded at the slim caramel chick on the left, with the silver dress, and silver eye shadow. The other chick, a dark haired Spanish looking girl in a tiny neon pink dress, said she wanted to play too. Lite played it cool, but he was thrilled that those bitches were on him. He felt of extreme importance. That let niggas know he had the bread to pay to play. His money was long.

Lite had a complex. The fact that he was just an ordinary Joe compared to some of the celebrities in the club bothered him. He was doing the damn thing down south, but up top they didn't respect him on the level he felt he deserved. Lite had changed now. The popularity had gone to his head. He was like a celebrity in the south. All them country niggas was on his shit. Even the haters. And that was good for his ego, because he liked to shine.

While he got his lap dance, Lite summoned another waitress, and ordered two bottles of Ace of Spades champagne. When the expensive champagne arrived, he cracked one of the bottles, and poured it out right on the floor. He said that was "for his dead homies." Jay and Cas weren't impressed. To them, it was actually a little ignorant, and disrespectful that he emptied the bottle on the floor.

Lite was one fronting ass nigga. But they got a good laugh. They especially found it comical the way he kept his top lip curled up, so everybody could see his iced out grill. He was a funny damn dude.

After those girls suckered Lite into a double table dance, they demanded fifty dollars apiece. He gave up the money, but you should've seen his face at first. He looked like he hadn't expected the dances to be so expensive. He counted out the bread, and rudely stuffed it in the back of the girls' thongs, and shooed them away.

By then, Lite was on his fourth glass of champagne, and he was getting a little too comfortable. The nigga just started running off at the mouth. Jay and Cas were both getting annoyed with him. They hadn't come out that night to listen to some little dude showboat.

And Lite kept lighting cigarette after cigarette, and it was really irritating them. Cas got sick and tired of inhaling his secondhand smoke, so he asked him to take it easy on the nicotine. Lite was like a hog. He smoked too much, and he drank too much. It was evident that he did not know when to stop. The dude was already sloshed, and he was still drinking.

Jay was thinking the same exact thing. Especially about Lite's constant smoking. That shit turned him off. Jay didn't like to judge people, but he thought too much of his body to chain-smoke cigarettes, and unnecessarily overindulge in alcohol. He and Cas drank, but just socially. Neither of them was a lush. And cigarette smoking was the biggest no-no of them all.

Lite kept talking about nothing. And he was the type of dude who got bold and stupid when he drank. Cas and Jay were on the verge of asking him to excuse himself from their table. They were fed up with his fronting.

Out of the blue, Lite grinned at Cas, and slurred, "Yo, Casino, there's somethin' I wanted to ask you for a long ass time, man. Yo, why you ain't shoot me that night? You wasn't supposed to leave any witnesses. Ya' heard? Ain't that the number one rule, Killah Cas?"

Cas didn't dignify what he said with a verbal response, but his left eyebrow rose in utter disbelief. His sixth sense kicked in, and a warning bell went of immediately. That fool was trying to come across as assertive. It seemed he had gotten pretty bigheaded, so Cas was forced to bring him back down to size.

He didn't bother to raise his voice. He just said, "Little Lite, what up? You tough now?"

Lite laughed, and brushed off his shoulders. He said, "Nah, I ain't tough, man. I just wanted to know why you ain't kill me. And I ain't lil' Lite no more. I'm a big dog. Check my credentials. You'll find that my résumé is pretty impressive. You see, I done put in a lotta work. And I haven't retired yet. Son." He smiled, and drank from his glass.

Cas was uneasy now. He wasn't stupid. Lite had directed has last words at him. He was trying to be funny. That boy must've really forgot, because if he was smart, he'd have known that that little indirect threat he'd left lingering in the air was enough to make Casino kill him. Cas didn't play with them young boys, and he refused to allow some young punk the opportunity to kill him, and come up in the streets off his name. He knew how some niggas thought.

It was sad, but the streets were fucked up like that. A little nigga could kill him, and then get big respect for taking out a legend. Cas didn't mean to toot his own horn, but he had made his mark on the streets. And mothafuckas knew that. His name rang a lot of bells. Jay's did too. They had come up in the streets together.

Cas didn't say a word, but now he had a serious dilemma on his hands. He might have to kill that fool that night. How'd he know that Lite hadn't come back to catch recognition on his good name? Now Cas' brain was in defensive battle mode. The type of person he was at this point in his life, and the level he was on now, he couldn't afford to feel threatened by anyone.

Casino had a lot to live for, his children especially, so whether Lite knew it or not, he was totally disposable to him. He could murder him right that second, and then go home and go to sleep without the slightest afterthought, or regret. Cas had a warm heart, but he was stone cold when appropriate. And when it came to his life, it was them or him.

Jay sat there watching that bitch nigga run his mouth, and he could vividly picture him in a casket. Lite should have already known that talking reckless that way would dig his own grave. Damn, he and Cas hadn't even come out for that tonight. But Jay refused to feel threatened by anything walking on two feet either. He stood with his man Cas on that. They both shared the same philosophy. "Eliminate the problem." So Lite's drunk, dumb ass didn't know it, but there was a strong possibility that he wouldn't make it back down south to "claim his throne".

It was a good thing that Jay and Cas were so much on point, because Lite was actually contemplating doing something to one of them. Especially to Cas. He heard them niggas were all "Hollywood" now, so he knew they weren't the gun busters they used to be. He believed he was more gangsta' than they were now, and he was anxious to prove it.

Lite knew their last encounter had ended with him pissing on himself in the back of the van, when Cas killed his man Miz. After that, Cas threw the heat in his face, and told him to disappear. He had ran around the corner, like the scared kid he was at the time. And he got lost, just like Cas said. That was the last time he was seen for about four whole years. But that cowardly exit out of the 'hood had been eating at Lite's ego for some time.

He'd always told himself that the next time he ran into that nigga Casino, he would make sure he knew he was no longer dealing with some young punk. He wasn't the same scared little dude anymore. He toted those big things now. And his guns went off loud, so there would be no more sucker moves. Over the years, there'd been times he'd vividly imagined pointing his gun at Cas, and telling him to get lost.

Lite didn't have the heart back then, but he really should've bodied all them niggas in retaliation for them killing his man Miz like that. Miz was his main man. He was supposed to have answered on his behalf. They did violate by running up in Jay's crib, but that was how the game went.

Lite was salty. He knew if he had taken care of that shit back then, he would've been real thorough in New York by now. He should've taken them niggas out when he had the chance. But now, the least he could do was let them know who the fuck he was. There was a new bad guy in town, and niggas better recognize.

Lite was still a novice. He hadn't mastered the art of maintaining a poker face like Jay and Cas had. At least not while he was drunk. His thoughts were spread all across his face. Jay and Cas could both read mothafuckas. That little nigga was looking at them like he had larceny in his heart.

Jay looked over at Cas. He had a little smile on his face. Jay already knew what it was. If Lite was smart, he'd have sensed danger. It had been a while, but he should've remembered the rumors about Killah Cas' homicidal smile. And Jay was on the same page he was. That nigga kept running off at the mouth, so he had sealed his own fate. Now he had to go.

Jay stood up first, and Cas followed. They told Lite they were going to the men's room. Lite stood up, and gave them each a phony pound, and they parted ways. Little did he know, his leaving the club that night could be his last walk of fame.

Lite watched Cas pull a big ass bankroll out of his pocket, and pay the tab. A light bulb came on in his head, and he got an idea. He went back to his table, and made a call on his cell phone. He quickly got in touch with this dude named Eighty, from around the way. Lite knew Eighty was infamous for sticking dudes up, so he told him he had some old dudes from the 'hood, Jay and Casino, lined up. Eighty knew them niggas were loaded, so Lite figured he would take the bait.

Eighty agreed to meet him in the city, and then he hung up the phone, and laughed. He had run into Lite the day before, when he came through the 'hood fronting. If Lite only knew, Eighty had thought about lining his ass fronting up. He was cool with Jay and Cas, and wouldn't dare violate them like that. He knew who to rob. And it wasn't a fear thing. It was about respect. Hell, he had just done a little job with Cas a few weeks ago. He had been paid ten thousand, just to take a ride with him. Them dudes were alright with him. They were so alright, he made a phone call to Cas' cell, and pulled his coat about Lite's plan.

When Cas got the call from Eighty, they spoke very briefly, and then he hung up the phone, and laughed. Eighty told him that Lite believed he was on his way to the city, to stick them up. He told them exactly where they had agreed to meet. On the corner, three blocks down.

Ironically, Cas and Jay had just discussed the notion of letting Lite live. They thought they might have been jumping the
gun if they killed him. They had figured he was probably more
talk than cock and balls. So Eighty's phone call came at the
perfect time. That was a sign to exterminate the vermin.

Lite left the club before Jay and Cas, He was trying to be
slick, but they saw him when he ducked out. They waited a few
seconds, and left right behind that snake. They knew exactly
where he was going.

Three blocks down, Lite stood in the shadows on a dark corner. He was waiting for Eighty. He hoped that nigga wouldn't
be late, and make them blow the opportunity.

Lite was just free-styling. He had never robbed anyone in his
life. But he knew that was Eighty's forte. He wasn't going to
inform Eighty, but after he robbed them, he planned on popping both of them niggas. Then the police would believe robbery was really the motive. Lite didn't have any robberies on
his rap sheet, so he figured he could get away with it.

A few minutes later, a yellow cab slowed down, and came to
a stop on the corner. Eighty had called him a minute ago, and
said he was in a taxi, so Lite assumed it was him. He walked up
to the car, and tapped on the back window impatiently.

When Eighty rolled the window down, Lite told him to
hurry. "Come on, nigga! What took you so long? Them niggas
Jay and Cas might be gone by the time we get back..."

Lite realized that was Jay, and he couldn't even finish his sentence. His stomach got weak. Wow, that fucking Eighty had
crossed him. And, oh shit, Cas was sitting in the driver's seat.
Again. What were the chances? Lite tried to think fast. He
opened his mouth, and started copping a plea.

But Jay didn't want to hear it. Not one word. He shot Lite
in the face at pointblank range, and literally blew his dumb expression off. He quickly rolled the window up, and Cas drove
off nonchalantly, before Lite's body even hit the ground.

They drove along with all the rest of the late night Manhattan
traffic, and got lost in a sea of yellow cabs. Cas headed back to
the cab stand they had gone to, on Twelfth Avenue.

When they got there, he parked down the street from the base, where the rightful driver of the car was waiting. He and Jay got out, and he gave Habib, the Arab cabbie, the other half of the ten thousand dollars he'd offered him, just to let them take a quick joy ride in his taxi.

Habib was relieved when they returned. He knew it was risky, but he hadn't been able to resist the cash. The offer came at a time when he really needed the extra money, for his daughter's upcoming tuition payment. He took a chance, but if they hadn't come back, he would've just reported his cab stolen. He had already rehearsed what he would say to the police. "Two black guys! They hit me, they rob me, and then they take my taxi!"

But luckily, Habib was able to call it a night now. And he could take the next day off too. There was a lot to do in the city, but he opted to go home to his wife and children. He never got a chance to spend enough time with them.

Jay and Cas thanked him again. They liked that dude. He hadn't asked any questions. With money, there was no limit to the things you could put together on short notice.

The crimies walked down the street together, and flagged another taxi. When one pulled over, they both hopped in the back. They needed to go back to the sports bar, because both of their cars were parked over there.

When they got back to Wings' spot, they both got their luxury foreign vehicles from valet parking. After that, they both hit the highway, and drove carefully home to Jersey. Lite had it coming, so neither of them really felt any remorse. That dude was mad grimy, so he had asked for it.

CHAPTER TWENTY NINE

A few days later, Jay was on his way to the studio to meet Cas. He was bumping a mix CD, and that Lil' Wayne and Game joint, "My Life" was playing. The words really had him thinking. Damn, he had lost a lot of people.

Jay sung along with the hook. "...so I'm grindin' with my eyes wide, lookin' to find a reason why... Dear Lord, you done took so many of my people, I'm just wondering why you haven't took my life. Like, what the hell am I doing right? My life..."

That was really something to think about. What the hell was he doing right? Why was he still there? Why did Wise have to be the one to go first? Why not him, or Cas? Jay had sense enough to know that it was unwise to question God's will, but it was definitely something to think about.

Jay didn't want anyone to get him wrong, he appreciated life. But he was also a realist. He was trying to live right at that point in his life, but he had a few blood stains on his clothes. Jay was a firm believer in karma. Like for instance, that time he got shot in the face, he knew that was payback for some of the dirt he'd done. So he just had to hold that.

Jay had respect for human life, and he also respected the laws of God. He was no hypocrite. He liked to take justice into his own hands, but he knew he wasn't God. His mother had raised him to believe that God was the highest power, and therefore the only judge of man. It was His job to dish out the wraths punishable to man for his misdeeds.

But Jay liked to be the judge sometimes. He, and a lot of other dudes in the world, liked to be the one to dish out the punishment. He considered every homicide he'd ever committed justifiable, but he knew it still wasn't right. He wasn't God, so he knew he would have to answer for his transgressions too.

It was just so hard not to kill niggas. Especially when they were always trying you. Even when you minded your own business, they still tried you. It was messed up, but it was a fact. That shit that had just happened with Lite was a prime example. Jay and Cas had decided to give him a pass, but he insisted on trying them. Jay wasn't proud of what he did, but he would do it all over again if he had to.

He thought about a conversation he and Portia had in the past. She'd asked him if he wanted to go to Heaven. He did. He really did. He had to get his life back on track. Jay said a quick prayer, and asked God to remove the malice from his heart. Then he prayed again to get his family back. He realized he was nothing without them.

$$$$$

Outside of smoking a little bit of weed, Fatima had been clean for a couple of months now. Now that she had returned to her right state of mind, she knew she wasn't crazy. She believed there might really be something supernatural going on in her home.

Falynn kept on insisting that she saw her daddy. Fatima was beginning to feel like they were living in the movie "Ghost". Sometimes she felt like she could feel Wise' presence too. Or was it just her imagination?

A couple of times, Falynn even said her daddy held her on his lap, and read her a story. Fatima was worried, and frightened. had her daughter somehow become traumatized? Or was Wise' spirit actually in the house walking around? Could the house really be haunted with his ghost?

Fatima confided in Portia and Laila, and told them about Falynn's sightings. At first, they just laughed at her, and told her to stop smoking so much weed. Then, on a serious note, Portia told her to sleep with her Bible under her pillow. Laila told her not to worry, because if Wise' spirit was really playing with Falynn, he would never harm her.

Fatima knew that was true, so she decided to just leave it alone, and let Wise roam free. She knew he loved his daughter, so he was probably just looking out for her, even after he was gone.

$$$$$

Ysatis had been trying to contact Jay hard body. She called him at least fifty times a day. But after a while, she came to the bitter realization that she had simply been shunned.

The news wasn't well received on her part. She was hurt, and she felt betrayed. She began to fantasize about paying Jay back for treating her the way he had. He was the only guy who'd ever acted like he really loved her, but now he had just turned on her. She was really taking it personal.

Ysatis had a lot of mental issues, because she was a victim of sexual abuse as a child. And at the hands of her own brother. Her older brother, Neal, had really treated her like trash. That was the main reason she had such a cold heart. For years, he had raped her, so she had set him up, and had him killed.

Jay was the only man she'd ever trusted, because he was the only one who'd ever had her best interest at heart. But she guessed not anymore. He had let her down too. She would never trust another man. She was hurt, and she wanted Jay to feel the same way.

Ysatis had been in contact with the police. They had questioned her a few times about her brother, Neal's whereabouts. When Neal hadn't reported to his parole officer, his P.O. went around asking questions in the 'hood. He'd found it strange that nobody had seen, or heard from Neal in so long, so he'd reported it to the police.

A detective named Davis had visited Neal's house after that, and discovered that his family had relocated. It was on record that his mother was sickly, and under the care of his younger sister, Ysatis. Detective Davis wanted to know why they suddenly moved down to North Carolina. He did a search on Ysatis, and found out that she was attending college down there.

He had tracked her down, and contacted her, and he questioned her about the whereabouts of her brother. There had been some inconsistencies in her story. She had been asked the same questions three different times, and she gave different answers. Only then did Detective Davis start to get a little suspicious. He had a feeling she was hiding something.

When Ysatis relocated back to New York, he paid her a visit, and let her know he had been tracking her moves. He assured her he had her best interest at heart, and asked once again that she cooperate with his investigation of her brother's disappearance, and assist him if she could.

Now that it seemed like Jay had crossed her, Ysatis thought about dropping his name. Getting him arrested for kidnapping and cold heartedly murdering her brother would sure enough be the big payback. Jay better smarten up, and start acting like he knew. If he knew what was good for him, he would love her back, and continue to provide for her.

$$\$\$\$\$\$$$

That night Portia dreamed of her mother. She got a chance to hold Patty Cake, and she could even smell her. She stroked her mama's hair, and kissed her on the cheek, and told her she loved her. The dream was so real. It was beautiful.

When Portia woke up and realized she was dreaming, she almost went into cardiac arrest. She just sat there for a moment, and cried her heart out. That dream had seemed so real. What she remembered most about the dream was her mother telling her to forgive Jay. She told her not to break her family apart. Patty Cake had come to her, and told her to go home.

Portia just laid there, and wept for about an hour. Dear God, she missed her mother. If she had one wish, it would be to bring her back. She would give up everything she had.

She glimpsed over at the time on the cable box. She hadn't realized how early in the morning it was. She had awakened just before dawn, and now she couldn't go back to sleep.

Portia got up, and went upstairs and checked on her daughters. They were both peacefully asleep. The girls were with her, but Jayquan had stayed at the house with Jay. Portia called over there, and checked on him all the time. Especially in the mornings, to make sure he got up and went to school. And she called him everyday after school, and before he went to bed every night.

Jayquan called her a lot too, and they talked like adults. That boy was so mature now. Portia knew she owed it to him to explain why she had just upped and left. She knew he was upset about her and Jay being split-up. Lil' Jay was her heart, and she let him know that her leaving had nothing to do with him. She told him that she and Jay just needed a "timeout". Nothing was permanent.

Jayquan actually asked her if she left because she didn't love Jay anymore. Portia was real with him. She told him it was more like she'd left because she loved him too much. She said she was just hurt about the way certain things had gone down, and she felt they needed a little time apart, so Jay would appreciate her more.

Portia knew that, as Lil' Jay's mother, it was her job to teach him certain things. So she also had to school her son about women. Someday he would love as well, and she wanted to make sure he knew how to. She told him to never, ever take someone he was fond of for granted.

$$$$$

That evening, Jayquan was at home alone for about an hour. Jay had called, and told him he was running a little late because he was caught up in City traffic. Jayquan didn't care. He wasn't afraid. He was thirteen years old now. He was finally in high school, so he was old enough to take care of himself.

He was chilling in the rec section, halfhearted playing a game on his Playstation III. He wasn't in the greatest mood, because he was busy thinking about the separation between his father and stepmother. He was a little tight at his pops for messing things up. Jayquan really missed Portia. And his little sisters.

He remembered when he was a little boy, and those goons broke in their house, when only he and Portia were there. They had tied him up, and put him in another room, and one of them had hurt her. He had been too small to help Portia at the time, but he told himself he would never let another man hurt her again. Jay hadn't physically harmed her, but he hurt Portia emotionally. That just didn't sit well with Jayquan.

He loved Portia like she was his real mother. She had taken care of him ever since his mom, Stacy, was killed in a car accident when he was four. Jay was his father, and he loved him, but Lil' Jay did not like the way he hurt Portia, and ran her away.

When given the choice, he had stayed in Jersey at the house with his dad. He was closer to his new high school there, so everybody thought that was best. But he let Jay know how uncool he thought him cheating on Portia was. Jayquan hadn't been disrespectful, but he gave Jay the business in his own way. He shot him little disapproving looks now and then, and shook his head at him a lot.

Nobody would actually come out and say it, but Jayquan wasn't stupid. He knew his father had cheated with another woman. He and Macy were close, so he had discussed the matter with her. They came to the conclusion that there couldn't be any other reason Portia had packed up, and jetted like that. Lil' Jay loved his dad, but he wasn't feeling him on that. Not at all.

That night when Jay came in, Jayquan asked him if he could have a word with him. Man to man. Jay noted that his boy was looking at him like he was tight about something. He pretty much already knew what that was about. Lil' Jay was disappointed in him. It showed all in his face. They needed to talk.

Jay felt horrible about having his son upset with him. And Jazmin was questioning him too. She wanted to know why her, her mommy, and her baby sister were living in another house, while him and Jayquan were still at home. Jay knew his dumb ass mistake affected a lot more than just him and Portia. He was on the whole team's shit list. He really felt like an asshole. He had a feeling he wouldn't like what his son had to say, but he encouraged him speak his mind.

Jayquan looked at him, and said, "Listen, Pop. Umm, I wanna go over there and stay with Portia for a little while. I know she could use a little help with my sisters. I kind of miss those little brats, you know?"

Jay just nodded. He couldn't talk. Not right then. There was a big lump in his throat, so his voice probably would've cracked.

Jayquan continued, "I can just go to school from over there for a few days. In a hired car. Right, Pop?"

It was hard, but Jay kept his composure. When Jayquan told him he wanted to leave, his heart broke completely in two. Damn, even his little man wanted to abandon him in his hour of need. He felt betrayed for some reason. Jayquan was his son. That was his boy. If nobody else stuck by him, he should have.

Jay swallowed the lump in his throat, and stopped himself from the pity trip he was about to go on. He had to be a man about it. Portia had raised Jayquan from a little boy. Of course he had love for her, and didn't appreciate him doing her wrong. Jay knew how protective sons were of their mothers. He was like that about his mom too.

Jay knew he was the bad guy, but it still hurt. He didn't even trip. He just told Jayquan, "Ayight, man. I ain't got no beef with that. I know your sisters miss you too."

Lil' Jay nodded at him, and he said, "Pop, thanks for understanding. Hopefully, we can all be a family again soon. I mean, under the same roof. You know?"

Jay just dropped his head, and replied quietly, "Yeah. I really hope so, son."

Jayquan knew his old man was sad, so he gave him a hug. His father was human. Parents needed love too.

That hug almost made Jay break, but he held it in like a man. He rubbed his son's head affectionately, and hugged him tight. He was really going to miss him for those few days he would be gone.

Jay silently said his eleven millionth prayer that Portia would forgive him. He made up his mind that second that he would get her back, if it took every breath in his body. Portia was his rib. He couldn't function without her much longer.

Just then, a light bulb came on in his head. He had an excellent idea. It was a little crazy, but there was a possibility that it

just might work. He made a mental note to call his realtor, Ms.
B the next morning.

CHAPTER THIRTY

It was finally Election Day. November 4th, 2008. Portia was registered to vote in New Jersey, so she got her daughters up, and got them ready early that morning. She knew this election was a historical one, and the news had warned voters of long lines at the polls.

Portia wanted to go vote early, and get it over with. She was taking her children with her, so they could witness history being made. She knew for a fact that Jay was taking Jayquan with him to the polls as well.

While Portia drove her and the girls to Jersey, she called her homegirls to see what time they were voting. She was glad to learn that Laila and Fatima were both up early, and ready to head to the polls. Everyone was anxious to make their contribution to change. It was time for a new America.

Portia thought about the irony of living in America, the land of the free. Fortunately, she and her family hadn't been faced with many financial struggles, but they were certainly aware of the racism and division in the country. It discouraged people to dream.

Just a few months before, Jayquan had got in trouble for wearing an "Obama" tee-shirt to school. He'd been sent home, because he refused to take it off. To Portia that was unbelievable. In this day and time. The thing that really got to her was, Jayquan told her that nobody had said anything to a white kid wearing a "McCain the Maverick" tee-shirt.

She wanted him to know he was free to have different views in the world, so she went up to that school, and voiced her unhappiness at their narrow-minded, one-sided attempt at censorship. They winded up apologizing to her son. Portia knew that incident had only happened because his school was predominantly white, and located in a wealthy, majority republican section of Jersey.

That was one of the reasons she was voting for change. So her kids would be free to be themselves, and have a chance to be whatever they wanted to be. A lot of people didn't think they'd live to see that day, but Portia was praying that America was ready to elect their first black president.

Portia had met up with Laila and Fatima in New Jersey, and they all casted their votes. Afterwards, they had headed to Laila's house to put together a little election party. It was just them and their children, but that was enough. They ordered pizza, and made the kids watch the news coverage with them. They kept drilling in them what a monumental occasion that day was. All three girlfriends were nervous, but full of hope that Obama would be elected.

At eleven o'clock that night, the results from the polls of the west coast states came in, and Barack Obama was elected the 44th president of the United States of America. Portia, Fatima, and Laila were so happy and proud, they broke down in tears. The kids were jubilant and exuberant too. They closely watched the huge crowds of people on television in Time's Square, and in the president-elect's hometown, Chicago. Jazmin and Falynn kept repeating what they heard Macy, and their mothers shouting. "Obama! Obama! Black to the future!"

At around twenty minutes pass eleven, Cas came home. And to Portia's surprise, Jay and Jayquan were with him. She was so caught up in the moment of black love, and racial pride, she hugged all of them tightly. She hugged Lil' Jay again, and showered his face with kisses. She told her son he could be anything he wanted to be.

Portia was a little choked up. She just felt particularly proud of all black men. It felt like the world was finally giving them their due respect. That night she felt like there was a part of Barack Obama inside of each and every one of them. Even the ones who didn't realize it. She wished her father could've lived to see this moment. Her mother too.

At that moment, there was joy in communities all across America. Especially in the black ones. But there were people of all colors rejoicing, all across the world. People were shouting, and shedding tears of joy, from America, all the way to Zimbabwe. There was a historically common cause for celebration. A new day had come. Portia, Jay, and all their friends had never in their lives been so proud to be Americans.

Portia had considered staying over Laila's house, so she wouldn't have to drive all the way back to Brooklyn that night. But the fact was that being around Jay was weakening her resistance. She wanted to forgive him, so they could celebrate black love. Especially after they watched Barack Obama's acceptance speech, and his wife Michelle stared on so proudly. And she watched how the president was with his daughters.

That stirred a strong sense of family in Portia. She knew Jay was a good man, and she wanted to be his first lady. But she couldn't forget about the fact that he had been seeing a younger woman on her. A younger woman that he was so fond of, he put her in a ritzy Central Park apartment, and paid her tuition to NYU. That was some major stuff.

Portia decided to take her daughters, and drive home that night. She had gotten caught up in the moment, but she was still hurting about what Jay had done. She couldn't just act like it was no big deal. He had betrayed her. She loved her husband, but she knew she couldn't trust him anymore.

$$$$$

That following Monday, Ysatis left the clinic smiling from ear to ear. She was in her best mood in months. Just days ago, she was salty at Jay for ignoring her calls, and ready to tell the police he killed her brother. Well, there was no need for that now. Not yet, anyhow. Her original plan had worked, and right on time.

She had desperately pricked a pinhole in the condom Jay used when they had sex, and that had proved to be the smartest thing she'd done all year. The test she had just taken confirmed it. She was pregnant. Eleven weeks. She had done the math, and realized she would be due sometime in late May, or early June of the following year.

She couldn't believe she had successfully gotten pregnant.

And she found out right on time, because Jay had pulled away from her. He'd been acting shady ever since his wife had come by her apartment acting crazy. Ysatis was pissed that he would leave her hanging like that. She was in love with him.

And then there was the fact that she couldn't afford to pay rent in New York City. Especially where she lived at now. Jay was the one who'd put her there. She hadn't asked him too, but she wanted to stay. And she also wanted to finish school. She only had a year and a half left until she graduated. Jay was her lifeline. If he cut her off, she was done.

That was the reason she had contemplated dropping his name to the police. She had felt like he was going to leave her high and dry. But now she had a little bun in the oven, so that was her safety net. Jay wasn't taking her calls, so it might be a long road. But she would find him when the time was right. She didn't even want him to know yet.

Ysatis patted herself on the back for a job well done. She felt a lot better now that she knew she had some security. Jay had paid her tuition for the year, so next semester was covered already. She also knew that he'd leased her apartment for a year. She was good until June, so that gave her a few months.

There was a reason she didn't plan on mentioning the pregnancy yet. She wanted to wait until she was too far gone to get an abortion. Then when she announced it to him, there would be nothing left to do but have the baby. She looked forward to having Jay's child. Being the type of dude he was, she was pretty sure she and her baby would be well taken care of. Hell, she would probably be set for life.

$$$$$

Most black men in the world were feeling positively motivated by the election of America's first black president. But not Smoke. He was a disgruntled dude, still negatively plotting, and scheming in life. He was in dire need of another vic. It was cool they had a black president, but that shit wasn't putting any money in his pocket. Hell, he didn't even vote.

Smoke was a cynic, and would always be. His skeptical views

and negative mind state would probably be the death of him. He sat there in his hotel room all alone. These days, he was usually uptight. That day was no different.

Smoke frowned in distaste at his surroundings. He was staying in a cheap, dirty ass, roach motel. He caught a glimpse of his face in the mirror on the hotel wall. Unsurprisingly, the expression on his face looked like he was constipated. That was a true reflection of the way he felt. He was constipated with fucking rage.

And he wouldn't be able to relieve himself until he saw that bitch Fatima. He was gonna shit all over that dyke. Once again, he replayed in his mind what he planned to do when he ran into her again. And he planned to run into her again, for sure.

Smoke was sick. He had finally touched the bread he needed to get right. He got a chance to live the life. He had money, cars, and clothes. But not for long. As soon as he got up, that bitch had singlehandedly destroyed his accomplishments. His star had rose, but it had fallen at the speed of light. He was broke again.

Every time he thought about the harshness of his reality, he wanted to cut Fatima's fucking throat. All that bitch had to do was mind her business, and him and Callie would've been out of the country. They had planned to leave the day after Callie got arrested. The very next day.

Smoke was giving things a little time to die down, but that Fatima broad was number one on his shit list. She really thought she was smart, but she wasn't going to get away with robbing him like that. He was no fucking sucker. That shit really pissed him off.

Smoke's mentality was such that of a criminal's, he actually believed he was the one who'd been done dirty. He really felt like Fatima had crossed him, and taken his bread. He never took the time to think that it was never rightfully his money from the gate. He was ready to kill Fatima for something that belonged to her.

It was personal for Smoke. He had found out about Fatima destroying Callie's car with a bat, and getting her arrested. After she did all that, she should've just left his money in their hotel suite. He had checked the room before the police did, and the money was gone. All that fucking money. He was ready to execute that bitch.

In minutes, Smoke had gone from buying a big mansion in Mexico, to being fucked up and dead broke, like a nigga just coming home. And he even had to sell his new Benz to a chop shop. He had let it go for dirt cheap, because he knew it was hot. He was really tight about that. Every time he thought about that shit, he was ready to murder something.

Fatima seemed to have this notion that she and her money would just return to safekeeping, but she must've been crazy. He was gonna get right again, if it had to be over her dead body. He and Callie had almost been in Mexico, home-free, but that bitch had to intervene.

Callie had got fucked up in the process, but that wasn't the reason he was upset. It wasn't even about that. That bitch Fatima had snatched away his dreams. He had finally touched it, and she took it all away. Smoke wanted that bread back.

He had left Callie out in L.A. fucked up in jail. She was a good girl, but he couldn't mess with her at the time. She had played her part, but now she was too hot. There was nothing he could do for her right now anyway, so they were at their crossroads.

Callie had called him when she first got locked up, and he had told her to keep her mouth shut. From what she told him, she was going to do some serious time.

Smoke had to disassociate himself from her, because he wasn't going back to jail. There was no way. He was just glad he got a chance to see where that bitch Fatima lived. She was responsible for his unhappiness, so he was gonna fix that bitch, if it was the last thing he did.

To be continued...

Order Form

Synergy Publications
P.O. Box 210-987   Brooklyn, NY 11221
www.SynergyPublications.com

_____ A Dollar Outta Fifteen Cent $14.95

_____ A Dollar Outta Fifteen Cent II: Money Talks… Bullsh*t Walks $14.95

_____ A Dollar Outta Fifteen Cent III: Mo' Money…Mo' Problems $14.95

_____ A Dollar Outta Fifteen Cent IV: $14.95
          Money Makes the World Go 'Round   *(Available Fall 2009)*

_____ Sex As a Weapon $14.95

_____ Sex As a Weapon 2: Steaming Hot Coffee   *(Available 2010)* $14.95

_____ Guns & Roses   *(Available 2010)* $14.95

          Shipping and Handling (plus $1 for each additional book) $ 4.00

          TOTAL   (for one book) $18.95

_____ TOTAL NUMBER OF BOOKS ORDERED

Name (please print) :_____
                      First   Last

Reg. # (Applies if Incarcerated): _____

Address: _____

         _____

City: _____ State: _____ Zip Code: _____

Email: _____

*25% Discount for Orders Being Shipped Directly to Prisons
Prison Discount: ($11.21+ $4.00 s & h = **$15.21**)
**Special Discounts for Book Clubs with 4 or more members
***Discount for Bulk Orders - please call for info (718) 930-8818
WE ACCEPT MONEY ORDERS ONLY for all mail orders
Credit Cards can be used for orders made online
Allow 2 -3 weeks for delivery
Purchase online at **www.SynergyPublications.com**